Praise for N...
au...

"Palmer demonst... queen of desperado quests for justice and true love."

—*Publishers Weekly* on *Dangerous*

"The popular Palmer has penned another winning novel, a perfect blend of romance and suspense."

—*Booklist* on *Lawman*

"Palmer knows how to make the sparks fly... heartwarming."

—*Publishers Weekly* on *Renegade*

"Diana Palmer is a mesmerizing storyteller who captures the essence of what a romance should be."

—*Affaire de Coeur*

Praise for author Caro Carson

"A heartbreaker... The treatment of both the heroine's insecurities and the hero's malady is awesome."

—*RT Book Reviews* on *A Texas Rescue Christmas*
(4.5 stars)

"The lonely hearts club is about to lose two members in Carson's amazingly heartfelt, love-at-first-sight Montana Mavericks holiday story."

—*RT Book Reviews* on
The Maverick's Holiday Masquerade

HOME ON THE RANCH:
TEXAS BLUE BLOOD

New York Times **Bestelling Author**
DIANA PALMER
CARO CARSON

HARLEQUIN® HOME ON THE RANCH

ISBN-13: 978-1-335-02037-6

Home on the Ranch: Texas Blue Blood

Copyright © 2018 by Harlequin Books S.A.

The publisher acknowledges the copyright holders of the individual works as follows:

The Rancher
Copyright © 2012 by Diana Palmer

Following Doctor's Orders
Copyright © 2015 by Caro Carson

PLEASE RECYCLE
THIS PRODUCT IS RECYCLABLE

Recycling programs
for this product may
not exist in your area.

HARLEQUIN®

TM www.Harlequin.com

Printed in U.S.A.

CONTENTS

The prolific author of more than one hundred books, **Diana Palmer** got her start as a newspaper reporter. A *New York Times* bestselling author who was voted one of the top ten romance writers in America, she has a gift for telling the most sensual tales with charm and humor. Diana lives with her family in Cornelia, Georgia.

THE RANCHER

DIANA PALMER

Chapter 1

Maddie Lane was worried. She was standing in her big yard, looking at her chickens, and all she saw was a mixture of hens. There were red ones and white ones and gray speckled ones. But they were all hens. Someone was missing: her big Rhode Island Red rooster, Pumpkin.

She knew where he likely was. It made her grind her teeth together. There was going to be trouble, again, and she was going to be on the receiving end of it.

She pushed back her short, wavy blond hair and grimaced. Her wide gray eyes searched the yard, hoping against hope that she was mistaken, that Pumpkin had only gone in search of bugs, not cowboys.

"Pumpkin?" she called loudly.

Great-Aunt Sadie came to the door. She was slight and a little dumpy, with short, thin gray hair, wearing glasses and a worried look.

"I saw him go over toward the Brannt place, Maddie," she said as she moved out onto the porch. "I'm sorry."

Maddie groaned aloud. "I'll have to go after him. Cort will kill me!"

"Well, he hasn't so far," Sadie replied gently. "And he could have shot Pumpkin, but he didn't…"

"Only because he missed!" Maddie huffed. She sighed and put her hands on her slim hips. She had a boyish figure. She wasn't tall or short, just sort of in the middle. But she was graceful, for all that. And she could work on a ranch, which she did. Her father had taught her how to raise cattle, how to market them, how to plan and how to budget. Her little ranch wasn't anything big or special, but she made a little money. Things had been going fine until she decided she wanted to branch out her organic egg-laying business and bought Pumpkin after her other rooster was killed by a coyote, along with several hens. But now things weren't so great financially.

Maddie had worried about getting a new rooster. Her other one wasn't really vicious, but she did have to carry a tree branch around with her to keep from getting spurred. She didn't want another aggressive one.

"Oh, he's gentle as a lamb," the former owner assured her. "Great bloodlines, good breeder, you'll get along just fine with him!"

Sure, she thought when she put him in the chicken yard and his first act was to jump on her foreman, old Ben Harrison, when he started to gather eggs.

"Better get rid of him now," Ben had warned as she doctored the cuts on his arms the rooster had made even through the fabric.

"He'll settle down, he's just excited about being in a new place," Maddie assured him.

Looking back at that conversation now, she laughed. Ben had been right. She should have sent the rooster back to the vendor in a shoebox. But she'd gotten attached to the feathered assassin. Sadly, Cort Brannt hadn't.

Cort Matthew Brannt was every woman's dream of the perfect man. He was tall, muscular without making it obvious, cultured, and he could play a guitar like a professional. He had jet-black hair with a slight wave, large dark brown eyes and a sensuous mouth that Maddie often dreamed of kissing.

The problem was that Cort was in love with their other neighbor, Odalie Everett. Odalie was the daughter of bigtime rancher Cole Everett and his wife, Heather, who was a former singer and songwriter. She had two brothers, John and Tanner. John still lived at home, but Tanner lived in Europe. Nobody talked about him.

Odalie loved grand opera. She had her mother's clear, beautiful voice and she wanted to be a professional soprano. That meant specialized training.

Cort wanted to marry Odalie, who couldn't see him for dust. She'd gone off to Italy to study with some famous voice trainer. Cort was distraught and it didn't help that Maddie's rooster kept showing up in his yard and attacking him without warning.

"I can't understand why he wants to go all the way over there to attack Cort," Maddie said aloud. "I mean, we've got cowboys here!"

"Cort threw a rake at him the last time he came over here to look at one of your yearling bulls," Sadie reminded her.

"I throw things at him all the time," Maddie pointed out.

"Yes, but Cort chased him around the yard, picked

him up by his feet, and carried him out to the hen yard to show him to the hens. Hurt his pride," Sadie continued. "He's getting even."

"You think so?"

"Roosters are unpredictable. That particular one," she added with a bite in her voice that was very out of character, "should have been chicken soup!"

"Great-Aunt Sadie!"

"Just telling you the way it is," Sadie huffed. "My brother—your granddaddy—would have killed him the first time he spurred you."

Maddie smiled. "I guess he would. I don't like killing things. Not even mean roosters."

"Cort would kill him for you if he could shoot straight," Sadie said with veiled contempt. "You load that .28 gauge shotgun in the closet for me, and I'll do it."

"Great-Aunt Sadie!"

She made a face. "Stupid thing. I wanted to pet the hens and he ran me all the way into the house. Pitiful, when a chicken can terrorize a whole ranch. You go ask Ben how he feels about that red rooster. I dare you. If you'd let him, he'd run a truck over it!"

Maddie sighed. "I guess Pumpkin is a terror. Well, maybe Cort will deal with him once and for all and I can go get us a nice rooster."

"In my experience, no such thing," the older woman said. "And about Cort dealing with him…" She nodded toward the highway.

Maddie grimaced. A big black ranch truck turned off the highway and came careening down the road toward the house. It was obviously being driven by a maniac.

The truck screeched to a stop at the front porch, sending chickens running for cover in the hen yard because of the noise.

"Great," Maddie muttered. "Now they'll stop laying for two days because he's terrified them!"

"Better worry about yourself," Great-Aunt Sadie said. "Hello, Cort! Nice to see you," she added with a wave and ran back into the house, almost at a run.

Maddie bit off what she was going to say about traitors. She braced herself as a tall, lean, furious cowboy in jeans, boots, a chambray shirt and a black Stetson cocked over one eye came straight toward her. She knew what the set of that hat meant. He was out for blood.

"I'm sorry!" she said at once, raising her hands, palms out. "I'll do something about him, I promise!"

"Andy landed in a cow patty," he raged in his deep voice. "That's nothing compared to what happened to the others while we were chasing him. I went headfirst into the dipping tray!"

She wouldn't laugh, she wouldn't laugh, she wouldn't…

"Oh, hell, stop that!" he raged while she bent over double at the mental image of big, handsome Cort lying facedown in the stinky stuff they dipped cattle in to prevent disease.

"I'm sorry. Really!" She forced herself to stop laughing. She wiped her wet eyes and tried to look serious. "Go ahead, keep yelling at me. Really. It's okay."

"Your stupid rooster is going to feed my ranch hands if you don't keep him at home!" he said angrily.

"Oh, my, chance would be a fine thing, wouldn't it?" she asked wistfully. "I mean, I guess I could hire an off-duty army unit to come out here and spend the next week trying to run him down." She gave him a droll look. "If you and your men can't catch him, how do you expect me to catch him?"

"I caught him the first day he was here," he reminded her.

"Yes, but that was three months ago," she pointed out. "And he'd just arrived. Now he's learned evasion techniques." She frowned. "I wonder if they've ever thought of using roosters as attack animals for the military? I should suggest it to someone."

"I'd suggest you find some way to keep him at home before I resort to the courts."

"You'd sue me over a chicken?" she exclaimed. "Wow, what a headline that would be. Rich, Successful Rancher Sues Starving, Female Small-Rancher for Rooster Attack. Wouldn't your dad love reading that headline in the local paper?" she asked with a bland smile.

His expression was growing so hard that his high cheekbones stood out. "One more flying red feather attack and I'll risk it. I'm not kidding."

"Oh, me, neither." She crossed her heart. "I'll have the vet prescribe some tranquilizers for Pumpkin to calm him down," she said facetiously. She frowned. "Ever thought about asking your family doctor for some? You look very stressed."

"I'm stressed because your damned rooster keeps attacking me! On my own damned ranch!" he raged.

"Well, I can see that it's a stressful situation to be in," she sympathized. "With him attacking you, and all." She knew it would make him furious, but she had to know. "I hear Odalie Everett went to Italy."

The anger grew. Now it was cold and threatening. "Since when is Odalie of interest to you?"

"Just passing on the latest gossip." She peered at him through her lashes. "Maybe you should study opera…"

"You venomous little snake," he said furiously. "As if you could sing a note that wasn't flat!"

She colored. "I could sing if I wanted to!"

He looked her up and down. "Sure. And get suddenly beautiful with it?"

The color left her face.

"You're too thin, too flat-chested, too plain and too untalented to ever appeal to me, just in case you wondered," he added with unconcealed distaste.

She drew herself up to her full height, which only brought the top of her head to his chin, and stared at him with ragged dignity. "Thank you. I was wondering why men don't come around. It's nice to know the reason."

Her damaged pride hit him soundly, and he felt small. He shifted from one big booted foot to the other. "I didn't mean it like that," he said after a minute.

She turned away. She wasn't going to cry in front of him.

Her sudden vulnerability hurt him. He started after her. "Listen, Madeline," he began.

She whirled on her booted heel. Her pale eyes shot fire at him. Her exquisite complexion went ruddy. Beside her thighs, her hands were clenched. "You think you're God's gift to women, don't you? Well, let me tell you a thing or two! You've traded on your good looks for years to get you what you want, but it didn't get you Odalie, did it?"

His face went stony. "Odalie is none of your damned business," he said in a soft, dangerous tone.

"Looks like she's none of yours, either," she said spitefully. "Or she'd never have left you."

He turned around and stomped back to his truck.

"And don't you dare roar out of my driveway and scare my hens again!"

He slammed the door, started the truck and deliberately gunned the engine as he roared out toward the main highway.

"Three days they won't lay, now," Maddie said to herself. She turned, miserable, and went up the porch steps. Her pride was never going to heal from that attack. She'd had secret feelings for Cort since she was sixteen. He'd never noticed her, of course, not even to tease her as men sometimes did. He simply ignored her existence most of the time, when her rooster wasn't attacking him. Now she knew why. Now she knew what he really thought of her.

Great-Aunt Sadie was waiting by the porch screen door. She was frowning. "No call for him to say that about you," she muttered. "Conceited man!"

Maddie fought tears and lost.

Great-Aunt Sadie wrapped her up tight and hugged her. "Don't you believe what he said. He was just mad and looking for a way to hurt you because you mentioned his precious Odalie. She's too good for any cowboy. At least, she thinks she is."

"She's beautiful and rich and talented. But so is Cort," Maddie choked out. "It really would have been a good match, to pair the Everett's Big Spur ranch with Skylance, the Brannt ranch. What a merger that would be."

"Except that Odalie doesn't love Cort and she probably never will."

"She may come home with changed feelings," Maddie replied, drawing away. "She might have a change of heart. He's always been around, sending her flowers, calling her. All that romantic stuff. The sudden stop might open her eyes to what a catch he is."

"You either love somebody or you don't," the older woman said quietly.

"You think?"

"I'll make you a nice pound cake. That will cheer you up."

"Thanks. That's sweet of you." She wiped her eyes. "Well, at least I've lost all my illusions. Now I can just deal with my ranch and stop mooning over a man who thinks he's too good for me."

"No man is too good for you, sweetheart," Great-Aunt Sadie said gently. "You're pure gold. Don't you ever let anyone tell you different."

She smiled.

When she went out late in the afternoon to put her hens in their henhouse to protect them from overnight predators, Pumpkin was right where he should be—back in the yard.

"You're going to get me sued, you red-feathered problem child," she muttered. She was carrying a small tree branch and a metal garbage can lid as she herded her hens into the large chicken house. Pumpkin lowered his head and charged her, but he bounced off the lid.

"Get in there, you fowl assassin," she said, evading and turning on him.

He ran into the henhouse. She closed the door behind him and latched it, leaned back against it with a sigh.

"Need to get rid of that rooster, Miss Maddie," Ben murmured as he walked by. "Be delicious with some dumplings."

"I'm not eating Pumpkin!"

He shrugged. "That's okay. I'll eat him for you."

"I'm not feeding him to you, either, Ben."

He made a face and kept walking.

She went inside to wash her hands and put antibiotic cream on the places where her knuckles were scraped from using the garbage can lid. She looked at her hands under the running water. They weren't elegant hands. They had short nails and they were functional, not pretty. She remembered Odalie Everett's long, beautiful white fingers on the keyboard at church, because Odalie could play as well as she sang. The woman was gorgeous, except for her snobbish attitude. No wonder Cort was in love with her.

Maddie looked in the mirror on the medicine cabinet above the sink and winced. She really was plain, she thought. Of course, she never used makeup or perfume, because she worked from dawn to dusk on the ranch. Not that makeup would make her beautiful, or give her bigger breasts or anything like that. She was basically just pleasant to look at, and Cort wanted beauty, brains and talent.

"I guess you'll end up an old spinster with a rooster who terrorizes the countryside."

The thought made her laugh. She thought of photographing Pumpkin and making a giant Wanted poster, with the legend, Wanted: Dead or Alive. She could hardly contain herself at the image that presented itself if she offered some outlandish reward. Men would wander the land with shotguns, looking for a small red rooster.

"Now you're getting silly," she told her image, and went back to work.

Cort Brannt slammed out of his pickup truck and into the ranch house, flushed with anger and self-contempt.

His mother, beautiful Shelby Brannt, glanced up as he passed the living room.

"Wow," she murmured. "Cloudy and looking like rain."

He paused and glanced at her. He grimaced, retraced his steps, tossed his hat onto the sofa and sat down beside her. "Yeah."

"That rooster again, huh?" she teased.

His dark eyes widened. "How did you guess?"

She tried to suppress laughter and lost. "Your father came in here bent over double, laughing his head off. He said half the cowboys were ready to load rifles and go rooster-hunting about the time you drove off. He wondered if we might need to find legal representation for you…?"

"I didn't shoot her," he said. He shrugged his powerful shoulders and let out a long sigh, his hands dangling between his splayed legs as he stared at the carpet. "But I said some really terrible things to her."

Shelby put down the European fashion magazine she'd been reading. In her younger days, she had been a world-class model before she married King Brannt. "Want to talk about it, Matt?" she asked gently.

"Cort," he corrected with a grin.

She sighed. "Cort. Listen, your dad and I were calling you Matt until you were teenager, so it's hard…"

"Yes, well, you were calling Morie 'Dana,' too, weren't you?"

Shelby laughed. "It was an inside-joke. I'll tell it to you one day." She smiled. "Come on. Talk to me."

His mother could always take the weight off his shoulders. He'd never been able to speak so comfortably about personal things to his father, although he loved the older man dearly. He and his mother were on the same wavelength. She could almost read his mind.

"I was pretty mad," he confessed. "And she was

cracking jokes about that stupid rooster. Then she made a crack about Odalie and I just, well, I just lost it."

Odalie, she knew, was a sore spot with her son. "I'm sorry about the way things worked out, Cort," she said gently. "But there's always hope. Never lose sight of that."

"I sent her roses. Serenaded her. Called her just to talk. Listened to her problems." He looked up. "None of that mattered. That Italian voice trainer gave her an invitation and she got on the next plane to Rome."

"She wants to sing. You know that. You've always known it. Her mother has the voice of an angel, too."

"Yes, but Heather never wanted fame. She wanted Cole Everett," he pointed out with a faint smile.

"That was one hard case of a man," Shelby pointed out. "Like your father." She shook her head. "We had a very, very rocky road to the altar. And so did Heather and Cole."

She continued pensively. "You and Odalie's brother, John Everett, were good friends for a while. What happened there?"

"His sister happened," Cort replied. "She got tired of having me at their place all the time playing video games with John and was very vocal about it, so he stopped inviting me over. I invited him here, but he got into rodeo and then I never saw him much. We're still friends, in spite of everything."

"He's a good fellow."

"Yeah."

Shelby got up, ruffled his hair and grinned. "You're a good fellow, too."

He laughed softly. "Thanks."

"Try not to dwell so much on things," she advised. "Sit back and just let life happen for a while. You're so intense, Cort. Like your dad," she said affectionately, her dark eyes soft on his face. "One day Odalie may discover that you're the sun in her sky and come home. But you have to let her try her wings. She's traveled, but only with her parents. This is her first real taste of freedom. Let her enjoy it."

"Even if she messes up her life with that Italian guy?"

"Even then. It's her life," she reminded him gently. "You don't like people telling you what to do, even if it's for your own good, right?"

He glowered at her. "If you're going to mention that time you told me not to climb up the barn roof and I didn't listen…"

"Your first broken arm," she recalled, and pursed her lips. "And I didn't even say I told you so," she reminded him.

"No. You didn't." He stared at his linked fingers. "Maddie Lane sets me off. But I should never have said she was ugly and no man would want her."

"You said that?" she exclaimed, wincing. "Cort…!"

"I know." He sighed. "Not my finest moment. She's not a bad person. It's just she gets these goofy notions about animals. That rooster is going to hurt somebody bad one day, maybe put an eye out, and she thinks it's funny."

"She doesn't realize he's dangerous," she replied.

"She doesn't want to realize it. She's in over her head with these expansion projects. Cage-free eggs. She hasn't got the capital to go into that sort of operation, and she's probably already breaking half a dozen laws by selling them to restaurants."

"She's hurting for money," Shelby reminded somberly. "Most ranchers are, even us. The drought is killing us. But Maddie only has a few head of cattle and she can't buy feed for them if her corn crop dies. She'll have to sell at a loss. Her breeding program is already losing money." She shook her head. "Her father was a fine rancher. He taught your father things about breeding bulls. But Maddie just doesn't have the experience. She jumped in at the deep end when her father died, but it was by necessity, not choice. I'm sure she'd much rather be drawing pictures than trying to produce calves."

"Drawing." He said it with contempt.

She stared at him. "Cort, haven't you ever noticed that?" She indicated a beautiful rendering in pastels of a fairy in a patch of daisies in an exquisite frame on the wall.

He glanced at it. "Not bad. Didn't you get that at an art show last year?"

"I got it from Maddie last year. She drew it."

He frowned. He actually got up and went to look at the piece. "She drew that?" he asked.

"Yes. She was selling two pastel drawings at the art show. This was one of them. She sculpts, too—beautiful little fairies—but she doesn't like to show those to people. I told her she should draw professionally, perhaps in graphic design or even illustration. She laughed. She doesn't think she's good enough." She sighed. "Maddie is insecure. She has one of the poorest self-images of anyone I know."

Cort knew that. His lips made a thin line. He felt even worse after what he'd said to her. "I should probably call and apologize," he murmured.

"That's not a bad idea, son," she agreed.

"And then I should drive over there, hide in the grass and shoot that damned red-feathered son of a…!"

"Cort!"

He let out a harsh breath. "Okay. I'll call her."

"Roosters don't live that long," she called after him. "He'll die of old age before too much longer."

"With my luck, he'll hit fifteen and keep going. Animals that nasty never die!" he called back.

He wanted to apologize to Maddie. But when he turned on his cell phone, he realized that he didn't even know her phone number. He tried to look it up on the internet, but couldn't find a listing.

He went back downstairs. His mother was in the kitchen.

"Do you know the Lanes' phone number?" he asked.

She blinked. "Well, no. I don't think I've ever tried to call them, not since Pierce Lane died last year, anyway."

"No number listed, anywhere," he said.

"You might drive by there later in the week," she suggested gently. "It's not that far."

He hesitated. "She'd lock the doors and hide inside when I drove up," he predicted.

His mother didn't know what to say. He was probably right.

"I need to get away," he said after a minute. "I'm wired like a piano. I need to get away from the rooster and Odalie and…everything."

"Why don't you go to Wyoming and visit your sister?" she suggested.

He sighed. "She's not expecting me until Thursday."

She laughed. "She won't care. Go early. It would do both of you good."

"It might at that."

"It won't take you long to fly up there," she added. "You can use the corporate jet. I'm sure your father wouldn't mind. He misses Morie. So do I."

"Yeah, I miss her, too," he said. He hugged his mother. "I'll go pack a bag. If that rooster shows up looking for me, put him on a plane to France, would you? I hear they love chicken over there. Get him a business-class ticket. If someone can ship a lobster from Maine," he added with a laugh, referring to a joke that had gone the rounds years before, "I can ship a chicken to France."

"I'll take it under advisement," she promised.

His mother was right, Cort thought that evening. He loved being with his sister. He and Morie were a lot alike, from their hot tempers to their very Puritan attitudes. They'd always been friends. When she was just five, she'd followed her big brother around everywhere, to the amusement of his friends. Cort was tolerant and he adored her. He never minded the kidding.

"I'm sorry about your rooster problems," Morie told him with a gentle laugh. "Believe me, we can understand. My poor sister-in-law has fits with ours."

"I like Bodie," he said, smiling. "Cane sure seems different these days."

"He is. He's back in therapy, he's stopped smashing bars and he seems to have settled down for good. Bodie's wonderful for him. She and Cane have had some problems, but they're mostly solved now," she said. She smiled secretly. "Actually, Bodie and I are going to have a lot more in common for the next few months."

Cort was quick. He glanced at her in the semidarkness of the front porch, with fireflies darting around. "A baby?"

She laughed with pure delight. "A baby," she said, and her voice was like velvet. "I only found out a little while ago. Bodie found out the day you showed up." She sighed. "So much happiness. It's almost too much to bear. Mal's over the moon."

"Is it a boy or a girl? Do you know yet?"

She shook her head. "Too early to tell. But we're not going to ask. We want it to be a surprise, however old-fashioned that might be."

He chuckled. "I'm going to be an uncle. Wow. That's super. Have you told Mom and Dad?"

"Not yet. I'll call Mom tonight, though."

"She'll be so excited. Her first grandchild."

Morie glanced at him. "You ever going to get married?" she asked.

"Sure, if Odalie ever says yes." He sighed. "She was warming up to me there just for a while. Then that Italian fellow came along and offered her voice training. He's something of a legend among opera stars. And that's what she wants, to sing at the Met." He grimaced. "Just my luck, to fall in love with a woman who only wants a career."

"I believe her mother was the same way, wasn't she?" Morie asked gently. "And then she and Cole Everett got really close. She gave up being a professional singer to come home and have kids. Although she still composes. That Wyoming group, Desperado, had a major hit from a song she wrote for them some years ago."

"I think she still composes. But she likes living on a ranch. Odalie hates it. She says she's never going to marry a man who smells like cow droppings." He looked at one of his big boots, where his ankle was resting on his other knee in the rocking chair. "I'm a rancher, damn it," he muttered. "I can't learn another trade. Dad's counting on me to take over when he can't do the work anymore."

"Yes, I know," she said sadly. "What else could you do?"

"Teach, I guess," he replied. "I have a degree in animal husbandry." He made a face. "I'd rather be shot. I'd rather let that red-feathered assassin loose on my nose. I hate the whole idea of routine."

"Me, too," Morie confessed. "I love ranching. I guess the drought is giving Dad problems, too, huh?"

"It's been pretty bad," Cort agreed. "People in Oklahoma and the other plains states are having it worse, though. No rain. It's like the Dust Bowl in the thirties, people are saying. So many disaster declarations."

"How are you getting around it?"

"Wells, mostly," he said. "We've drilled new ones and filled the tanks to the top. Irrigating our grain crops. Of course, we'll still have to buy some feed through the winter. But we're in better shape than a lot of other cattle producers. Damn, I hate how it's going to impact small ranchers and farmers. Those huge combines will be standing in the shadows, just waiting to pounce when the foreclosures come."

"Family ranches are going to be obsolete one day, like family farms," Morie said sadly. "Except, maybe, for the big ones, like ours."

"True words. People don't realize how critical this really is."

She reached over and squeezed his hand. "That's why we have the National Cattleman's Association and the state organizations," she reminded him. "Now, stop worrying. We're going fishing tomorrow!"

"Really?" he asked, delighted. "Trout?"

"Yes. The water's just cold enough, still. When it heats up too much, you can't eat them." She sighed. "This may be the last chance we'll get for a while, if this heat doesn't relent."

"Tell me about it. We hardly had winter at all in Texas. Spring was like summer, and it's gone downhill since. I'd love to stand in a trout stream, even if I don't catch a thing."

"Me, too."

"Does Bodie fish?"

"You know, I've never asked. We'll do that tomorrow. For now," she said, rising, "I'm for bed." She paused and hugged him. "It's nice to have you here for a while."

"For me, too, little sis." He hugged her back, and kissed her forehead. "See you in the morning."

Chapter 2

Maddie hadn't thought about Cort for one whole hour. She laughed at herself while she fed her hens. Pumpkin was in the henhouse, locked in for the time being, so that she could feed the chickens without having to defend herself.

The laughter died away as she recalled the things Cort had said to her. She was ugly and flat-chested and he could never be attracted to her. She looked down at her slender body and frowned. She couldn't suddenly become beautiful. She didn't have the money to buy fancy clothes that flattered her, like Odalie did. In fact, her wardrobe was two years old.

When her father had been dying of cancer, every penny they had was tied up trying to keep up with doctor bills that the insurance didn't cover. Her father did carry life insurance, which was a lucky break because at his death, it was enough to pay back everybody.

But things were still hard. This year, they'd struggled to pay just the utility bills. It was going to come down to a hard choice, sell off cattle or sell off land. There was a developer who'd already been to see Maddie about selling the ranch. He wanted to build a huge hotel and amusement park complex. He was offering her over a million dollars, and he was persistent.

"You just run a few head of cattle here, don't you?" the tall man in the expensive suit said, but his smile didn't really reach his eyes. He was an opportunist, looking for a great deal. He thought Maddie would be a pushover once he pulled out a figure that would tempt a saint.

But Maddie's whole heritage was in that land. Her great-grandfather had started the ranch and suffered all sorts of deprivations to get it going. Her grandfather had taken over where he left off, improving both the cattle herd and the land. Her father had toiled for years to find just the right mix of grasses to pursue a purebred cattle breeding herd that was now the envy of several neighbors. All that would be gone. The cattle sold off, the productive grasslands torn up and paved for the complex, which would attract people passing by on the long, monotonous interstate highway that ran close to the border of the ranch.

"I'll have to think about it," she told him, nodding. Her smile didn't reach her eyes, either.

He pursed his lips. "You know, we're looking at other land in the area, too. You might get left out in the cold if we find someone who's more enthusiastic about the price we're offering."

Maddie didn't like threats. Even nice ones, that came with soft words and smiles.

"Whatever," she said. She smiled again. "I did say I'd have to think about it."

His smile faded, and his eyes narrowed. "You have a prime location here, only one close neighbor and a nearby interstate. I really want this place. I want it a lot."

"Listen, I hate being pressured…!"

He held up both hands. "Okay! But you think about it. You think hard." His expression became dangerous-looking. "We know how to deal with reluctant buyers. That's not a threat, it's just a statement. Here's my card."

She took it gingerly, as if she thought it had germs.

He made a huffing sound and climbed back into his fantastically expensive foreign car. He roared out of the driveway, scattering chickens.

She glared after it. No more eggs for two more days, she thought irritably. She'd rather starve than sell the ranch. But money was getting very tight. The drought was going to be a major hit to their poor finances, she thought dismally.

"Miss Maddie, you got that rooster locked up?" Ben called at the fence, interrupting her depressing reverie.

She turned. "Yes, Ben, he's restrained." She laughed.

"Thanks." He grimaced. "Going to feed the livestock and I'd just as soon not be mauled in the process."

"I know." She glanced at the wire door behind which Pumpkin was calling to the hens in that odd tone that roosters used when there was some special treat on the ground for them. It was actually a handful of mealworms that Maddie had tossed in the henhouse to keep him occupied while she locked him in.

Two of the hens went running to the door.

"He's lying," Maddie told them solemnly. "He's already eaten the mealworms, he just wants out."

"Cort left town, you hear?" Ben asked.

Her heart jumped. "Where did he go?" she asked miserably, waiting to hear that he'd flown to Italy to see Odalie.

"Wyoming, one of his cowboys said, to see his sister."

"Oh."

"Mooning over that Odalie girl, I guess," he muttered. "She said she hated men who smelled like cattle. I guess she hates her dad, then, because he made his fortune on the Big Spur raising cattle, and he still does!"

"She's just been spoiled," Maddie said quietly.

Ben glanced at her irritably. "She was mean to you when you were in school. Your dad actually went to the school to get it stopped. He went to see Cole Everett about it, too, didn't he?"

"Yes." She flushed. She didn't like remembering that situation, although Odalie had quickly stopped victimizing her after her father got involved.

"Had a nasty attitude, that one," Ben muttered. "Looked down her nose at every other girl and most of the boys. Thought she was too good to live in a hick town in Texas." His eyes narrowed. "She's going to come a cropper one day, you mark my words. What's that quote, 'pride goeth after a fall'? And she's got a lot farther to fall than some women."

"There's another quote, something about love your enemies?" she teased.

"Yes, well, she's given a lot of people reason to put that one into practice."

Maddie grimaced. "It must be nice, to have beauty and talent. I'd settle for one or the other myself." She laughed.

"You ought to be selling them little fairy statues you make," he advised. "Prettiest little things I ever saw. That one you sent my granddaughter for her birthday sits in the living room, because her mother loves to look at it. One of her friends has an art gallery in San Antonio. She said," he emphasized, "that you could make a fortune with those things."

Maddie flushed. "Wow."

"Not that those pretty drawings are bad, either. Sold one to Shelby Brannt, didn't you?"

"Yes." She'd loved the idea of Cort having to see her artwork every day, because she knew that Shelby had mounted it on a wall in the dining room of her home. But he probably never even looked at it. Though cultured, Cort had little use for art or sculpture. Unless it was a sculpture of one of the ranch's prize bulls. They had one done in bronze. It sat on the mantel in the living room of the Brannt home.

"Ought to paint that rooster while he's still alive," Ben said darkly.

"Ben!"

He held up both hands. "Didn't say I was going to hurt him."

"Okay."

"But somebody else might." He pursed his lips. "You know, he could be the victim of a terrible traffic accident one day. He loves to run down that dirt road in front of the house."

"You bite your tongue," she admonished.

"Spoilsport."

"That visitor who came the other day, that developer, you see him again?" Ben asked curiously.

"No, but he left his name." She pulled his business

card out of her pocket and held it up. "He's from Las Vegas. He wants to build a hotel and amusement park complex right here." She looked around wistfully. "Offered me a million dollars. Gosh, what I could do with that!"

"You could sell and throw away everything your family worked for here?" Ben asked sadly. "My great-grandfather started working here with your great-grandfather. Our families have been together all that time." He sighed. "Guess I could learn to use a computer and make a killing with a dot-com business," he mused facetiously.

"Aw, Ben," she said gently. "I don't want to sell up. I was just thinking out loud." She smiled, and this time it was genuine. "I'd put a lot of people out of work, and God knows what I'd do with all the animals who live here."

"Especially them fancy breeding bulls and cows," he replied. "Cort Brannt would love to get his hands on them. He's always over here buying our calves."

"So he is."

Ben hesitated. "Heard something about that developer, that Archie Lawson fellow."

"You did? What?"

"Just gossip, mind."

"So? Tell me!" she prodded.

He made a face. "Well, he wanted a piece of land over around Cheyenne, on the interstate. The owner wouldn't sell. So cattle started dying of mysterious causes. So did the owner's dog, a big border collie he'd had for years. He hired a private investigator, and had the dog autopsied. It was poison. They could never prove it was Lawson, but they were pretty sure of it. See, he has a background in chemistry. Used to work at a big government lab, they say, before he started buying and selling land."

Her heart stopped. "Oh, dear." She bit her lip. "He said something about knowing how to force deals…"

"I'll get a couple of my pals to keep an eye on the cattle in the outer pastures," Ben said. "I'll tell them to shoot first and ask questions later if they see anybody prowling around here."

"Thanks, Ben," she said heavily. "Good heavens, as if we don't already have enough trouble here with no rain, for God knows how long."

"Everybody's praying for it." He cocked his head. "I know a Cheyenne medicine man. Been friends for a couple of years. They say he can make rain."

"Well!" She hesitated. "What does he charge?"

"He doesn't. He says he has these abilities that God gave him, and if he ever takes money for it, he'll lose it. Seems to believe it, and I hear he's made rain at least twice in the area. If things go from bad to worse, maybe we should talk to him."

She grinned. "Let's talk to him."

He chuckled. "I'll give him a call later."

Her eyebrows arched. "He has a telephone?"

"Miss Maddie," he scoffed, "do you think Native American people still live in teepees and wear head-dresses?"

She flushed. "Of course not," she lied.

"He lives in a house just like ours, he wears jeans and T-shirts mostly and he's got a degree in anthropology. When he's not fossicking, they say he goes overseas with a group of mercs from Texas for top secret operations."

She was fascinated. "Really!"

"He's something of a local celebrity on the rez. He lives there."

"Could you call him and ask him to come over when he has time?"

He laughed. "I'll do that tonight."

"Even if he can't make rain, I'd love to meet him," she said. "He sounds very interesting."

"Take my word for it, he is. Doesn't talk much, but when he does, it's worth hearing. Well, I'll get back to work."

"Thanks, Ben."

He smiled. "My pleasure. And don't let that developer bully you," he said firmly. "Maybe you need to talk to Cort's dad and tell him what's going on. He's not going to like that, about the development. It's too close to his barns. In these hard times, even the Brannts couldn't afford to build new ones with all that high tech they use."

"Got a point. I'll talk to him."

Maddie went back to the house. She put the feed basket absently on the kitchen counter, mentally reviewing all the things she had planned for the week. She missed Cort already. But at least it meant the rooster was likely to stay at home. He only went over to the Brannt ranch when Cort was in residence, to attack him.

"Better wash those eggs and put them in the refrigerator," Great-Aunt Sadie advised. "They're the ones for the restaurant, aren't they?"

"Yes. Old Mr. Bailey said his customers have been raving about the taste of his egg omelets lately." She laughed. "I'll have to give my girls a treat for that."

Great-Aunt Sadie was frowning. "Maddie, did you ever look up the law about selling raw products?"

Maddie shook her head. "I meant to. But I'm sure it's not illegal to sell eggs. My mother did it for years before she died…"

"That was a long time ago, honey. Don't you remember that raid a few years ago on those poor farmers who were selling raw milk?" She made a face. "What sort of country do we live in? Sending an armed raid team after helpless farmers for selling milk!"

Maddie felt uneasy. "I'd forgotten that."

"I hadn't. In my day we had homemade butter and we could drink all the raw milk we wanted—didn't have all this fancy stuff a hundred years ago and it seems to me people were a whole lot healthier."

"You weren't here a hundred years ago," Maddie pointed out with a grin. "Anyway, the government's not going to come out here and attack me for selling a few eggs!"

She did look on the internet for the law pertaining to egg production and found that she was in compliance. In fact, there were even places in the country licensed to sell raw milk. She'd have to tell Great-Aunt Sadie about that, she mused. Apparently armed teams weren't raiding farms out west.

Meanwhile, a day later, she did call King Brannt. She was hesitant about it. Not only was he Cort's father, he had a reputation in the county for being one tough customer, and difficult to get along with. He had a fiery temper that he wasn't shy about using. But the developer's determination to get the Lane ranch could have repercussions. A lot of them.

She picked up the phone and dialed the ranch.

The housekeeper answered.

"Could I speak to King Brannt, please?" she asked. "It's Maddie Lane."

There was a skirl of laughter. "Yes, you've got a rooster named Pumpkin."

Maddie laughed. "Is he famous?"

"He is around here," the woman said. "Cort isn't laughing, but the rest of us are. Imagine having a personal devil in the form of a little red rooster! We've been teasing Cort that he must have done something terrible that we don't know about."

Maddie sighed. "I'm afraid Pumpkin has it in for Cort. See, he picked him up by the feet and showed him to my girls, my hens, I mean, and hurt his pride. That was when he started looking for Cort."

"Oh, I see. It's vengeance." She laughed again. "Nice talking to you, I'll go get Mr. Brannt. Take just a minute…"

Maddie held on. Her gaze fell on one of her little fairy statues. It was delicate and beautiful; the tiny face perfect, lovely, with sculpted long blond hair, sitting on a stone with a butterfly in its hand. It was a new piece, one she'd just finished with the plastic sculpture mix that was the best on the market. Her egg money paid for the materials. She loved the little things and could never bear to sell one. But she did wonder if there was a market for such a specialized piece.

"Brannt," a deep voice said curtly.

She almost jumped. "Mr. Brannt? It's… I mean, I'm Maddie Lane. I live on the little ranch next door to yours," she faltered.

"Hi, Maddie," he said, and his voice lost its curt edge and was pleasant. "What can I do for you?"

"I've got sort of a situation over here. I wanted to tell you about it."

"What's wrong? Can we help?"

"That's so nice of you." She didn't add that she'd been told some very scary things about his temper. "It's this developer. He's from Las Vegas…"

"Yes. Archie Lawson. I had him investigated."

"He's trying to get me to sell my ranch to him. I don't want to. This ranch has been in my family for generations. But he's very pushy and he made some threats."

"He's carried them out in the past," King said, very curtly. "But you can be sure I'm not going to let him hurt you or your cattle herd. I'll put on extra patrols on the land boundary we share, and station men at the cabin out there. We use it for roundup, but it's been vacant for a week or so. I'll make sure someone's there at all times, and we'll hook up cameras around your cattle herd and monitor them constantly."

"You'd do that for me?" she faltered. "Cameras. It's so expensive." She knew, because in desperation she'd looked at them and been shocked at the prices for even a cheap system.

"I'd do that for you," he replied. "You have one of the finest breeding herds I know of, which is why we buy so many of your young bulls."

"Why, thank you."

"You're welcome. You see, it's looking out for our interests as well as yours. I can't have a complex so close to my barns, or my purebred herd. The noise of construction would be bad enough, but the constant traffic would injure production."

"Yes, I know what you mean."

"Besides that, Lawson is unscrupulous. He's got his fingers in lots of dirty pies. He's had several brushes with the law, too."

"I'm not surprised. He was a little scary."

"Don't you worry. If he comes back and makes any threat at all, you call over here. If you can't find me, talk to Cort. He'll take care of it."

She hesitated. "Actually Cort isn't speaking to me right now."

There was a pause. "Because of the rooster?" His voice was almost smiling.

"Actually because I made a nasty crack about Odalie Everett," she confessed heavily. "I didn't mean to. He made me mad. I guess he was justified to complain. Pumpkin is really mean to him."

"So I heard. That rooster has had brushes with several of our cowboys." She could tell that he was trying not to laugh.

"The man who sold him to me said he was real gentle and wouldn't hurt a fly. That's sort of true. I've never seen Pumpkin hurt a fly." She laughed. "Just people."

"You need a gentle rooster, especially if you're going to be selling eggs and baby chicks."

"The baby chick operation is down the road, but I'm doing well with my egg business."

"Glad to hear it. Our housekeeper wants to get on your customer list, by the way."

"I'll talk to her, and thanks!"

He chuckled. "My pleasure."

"If Mr. Lawson comes back, I'll let you know."

"Please do. The man is trouble."

"I know. Thanks again, Mr. Brannt. I feel better now."

"Your dad was a friend of mine," he said quietly. "I miss him. I know you do, too."

"I miss him a lot," she said. "But Great-Aunt Sadie and I are coping. It's just this ranching thing," she added miserably. "Dad was good at it, he had charts in the barn, he knew which traits to breed for, all that technical stuff. He taught me well, but I'm not as good as he was at it. Not at all. I like to paint and sculpt." She hesitated. "Creative people shouldn't have to breed cattle!" she burst out.

He laughed. "I hear you. Listen, suppose I send Cort over there to help you with the genetics? He's even better at it than I am. And I'm good. No conceit, just fact."

She laughed, too. "You really are. We read about your bulls in the cattle journals." She paused. "I don't think Cort would come."

"He'll come." He sounded certain of it. "He needs something to take his mind off that woman. She's a sweet girl, in her way, but she's got some serious growing up to do. She thinks the world revolves around her. It doesn't."

"She's just been a little spoiled, I think." She tried to be gracious.

"Rotten," he replied. "My kids never were."

"You and Mrs. Brannt did a great job with yours. And John Everett is a really nice man. So the Everetts did a great job there, too." She didn't mention the second Everett son, Tanner. The Everetts never spoke about him. Neither did anyone else. He was something of a mystery man. But gossip was that he and his dad didn't get along.

"They did a great job on John, for sure." He let out a breath. "I just wish Cort would wake up. Odalie is never going to settle in a small community. She's meant for high society and big cities. Cort would die in a high-rise apartment. He's got too much country in him, although he'd jump at the chance if Odalie would offer him one. Just between us," he added quietly, "I hope she doesn't. If she makes it in opera, and I think she can, what would Cort do with himself while she trained and performed?

He'd be bored out of his mind. He doesn't even like opera. He likes country-western."

"He plays it very well," Maddie said softly. "I loved coming to the barbecue at your place during the spring sale and hearing him sing. It was nice of you to invite all of us. Even old Ben. He was over the moon."

He laughed. "You're all neighbors. I know you think of Ben as more family than employee. His family has worked for your family for four generations."

"That's a long time," she agreed. "I'm not selling my place," she added firmly. "No matter what that fancy Las Vegas man does."

"Good for you. I'll help you make sure of that. I'll send Cort on over."

"He's back from visiting his sister?" she stammered.

"Yes. Got back yesterday. They went trout fishing."

She sighed. "I'd love to go trout fishing."

"Cort loves it. He said they did close the trout streams for fishing a couple of days after he and Dana—Morie, I mean, went. The heat makes it impossible. "

"That's true." She hesitated. "Why do you call Morie Dana?" she blurted out.

He laughed. "When Shelby was carrying them, we called them Matt and Dana. Those were the names we picked out. Except that two of our friends used those names for theirs and we had to change ours. It got to be a habit, though, until the kids were adolescents.

"Hey, Cort," she heard King call, his hand covering the receiver so his voice was a little muffled.

"Yes, Dad?" came the reply.

"I want you to go over to the Lane place and give Maddie some help with her breeding program."

"The hell I will!" Cort burst out.

The hand over the phone seemed to close, because the rest of it was muffled. Angry voices, followed by more discussion, followed like what seemed a string of horrible curses from Cort.

King came back on the line. "He said he'd be pleased to come over and help," he lied. "But he did ask if you'd shut your rooster up first." He chuckled.

"I'll put him in the chicken house right now." She tried not to sound as miserable as she felt. She knew Cort didn't want to help her. He hated her. "And thank you again."

"You're very welcome. Call us if you need help with Lawson. Okay?"

"Okay."

True to his father's words, Cort drove up in front of the house less than an hour later. He wasn't slamming doors or scattering chickens this time, either. He looked almost pleasant. Apparently his father had talked to him very firmly.

Maddie had combed her hair and washed her face. She still wasn't going to win any beauty contests. She had on her nicest jeans and a pink T-shirt that said *La Vie en Rose*.

It called attention, unfortunately, to breasts that were small and pert instead of big and tempting. But Cort was looking at her shirt with his lips pursed.

"The world through rose-colored glasses?" he mused.

"You speak French."

"Of course. French, Spanish and enough German to get me arrested in Munich. We do cattle deals all over the world," he added.

"Yes, I remember." She swallowed, hard, recalling the

things he'd said at their last unfortunate meeting. "Your father said you could help me figure out Dad's breeding program."

"I think so. I helped him work up the new one before he passed away," he added quietly. "We were all shocked by how fast it happened."

"So were we," Maddie confessed. "Two months from the time he was diagnosed until he passed on." She drew in a long breath. "He hated tests, you know. He wouldn't go to the doctor about anything unless he was already at death's door. I think the doctor suspected something, but Dad just passed right over the lecture about tests being necessary and walked out. By the time they diagnosed the cancer, it was too late for anything except radiation. And somebody said that they only did that to help contain the pain." Her pale eyes grew sad. "It was terrible, the pain. At the last, he was so sedated that he hardly knew me. It was the only way he could cope."

"I'm sorry," he said. "I haven't lost parents, but I lost both my grandparents. They were wonderful people. It was hard to let them go."

"Life goes on," she said quietly. "Everybody dies. It's just a matter of how and when."

"True."

She swallowed. "Dad kept his chalkboard in the barn, and his books in the library, along with his journals. I've read them all, but I can't make sense of what he was doing. I'm not college educated, and I don't really know much about animal husbandry. I know what I do from watching Dad."

"I can explain it to you."

She nodded. "Thanks."

She turned and led the way to the house.

"Where's that...rooster?" he asked.

"Shut up in the henhouse with a fan."

"A fan?" he exclaimed and burst out laughing.

"It really isn't funny," she said softly. "I lost two of my girls to the heat. Found them dead in the henhouse, trying to lay. I had Ben go and get us a fan and install it there. It does help with the heat, a little at least."

"My grandmother used to keep hens," he recalled. "But we only have one or two now. Foxes got the rest." He glanced at her. "Andie, our housekeeper, wants to get on your egg customer list for two dozen a week."

She nodded. "Your dad mentioned that. I can do that. I've got pullets that should start laying soon. My flock is growing by leaps and bounds." She indicated the large fenced chicken yard, dotted with all sorts of chickens. The henhouse was huge, enough to accommodate them all, complete with perches and ladders and egg boxes and, now, a fan.

"Nice operation."

"I'm going to expand it next year, if I do enough business."

"Did you check the law on egg production?"

She laughed. "Yes, I did. I'm in compliance. I don't have a middleman, or I could be in trouble. I sell directly to the customer, so it's all okay."

"Good." He shrugged, his hands in his jean pockets. "I'd hate to have to bail you out of jail."

"You wouldn't." She sighed.

He stopped and looked down at her. She seemed so dejected. "Yes, I would," he said, his deep voice quiet and almost tender as he studied her small frame, her short wavy blond hair, her wide, soft gray eyes. Her complexion was exquisite, not a blemish on it except for one small mole on her cheek. She had a pretty mouth, too. It looked tempting. Bow-shaped, soft, naturally pink...

"Cort?" she asked suddenly, her whole body tingling, her heart racing at the way he was staring at her mouth.

"What? Oh. Yes. The breeding books." He nodded. "We should get to it."

"Yes." She swallowed, tried to hide her blush and opened the front door.

Chapter 3

Maddie couldn't help but stare at Cort as he leaned over the desk to read the last page of her father's breeding journal. He was the handsomest man she'd ever seen. And that physique! He was long and lean, but also muscular. Broad-shouldered, narrow-hipped, and in the opening of his chambray shirt, thick curling black hair peeked out.

She'd never been overly interested in intimacy. Never having indulged, she had no idea how it felt, although she'd been reading romance novels since her early teens. She did know how things worked between men and women from health class. What she didn't know was why women gave in to men. She supposed it came naturally.

Cort felt her eyes on him and turned, so that he was looking directly into her wide, shocked gray eyes. His own dark ones narrowed. He knew that look, that expression. She was trying to hide it, but he wasn't fooled.

"Take a picture," he drawled, because her interest irritated him. She wasn't his type. Not at all.

Her reaction shamed him. She looked away, cleared her throat and went beet-red. "Sorry," she choked. "I was just thinking. You were sort of in the way. I was thinking about my fairies..."

He felt guilty. That made him even more irritable. "What fairies?"

She stumbled and had to catch herself as she went past him. She was so embarrassed she could hardly even walk.

She went to the shelf where she'd put the newest one. Taking it down very carefully, she carried it to the desk and put it in front of him.

He caught his breath. He picked it up, delicately for a man with such large, strong hands, and held it up to his eyes. He turned it. He was smiling. "This is really beautiful," he said, as if it surprised him. He glanced at her. "You did this by yourself?"

She moved uneasily. "Yes," she muttered. What did he think—that she had somebody come in and do the work so she could claim credit for it?

"I didn't mean it like that, Maddie," he said gently. The sound of her name on his lips made her tingle. She didn't dare look up, because her attraction to him would surely show. He knew a lot more about women than she knew about men. He could probably tell already that she liked him. It had made him mad. So she'd have to hide it.

"Okay," she said. But she still wouldn't look up.

He gave the beautiful little statuette another look before he put it down very gently on the desk. "You should be marketing those," he said firmly. "I've seen things half as lovely sell for thousands of dollars."

"Thousands?" she exclaimed.

"Yes. Sometimes five figures. I was staying at a hotel in Arizona during a cattlemen's conference and a doll show was exhibiting at the same hotel. I talked to some of the artists." He shook his head. "It's amazing how much collectors will pay for stuff like that." He indicated the fairy with his head. "You should look into it."

She was stunned. "I never dreamed people would pay so much for a little sculpture."

"Your paintings are nice, too," he admitted. "My mother loves the drawing you did. She bought it at that art show last year. She said you should be selling the sculptures, too."

"I would. It's just that they're like my children," she confessed, and flushed because that sounded nutty. "I mean...well, it's hard to explain."

"Each one is unique and you put a lot of yourself into it," he guessed. "So it would be hard to sell one."

"Yes." She did look up then, surprised that he was so perceptive.

"You have the talent. All you need is the drive."

"Drive." She sighed. She smiled faintly. "How about imminent starvation? Does that work for drive?"

He laughed. "We wouldn't let you starve. Your bull calves are too valuable to us," he added, just when she thought he might actually care.

"Thanks," she said shyly. "In that journal of Dad's—" she changed the subject "—he talks about heritability traits for lean meat with marbling to produce cuts that health-conscious consumers will buy. Can you explain to me how I go about producing herd sires that carry the traits we breed for?"

He smiled. "It's complicated. Want to take notes?"

She sighed. "Just like going back to school." Then she

remembered school, and the agonies she went through in her junior and senior years because of Odalie Everett, and her face clenched.

"What's wrong?" he asked, frowning.

She swallowed. She almost said what was wrong. But she'd been down that road with him already, making comments she shouldn't have made about Odalie. She wasn't going to make him mad. Not now, when he was being pleasant and helpful.

"Nothing. Just a stray thought." She smiled. "I'll get some paper and a pencil."

After a half hour she put down the pencil. "It's got to be like learning to speak Martian," she muttered.

He laughed out loud. "Listen, I didn't come into the world knowing how this stuff worked, either. I had to learn it, and if my dad hadn't been a patient man, I'd have jumped off a cliff."

"Your dad is patient?" she asked, and couldn't help sounding surprised.

"I know he's got a reputation for being just the opposite. But he really is patient. I had a hard time with algebra in high school. He'd take me into the office every night and go over problems with me until I understood how to do them. He never fussed, or yelled, or raised his voice. And I was a problem child." He shook his head. "I'm amazed I got through my childhood in one piece. I've broken half the bones in my body at some point, and I know my mother's gray hairs are all because of me. Morie was a little lady. She never caused anybody any trouble."

"I remember," Maddie said with a smile. "She was always kind to me. She was a couple of years ahead of me, but she was never snobby."

His dark eyes narrowed. "There's a hidden comment in there."

She flushed. "I didn't mention anybody else."

"You meant Odalie," he said. "She can't help being beautiful and rich and talented," he pointed out. "And it wasn't her fault that her parents put her in public school instead of private school, where she might have been better treated."

"Better treated." She glared at him. "Not one teacher or administrator ever had a bad word to say about her, even though she bullied younger girls mercilessly and spent most of her time bad-mouthing people she didn't like. One year she had a party for our whole class, at the ranch. She invited every single girl in the class—except me."

Cort's eyes narrowed. "I'm sure it wasn't intentional."

"My father went to see her father, that's how unintentional it was," she replied quietly. "When Cole Everett knew what she'd done to me, he grounded her for a month and took away her end-of-school trip as punishment."

"That seems extreme for not inviting someone to a party," he scoffed.

"I guess that's because you don't know about the other things she did to me," she replied.

"Let me guess—she didn't send you a Valentine's Day card, either," he drawled in a tone that dripped sarcasm.

She looked at him with open sadness. "Sure. That's it. I held a grudge because she didn't send me a holiday card and my father went to see the school principal and Odalie's father because he liked starting trouble."

Cort remembered her father. He was the mildest, most forgiving man anywhere around Branntville. He'd walk away from a fight if he could. The very fact that he got involved meant that he felt there was more than a slight problem.

But Cort loved Odalie, and here was this bad-tempered little frump making cracks about her, probably because she was jealous.

"I guess if you don't have a real talent and you aren't as pretty, it's hard to get along with someone who has it all," he commented.

Her face went beet-red. She stood up, took her father's journal, closed it and put it back in the desk drawer. She faced him across the width of the desk.

"Thank you for explaining the journal to me," she said in a formal tone. "I'll study the notes I took very carefully."

"Fine." He started to leave, hesitated. He turned and looked back at her. He could see an unusual brightness in her eyes. "Look, I didn't mean to hurt your feelings. It's just, well, you don't know Odalie. She's sweet and kind, she'd never hurt anybody on purpose."

"I don't have any talent, I'm ugly and I lie." She nodded. "Thanks."

"Hell, I never said you lied!"

She swallowed. Loud voices and curses made her nervous. She gripped the edge of the desk.

"Now what's wrong?" he asked angrily.

She shook her head. "Nothing," she said quickly.

He took a sudden, quick step toward her. She backed up, knocked over the desk chair and almost fell again getting it between him and herself. She was white in the face.

He stopped in his tracks. His lips fell open. In all his life, he'd never seen a woman react that way.

"What the hell is wrong with you?" he asked, but not in a loud or menacing tone.

She swallowed. "Nothing. Thanks for coming over."

He scowled. She looked scared to death.

Great-Aunt Sadie had heard a crash in the room. She opened the door gingerly and looked in. She glanced from Maddie's white face to Cort's drawn one. "Maddie, you okay?" she asked hesitantly, her eyes flicking back and forth to Cort's as if she, too, was uneasy.

"I'm fine. I just…knocked the chair over." She laughed, but it was a nervous, quick laugh. "Cort was just leaving. He gave me lots of information."

"Nice of him," Sadie agreed. She moved closer to Maddie, as if prepared to act as a human shield if Cort took another step toward the younger woman. "Good night, Cort."

He wanted to know what was wrong. It was true he'd said some mean things, but the fear in Maddie's eyes, and the looks he was getting, really disturbed him. He moved to the door, hesitated. "If you need any more help…" he began.

"I'll call. Sure. Thanks for offering." Maddie's voice sounded tight. She was standing very still. He was reminded forcibly of deer's eyes in headlights.

"Well, I'll get on home. Good night."

"Night," Maddie choked out.

He glanced from one woman to the other, turned and pulled the door closed behind him.

Maddie almost collapsed into the chair. Tears were running down her cheeks. Great-Aunt Sadie knelt beside the chair and pulled her close, rocking her. "There, there, it's all right. He's gone. What happened?"

"I mentioned about Odalie not inviting me to the party

and he said I was just jealous of her. I said something, I don't…remember what, and he started toward me, all mad and impatient…" She closed her eyes, shivering. "I can't forget. All those years ago, and I still can't forget!"

"Nobody ever told Cort just what Odalie did to you, did they?"

"Apparently not," Maddie said heavily. She wiped her eyes. "Her dad made her apologize, but I know she never regretted it." She drew in a breath. "I told her that one day somebody was going to pay her back for all the mean things she did." She looked up. "Cort thinks she's a saint. If he only knew what she's really like…"

"It wouldn't matter," the older woman said sadly. "Men get hooked on a pretty face and they'd believe white was black if the woman told them it was. He's infatuated, baby. No cure for that but time."

"I thought he was so sexy." Maddie laughed. She brushed at her eyes again. "Then he lost his temper like that. He scared me," she said on a nervous smile.

"It's all right. Nobody's going to hurt you here. I promise."

She hugged the older woman tight. "Thanks."

"At the time, that boy did apologize, and he meant it," Sadie reminded her. "He was as much a victim as you were."

"Yes, but he got in trouble and he should have. No man, even an angry young one with justification, should ever do what he did to a girl. He didn't have nightmares for a month, either, did he, or carry emotional scars that never go away? Sad thing about him," she added quietly, "he died overseas when a roadside bomb blew up when he was serving in the Middle East. With a temper like that,

I often wondered what he might do to a woman if he got even more upset than he was at me that time."

"No telling. And just as well we don't have to find out." Her face hardened. "But you're right about that Odalie girl. Got a bad attitude and no compassion for anybody. One of these days, life is going to pay her out in her own coin. She'll be sorry for the things she's done, but it will be too late. God forgives," she added. "But there's a price."

"What's that old saying, 'God's mill grinds slowly, but relentlessly'?"

"Something like that. Come on. I'll make you a nice cup of hot coffee."

"Make that a nice cup of hot chocolate instead," Maddie said. "I've had a rough day and I want to go to bed."

"I don't blame you. Not one bit."

Cort was thoughtful at breakfast the next morning. He was usually animated with his parents while he ate. But now he was quiet and retrospective.

"Something wrong?" his dad asked.

Cort glanced at him. He managed a smile. "Yeah. Something." He sipped coffee. "I went over her dad's journal with Maddie. We had sort of an argument and I started toward her while I was mad." He hesitated. "She knocked over a chair getting away from me. White in the face, shaking all over. It was an extreme reaction. We've argued before, but that's the first time she's been afraid of me."

"And you don't understand why." His father's expression was troubled.

"I don't." Cort's eyes narrowed. "But you do, don't you?"

He nodded.

"King, should you tell him?" Shelby asked worriedly.

"I think I should, honey," he said gently, and his dark eyes smiled with affection. "Somebody needs to."

"Okay then." She got up with her coffee. "You men talk. I'm going to phone Morie and see how she's doing."

"Give her my love," King called after her.

"Mine, too," Cort added.

She waved a hand and closed the door behind her. "Tell me," Cort asked his dad.

King put down his coffee cup. "In her senior year, Maddie was Odalie's worst enemy. There was a boy, seemingly a nice boy, who liked Maddie. But Odalie liked him, and she was angry that Maddie, a younger girl who wasn't pretty or rich or talented, seemed to be winning in the affection sweepstakes."

"I told Maddie, Odalie's not like that," Cort began angrily.

King held up a hand. "Just hear me out. Don't interrupt."

Cort made a face, but he shut up.

"So Odalie and a girlfriend got on one of the social websites and started posting things that she said Maddie told her about the boy. She said Maddie thought he was a hick, that his mother was stupid, that both his parents couldn't even pass a basic IQ test."

"What? That's a lie…!"

"Sit down!" King's voice was soft, but the look in his eyes wasn't. Cort sat.

"The boy's mother was dying of cancer. He was outraged and furious at what Maddie had allegedly said about his family. His mother had just been taken to the hospital, not expected to live. She died that same day.

He went to school just to find Maddie. She was in the library." He picked up his cup and sipped coffee. "He jerked her out of her chair, slapped her over a table and pulled her by her hair to the window. He was in the act of throwing her out—and it was on the second floor—when the librarian screamed for help and two big, stronger boys restrained him, in the nick of time."

Cort's face froze. "Maddie told you that?"

"Her father's lawyer told Cole Everett that," came the terse reply. "There were at least five witnesses. The boy was arrested for assault. It was hushed up, because that's what's done in small communities to protect the families. Odalie was implicated, because the attorney hired a private investigator to find the source of the allegations. They traced the posts to her computer."

Cort felt uneasy. He was certain Odalie couldn't have done such a thing. "Maybe somebody used her computer," he began.

"She confessed," King said curtly.

Cort was even more uneasy now.

"Cole Everett had his own attorney speak to the one Maddie's father had hired. They worked out a compromise that wouldn't involve a trial. But Odalie had to toe the line from that time forward. They put her on probation, you see. She had first-offender status, so her record was wiped when she stayed out of trouble for the next two years. She had a girlfriend who'd egged her on. The girlfriend left town shortly thereafter."

"Yes," Cort replied, relaxing. "I see now. The girlfriend forced her to do it."

King made a curt sound deep in his throat. "Son, nobody forced her to do a damned thing. She was jealous of Maddie. She was lucky the boy didn't kill Maddie, or she'd have been an accessory to murder." He watched Cort's face pale. "That's right. And I don't think even Cole Everett could have kept her out of jail if that had happened."

Cort leaned back in his chair. "Poor Odalie."

"Funny," King said. "I would have said, 'Poor Maddie.'"

Cort flushed. "It must have been terrible for both of them, I suppose."

King just shook his head. He got up. "Blind as a bat," he mused. "Just like me, when I was giving your mother hell twice a day for being engaged to my little brother. God, I hated him. Hated them both. Never would admit why."

"Uncle Danny?" Cort exclaimed. "He was engaged to Mom?"

"He was. It was a fake engagement, however." He chuckled. "He was just trying to show me what my feelings for Shelby really were. I forgave him every minute's agony. She's the best thing that ever happened to me. I didn't realize how deeply a man could love a woman. All these years," he added in a soft tone, "and those feelings haven't lessened a bit. I hope you find that sort of happiness in your life. I wish it for you."

"Thanks," Cort said. He smiled. "If I can get Odalie to marry me, I promise you, I'll have it."

King started to speak, but thought better of it. "I've got some book work to do."

"I've got a new video game I'm dying to try." Cort chuckled. "It's been a long day."

"I appreciate you going over to talk to Maddie."

"No problem. She just needed a few pointers."

"She's no cattlewoman," King said worriedly. "She's

swimming upstream. She doesn't even like cattle. She likes chickens."

"Don't say chickens," Cort pleaded with a groan.

"Your problem isn't with chickens, it's with a rooster."

"I'd dearly love to help him have a fatal heart attack," Cort said irritably.

"He'll die of old age one day." His dad laughed.

"Maddie said that developer had been putting pressure on her to sell," King added solemnly. "I've put on some extra help to keep an eye over that way, just to make sure her breeding stock doesn't start dying mysteriously."

"What?" Cort asked, shocked. "She didn't say anything about that."

"Probably wouldn't, to you. It smacks of weakness to mention such things to the enemy."

"I'm not the enemy."

King smiled. "Aren't you?"

He left his son sitting at the table, deep in thought.

Maddie was working in the yard when the developer drove up a week later. She leaned on the pitchfork she was using to put hay into a trough, and waited, miserable, for him to get out of his car and talk to her.

"I won't sell," she said when he came up to her. "And in case you feel like high pressure tactics, my neighbor has mounted cameras all over the ranch." She flushed at his fury.

"Well, how about that?" he drawled, and his eyes were blazing with anger. He forced a smile. "You did know that cameras can be disabled?" he asked.

"The cameras also have listening devices that can pick up a whisper."

He actually seemed to go pale. He looked at the poles

that contained the outside lighting and mumbled a curse under his breath. There was some sort of electronic device up there.

"I'll come back again one day and ask you the same question," he promised, but he smiled and his voice was pleasant. "Maybe you'll change your mind."

"We also have cowboys in the line cabins on the borders of this ranch. Mr. Brannt is very protective of me since my father died. He buys many of our young breeding bulls," she added for good measure.

He was very still. "King Brannt?"

"Yes. You've heard of him, I gather."

He didn't reply. He turned on his heel and marched back to his car. But this time he didn't spin his wheels.

Maddie almost fell over with relief.

Just as the developer left, another car drove up, a sleek Jaguar, black with silver trim. Maddie didn't recognize it. Oh, dear, didn't some hit men drive fancy cars...?

The door opened and big John Everett climbed out of the low-slung luxury car, holding on to his white Stetson so that it wouldn't be dislodged from his thick head of blond hair. Maddie almost laughed with relief.

John grinned as he approached her. He had pale blue eyes, almost silver-colored, like his dad's, and he was a real dish. He and Odalie both had their mother's blond fairness, instead of Cole Everett's dark hair and olive complexion.

"What the hell's wrong with you?" he drawled. "Black cars make you twitchy or something?"

"I think hit men drive them, is all."

He burst out laughing. "I've never shot one single person. A deer or two, maybe, in season." He moved toward her and stopped, towering over her. His pale eyes were dancing on her flushed face. "I ran into King Brannt at a cattlemen's association meeting last night. He said you were having some problems trying to work out your father's breeding program. He said Cort explained it to you."

"Uh, well, yes, sort of." It was hard to admit that even taking notes, she hadn't understood much of what Cort had told her.

"Cort tried to tutor me in biology in high school. I got a D on the test. He's good at genetics, lousy at trying to explain them." He shoved his hat back on his head and grinned. "So I thought, maybe I'll come over and have a try at helping you understand it."

"You're a nice guy, John," she said gently. And he was. At the height of his sister's intimidation, John had been on Maddie's side.

He shrugged. "I'm the flower of my family." His face hardened. "Even if she is my sister, Odalie makes me ashamed sometimes. I haven't forgotten the things she did to you."

"We all make mistakes when we're young," she faltered, trying to be fair.

"You have a gentle nature," he observed. "Like Cort's mother. And mine," he added with a smile. "Mom can't bear to see anything hurt. She cried for days when your father's lawyer came over and told her and Dad what Odalie had done to you."

"I know. She called me. Your dad did, too. They're good people."

"Odalie might be a better person if she had a few disadvantages," John said coldly. "As things stand, she'll give in to Cort's persuasion one day and marry him. He'll be in hell for the rest of his life. The only person she's ever really loved is herself."

"That's harsh, John," she chided gently.

"It's the truth, Maddie." He swung his pointing finger at her nose. "You're like my mother...she'd find one nice thing to say about the devil." He smiled. "I'm in the mood to do some tutoring today. But I require payment. Your great-aunt makes a mean cup of coffee, and I'm partial to French vanilla."

"That's my favorite."

He chuckled. "Mine, too." He went back to the car, opened the passenger seat, took out a big box and a bag. "So since I drink a lot of it, I brought my own."

She caught her breath. It was one of those European coffee machines that used pods. Maddie had always wanted one, but the price was prohibitive.

"Sad thing is it only brews one cup at a time, but we'll compensate." He grinned. "So lead the way to the kitchen and I'll show you how to use it."

Two cups of mouthwatering coffee later, they were sitting in Maddie's father's office, going over breeding charts. John found the blackboard her father had used to map out the genetics. He was able to explain it so simply that Maddie understood almost at once which herd sires to breed to which cows.

"You make it sound so simple!" she exclaimed. "You're a wonder, John!"

He laughed. "It's all a matter of simplification," he drawled. He leaned back in the chair and sketched Maddie's radiant face with narrowed pale blue eyes. "You sell yourself short. It's not that you can't understand. You just have to have things explained. Cort's too impatient."

She averted her eyes. Mention of Cort made her uneasy.

"Yes, he loses his temper," John said thoughtfully. "But he's not dangerous. Not like that boy."

She paled. "I can't talk about it."

"You can, and you should," he replied solemnly. "Your father was advised to get some counseling for you, but he didn't believe in such things. That boy had a record for domestic assault, did you ever know? He beat his grandmother almost to death one day. She refused to press charges, or he would have gone to jail. His parents jumped in and got a fancy lawyer and convinced the authorities that he wasn't dangerous. I believe they contributed to the reelection campaign of the man who was police chief at the time as well."

"That's a harsh accusation," she said, shocked.

"It's a harsh world, and politics is the dirtiest business in town. Corruption doesn't stop at criminals, you know. Rich people have a way of subverting justice from time to time."

"You're rich, and you don't do those types of things."

"Yes, I am rich," he replied honestly. "And I'm honest. I have my own business, but I didn't get where I am by depending on my dad to support me."

She searched his eyes curiously. "Is that a dig at Cort?"

"It is," he replied quietly. "He stays at home, works on the ranch and does what King tells him to do. I told him some time ago that he's hurting himself by doing no more than wait to inherit Skylance, but he just nods and walks off."

"Somebody will have to take over the ranch when King is too old to manage it," she pointed out reasonably. "There isn't anybody else."

John grimaced. "I suppose that's true. But it's the same

with me. Can you really see Odalie running a ranch?" He burst out laughing. "God, she might chip a fingernail!"

She grinned from ear to ear.

"Anyway, I was a maverick. I wanted my own business. I have a farm-equipment business and I also specialize in marketing native grasses for pasture improvement."

"You're an entrepreneur," she said with a chuckle.

"Something like that, I guess." He cocked his head and studied her. "You know I don't date much."

"Yes. Sort of like me. I'm not modern enough for most men."

"I'm not modern enough for most women," he replied, and smiled. "Uh, there's going to be a dressy party over at the Hancock place to introduce a new rancher in the area. I wondered if you might like to go with me?"

"A party?" she asked. She did have one good dress. She'd bought it for a special occasion a while ago, and she couldn't really afford another one with the ranch having financial issues. But it was a nice dress. Her eyes brightened. "I haven't been to a party in a long time. I went with Dad to a conference in Denver before he got sick."

"I remember. You looked very nice."

"Well, I'd be wearing the same dress I had on then," she pointed out.

He laughed. "I don't follow the current fashions for women," he mused. "I'm inviting you, not the dress."

"In that case," she said with a pert smile, "I'd be delighted!"

Chapter 4

Some men dragged their feet around the room and called it dancing. John Everett could actually dance! He knew all the Latin dances and how to waltz, although he was uncomfortable with some of the newer ways to display on a dance floor. Fortunately the organizers of the party were older people and they liked older music.

Only a minute into an enthusiastic samba, John and Maddie found themselves in the middle of the dance floor with the other guests clapping as they marked the fast rhythm.

"We should take this show on the road." John chuckled as they danced.

"I'm game. I'll give up ranching and become a professional samba performer, if you'll come, too," she suggested.

"Maybe only part of the year," he mused. "We can't let our businesses go to pot."

"Spoilsport."

He grinned.

While the two were dancing, oblivious to the other guests, a tall, dark man in a suit walked in and found himself a flute of champagne. He tasted it, nodding to other guests. Everyone was gathered around the dance floor of the ballroom in the Victorian mansion. He wandered to the fringes and caught his breath. There, on the dance floor, was Maddie Lane.

She was wearing a dress, a sheath of black slinky material that dipped in front to display just a hint of the lovely curve of her breasts and display her long elegant neck and rounded arms. Her pale blond hair shone like gold in the light from the chandeliers. She was wearing makeup, just enough to enhance what seemed to be a rather pretty face, and the pretty calves of her legs were displayed to their best advantage from the arch of her spiked high-heel shoes. He'd rarely seen her dressed up. Not that he'd been interested in her or anything.

But there she was, decked out like a Christmas tree, dancing with his best friend. John didn't date anybody. Until now.

Cort Brannt felt irritation rise in him like bile. He scowled at the display they were making of themselves. Had they no modesty at all? And people were clapping like idiots.

He glared at Maddie. He remembered the last time he'd seen her. She backed away from Cort, but she was dancing with John as if she really liked him. Her face was radiant. She was smiling. Cort had rarely seen her smile at all. Of course, usually he was yelling at her or making hurtful remarks. Not much incentive for smiles.

He sipped champagne. Someone spoke to him. He

just nodded. He was intent on the dancing couple, focused and furious.

Suddenly he noticed that the flute was empty. He turned and went back to the hors d'oeuvres table and had them refill it. But he didn't go back to the dance floor. Instead he found a fellow cattleman to talk to about the drought and selling off cattle.

A few minutes later he was aware of two people helping themselves to punch and cake.

"Oh, hi, Cort," John greeted him with a smile. "I didn't think you were coming."

"Hadn't planned to," Cort said in a cool tone. "My dad had an emergency on the ranch, so I'm filling in. One of the officers of the cattlemen's association is here." He indicated the man with a nod of his head. "Dad wanted me to ask him about any pending legislation that might help us through the drought. We've heard rumors, but nothing substantial."

"My dad was wondering the same." John frowned. "You okay?"

"I'm fine," Cort said, making sure that he enunciated as plainly as possible. He stood taller, although he still wasn't as tall, or as big, as his friend. "Why do you ask?"

"Because that's your second glass of champagne and you don't drink," John said flatly.

Cort held the flute up and looked at it. It was empty. "Where did that go?" he murmured.

"Just a guess, but maybe you drank it?" John replied.

Cort set the flute on the spotless white tablecloth and looked down at Maddie. "You're keeping expensive company these days."

She was shocked at the implication.

"Hold it right there," John said, and his deep tone was menacing. "I invited her."

"Got plans, have you?" Cort replied coldly.

"Why shouldn't I?" came the droll reply. "Oh, by the way, Odalie says her Italian voice teacher is an idiot. He doesn't know beans about how to sing, and he isn't teaching her anything. So she thinks she may come home soon."

Maddie felt her heart sink. Cort's expression lightened. "You think she might?"

"It's possible. You should lay off that stuff."

Cort glanced at the flute. "I suppose so."

"Hey, John, can I talk to you for a minute?" a man called to him. "I need a new combine!"

"I need a new sale," John teased. He glanced at Maddie. "I won't be a minute, okay?"

"Okay," she said. But she was clutching her small evening bag as if she was afraid that it might escape. She started looking around for someone, anyone, to talk to besides Cort Brannt.

While she was thinking about running, he slid his big hand into her small one and pulled her onto the dance floor. He didn't even ask. He folded her into his arms and led her to the lazy, slow rhythm.

He smelled of spicy, rich cologne. He was much taller than she was, so her she couldn't see his face. She felt his cheek against the big wave of blond hair at her temple and her body began to do odd things. She felt uneasy, nervous. She felt…safe, excited.

"Your hand is like ice," he murmured as he danced with her around the room.

"They get cold all the time," she lied.

He laughed deep in his throat. "Really."

She wondered why he was doing this. Surely he should be pleased about Odalie's imminent reappearance in his life. He hated Maddie. Why was he dancing with her?

"I've never raised my hand to a woman," he said at her ear. "I never would, no matter how angry I was."

She swallowed and stopped dancing. She didn't want to talk about that.

He coaxed her eyes up. His were dark, narrow, intent. He was remembering what his father had told him, about the boy who tried to throw Maddie out a second-story window because of Odalie's lies. He didn't want to believe that Odalie had meant that to happen. Surely her female visitor had talked her into putting those nasty things about the boy and his family on the internet. But however it had happened, the thought of someone manhandling Maddie made him angry. It upset him.

He didn't really understand why. He'd never thought of her in any romantic way. She was just Pierce Lane's daughter. He'd known her since she was a child, watched her follow her dad around the ranch. She was always petting a calf or a dog, or carrying chickens around because she liked the sounds they made.

"Why are you watching me like that?" she faltered.

"You love animals, don't you?" he asked, and there was an odd, soft glow about his dark eyes. "I remember you carrying Mom's chickens around like cuddly toys when you'd come over to the ranch with your dad. You were very small then. I had to rescue you from one of the herding dogs. You tried to pet him, and he wasn't a pet."

"His name was Rowdy," she recalled. "He was so pretty."

"We never let anybody touch those dogs except the man who trains and uses them. They have to be focused. You didn't know." He smiled. "You were a cute little kid.

Always asking questions, always curious about everything."

She shifted uncomfortably. He wasn't dancing and they were drawing attention.

He looked around, cocked an eyebrow and moved her back around the room in his arms. "Sorry."

She didn't know what to think. She was tingling all over. She wanted him to hold her so close that she could feel every inch of his powerful frame against her. She wanted him to bend his head and kiss her so hard that her lips would sting. She wanted…something. Something more. She didn't understand these new and unexpected longings. It was getting hard to breathe and her heartbeat was almost shaking her. She couldn't bear it if he noticed.

He did notice. She was like melting ice in his arms. He felt her shiver when he drew her even closer, so that her soft, pert little breasts were hard against his chest through the thin suit jacket he was wearing. He liked the way she smelled, of wildflowers in the sun.

He drank in that scent. It made his head swim. His arm contracted. He was feeling sensations that he'd almost forgotten. Odalie didn't like him close to her, so his longing for her had been stifled. But Maddie was soft and warm and receptive. Too receptive.

His mouth touched her ear. "You make me hungry," he whispered roughly.

"Ex-excuse me?" she stammered.

"I want to lay you down on the carpet and kiss your breasts until my body stops hurting."

She caught her breath and stopped dancing. She pushed back from him, her eyes blazing, her face red with embarrassment. She wanted to kick him in the shin, but that would cause more problems.

She turned away from him, almost shivering with the emotions he'd kindled in her, shocked at the things he'd said to her. She almost ran toward John, who was walking toward her, frowning.

"What is it?" he asked suddenly, putting his arm around her.

She hid her face against him.

He glared at Cort, who was approaching them with more conflicting emotions than he'd ever felt in his life.

"You need to go home," John told Cort in a patient tone that was belied by his expression. "You've had too much to drink and you're going to make a spectacle of yourself and us if you keep this up."

"I want to dance with her," Cort muttered stubbornly.

"Well, it's pretty obvious that she doesn't want to dance with you." John leaned closer. "I can pick you up over my shoulder and carry you out of here, and I will."

"I'd like to see you try it," Cort replied, and his eyes blazed with anger.

Another cattleman, seeing a confrontation building, came strolling over and deliberately got between the two men.

"Hey, Cort," he said pleasantly, "I need to ask you about those new calves your dad's going to put up at the fall production sale. Can I ride home with you and see them?"

Cort blinked. "It's the middle of the night."

"The barn doesn't have lights?" the older man asked, raising an eyebrow.

Cort was torn. He knew the man. He was from up around the Frio river. He had a huge ranch, and Cort's dad was hungry for new customers.

"The barn has lights. I guess we could…go look at

the calves." He was feeling very light-headed. He wasn't used to alcohol. Not at all.

"I'll drive you home," the rancher said gently. "You can have one of your cowboys fetch your car, can't you?"

"Yeah. I guess so."

"Thanks," John told the man.

He shrugged and smiled. "No problem."

He indicated the door. Cort hesitated for just a minute. He looked back at Maddie with dark, stormy eyes, long enough that she dropped her own like hot bricks. He gave John a smug glance and followed the visiting cattleman out the door.

"Oh, boy," John said to himself. "Now we get to the complications."

"Complications?" Maddie was only half listening. Her eyes were on Cort's long, elegant back. She couldn't remember ever being so confused.

After the party was over, John drove her to her front door and cut off the engine.

"What happened?" he asked her gently, because she was still visibly upset.

"Cort was out of line," she murmured without lifting her eyes.

"Not surprising. He doesn't drink. I can't imagine what got him started."

"I guess he's missing your sister," she replied with a sigh. She looked up at him. "She's really coming home?"

"She says she is," he told her. He made a face. "That's Odalie. She always knows more than anybody else about any subject. My parents let her get away with being sassy because she was pretty and talented." He laughed shortly.

"My dad let me have it if I was ever rude or impolite or spoke out of turn. My brother had it even rougher."

She cocked her head. "You never talk about Tanner."

He grimaced. "I can't. It's a family thing. Maybe I'll tell you one day. Anyway, Dad pulled me up short if I didn't toe the line at home." He shook his head. "You wouldn't believe how many times I had to clean the horse stalls when I made him mad."

"Odalie is beautiful," Maddie conceded, but in a subdued tone.

"Only a very few people know what she did to you," John said quietly. "It shamed the family. Odalie was only sorry she got caught. I think she finally realized how tragic the results could have been, though."

"How so?"

"For one thing, she never spoke again to the girlfriend who put her up to it," he said. "After she got out of school, she stopped posting on her social page and threw herself into studying music."

"The girlfriend moved away, didn't she, though?"

"She moved because threats were made. Legal ones," John confided. "My dad sent his attorneys after her. He was pretty sure that Odalie didn't know how to link internet sites and post simultaneously, which is what was done about you." He touched her short hair gently. "Odalie is spoiled and snobbish and she thinks she's the center of the universe. But she isn't cruel."

"Isn't she?"

"Well, not anymore," he added. "Not since the lawyers got involved. You weren't the only girl she victimized. Several others came forward and talked to my dad when they heard about what happened to you in the library. He was absolutely dumbfounded. So was my mother." He shook his head. "Odalie never got over what they said to her. She started making a real effort to consider the feelings of other people. Years too late, of course, and she's still got that bad attitude."

"It's a shame she isn't more like your mother," Maddie said gently, and she smiled. "Mrs. Everett is a sweet woman."

"Yes. Mom has an amazing voice and is not conceited. She was offered a career in opera but she turned it down. She liked singing the blues, she said. Now, she just plays and sings for us, and composes. There's still the occasional journalist who shows up at the door when one of her songs is a big hit, like Desperado's."

"Do they still perform… I mean, Desperado?" she qualified.

"Yes, but not so much. They've all got kids now. It makes it tough to go on the road, except during summer holidays."

She laughed. "I love their music."

"Me, too." He studied her. "Odd."

"What is?"

"You're so easy to talk to. I don't get along with most women. I'm strung up and nervous and the aggressive ones make me uncomfortable. I sort of gave up dating after my last bad experience." He laughed. "I don't like women making crude remarks to me."

"Isn't it funny how things have changed?" she wondered aloud. "Not that I'm making fun of you. It's just that women used to get hassled. They still do, but it's turned around somewhat—now men get it, too."

"Yes, life is much more complicated now."

"I really enjoyed the party. Especially the dancing."

"Me, too. We might do that again one day."

She raised both eyebrows. "We might?"

He chuckled. "I'll call you."

"That would be nice."

He smiled, got out, went around and opened the door for her. He seemed to be debating whether or not to kiss her. She liked that lack of aggression in him. She smiled, went on tiptoe and kissed him right beside his chiseled mouth.

"Thanks again," she said. "See you!"

She went up the steps and into the house. John Everett stood looking after her wistfully. She thought he was nice. She liked him. But when she'd come off the dance floor trailing Cort Brannt, she'd been radiating like a furnace. Whether she knew it or not, she was in love with Cort. Shame, he thought as he drove off. She was just the sort of woman he'd like to settle down with. Not much chance of that, now.

Maddie didn't sleep at all. She stared at the ceiling. Her body tingled from the long contact with Cort's. She could feel his breath on her forehead, his lips in her hair. She could hear what he'd whispered.

She flushed at the memory. It had evoked incredible hunger. She didn't understand why she had these feelings now, when she hadn't had them for that boy who'd tried to hurt her so badly. She'd really thought she was crazy about him. But it was nothing like this.

Since her bad experience, she hadn't dated much. She'd seen her father get mad, but it was always quick and never physical. She hadn't been exposed to men who hit women. Now she knew they existed. It had been a worrying discovery.

Cort had frightened her when he'd lost his temper so violently in her father's office. She didn't think he'd attack her. But she'd been wary of him, until they danced together. Even if he was drunk, it had been the experience of a lifetime. She thought she could live on it forever, even if Odalie came home and Cort married her. He was never going to be happy with her, though. Odalie loved herself so much that there was no room in her life for a man.

If only the other woman had fallen in love with the Italian voice trainer and married him. Then Cort would have to let go of his unrequited feelings for Odalie, and maybe look in another direction. Maybe look in Maddie's direction.

On the other hand, he'd only been teasing at the dance. He wasn't himself.

Cold sober, he'd never have anything to do with Maddie. Probably, he'd just been missing Odalie and wanted a warm body to hold. Yes. That was probably it.

Just before dawn she fell asleep, but all too soon it was time to get up and start doing the chores around the ranch.

She went to feed her flock of hens, clutching the metal garbage can lid and the leafy limb to fend off Pumpkin. Somewhere in the back of her mind, she realized that it was going to come down to a hard decision one day. Pumpkin protected her hens, yes; he would be the bane of predators everywhere. But he was equally dangerous to people. What if he flew up and got one of her cowboys in the eye? She'd been reading up on rooster behavior, and she'd read some horror stories.

There had been all sorts of helpful advice, like giving him special treats and being nice to him. That had resulted in more gouges on her legs, even through her slacks, where his spurs had landed. Then there was the advice about having his spurs trimmed. Good advice, but who was going to catch and hold him while someone did that? None of her cowboys were lining up to volunteer.

"You problem child," she told Pumpkin as he chased her toward the gate. "One day, I'll have to do something about you!"

She got through the gate in the nick of time and shut it, hard. At least he wasn't going to get out of there, she told herself. She'd had Ben go around the perimeter of the large fenced area that surrounded the henhouse and plug any openings where that sneaky feathered fiend could possibly get out. If she kept him shut up, he couldn't hurt anybody, and the fence was seven feet high. No way he was jumping that!

She said so to Ben as she made her way to the barn to check on a calf they were nursing; it had dropped late and its mother had been killed by predators. They found it far on the outskirts of the ranch. They couldn't figure how it had wandered so far, but then, cattle did that. It was why you brought pregnant cows up close to the barn, so that you'd know when they were calving. It was especially important to do that in winter, just before the spring calves were due.

She looked over the gate at the little calf in the stall and smiled. "Pretty boy," she teased.

He was a purebred Santa Gertrudis bull. Some were culled and castrated and became steers, if they had poor conformation or were less than robust. But the best ones were treated like cattle royalty, spoiled rotten and watched over. This little guy would one day bring a handsome price as a breeding bull.

She heard a car door slam and turned just as Cort came into the barn.

She felt her heartbeat shoot off like a rocket.

He tilted his hat back and moved to the stall, peering over it. "That's a nice young one," he remarked.

"His mother was killed, so we're nursing him," she faltered.

He frowned. "Killed?"

"Predators, we think," she replied. "She was pretty torn up. We found her almost at the highway, out near your line cabin. Odd, that she wandered so far."

"Very odd," he agreed.

Ben came walking in with a bottle. "'Day, Cort," he said pleasantly.

"How's it going, Ben?" the younger man replied.

"So far so good."

Maddie smiled as Ben settled down in the hay and fed the bottle to the hungry calf.

"Poor little guy," Maddie said.

"He'll make it," Ben promised, smiling up at her.

"Well, I'll leave you to it," Maddie said. She was reluctant to be alone with Cort after the night before, but she couldn't see any way around it.

"You're up early," she said, fishing for a safe topic.

"I didn't sleep." He stuck his hands into his pockets as he strolled along with her toward the house.

"Oh?"

He stopped, so that she had to. His eyes were bloodshot and they had dark circles under them. "I drank too much," he said. "I wanted to apologize for the way I behaved with you."

"Oh." She looked around for anything more than one syllable that she could reply with. "That's…that's okay."

He stared down at her with curiously intent eyes. "You're incredibly naive."

She averted her eyes and her jaw clenched. "Yes, well,

with my background, you'd probably be the same way. I haven't been anxious to repeat the mistakes of the past with some other man who wasn't what he seemed to be."

"I'm sorry. About what happened to you."

"Everybody was sorry," she replied heavily. "But nobody else has to live with the emotional baggage I'm carrying around."

"How did you end up at the party with John?"

She blinked. "Well, he came over to show me some things about animal husbandry, and he asked me to go with him. It was sort of surprising, really. He doesn't date anybody."

"He's had a few bad experiences with women. So have I."

She'd heard about Cort's, but she wasn't opening that topic with him. "Would you like coffee?" she asked. "Great-Aunt Sadie went shopping, but she left a nice coffee cake baking in the oven. It should be about ready."

"Thanks. I could use a second cup," he added with a smile.

But the smile faded when he saw the fancy European coffee machine on the counter. "Where the hell did you buy that?" he asked.

She flushed. "I didn't. John likes European coffee, so he brought the machine and the pods over with him."

He lifted his chin. "Did he, now? I gather he thinks he'll be having coffee here often, then?"

She frowned. "He didn't say anything about that."

He made a huffing sound in his throat, just as the stove timer rang. Maddie went to take the coffee cake out of the oven. She was feeling so rattled, it was a good thing she'd remembered that it was baking. She placed it on a trivet. It smelled of cinnamon and butter.

"My great-aunt can really cook," she remarked as she took off the oven mitts she'd used to lift it out.

"She can, can't she?"

She turned and walked right into Cort. She hadn't realized he was so close. He caught her small waist in his big hands and lifted her right onto the counter next to the coffee cake, so that she was even with his dark, probing eyes.

"You looked lovely last night," he said in a strange, deep tone. "I've never really seen you dressed up before."

"I...I don't dress up," she stammered. He was tracing her collarbone and the sensations it aroused were delicious and unsettling. "Just occasionally."

"I didn't know you could do those complicated Latin dances, either," he continued.

"I learned them from watching television," she said.

His head was lower now. She could feel his breath on her lips; feel the heat from his body as he moved closer, in between her legs so that he was right up against her.

"I'm not in John Everett's class as a dancer," he drawled, tilting her chin up. "But, then, he's not in my class...at this..."

His mouth slowly covered hers, teasing gently, so that he didn't startle her. He tilted her head just a little more, so that her mouth was at just the right angle. His firm lips pushed hers apart, easing them back, so that he had access to the soft, warm depths of her mouth.

He kissed her with muted hunger, so slowly that she didn't realize until too late how much a trap it was. He grew insistent then, one lean hand at the back of her head, holding it still, as his mouth devoured her soft lips.

"Sweet," he whispered huskily. "You taste like honey..."

His arms went under hers and around her, lifting

her, so that her breasts were flattened against his broad, strong chest.

Involuntarily her cold hands snaked around his neck. She'd never felt hunger like this. She hadn't known it was possible. She let him open her mouth with his, let him grind her breasts against him. She moaned softly as sensations she'd never experienced left her helpless, vulnerable.

She felt his hand in her hair, tangling in it, while he kissed her in the soft silence of the kitchen. It was a moment out of time when she wished it could never end, that she could go on kissing him forever.

But just when he lifted his head, and looked into her eyes, and started to speak…

A car pulled up at the front porch and a door slammed.

Maddie looked into Cort's eyes with shock. He seemed almost as unsettled as she did. He moved back, helping her off the counter and onto her feet. He backed up just as Great-Aunt Sadie walked in with two bags of groceries.

"Didn't even have fresh mushrooms, can you believe it?" she was moaning, her mind on the door that was trying to close in her face rather than the two dazed people in the kitchen.

"Here, let me have those," Cort said politely, and he took the bags and put them on the counter. "Are there more in the car?" he asked.

"No, but thank you, Cort," Sadie said with a warm smile.

He grinned. "No problem." He glanced at Maddie, who still looked rattled. "I have to go. Thanks for the offer of coffee. Rain check?" he added, and his eyes were almost black with feeling.

"Oh, yes," Maddie managed breathlessly. "Rain check."

He smiled at her and left her standing there, vibrating with new hope.

Chapter 5

Maddie still couldn't believe what had happened right there in her kitchen. Cort had kissed her, and as if he really did feel something for her. Besides that, he was very obviously jealous of John Everett. She felt as if she could actually walk on air.

"You look happier than I've seen you in years, sweetie," Great-Aunt Sadie said with a smile.

"I am."

Sadie grinned. "It's that John Everett, isn't it?" she teased. She indicated the coffeemaker. "Thought he was pretty interested. I mean, those things cost the earth. Not every man would start out courting a girl with a present like that!"

"Oh. Well, of course, I like John," Maddie stammered. And then she realized that she couldn't very well tell her great-aunt what was going on. Sadie might start gossiping. Maddie's ranch hands had friends who worked for the Brannts. She didn't want Cort to think she was telling tales about him, even in an innocent way. After all, it might have been a fluke. He could be missing Odalie and just reacted to Maddie in unexpected ways.

"He's a dish," Sadie continued as she peeled potatoes in the kitchen. "Handsome young man, just like his dad." She grimaced. "I'm not too fond of his sister, but, then, no family is perfect."

"No." She hesitated. "Sadie, do you know why nobody talks about the oldest brother, Tanner?"

Sadie smiled. "Just gossip. They said he and his dad had a major falling out over his choice of careers and he packed up and went to Europe. That was when he was in his late teens. As far as I know, he's never contacted the family since. It's a sore spot with the Everetts, so they don't talk about him anymore. Too painful, I expect."

"That's sad."

"Yes, it is. There was a rumor that he was hanging out with some dangerous people as well. But you know what rumors are."

"Yes," Maddie said.

"What was Cort doing over here earlier in the week?" Sadie asked suddenly.

"Oh, he was just…giving me some more pointers on dad's breeding program," Maddie lied.

"Scared you to death, too," Sadie said irritably. "I don't think he'd hurt you, but he's got a bad temper, sweetie."

Maddie had forgotten that, in the new relationship she seemed to be building with Cort. "People say his father was like that, when he was young. But Shelby married him and tamed him," she added with a secret smile.

Sadie glanced at her curiously. "I guess that can happen. A good woman can be the salvation of a man. But just…be careful."

"I will," she promised. "Cort isn't a mean person."

Sadie gave her a careful look. "So that's how it is."

Maddie flushed. "I don't know what you mean."

"John likes you, a lot," she replied.

Maddie sighed. "John's got a barracuda for a sister, too," she reminded the older woman. "No way in the world am I having her for a sister-in-law, no matter how nice John is."

Sadie grimaced. "Should have thought of that, shouldn't I?"

"I did."

She laughed. "I guess so. But just a suggestion, if you stick your neck out with Cort," she added very seriously. "Make him mad. Make him really mad, someplace where you can get help if you need to. Don't wait and find out when it's too late if he can't control his temper."

"I remember that boy in high school," Maddie reminded her. "He didn't stop. Cort frightened me, yes, but when he saw I was afraid, he started apologizing. If he couldn't control his temper, he'd never have been able to stop."

Sadie looked calmer. "No. I don't think he would."

"He's still apologizing for it, in fact," Maddie added.

Sadie smiled and her eyes were kind. "All right, then. I won't harp on it. He's a lot like his father, and his dad is a good man."

"They're all nice people. Morie was wonderful to me in school. She stuck up for me when Odalie and her girlfriend were making my life a daily purgatory."

"Pity Odalie never really gets paid back for the things she does," Sadie muttered.

Maddie hugged her. "That mill grinds slowly but relentlessly," she reminded her. She grinned. "One day…"

Sadie laughed. "One day."

Maddie let her go with a sigh. "I hope I can learn enough of this stuff not to sink dad's cattle operation," she moaned. "I wasn't really faced with having to deal with the breeding aspect until now, with roundup ahead and fall breeding standing on the line in front of me. Which bull do I put on which cows? Gosh! It's enough to drive you nuts!"

"Getting a lot of help in that, though, aren't you?" Sadie teased. "Did you tell Cort that John had been coaching you, too?"

"Yes." She sighed. "Cort wasn't overjoyed about it, either. But John makes it understandable." She threw up her hands. "I'm just slow. I don't understand cattle. I love to paint and sculpt. But Dad never expected to go so soon and have to leave me in charge of things. We're going in the hole because I don't know what I'm doing." She glanced at the older woman. "In about two years, we're going to start losing customers. It terrifies me. I don't want to lose the ranch, but it's going to go downhill without dad to run it." She toyed with a bag on the counter. "I've been thinking about that developer…"

"Don't you dare," Sadie said firmly. "Darlin', do you realize what he'd do to this place if he got his hands on it?" she exclaimed. "He'd sell off all the livestock to anybody who wanted it, even for slaughter, and he'd rip the land to pieces. All that prime farmland, gone, all the native grasses your dad planted and nurtured, gone. This house—" she indicated it "—where your father and your grandfather and I were born! Gone!"

Maddie felt sick. "Oh, dear."

"You're not going to run the ranch into the ground. Not when you have people, like King Brannt, who want to help you get it going again," she said firmly. "If you ever want to sell up, you talk to him. I'll bet he'd offer for it and put in a manager. We could probably even stay on and pay rent."

"With what?" Maddie asked reasonably. "Your social security check and my egg money?" She sighed. "I can't sell enough paintings or enough eggs to pay for lunch in town," she added miserably. "I should have gone to school and learned a trade or something." She grimaced. "I don't know what to do."

"Give it a little time," the older woman said gently. "I know it's overwhelming, but you can learn. Ask John to make you a chart and have Ben in on the conversation. Your dad trusted Ben with everything, even the finances. I daresay he knows as much as you do about things."

"That's an idea." She smiled sadly. "I don't really want to sell that developer anything. He's got a shady look about him."

"You're telling me."

"I guess I'll wait a bit."

"Meanwhile, you might look in that bag I brought home yesterday."

"Isn't it groceries…dry goods?"

"Look."

She peered in the big brown bag and caught her breath. "Sculpting material. Paint! Great-Aunt Sadie!" she exclaimed, and ran and hugged the other woman. "That's so sweet of you!"

"Looking out for you, darling," she teased. "I want you to be famous so those big TV people will want to interview me on account of we're related!" She stood up and struck a pose. "Don't you think I'd be a hit?"

Maddie hugged her even tighter. "I think you're already a hit. Okay. I can take a hint. I'll get to work right now!"

Sadie chortled as she rushed from the room.

Cort came in several days later while she was retouching one of the four new fairies she'd created, working where the light was best, in a corner of her father's old office. She looked up, startled, when Great-Aunt Sadie let him in.

She froze. "Pumpkin came after you again?" she asked, worried.

"What?" He looked around, as if expecting the big red rooster to appear. "Oh, Pumpkin." He chuckled. "No. He was in the hen yard giving me mean looks, but he seems to be well contained."

"Thank goodness!"

He moved to the table and looked at her handiwork. "What a group," he mused, smiling. "They're all beautiful."

"Thanks." She wished she didn't sound so breathless, and that she didn't have paint dabbed all over her face from her days' efforts. She probably looked like a painting herself.

"Going to sell them?"

"Oh, I couldn't," she said hesitantly. "I mean, I…well, I just couldn't."

"Can't you imagine what joy they'd bring to other people?" he asked, thinking out loud. "Why do you think doll collectors pay so much for one-of-a-kind creations like those? They build special cabinets for them, take them out and talk to them…"

"You're kidding!" she exclaimed, laughing. "Really?"

"This one guy I met at the conference said he had about ten really rare dolls. He sat them around the dining room table every night and talked to them while he ate. He was very rich and very eccentric, but you get the idea. He loved his dolls. He goes to all the doll collector conventions. In fact, there's one coming up in Denver, where they're holding a cattlemen's workshop." He smiled. "Anyway, your fairies wouldn't be sitting on a shelf collecting dust on the shelf of a collector like that. They'd be loved."

"Wow." She looked back at the little statuettes. "I never thought of it like that."

"Maybe you should."

She managed a shy smile. He looked delicious in a pair of beige slacks and a yellow, very expensive pullover shirt with an emblem on the pocket. Thick black hair peeked out where the top buttons were undone. She wondered how his bare chest would feel against her hands. She blushed. "What can I do for you?" she asked quickly, trying to hide her interest.

Her reaction to him was amusing. He found it really touching. Flattering. He hadn't been able to get her out of his mind since he'd kissed her so hungrily in her kitchen. He'd wanted to come back sooner than this, but business had overwhelmed him.

"I have to drive down to Jacobsville, Texas, to see a rancher about some livestock," he said. "I thought you might like to ride with me."

She stared at him as if she'd won the lottery. "Me?"

"You." He smiled. "I'll buy you lunch on the way. I

know this little tearoom off the beaten path. We can have high tea and buttermilk pie."

She caught her breath. "I used to hear my mother talk about that one. I've never had high tea. I'm not even sure what it is, exactly."

"Come with me and find out."

She grinned. "Okay! Just let me wash up first."

"Take your time. I'm not in any hurry."

"I'll just be a few minutes."

She almost ran up the staircase to her room.

Cort picked up one of the delicate little fairies and stared at it with utter fascination. It was ethereal, beautiful, stunning. He'd seen such things before, but never anything so small with such personality. The little fairy had short blond hair, like Maddie's, and pale eyes. It amused him that she could paint something so tiny. He noted the magnifying glass standing on the table, and realized that she must use it for the more detailed work. Still, it was like magic, making something so small look so realistic.

He put it down, very carefully, and went into the kitchen to talk to Sadie while he waited for Maddie to get ready.

"Those little fairies she makes are amazing," he commented, lounging against the counter.

Sadie smiled at him. "They really are. I don't know how she does all that tiny detailed work without going blind. The little faces are so realistic. She has a gift."

"She does. I wish she'd do something with it."

"Me, too," Sadie replied. "But she doesn't want to sell her babies, as she calls them."

"She's sitting on a gold mine here." Cort sighed. "You

know, breeding herd sires is hard work, even for people who've done it for generations and love it."

She glanced at him and she looked worried. "I know. She doesn't really want to do it. My nephew had to toss her in at the deep end when he knew his cancer was fatal." She shook her head. "I hate it for her. You shouldn't be locked into a job you don't want to do. But she's had no training. She really can't do anything else."

"She can paint. And she can sculpt."

"Yes, but there's still the ranch," Sadie emphasized.

"Any problem has a solution. It's just a question of finding it." He sighed. "Ben said you'd had another cow go missing."

"Yes." She frowned. "Odd thing, too, she was in a pasture with several other cows, all of them healthier than her. I can't think somebody would steal her."

"I know what you mean. They do wander off. It's just that it looks suspicious, having two go missing in the same month."

"Could it be that developer man?"

Cort shook his head. "I wouldn't think so. We've got armed patrols and cameras mounted everywhere. If anything like that was going on, we'd see it."

"I suppose so."

There was the clatter of footsteps almost leaping down the staircase.

"Okay, I'm ready," Maddie said, breathless. She was wearing jeans and boots and a pretty pink button-up blouse. She looked radiant.

"Where are you off to?" Sadie asked, laughing.

"I'm going to Jacobsville with Cort to look at livestock."

"Oh." Sadie forced a smile. "Well, have fun, then."

Cort started the sleek two-seater Jaguar. He glanced at Maddie, who was looking at everything with utter fascination.

"Not quite like your little Volkswagen, huh?" he teased.

"No! It's like a spaceship or something."

"Watch this."

As he started the car, the air vents suddenly opened up and the Jaguar symbol lit up on a touch screen between the steering wheel and the glove compartment. At the same time, the gearshift rose up from the console, where it had been lying flat.

"Oh, gosh!" she exclaimed. "That's amazing!"

He chuckled. "I like high-tech gadgets."

"John has one of these," she recalled.

His eyes narrowed. "So he does. I rode him around in mine and he found a dealership the next day. His is more sedate."

"I just think they're incredible."

He smiled. "Fasten your seat belt."

"Oops, sorry, wasn't thinking." She reached up and drew it between her breasts, to fasten it beside her hip.

"I always wear my seat belt," he said. "Dad refused to drive the car until we were all strapped in. He was in a wreck once. He said he never forgot that he'd be dead except for the seat belt."

"My dad wasn't in a wreck, but he was always careful about them, too." She put her strappy purse on the floorboard. "Did Odalie come home?" she asked, trying not to sound too interested.

"Not yet," he said. He had to hide a smile, because the question lacked any subtlety.

"Oh."

He was beginning to realize that Odalie had been a

major infatuation for him. Someone unreachable that he'd dreamed about, much as young boys dreamed about movie stars. He knew somewhere in the back of his mind that he and Odalie were as different as night and day. She wanted an operatic career and wasn't interested in fitting him into that picture. Would he be forever hanging around opera houses where she performed, carrying bags and organizing fans? Or would he be in Texas, waiting for her rare visits? She couldn't have a family and be a performer, not in the early stages of her career, maybe never. Cort wanted a family. He wanted children.

Funny, he'd never thought of himself as a parent before. But when he'd listened to Maddie talk about her little fairy sculptures and spoke of them as her children, he'd pictured her with a baby in her arms. It had shocked him how much he wanted to see that for real.

"You like kids, don't you?" he asked suddenly.

"What brought that on?" She laughed.

"What you said, about your little fairy sculptures. They're beautiful kids."

"Thanks." She looked out the window at the dry, parched grasslands they were passing through. "Yes, I love kids. Oh, Cort, look at the poor corn crops! That's old Mr. Raines's land, isn't it?" she added. "He's already holding on to his place by his fingernails I guess he'll have to sell if it doesn't rain."

"My sister said they're having the same issues up in Wyoming." He glanced at her. "Her husband knows a medicine man from one of the plains tribes. She said that he actually did make it rain a few times. Nobody understands how, and most people think it's fake, but I wonder."

"Ben was talking about a Cheyenne medicine man

who can make rain. He's friends with him. I've known people who could douse for water," she said.

"Now, there's a rare talent indeed," he commented. He pursed his lips. "Can't Ben do that?"

"Shh," she said, laughing. "He doesn't want people to think he's odd, so he doesn't want us to tell anybody."

"Still, you might ask him to go see if he could find water. If he does, we could send a well-borer over to do the job for him."

She looked at him with new eyes. "That's really nice of you."

He shrugged. "I'm nice enough. From time to time." He glanced at her pointedly. "When women aren't driving me to drink."

"What? I didn't drive you to drink!"

"The hell you didn't," he mused, his eyes on the road so that he missed her blush. "Dancing with John Everett. Fancy dancing. Latin dancing." He sighed. "I can't even do a waltz."

"Oh, but that doesn't matter," she faltered, trying to deal with the fact that he was jealous. Was he? That was how it sounded! "I mean, I think you dance very nicely."

"I said some crude things to you," he said heavily. "I'm really sorry. I don't drink, you see. When I do…" He let the sentence trail off. "Anyway, I apologize."

"You already apologized."

"Yes, but it weighs on my conscience." He stopped at a traffic light. He glanced at her with dark, soft eyes. "John's my friend. I think a lot of him. But I don't like him taking you out on dates and hanging around you."

She went beet-red. She didn't even know what to say.

"I thought it might come as a shock," he said softly. He reached a big hand across the console and caught hers in it. He linked her fingers with his and looked into her eyes while he waited for the lights to change. "I thought we might take in a movie Friday night. There's that new Batman one."

"There's that new Ice Age one," she said at the same time.

He gave her a long, amused look. "You like cartoon movies?"

She flushed. "Well…"

He burst out laughing. "So do I. Dad thinks I'm nuts."

"Oh, I don't!"

His fingers contracted around hers. "Well, in that case, we'll see the Ice Age one."

"Great!"

The light changed and he drove on. But he didn't let go of her hand.

High tea was amazing! There were several kinds of tea, china cups and saucers to contain it, and little cucumber sandwiches, chicken salad sandwiches, little cakes and other nibbles. Maddie had never seen anything like it. The tearoom was full, too, with tourists almost overflowing out of the building, which also housed an antiques shop.

"This is awesome!" she exclaimed as she sampled one thing after another.

"Why, thank you." The owner laughed, pausing by their table. "We hoped it would be a success." She shook her head. "Everybody thought we were crazy. We're from Charleston, South Carolina. We came out here when my husband was stationed in the air force base at San Antonio, and stayed. We'd seen another tearoom, way north, almost in Dallas, and we were so impressed with it that we thought we might try one of our own. Neither of us knew a thing about restaurants, but we learned, with help from our staff." She shook her head. "Never dreamed we'd have this kind of success," she added, looking around. "It's quite a dream come true."

"That cameo," Maddie said hesitantly, nodding toward a display case close by. "Does it have a story?"

"A sad one. The lady who owned it said it was handed down in her family for five generations. Finally there was nobody to leave it to. She fell on hard times and asked me to sell it for her." She sighed. "She died a month ago." She opened the case with a key and pulled out the cameo, handing it to Maddie. It was black lacquer with a beautiful black-haired Spanish lady painted on it. She had laughing black eyes and a sweet smile. "She was so beautiful."

"It was the great-great-grandmother of the owner. They said a visiting artist made it and gave it to her. She and her husband owned a huge ranch, from one of those Spanish land grants. Pity there's nobody to keep the legend going."

"Oh, but there is." Cort took it from the woman and handed it to Maddie. "Put it on the tab, if you will," he told the owner. "I can't think of anyone who'll take better care of her."

"No, you can't," Maddie protested, because she saw the price tag.

"I can," Cort said firmly. "It was a family legacy. It still is." His dark eyes stared meaningfully into hers. "It can be handed down, to your own children. You might have a daughter who'd love it one day."

Maddie's heart ran wild. She looked into Cort's dark eyes and couldn't turn away.

"I'll put the ticket with lunch," the owner said with

a soft laugh. "I'm glad she'll have a home," she added gently.

"Can you write down the woman's name who sold it to you?" Maddie asked. "I want to remember her, too."

"That I can. How about some buttermilk pie? It's the house specialty," she added with a grin.

"I'd love some."

"Me, too," Cort said.

Maddie touched the beautiful cheek of the cameo's subject. "I should sculpt a fairy who looks like her."

"Yes, you should," Cort agreed at once. "And show it with the cameo."

She nodded. "How sad," she said, "to be the last of your family."

"I can almost guarantee that you won't be the last of yours," he said in a breathlessly tender tone.

She looked up into his face and her whole heart was in her eyes.

He had to fight his first impulse, which was to drag her across the table into his arms and kiss the breath out of her.

She saw that hunger in him and was fascinated that she seemed to have inspired it. He'd said that she was plain and uninteresting. But he was looking at her as if he thought her the most beautiful woman on earth.

"Dangerous," he teased softly, "looking at me like that in a public place."

"Huh?" She caught her breath as she realized what he was saying. She laughed nervously, put the beautiful cameo beside her plate and smiled at him. "Thank you, for the cameo."

"My pleasure. Eat up. We've still got a long drive ahead of us!"

Jacobsville, Texas, was a place Maddie had heard of all her life, but she'd never seen it before. In the town square, there was a towering statue of Big John Jacobs, the founder of Jacobsville, for whom Jacobs County was named. Legend had it that he came to Texas from Georgia after the Civil War, with a wagonload of black sharecroppers. He also had a couple of Comanche men who helped him on the ranch. It was a fascinating story, how he'd married the spunky but not so pretty daughter of a multimillionaire and started a dynasty in Texas.

Maddie shared the history with Cort as they drove down a long dirt road to the ranch, which was owned by Cy Parks. He was an odd sort of person, very reticent, with jet-black hair sprinkled with silver and piercing green eyes. He favored one of his arms, and Maddie could tell that it had been badly burned at some point. His wife was a plain little blonde woman who wore glasses and obviously adored her husband. The feeling seemed to be mutual. They had two sons who were in school, Lisa explained shyly. She was sorry she couldn't introduce them to the visitors.

Cy Parks showed them around his ranch in a huge SUV. He stopped at one pasture and then another, grimacing at the dry grass.

"We're having to use up our winter hay to feed them," he said with a sigh. "It's going to make it a very hard winter if we have to buy extra feed to carry us through." He glanced at Cort and laughed. "You'll make my situation a bit easier if you want to carry a couple of my young bulls home with you."

Cort grinned, too. "I think I might manage that. Although we're in the same situation you are. Even my sister's husband, who runs purebred cattle in Wyoming, is having it rough. This drought is out of anybody's experience. People are likening it to the famous Dust Bowl of the thirties."

"There was another bad drought in the fifties," Parks added. "When we live on the land, we always have issues with weather, even in good years. This one has been a disaster, though. It will put a lot of the family farms and ranches out of business." He made a face. "They'll be bought up by those damned great combines, corporate ranching, I call it. Animals pumped up with drugs, genetically altered—damned shame. Pardon the language," he added, smiling apologetically at Maddie.

"She's lived around cattlemen all her life," Cort said affectionately, smiling over the back of the seat at her.

"Yes, I have." Maddie laughed. She looked into Cort's dark eyes and blushed. He grinned.

They stopped at the big barn on the way back and Cy led them through it to a stall in the rear. It connected to a huge paddock with plenty of feed and fresh water.

"Now this is my pride and joy," he said, indicating a sleek, exquisite young Santa Gertrudis bull.

"That is some conformation," Cort said, whistling. "He's out of Red Irony, isn't he?" he added.

Cy chuckled. "So you read the cattle journals, do you?"

"All of them. Your ranch has some of the best breeding stock in Texas. In the country, in fact."

"So does Skylance," Parks replied. "I've bought your own bulls over the years. And your father's," he added to Maddie. "Good stock."

"Thanks," she said.

"Same here," Cort replied. He drew in a breath. "Well, if this little fellow's up for bids, I'll put ours in."

"No bids. He's yours if you want him." He named a price that made Maddie feel faint, but Cort just smiled.

"Done," he said, and they shook hands.

On the way back home, Maddie was still astonished at the price. "That's a fortune," she exclaimed.

"Worth every penny, though," Cort assured her. "Healthy genetics make healthy progeny. We have to put new bulls on our cows every couple of years to avoid any defects. Too much inbreeding can be dangerous to the cattle and disastrous for us."

"I guess so. Mr. Parks seems like a very nice man," she mused.

He chuckled. "You don't know his history, do you? He led one of the most respected groups of mercenaries in the world into small wars overseas. His friend Eb Scott still runs a world-class counterterrorism school on his ranch. He was part of the merc group, along with a couple of other citizens of Jacobsville."

"I didn't know!"

"He's a good guy. Dad's known him for years."

"What a dangerous way to make a living, though."

"No more dangerous than dealing with livestock," Cort returned.

That was true. There were many pitfalls of working with cattle, the least of which was broken bones. Concussions could be, and sometimes were, fatal. You could drown in a river or be trampled…the list went on and on.

"You're very thoughtful," Cort remarked.

She smiled. "I was just thinking."

"Me, too." He turned off onto a side road that led to a park. "I want to stretch my legs for a bit. You game?"

"Of course."

He pulled into the car park and led the way down a

small bank to the nearby river. The water level was down, but flowing beautifully over mossy rocks, with mesquite trees drooping a little in the heat, but still pretty enough to catch the eye.

"It's lovely here."

"Yes." He turned and pulled her into his arms, looking down into her wide eyes. "It's very lovely here." He bent his head and kissed her.

Chapter 6

Maddie's head was swimming. She felt the blood rush to her heart as Cort riveted her to his long, hard body and kissed her as if he might never see her again. She pressed closer, wrapping her arms around him, holding on for dear life.

His mouth tasted of coffee. It was warm and hard, insistent as it ground into hers. She thought if she died now, it would be all right. She'd never been so happy.

She heard a soft groan from his mouth. One lean hand swept down her back and pressed her hips firmly into his. She stiffened a little. She didn't know much about men, but she was a great reader. The contours of his body had changed quite suddenly.

"Nothing to worry about," he whispered into her mouth. "Just relax…"

She did. It was intoxicating. His free hand went under

her blouse and expertly unclasped her bra to give free rein to his searching fingers. They found her breast and teased the nipple until it went hard. He groaned and bent his head, putting his mouth right over it, over the cloth. She arched up to him, so entranced that she couldn't even find means to protest.

"Yes," he groaned. "Yes, yes…!"

Her hands tangled in his thick black hair, tugging it closer. She arched backward, held by his strong arms as he fed on the softness of her breast under his demanding mouth. His hand at her back was more insistent now, grinding her against the growing hardness of his body.

She was melting, dying, starving to death. She wanted him to take off her clothes; she wanted to lie down with him and she wanted something, anything that would ease the terrible ache in her young body.

And just when she was certain that it would happen, that he wasn't going to stop, a noisy car pulled into the car park above and a car door slammed.

She jerked back from him, tugging down her blouse, shivering at the interruption. His eyes were almost black with hunger. He cursed under his breath, biting his lip as he fought down the need that almost bent him over double.

From above there were children's voices, laughing and calling to each other. Maddie stood with her back to him, her arms wrapped around her body, while she struggled with wild excitement, embarrassment and confusion. He didn't like her. He thought she was ugly. But he'd kissed her as if he were dying for her mouth. It was one big puzzle…

She felt his big, warm hands on her shoulders. "Don't sweat it," he said in a deep, soft tone. "Things happen."

She swallowed and forced a smile. "Right."

He turned her around, tipping her red face up to his eyes. He searched them in a silence punctuated with the screams and laughter of children. She was very pretty like that, her mouth swollen from his kisses, her face shy, timid. He was used to women who demanded. Aggressive women. Even Odalie, when he'd kissed her once, had been very outspoken about what she liked and didn't like. Maddie simply…accepted.

"Don't be embarrassed," he said softly. "Everything's all right. But we should probably go now. It's getting late."

She nodded. He took her small hand in his, curled his fingers into hers and drew her with him along the dirt path that led back up to the parking lot.

Two bedraggled parents were trying to put out food in plastic containers on a picnic table, fighting the wind, which was blowing like crazy in the sweltering heat. They glanced at the couple and grinned.

Cort grinned back. There were three children, all under school age, one in his father's arms. They looked happy, even though they were driving a car that looked as if it wouldn't make it out of the parking lot.

"Nice day for a picnic," Cort remarked.

The father made a face. "Not so much, but we've got a long drive ahead of us and it's hard to sit in a fast-food joint with this company." He indicated the leaping, running toddlers. He laughed. "Tomorrow, they'll be hijacking my car," he added with an ear-to-ear smile, "so we're enjoying it while we can."

"Nothing like kids to make a home a home," the mother commented.

"Nice looking kids, too," Cort said.

"Very nice," Maddie said, finally finding her voice.

"Thanks," the mother said. "They're a handful, but we don't mind."

She went back to her food containers, and the father went running after the toddlers, who were about to climb down the bank.

"Nice family," Cort remarked as they reached his car.

"Yes. They seemed so happy."

He glanced down at her as he stopped to open the passenger door. He was thoughtful. He didn't say anything, but his eyes were soft and full of secrets. "In you go."

She got in, fastened her seat belt without any prompting and smiled all the way back home.

Things were going great, until they got out of the car in front of Maddie's house. Pumpkin had found a way out of the hen enclosure. He spotted Cort and broke into a halting run, with his head down and his feathers ruffled.

"No!" Maddie yelled. "Pumpkin, no!"

She tried to head him off, but he jumped at her and she turned away just in time to avoid spurs in her face. "Cort, run! It's okay, just run!" she called when he hesitated.

He threw his hands up and darted toward his car. "You have to do something about that damned rooster, Maddie!" he called back.

"I know," she wailed. "I will, honest! I had fun. Thanks so much!"

He threw up his hands and dived into the car. He started it and drove off just before Pumpkin reached him.

"You stupid chicken! I'm going to let Ben eat you, I swear I am!" she raged.

But when he started toward her, she ran up the steps, into the house and slammed the door.

She opened her cell phone and called her foreman.

"Ben, can you please get Pumpkin back into the hen

lot and try to see where he got out? Be sure to wear your chaps and carry a shield," she added.

"Need to eat that rooster, Maddie," he drawled.

"I know." She groaned. "Please?"

There was a long sigh. "All right. One more time..." He hung up.

Great-Aunt Sadie gave her a long look. "Pumpkin got out again?"

"Yes. There must be a hole in the fence or something," she moaned. "I don't know how in the world he does it!"

"Ben will find a way to shut him in, don't worry. But you are going to have to do something, you know. He's dangerous."

"I love him," Maddie said miserably.

"Well, sometimes things we love don't love us back and should be made into chicken and dumplings," Sadie mused with pursed lips.

Maddie made a face at her. She opened her shoulder bag and pulled out a box. "I want to show you something. Cort bought it for me."

"Cort's buying you presents?" Sadie exclaimed.

"It's some present, too," Maddie said with a flushed smile.

She opened the box. There, inside, was the hand-painted cameo of the little Spanish lady, with a card that gave all the information about the woman, now deceased, who left it with the antiques dealer.

"She's lovely," Sadie said, tracing the face with a fore-finger very gently.

"Read the card." Maddie showed it to her.

When Sadie finished reading it, she was almost in tears. "How sad, to be the last one in your family."

"Yes. But this will be handed down someday." She was

remembering the family at the picnic tables and Cort's strange smile, holding hands with him, kissing him. "Someday," she said again, and she sounded as breathless as she felt.

Sadie didn't ask any questions. But she didn't have to. Maddie's bemused expression told her everything she needed to know. Apparently Maddie and Cort were getting along very well, all of a sudden.

Cort walked into the house muttering about the rooster.

"Trouble again?" Shelby asked. She was curled up on the sofa watching the news, but she turned off the television when she saw her son. She smiled; dark-eyed and still beautiful.

"The rooster." He sighed. He tossed his hat into a chair and dropped down into his father's big recliner. "I bought us a bull. He's very nice."

"From Cy Parks?"

He nodded. "He's quite a character."

"So I've heard."

"I bought Maddie a cameo," he added. "In that tearoom halfway between here and Jacobsville. It's got an antiques store in with it." He shook his head. "Beautiful thing. It's hand-painted...a pretty Spanish lady with a fan, enameled. She had a fit over it. The seller died recently and had no family."

"Sad. But it was nice of you to buy it for Maddie."

He pursed his lips. "When you met Dad, you said you didn't get along."

She shivered dramatically. "That's putting it mildly. He hated me. Or he seemed to. But when my mother, your grandmother, died, I was alone in a media circus. They think she committed suicide and she was a big-name movie star, you see. So there was a lot of publicity. I was almost in hysterics when your father showed up out of nowhere and managed everything."

"Well!"

"I was shocked. He'd sent me home, told me he had a girlfriend and broke me up with Danny. Not that I needed breaking-up, Danny was only pretending to be engaged to me to make King face how he really felt. But it was fireworks from the start." She peered at him through her thick black eyelashes. "Sort of the way it was with you and Maddie, I think."

"It's fireworks, now, too. But of a different sort," he added very slowly.

"Oh?" She didn't want to pry, but she was curious.

"I'm confused. Maddie isn't pretty. She can't sing or play anything. But she can paint and sculpt and she's sharp about people." He grimaced. "Odalie is beautiful, like the rising sun, and she can play any instrument and sing like an angel."

"Accomplishments and education don't matter as much as personality and character," his mother replied quietly. "I'm not an educated person, although I've taken online courses. I made my living modeling. Do you think I'm less valuable to your father than a woman with a college degree and greater beauty?"

"Goodness, no!" he exclaimed at once.

She smiled gently. "See what I mean?"

"I think I'm beginning to." He leaned back. "It was a good day."

"I'm glad."

"Except for that damned rooster," he muttered. "One of these days...!"

She laughed.

He was about to call Maddie, just to talk, when his cell phone rang.

He didn't recognize the number. He put it up to his ear. "Hello?"

"Hello, Cort," Odalie's voice purred in his ear. "Guess what. I'm home! Want to come over for supper tonight?"

He hesitated. Things had just gotten complicated.

Maddie half expected Cort to phone her, after their lovely day together, but he didn't. The next morning, she heard a car pull up in the driveway and went running out. But it wasn't Cort. It was John Everett.

She tried not to let her disappointment show. "Hi!" she said. "Would you like a cup of very nice European coffee from a fancy European coffeemaker?" she added, grinning.

He burst out laughing. "I would. Thanks. It's been a hectic day and night."

"Has it? Why?" she asked as they walked up the steps.

"I had to drive up to Dallas-Fort Worth airport to pick up Odalie yesterday."

Her heart did a nosedive. She'd hoped against hope that the other woman would stay in Italy, marry her voice teacher, get a job at the opera house, anything but come home, and especially right now! She and Cort were only just beginning to get to know each other. It wasn't fair!

"How is she?" she asked, her heart shattering.

"Good," he said heavily. "She and the voice teacher disagreed, so she's going to find someone in this country to take over from him." He grimaced. "I don't know who. Since she knows more than the voice trainers do, I don't really see the point in it. She can't take criticism."

She swallowed, hard, as she went to work at the coffee machine. "Has Cort seen her?"

"Oh, yes," he said, sitting down at the little kitchen table. "He came over for supper last night. They went driving."

She froze at the counter. She didn't let him see her face, but her stiff back was a good indication of how she'd received the news.

"I'm really sorry," he said gently. "But I thought you should know before you heard gossip."

She nodded. Tears were stinging her eyes, but she hid them. "Thanks, John."

He drew in a long breath. "She doesn't love him," he said. "He's just a habit she can't give up. I don't think he loves her, either, really. It's like those crushes we get on movie stars. Odalie is an image, not someone real who wants to settle down and have kids and live on a ranch. She can't stand cattle!"

She started the coffee machine, collected herself, smiled and turned around. "Good thing your parents don't mind them," she said.

"And I've told her so. Repeatedly." He studied her through narrowed eyes. His thick blond hair shone like pale yellow diamonds in the overhead light. He was so good-looking, she thought. She wished she could feel for him what she felt for Cort.

"People can't help being who they are," she replied quietly.

"You're wise for your years," he teased.

She laughed. "Not so wise, or I'd get out of the cattle business." She chuckled. "After we have coffee, want to have another go at explaining genetics to me? I'm a lost cause, but we can try."

"You're not a lost cause, and I'd love to try."

* * *

Odalie was irritable and not trying to hide it. "What's the matter with you?" she snapped at Cort. "You haven't heard a word I've said."

He glanced at her and grimaced. "Sorry. We've got a new bull coming. I'm distracted."

Her pale blue eyes narrowed. "More than distracted, I think. What's this I hear about you taking that Lane girl with you to buy the new bull?"

He gave her a long look and didn't reply.

She cleared her throat. Cort was usually running after her, doing everything he could to make her happy, make her smile. She'd come home to find a stranger, a man she didn't know. Her beauty hadn't interested the voice trainer; her voice hadn't really impressed him. She'd come home with a damaged ego and wanted Cort to fix it by catering to her. That hadn't happened. She'd invited him over today for lunch and he'd eaten it in a fog. He actually seemed to not want to be with her, and that was new and scary.

"Well, she's plain as toast," Odalie said haughtily. "She has no talent and she's not educated."

He cocked his head. "And you think those are the most important character traits?"

She didn't like the way he was looking at her. "None of my friends had anything to do with her in school," she muttered.

"You had plenty to do with that, didn't you?" Cort asked with a cold smile. "I believe attorneys were involved...?"

"Cort!" She went flaming red. She turned her head. "That was a terrible misunderstanding. And it was Millie who put me up to it. That's the truth. I didn't like Maddie, but I'd never have done it if I'd realized what that boy might do." She bit her lip. She'd thought about that a lot in recent weeks, she didn't know why. "He could have killed her. I'd have had it on my conscience forever," she added in a strange, absent tone.

Cort was not impressed. This was the first time he'd heard Odalie say anything about the other woman that didn't have a barb in it, and even this comment was self-centered. Though it was small, he still took her words as a sign that maybe she was changing and becoming more tolerant...

"Deep thoughts," he told her.

She glanced at him and smiled. "Yes. I've become introspective. Enjoy it while it lasts." She laughed, and she was so beautiful that he was really confused.

"I love your car," she said, glancing out the window. "Would you let me drive it?"

He hesitated. She was the worst driver he'd ever known. "As long as I'm in it," he said firmly.

She laughed. "I didn't mean I wanted to go alone," she teased.

She knew where she wanted to drive it, too. Right past Maddie Lane's house, so that she'd see Odalie with Cort. So she'd know that he was no longer available. Odalie seemed to have lost her chance at a career in opera, but here was Cort, who'd always loved her. Maybe she'd settle down, maybe she wouldn't, but Cort was hers. She wanted Maddie to know it.

She'd never driven a Jaguar before. This was a very fast, very powerful, very expensive two-seater. Cort handed her the key.

She clicked it to open the door. She frowned. "Where's the key?" she asked.

"You don't need a key. It's a smart key. You just keep it in your pocket or lay it in the cup holder."

"Oh."

She climbed into the car and put the smart key in the cup holder.

"Seat belt," he emphasized.

She glared at him. "It will wrinkle my dress," she said fussily, because it was delicate silk, pink and very pretty.

"Seat belt or the car doesn't move," he repeated.

She sighed. He was very forceful. She liked that. She smiled at him prettily. "Okay."

She put it on, grimacing as it wrinkled the delicate fabric. Oh, well, the dry cleaners could fix it. She didn't want to make Cort mad. She pushed the button Cort showed her, the button that would start the car, but nothing happened.

"Brake," he said.

She glared at him. "I'm not going fast enough to brake!"

"You have to put your foot on the brake or it won't start," he explained patiently.

"Oh."

She put her foot on the brake and it started. The air vents opened and the touch screen came on. "It's like something out of a science-fiction movie," she said, impressed.

"Isn't it, though?" He chuckled.

She glanced at him, her face radiant. "I have got to have Daddy get me one of these!" she exclaimed.

Cort hoped her father wouldn't murder him when he saw what they cost.

Odalie pulled the car out of the driveway in short jerks. She grimaced. "I haven't driven in a while, but it will come back to me, honest."

"Okay. I'm not worried." He was petrified, but he wasn't showing it. He hoped he could grab the wheel if he had to.

She smoothed out the motions when she got onto the highway. "There, better?" she teased, looking at him.

"Eyes on the road," he cautioned.

She sighed. "Cort, you're no fun."

"It's a powerful machine. You have to respect it. That means keeping your eyes on the road and paying attention to your surroundings."

"I'm doing that," she argued, looking at him again.

He prayed silently that they'd get home again.

She pulled off on a side road and he began to worry.

"Why are we going this way?" he asked suspiciously.

"Isn't this the way to Catelow?" she asked in all innocence.

"No, it's not," he said. "It's the road that leads to the Lane ranch."

"Oh, dear, I don't want to go there. But there's no place to turn off," she worried. "Anyway, the ranch is just ahead, I'll turn around there."

Cort had to bite his lip to keep from saying something.

Maddie was out in the yard with her garbage can lid. This time Pumpkin had gotten out of the pen when she was looking. He'd jumped a seven-foot-high fence. If she hadn't seen it with her own eyes, she'd never have believed it.

"Pumpkin, you fool!" she yelled at him. "Why can't you stay where I put you? Get back in there!"

But he ran around her. This time he wasn't even trying to spur her. He ran toward the road. It was his favorite place, for some reason, despite the heat that made the ribbon of black asphalt hotter than a frying pan.

"You come back here!" she yelled.

Just as she started after him, Odalie's foot hit the accelerator pedal too hard, Cort called out, Odalie looked at him instead of the road…

Maddie heard screaming. She was numb. She opened her eyes and there was Cort, his face contorted with horror. Beside him, Odalie was screaming and crying.

"Just lie still," Cort said hoarsely. "The ambulance is on the way. Just lie still, baby."

"I hit her, I hit her!" Odalie screamed. "I didn't see her until it was too late! I hit her!"

"Odalie, you have to calm down. You're not helping!" Cort snapped at her. "Find something to cover her. Hurry!"

"Yes…there's a blanket…in the backseat, isn't there…?"

Odalie fetched it with cold, shaking hands. She drew it over Maddie's prone body. There was blood. So much blood. She felt as if she were going to faint, or throw up. Then she saw Maddie's face and tears ran down her cheeks. "Oh, Maddie," she sobbed, "I'm so sorry!"

"Find something to prop her head, in case her spine is injured," Cort gritted. He was terrified. He brushed back Maddie's blond hair, listened to her ragged breathing, saw her face go even paler. "Please hurry!" he groaned.

There wasn't anything. Odalie put her beautiful white leather purse on one side of Maddie's head without a single word, knowing it would ruin the leather and not caring at all. She put her knit overblouse on the other, crumpled up. She knelt in the dirt road beside Maddie and sat down, tears in her eyes. She touched Maddie's arm. "Help is coming," she whispered brokenly. "You hold on, Maddie. Hold on!"

Maddie couldn't believe it. Her worst enemy was sitting beside her in a vision of a horrifically expensive pink silk dress that was going to be absolutely ruined, and apparently didn't mind at all.

She tried to speak. "Pum… Pumpkin?" she rasped.

Cort looked past her and grimaced. He didn't say anything. He didn't have to.

Maddie started to cry, great heaving sobs.

"We'll get you another rooster," Cort said at once. "I'll train him to attack me. Anything. You just have to…hold on, baby," he pleaded. "Hold on!"

She couldn't breathe. "Hurts," she whispered as sensation rushed back in and she began to shudder.

Cort was in hell. There was no other word that would express what he felt as he saw her lying there in bloody clothing, maybe dying, and he couldn't do one damned thing to help her. He was sick to his soul.

He brushed back her hair, trying to remember anything else, anything that would help her until the ambulance arrived.

"Call them again!" Odalie said firmly.

He did. The operator assured them that the ambulance was almost there. She began asking questions, which Cort did his best to answer.

"Where's your great-aunt?" he asked Maddie softly.

"Store," she choked out.

"It's okay, I'll call her," he said when she looked upset.

Odalie had come out of her stupor and she was checking for injuries while Cort talked to the 911 operator. "I don't see anything that looks dangerous, but I'm afraid to move her," she said, ignoring the blood in her efforts to give aid. "There are some abrasions, pretty raw ones. Maddie, can you move your arms and legs?" she asked in a voice so tender that Maddie thought maybe she really was just dreaming all this.

She moved. "Yes," she said. "But…it hurts…"

"Move your ankles."

"Okay."

Odalie looked at Cort with horror.

"I moved…them," Maddie said, wincing. "Hurts!"

"Please, ask them to hurry," Cort groaned into the phone.

"No need," Odalie said, noting the red-and-white vehicle that was speeding toward them.

"No sirens?" Cort asked blankly.

"They don't run the sirens or lights unless they have to," the operator explained kindly. "It scares people to death and can cause wrecks. They'll use them to get the victim to the hospital, though, you bet," she reassured him.

"Thanks so much," Cort said.

"I hope she does well."

"Me, too," he replied huskily and hung up.

Odalie took one of the EMTs aside. "She can't move her feet," she whispered.

He nodded. "We won't let her know."

They went to the patient.

Maddie wasn't aware of anything after they loaded her into the ambulance on a backboard. They talked to someone on the radio and stuck a needle into her arm. She slept.

When she woke again, she was in a hospital bed with two people hovering. Cort and Odalie. Odalie's dress was dirty and bloodstained.

"Your…beautiful dress," Maddie whispered, wincing.

Odalie went to the bed. She felt very strange. Her whole life she'd lived as if there was nobody else around. She'd never been in the position of nursing anybody—her parents and brother had never even sprained a hand. She'd been petted, spoiled, praised, but never depended upon.

Now here was this woman, this enemy, whom her actions had placed almost at death's door. And suddenly she was needed. Really needed.

Maddie's great-aunt had been called. She was in the waiting room, but in no condition to be let near the patient. The hospital staff had to calm her down, she was so terrified.

They hadn't told Maddie yet. When Sadie was calmer, they'd let her in to see the injured woman.

"Your great-aunt is here, too," Odalie said gently. "You're going to be fine."

"Fine." Maddie felt tears run down her cheeks. "So much…to be done at the ranch, and I'm stove up…!"

"I'll handle it," Cort said firmly. "No worries there."

"Pumpkin," she sobbed. "He was horrible. Just horrible. But I loved him." She cried harder.

Odalie leaned down and kissed her unkempt hair. "We'll find you another horrible rooster. Honest."

Maddie sobbed. "You hate me."

"No," Odalie said softly. "No, I don't. And I'm so sorry that I put you in here. I was driving." She bit her lip. "I wasn't watching the road," she said stiffly. "God, I'm sorry!"

Maddie reached out a lacerated hand and touched Odalie's. "I ran into the road after Pumpkin… I wasn't looking. Not your fault. My fault."

Odalie was crying, too. "Okay. Both our faults. Now we have to get you well."

"Both of us," Cort agreed, touching Maddie's bruised cheek.

Maddie swallowed, hard. She wanted to say something else, but they'd given her drugs to make her comfortable, apparently. She opened her mouth to speak and went right to sleep.

Chapter 7

"Is she going to be all right?" Great-Aunt Sadie asked when Odalie and Cort dropped into chairs in the waiting room while Maddie was sleeping.

"Yes, but it's going to be a long recovery," Cort said heavily.

"You can't tell her," Odalie said gently, "but there seems to be some paralysis in her legs. No, it's all right," she interrupted when Sadie looked as if she might start crying. "We've called one of the foremost orthopedic surgeons in the country at the Mayo Clinic. We're flying him down here to see her. We'll go from there, once he's examined her."

"But the expense," Sadie exclaimed.

"No expense. None. This is my fault and I'm paying for it," Odalie said firmly.

"It's my car, I'm helping," Cort added.

She started crying again. "It's so nice of you, both of you."

Odalie hugged her. "I'm so sorry," she said sadly. "I didn't mean to hit her. I wasn't looking, and I should have been."

Sadie hugged her back. "Accidents happen," she sobbed. "It was that stupid rooster, wasn't it?"

"It was." Cort sighed. "He ran right into the road and Maddie ran after him. The road was clear and then, seconds later, she was in the middle of it."

Odalie couldn't confess that she'd gone that way deliberately to show Maddie she was with Cort. She was too ashamed. "She'll be all right," she promised.

"Oh, my poor little girl," Sadie said miserably. "She'll give up, if she knows she might not be able to walk again. She won't fight!"

"She will. Because we'll make her," Odalie said quietly.

Sadie looked at her with new eyes. Her gaze fell to Odalie's dress. "Oh, your dress," she exclaimed.

Odalie just smiled. "I can get another dress. It's Maddie I'm worried about." It sounded like a glib reply, but it wasn't. In the past few hours, Odalie's outlook had totally shifted from herself to someone who needed her. She knew that her life would never be the same again.

A sheriff's deputy came into the waiting room, spotted Odalie and Cort and approached them, shaking his head.

"I know," Odalie said. "It's my fault. I was driving his car—" she indicated Cort "—and not looking where I was going. Maddie ran out into the road after her stupid rooster, trying to save him. She's like that."

The deputy smiled. "We know all that from the

re-creation of the scene that we did," he said. "It's very scientific," he added. "How is she?"

"Bad," Odalie said heavily. "They think she may lose the use of her legs. But we've called in a world-famous surgeon. If anything can be done, it will be. We're going to take care of her."

The deputy looked at the beautiful woman, at her bloodstained, dirty, expensive dress, with kind eyes. "I know some women who would be much more concerned with the state of their clothing than the state of the victim. Your parents must be very proud of you, young lady. If you were my daughter, I would be."

Odalie flushed and smiled. "I feel pretty guilty right now. So thanks for making me feel better."

"You going to charge her?" Cort asked.

The deputy shook his head. "Probably not, as long as she survives. In the law, everything is intent. You didn't mean to do it, and the young lady ran into the road by her own admission." He didn't add that having to watch the results of the accident day after day would probably be a worse punishment than anything the law could prescribe. But he was thinking it.

"That doesn't preclude the young lady pressing charges, however," the deputy added.

Odalie smiled wanly. "I wouldn't blame her if she did."

He smiled back. "I hope she does well."

"So do we," Odalie agreed. "Thanks."

He nodded and went back out again.

"Tell me what the doctor said about her legs," Sadie said sadly, leaning toward them.

Odalie took a long breath. She was very tired and she had no plans to go home that night. She'd have to call her family and tell them what was happening here. She hadn't had time to do that yet, nor had Cort.

"He said that there's a great deal of bruising, with inflammation and swelling. That can cause partial paralysis, apparently. He's started her on anti-inflammatories and when she's able, he'll have her in rehab to help get her moving," she added gently.

"But she was in so much pain…surely they won't make her get up!" Sadie was astonished.

"The longer she stays there, the stronger the possibility that she won't ever get up, Sadie," Odalie said gently. She patted the other woman's hands, which were resting clenched in her lap. "He's a very good doctor."

"Yes," Sadie said absently. "He treated my nephew when he had cancer. Sent him to some of the best oncologists in Texas." She looked up. "So maybe it isn't going to be permanent?"

"A good chance. So you stop worrying. We all have to be strong so that we can make her look ahead instead of behind, so that we can keep her from brooding." She bit her lower lip. "It's going to be very depressing for her, and it's going to be a long haul, even if it has a good result."

"I don't care. I'm just so happy she's still alive," the older woman cried.

"Oh, so am I," Odalie said heavily. "I can't remember ever feeling quite so bad in all my life. I took my eyes off the road, just for a minute." Her eyes closed and she shuddered. "I'll be able to hear that horrible sound when I'm an old lady…"

Cort put his arm around her. "Stop that. I shouldn't have let you drive the car until you were familiar with it. My fault, too. I feel as bad as you do. But we're going to get Maddie back on her feet."

"Yes," Odalie agreed, forcing a smile. "Yes, we are."

Sadie wiped her eyes and looked from one young determined face to the other. Funny how things worked out, she was thinking. Here was Odalie, Maddie's worst enemy, being protective of her, and Cort just as determined to make her walk again when he'd been yelling at her only a week or so earlier. What odd companions they were going to be for her young great-niece. But what a blessing.

She considered how it could have worked out, if Maddie had chased that stupid red rooster out into the road and been hit by someone else, maybe someone who ran and left her there to die. It did happen. The newspapers were full of such cases.

"What are you thinking so hard about?" Cort asked with a faint smile.

Sadie laughed self-consciously. "That if she had to get run over, it was by such nice people who stopped and rendered aid."

"I know what you mean," Cort replied. "A man was killed just a couple of weeks ago by a hit-and-run driver who was drunk and took off. The pedestrian died. I wondered at the time if his life might have been spared, if the man had just stopped to call an ambulance before he ran." He shook his head. "So many cases like that."

"Well, you didn't run, either of you." Sadie smiled. "Thanks, for saving my baby."

Odalie hugged her again, impulsively. "For the foreseeable future, she's my baby, too," she said with a laugh. "Now, how about some coffee? I don't know about you, but I'm about to go to sleep out here and I have no intention of leaving the hospital."

"Nor do I," Cort agreed. He stood up. "Let's go down

to the cafeteria and see what we can find to eat, too. I just realized I'm starving."

The women smiled, as they were meant to.

Maddie came around a long time later, or so it seemed. A dignified man with black wavy hair was standing over her with a nurse. He was wearing a white lab coat with a stethoscope draped around his neck.

"Miss Lane?" the nurse asked gently. She smiled. "This is Dr. Parker from the Mayo Clinic. He's an orthopedic specialist, and we'd like him to have a look at your back. If you don't mind."

Maddie cleared her throat. She didn't seem to be in pain, which was odd. She felt very drowsy. "Of course," she said, puzzled as to why they would have such a famous man at such a small rural hospital.

"Just a few questions first," he said in a deep, pleasant tone, "and then I'll examine you." He smiled down at her.

"Okay."

The pain came back as the examination progressed, but he said it was a good sign. Especially the pain she felt in one leg. He pressed and poked and asked questions while he did it. After a few minutes she was allowed to lie down in the bed, which she did with a grimace of pure relief.

"There's a great deal of edema—swelling," he translated quietly. "Bruising of the spinal column, inflammation, all to be expected from the trauma you experienced."

"I can't feel my legs. I can't move them," Maddie said with anguish in her wan face.

He dropped down elegantly into the chair by her bed, crossed his legs and picked up her chart. "Yes, I know. But you mustn't give up hope. I have every confidence that you'll start to regain feeling in a couple of weeks, three at the outside. You have to believe that as well." He made notations and read what her attending physician had written in the forms on the clipboard, very intent on every word. "He's started you on anti-inflammatories," he murmured. "Good, good, just what I would have advised. Getting fluids into you intravenously, anti-biotics…" He stopped and made another notation. "And then, physical therapy."

"Physical therapy." She laughed and almost cried. "I can't stand up!"

"It's much more than just exercise," he said and smiled gently. "Heat, massage, gentle movements, you'll see. You've never had physical therapy I see."

She shook her head. "I've never really had an injury that required it."

"You're very lucky, then," he said.

"You think I'll walk again?" she prompted, her eyes wide and full of fear.

"I think so," he said. "I won't lie to you, there's a possibility that the injury may result in permanent disability." He held up a hand when she seemed distraught. "If that happens, you have a wonderful support group here. Your family. They'll make sure you have everything you need. You'll cope. You'll learn how to adapt. I've seen some miraculous things in my career, Miss Lane," he added. "One of my newest patients lost a leg overseas in a bombing. We repaired the damage, got him a prosthesis and now he's playing basketball."

She caught her breath. "Basketball?"

He grinned, looking much younger. "You'd be amazed at the advances science has made in such things. Right now, they're working on an interface that will allow quadriplegics to use a computer with just thought. Sounds like science fiction, doesn't it? But it's real. I watched a video of a researcher who linked a man's mind electronically to a computer screen, and he was able to move a curser just with the power of his thoughts." He shook his head. "Give those guys ten years and they'll build something that can read minds."

"Truly fascinating," she agreed.

"But right now, what I want from you is a promise that you'll do what your doctor tells you and work hard at getting back on your feet," he said. "No brooding. No pessimism. You have to believe you'll walk again."

She swallowed. She was bruised and broken and miserable. She drew in a breath. "I'll try," she said.

He stood up and handed the chart to the nurse with a smile. "I'll settle for that, as long as it's your very best try," he promised. He shook hands with her. "I'm going to stay in touch with your doctor and be available for consultation. If I'm needed, I can fly back down here. Your friends out there sent a private jet for me." He chuckled. "I felt like a rock star."

She laughed, then, for the first time since her ordeal had begun.

"That's more like it," he said. "Ninety-nine percent of recovery is in the mind. You remember that."

"I'll remember," she promised. "Thanks for coming all this way."

He threw up a hand. "Don't apologize for that. It got me out of a board meeting," he said. "I hate board meetings."

She grinned.

Later, after she'd been given her medicines and fed, Odalie and Cort came into the private room she'd been moved to.

"Dr. Parker is very nice," she told them. "He came all the way from the Mayo Clinic, though…!"

"Whatever it takes is what you'll get," Odalie said with a smile.

Maddie grimaced as she looked at Odalie's beautiful pink dress, creased and stained with blood and dirt. "Your dress," she moaned.

"I've got a dozen pretty much just like it," Odalie told her. "I won't even miss it." She sighed. "But I really should go home and change."

"Go home and go to bed," Maddie said softly. "You've done more than I ever expected already…"

"No," Odalie replied. "I'm staying with you. I got permission."

"But there's no bed," Maddie exclaimed. "You can't sleep in a chair…!"

"There's a roll-away bed. They're bringing it in." She glanced at Cort with a wicked smile. "Cort gets to sleep in the chair."

He made a face. "Don't rub it in."

"But you don't have to stay," Maddie tried to reason with them. "I have nurses. I'll be fine, honest I will."

Odalie moved to the bed and brushed Maddie's unkempt hair away from her wan face. "You'll brood if we leave you alone," she said reasonably. "It's not as if I've got a full social calendar these days, and I'm not much for cocktail parties. I'd just as soon be here with you. We can talk about art. I majored in it at college."

"I remember," Maddie said slowly. "I don't go to college," she began.

"I'll wager you know more about it than I do," Odalie returned. "You had to learn something of anatomy to make those sculptures so accurate."

"Well, yes, I did," Maddie faltered. "I went on the internet and read everything I could find."

"I have all sorts of books on medieval legends and romances, I'll bring them over for you to read when they let you go home. Right now you have to rest," Odalie said.

Maddie flushed. "That would be so nice of you."

Odalie's eyes were sad. "I've been not so nice to you for most of the time we've known one another," she replied. "You can't imagine how I felt, after what happened because I let an idiot girl talk me into telling lies about you online. I've had to live with that, just as you have. I never even said I was sorry for it. But I am," she added.

Maddie drew in a breath. She was feeling drowsy. "Thanks," she said. "It means a lot."

"Don't you worry about a thing," Odalie added. "I'll take care of you."

Maddie flushed. She'd never even really had a girlfriend, and here was Odalie turning out to be one.

Odalie smiled. "Now go to sleep. Things will look brighter tomorrow. Sometimes a day can make all the difference in how we look at life."

"I'll try."

"Good girl." She glanced at Cort. "Can you drive me home and bring me back?"

"Sure," he said. "I need a change of clothes, too. I'll drop you off at Big Spur, go home and clean up and we'll both come back. We need to tell our parents what's going on, too."

"John will be beside himself," Odalie said without thinking. "All I've heard since I got home is how sweet Maddie is," she added with a smile.

She didn't see Cort's expression, and she couldn't

understand why Maddie suddenly looked so miserable at the mention of her brother's name.

"Well, don't worry about that right now," Odalie said quickly. "But I'm sure he'll be in to see you as soon as he knows what happened."

Maddie nodded.

"I'll be right out," Cort said, smiling at Odalie.

"Sure. Sleep tight," she told Maddie. She hesitated. "I'm sorry about your rooster, too. Really sorry," she stammered, and left quickly.

Maddie felt tears running down her cheeks.

Cort picked a tissue out of the box by the bed, bent down and dabbed at both her eyes. "Stop that," he said softly. "They'll think I'm pinching you and throw me out."

She smiled sadly. "Nobody would ever think you were mean."

"Don't you believe it."

"You and Odalie...you've both been so kind," she said hesitantly. "Thank you."

"We feel terrible," he replied, resting his hand beside her tousled hair on the pillow. "It could have been a worse tragedy than it is. And Pumpkin..." He grimaced and dabbed at more tears on her face. "As much as I hated him, I really am sorry. I know you loved him."

She sniffed, and he dabbed at her nose, too. "He was so mean," she choked out. "But I really did love him."

"We'll get you a new rooster. I'll train him to attack me," he promised.

She laughed through her tears.

"That's better. The way you looked just now was breaking my heart."

She searched his eyes. He wasn't joking. He meant it.

He brushed back her hair. "God, I don't know what I would have done if you'd died," he whispered hoarsely. He bent and crushed his mouth down over hers, ground into it with helpless need. After a few seconds, he forced himself to pull back. "Sorry," he said huskily. "Couldn't help myself. I was terrified when I saw you lying there so still."

"You were?" She looked fascinated.

He shook his head and forced a smile. "Clueless," he murmured. "I guess that's not such a bad thing. Not for the moment anyway." He bent and brushed his mouth tenderly over hers. "I'll be back. Don't go anywhere."

"If I tried to, three nurses would tackle me, and a doctor would sit on me while they sent for a gurney," she assured him, her eyes twinkling.

He wrinkled his nose and kissed her again. "Okay. He stood up. "Anything you want me to bring you?"

"A steak dinner, two strawberry milk shakes, a large order of fries…"

"For that, they'd drag me out the front door and pin me to a wall with scalpels," he assured her.

She sighed. "Oh, well. It was worth a try. They fed me green gelatin." She made a face.

"When we get you out of here, I'll buy you the tastiest steak in Texas, and that's a promise. With fries."

"Ooooh," she murmured.

He grinned. "Incentive to get better. Yes?"

She nodded. "Yes." The smile faded. "You don't have to come back. Odalie, either. I'll be okay."

"We're coming back, just the same. We'll drop Great-Aunt Sadie off at the house, but she can stay at Skylance if she's nervous about being there alone. She's been a real trooper, but she's very upset."

"Can I see her?"

"For just a minute. I'll bring her in. You be good."

She nodded.

Great-Aunt Sadie was still crying when she went to the bed and very carefully bent down to hug Maddie. "I'm so glad you're going to be all right," she sobbed.

Maddie touched her gray hair gently. "Can't kill a weed." She laughed.

"You're no weed, my baby." She smoothed back her hair. "You keep getting better. I'll bring your gown and robe and slippers and some cash when I come back. Here. This is for the machines if you want them to get you anything..."

"Put that back," Cort said, "Maddie won't need cash."

"Oh, but—" Sadie started to argue.

"It won't do any good," Cort interrupted with a grin. "Ask my dad."

"He's right," Maddie said drowsily. "I heard one of his cowboys say that it's easier to argue with a signpost, and you'll get further."

"Stop bad-mouthing me. Bad girl," he teased.

She grinned sleepily.

"You go to sleep," he told her. "Odalie and I will be back later, and we'll bring Sadie in the morning."

"You're a nice boy, Cort," Sadie said tearfully.

He hugged her. "You're a nice girl," he teased. "Good night, honey," he told Maddie, and didn't miss the faint blush in her cheeks as she registered the endearment.

"Good night," she replied.

She drifted off to sleep before they got out of the hospital. In her mind, she could still hear that soft, deep voice drawling "honey."

The next morning, Maddie opened her eyes when she heard a commotion.

"I can't bathe her with you sitting there," the nurse was saying reasonably.

Cort frowned as he stood up. "I know, I know. Sorry. I only fell asleep about four," he added with a sheepish smile.

The nurse smiled back. "It's all right. A lot of patients don't have anybody who even cares if they live or die. Your friend's very fortunate that the two of you care so much."

"She's a sweet girl," Odalie said gently.

"So are you," Cort said, and smiled warmly at her.

She flushed a little.

Maddie, watching, felt her heart sink. They'd both been so caring and attentive that she'd actually forgotten how Cort felt about Odalie. And now it seemed that Odalie was seeing him with new eyes.

Cort turned, but Maddie closed her eyes. She couldn't deal with this. Not now.

"Tell her we went to have breakfast and we'll be back," Cort said, studying Maddie's relaxed face.

"I will," the nurse promised.

Cort let Odalie go out before him and closed the door as he left.

"Time to wake up, sweetie," the nurse told Maddie. "I'm going to give you your bath and then you can have breakfast."

"Oh, is it morning?" Maddie asked, and pretended to yawn. "I slept very well."

"Good. Your friends went to have breakfast. That handsome man said they'd be back," she added with a laugh. "And that woman. What I wouldn't give to be that beautiful!"

"She sings like an angel, too," Maddie said.

"My, my, as handsome as he is, can you imagine what beautiful children they'd have?" the nurse murmured as she got her things together to bathe Maddie.

"Yes, wouldn't they?" Maddie echoed.

Something in her tone made the other woman look at her curiously.

But Maddie just smiled wanly. "They've both been very kind," she said. "They're my neighbors."

"I see."

No, she didn't, but Maddie changed the subject to a popular television series that she watched. The nurse watched it, too, which gave them a talking point.

Later, Sadie came in with a small overnight bag.

"I brought all your stuff," she told Maddie. "You look better," she lied, because Maddie was pale and lethargic and obviously fighting pain.

"It's a little worse today," she replied heavily. "You know what they say about injuries, they're worse until the third day and then they start getting better."

"Who said that?" Sadie wondered.

"Beats me, but I've heard it all my life. Did you bring me anything to read?" she added curiously.

"I didn't. But somebody else did." She glanced at the door. Odalie came in with three beautifully illustrated fairy-tale books. After breakfast, both Odalie and Cort had gone home to change, and then picked up Great-Aunt Sadie when returning to the hospital.

"I bought these while I was in college," Odalie said,

handing one to Maddie. "I thought they had some of the most exquisite plates I'd ever seen."

And by plates, she meant paintings. Maddie caught her breath as she opened the book and saw fairies, like the ones she made, depicted in a fantasy forest with a shimmering lake.

"Oh, this is… It's beyond words," she exclaimed, breathlessly turning pages.

"Yes. I thought you'd like them." She beamed. "These are updated versions of the ones I have. I bought these for you."

"For me?" Maddie looked as if she'd won the lottery. "You mean it?"

"I mean it. I'm so glad you like them."

"They're beautiful," she whispered reverently. She traced one of the fairies. "I have my own ideas about faces and expressions, but these are absolutely inspiring!"

"Fantasy art is my favorite."

"Mine, too." She looked up, flushing a little. "How can I ever thank you enough?"

"You can get better so that my conscience will stop killing me," Odalie said gently.

Maddie smiled. "Okay. I promise to try."

"I'll settle for that."

"I put your best gowns and slippers in the bag," Sadie told her. "And Cort brought you something, too."

"Cort?"

She looked toward the door. He was smiling and nodding at the nurses, backing into the room. Behind his back was a strange, bottom-heavy bear with a big grin and bushy eyebrows.

He turned into the room and handed it to Maddie. "I don't know if they'll let you keep it, but if they won't,

I'll let Sadie take him home and put him in your room. His name's Bubba."

"Bubba?" She burst out laughing as she took the bear from him. It was the cutest stuffed bear she'd ever seen. "Oh, he's so cute!"

"I'm glad you like him. I wanted to smuggle in a steak, but they'd have smelled it at the door."

"Thanks for the thought," she said shyly.

"You're welcome."

"Bears and books." She sighed. "I feel spoiled."

"I should hope so," Odalie said with a grin. "We're doing our best."

"When we get you out of here, we're taking you up to Dallas and we'll hit all the major museums and art galleries," Cort said, dropping into a chair. "Culture. Might give you some new ideas for your paintings and sculptures."

"Plus we bought out an art supply store for you," Odalie said with twinkling eyes. "You'll have enough to make all sorts of creations when you get home."

"Home." Maddie looked from one of them to the other. "When? When can I go home?"

"In a few days." Cort spoke for the others. "First they have to get you stabilized. Then you'll be on a regimen of medicine and physical therapy. We'll go from there."

Maddie drew in a long breath. It sounded like an ordeal. She wasn't looking forward to it. And afterward, what if she could never walk again? What if…?

"No pessimistic thoughts." Odalie spoke for the visitors. "You're going to get well. You're going to walk. Period."

"Absolutely," Sadie said.

"Amen," Cort added.

Maddie managed a sheepish smile. With a cheering section like that, she thought, perhaps she could, after all.

Chapter 8

The third day was definitely the worst. Maddie was in incredible pain from all the bruising. It was agony to move at all, and her legs were still numb. They kept her sedated most of the day. And at night, as usual, Cort and Odalie stayed with her.

"How are you getting away with this?" Maddie asked Odalie when Cort left to get them both a cup of coffee.

"With this?" Odalie asked gently.

"Staying in the room with me," she replied drowsily. "I thought hospitals made people leave at eight-thirty."

"Well, they mostly do," Odalie said sheepishly. "But, you see, Cort's Dad endowed the new pediatric unit, and mine paid for the equipment in the physical therapy unit. So, they sort of made an exception for us."

Maddie laughed in spite of the pain. "Oh, my."

"As my dad explained it, you can do a lot of good for

other people and help defray your own taxes, all at once. But, just between us, my dad would give away money even if it didn't help his tax bill. So would Cort's. It's just the sort of people they are."

"It's very nice of them." She shifted and grimaced. "How are things at my ranch, do you know?" she asked worriedly.

"Great. Not that the boys don't miss you. But Cort's been over there every day getting roundup organized and deciding on your breeding program. I hope you don't mind."

"Are you kidding? I make fairies… I don't know anything about creating bloodlines." She sighed. "My dad knew all that stuff. He was great at it. But he should have had a boy who'd have loved running a ranch. I just got stuck with it because there was nobody else he could leave it to."

"Your father must have known that you'd do the best you could to keep it going," Odalie said gently.

"I am. It's just I have no aptitude for it, that's all."

"I think…"

"Finally!" John Everett said as he walked in, frowning at his sister. "There was such a conspiracy of silence. I couldn't get Cort to tell me where you were. I called every hospital in Dallas…"

"I left you seven emails and ten text messages!" Odalie gasped. "Don't tell me you never read them?"

He glowered at her. "I don't read my personal email because it's always advertisements, and I hate text messages. I disabled them from coming to my phone. You couldn't have called me in Denver and told me what happened?"

Odalie would have told him that Cort talked her out

of it, but he was mad, and John in a temper would discourage most people from confessing that.

"Sorry," she said instead.

He turned his attention to Maddie and grimaced. The bruises were visible around the short-sleeved gown she was wearing. "Poor little thing," he said gently. "I brought you flowers."

He opened the door and nodded to a lady standing outside with a huge square vase full of every flower known to man—or so it seemed. "Right over there looks like a good place," he said, indicating a side table.

The lady, probably from the gift shop, smiled at Maddie and placed the flowers on the table. "I hope you feel better soon," she told her.

"The flowers are just lovely," Maddie exclaimed.

"Thanks," the lady replied, smiled at John and left them to it.

"Oh, how beautiful. Thanks, John!" she exclaimed.

Odalie looked very uncomfortable. John didn't even look at her. He went to the bedside, removed his Stetson and sat down in the chair by the bed, grasping one of Maddie's hands in his. "I've been beside myself since I knew what happened. I wanted to fly right home, but I was in the middle of negotiations for Dad and I couldn't. I did try to call your house, but nobody answered, and I didn't have your cell phone number." He glared at his sister again. "Nobody would even tell me which hospital you were in!"

"I sent you emails," Odalie said again.

"The telephone has a voice mode," he drawled sarcastically.

Odalie swallowed hard and got to her feet. "Maybe

I should help Cort carry the coffee," she said. "Do you want some?"

"Don't be mean to her," Maddie said firmly. "She's been wonderful to me."

John blinked. He glanced at Odalie with wide-eyed surprise. "Her?"

"Yes, her," Maddie replied. "She hasn't left me since I've been in here. She brought me books…"

"Her?" John exclaimed again.

Odalie glared at him. "I am not totally beyond redemption," she said haughtily.

"Maybe I have a fever," John mused, touching his forehead as he looked back down into Maddie's eyes. "I thought you said she stayed with you in the hospital. She hates hospitals."

"She's been here all night every night," Maddie said softly. She smiled at Odalie. "She's been amazing."

Odalie went beet-red. She didn't know how to handle the compliment. She'd had so many, all her life, about her beauty and her talent. But nobody had ever said she was amazing for exhibiting compassion. It felt really good.

"It was my fault, what happened," Odalie said quietly. "I was driving."

"Who the hell let you drive a car?" John exclaimed.

"I did," Cort said heavily as he joined them. He looked at John's hand holding Maddie's and his dark eyes began to burn with irritation. "Don't hold her hand, it's bruised," he blurted out before he thought.

John's blue eyes twinkled suddenly. "It is?" He turned it over and looked at it. "Doesn't look bruised. That hurt?" he asked Maddie.

"Well, no," she answered. The way Cort was looking at John was very odd.

"Yes, he let me drive because I badgered him into it," Odalie broke in. "Poor Maddie tried to save her rooster and ran out into the road. I didn't see her until it was too late."

"Oh, no," John said, concerned. "Will you be all right?" he asked Maddie.

"I'm going to be fine," she assured him with more confidence than she really felt.

"Yes, she is," Odalie said, smiling. "We're all going to make sure of it."

"What about Pumpkin?" John asked.

Odalie tried to stop him from asking, but she was too late.

"It's all right," Maddie said gently. "I'm getting used to it. Pumpkin…didn't make it."

Sadie had told her that Ben had buried the awful rooster under a mesquite tree and even made a little headstone to go on the grave. Considering how many scars Ben had, it was quite a feat of compassion.

"I'll get you a new rooster," John said firmly.

"Already taken care of," Cort replied. "You're in my seat, bro."

John gave him a strange look. "Excuse me?"

"That's my seat. I've got it just the way I like it, from sleeping in it for two nights."

John was getting the picture. He laughed inside. Amazing how determined Cort was to get him away from Maddie. He glanced at his sister, who should be fuming. But she wasn't. Her eyes were smiling. She didn't even seem to be jealous.

Maddie was so out of it that she barely noticed the byplay. The sedative was working on her. She could barely keep her eyes open.

As she drifted off, Cort was saying something about a rooster with feathers on his feet...

A week after the accident, Maddie began to feel her back again. It was agonizing pain. Dr. Brooks came in to examine her, his face impassive as he had her grip his fingers. He used a pin on the bottom of her feet, and actually grinned when she flinched.

"I'm not going to be paralyzed?" she asked, excited and hopeful.

"We can't say that for sure," Dr. Brooks said gently. "Once the swelling and edema are reduced, there may be additional injuries that become apparent. But I will say it's a good sign."

She let out a breath. "I'd have coped," she assured him. "But I'm hoping I won't have to."

He smiled and patted her on the shoulder. "One step at a time, young lady. Recovery first, then rehabilitation with physiotherapy. Meanwhile I'm going to consult with your orthopedic surgeon and put in a call to a friend of mine, a neurologist. We want to cover all our bases."

"You're being very cautious," she murmured.

"I have to be. The fact that you got excellent immediate care at the scene is greatly in your favor, however. Cort knew exactly what to do, and the paramedics followed up in textbook perfection. However," he added with a smile, "my personal opinion is your condition comes from bad bruising and it is not a permanent injury. We saw nothing on the tests that indicated a tearing of the spinal cord or critical damage to any of your lumbar vertebrae."

"You didn't say," she replied.

"Until the swelling goes down, we can't be absolutely

sure of anything, which is why I'm reluctant to go all bright-eyed over a cheery prognosis," he explained. "But on the evidence of what I see, I think you're going to make a complete recovery."

She beamed. "Thank you!"

He held up a hand. "We'll still wait and see."

"When can I go home?" she asked.

"Ask me next week."

She made a face. "I'm tired of colored gelatin," she complained. "They're force feeding me water and stuff with fiber in it."

"To keep your kidney and bowel function within acceptable levels," he said. "Don't fuss. Do what they tell you."

She sighed. "Okay. Thanks for letting Cort and Odalie stay with me at night. One of the nurses said you spoke to the administrator himself."

He shrugged. "He and I were at med school together. I beat him at chess regularly."

She laughed. "Can you thank him for me? You don't know what it meant, that they wanted to stay."

"Yes, I do," he replied solemnly. "I've never seen anybody do a greater turnaround than your friend Odalie." He was the doctor who'd treated Maddie after the boy tried to throw her out of the window at school. He'd given a statement to the attorneys who went to see Cole Everett, as well. He shook his head. "I've known your families since you were children. I know more about Odalie than most people do. I must say, she's impressed me. And I'm hard to impress."

Maddie smiled. "She's impressed me, too. I never expected her to be so compassionate. Of course, it could be guilt," she said hesitantly. She didn't add that Odalie could be trying to win back Cort. She made a face. "I'm ashamed that I said that."

"Don't be. It's natural to be suspicious of someone who's been nothing short of an enemy. But this time, I believe her motives are quite sincere."

"Thanks. That helps."

He smiled. "You keep improving. I'll be back to see you from time to time. But I'm pleased with the progress I see."

"Thanks more for that."

He chuckled. "I love my job," he said at the door.

Late at night, Maddie was prey to her secret fears of losing the use of her legs. Despite Dr. Brooks's assurances, she knew that the prognosis could change. The traumatic nature of her injury made it unpredictable.

"Hey," Cort said softly, holding her hand when she moved restlessly in bed. "Don't think about tomorrow. Just get through one day at a time."

She rolled her head on the pillow and looked at him with tormented eyes. Odalie was sound asleep on the rollaway bed nearby, oblivious. But last night, it had been the other woman who'd been awake while Cort slept, to make sure Maddie had anything she needed.

"It's hard not to think about it," she said worriedly. "I'm letting everybody at the ranch down…"

"Baloney," he mused, smiling. "I've got Ben and the others organized. We're making progress on your breeding program." He made a face. "John went over there today to oversee things while I was here with you."

"John's your best friend," she reminded him.

He didn't want to tell her that he was jealous of his friend. He'd wanted to thump John when he walked in and found him holding Maddie's hand. But he was trying to be reasonable. He couldn't be here and at the ranch. And John was talented with breeding livestock. He'd learned from Cole Everett, whose skills were at least equal with King Brannt's and, some people said, just a tad more scientific.

"That's nice of John," she remarked.

He forced a smile. "Yeah. He's a good guy."

She searched his eyes.

"Oh, hell," he muttered, "he's got an honors degree in animal husbandry. I've got an associate's."

She brightened. "Doesn't experience count for something?" she teased lightly.

He chuckled deep in his throat. "Nice of you, to make me feel better, when I've landed you in that hospital bed," he added with guilt in his eyes.

She squeezed his hand. "My dad used to say," she said softly, "that God sends people into our lives at various times, sometimes to help, sometimes as instruments to test us. He said that you should never blame people who cause things to happen to you, because that might be a test to teach you something you needed to know." She glanced at Odalie. "I can't be the only person who's noticed how much she's changed," she added in a low tone. "She's been my rock through all this. You have, too, but…"

"I understand." He squeezed her hand back, turning it over to look at the neat, clean fingernails tipping her small, capable fingers. "I've been very proud of her."

"Me, too," Maddie confessed. "Honestly this whole experience has changed the way I look at the world, at people."

"Your dad," he replied, "was a very smart man. And not just with cattle."

She smiled. "I always thought so. I do miss him."

He nodded. "I know you do."

He put her hand back on the bed. "You try to go back to sleep. Want me to call the nurse and see if she can give you something else for pain?"

She laughed softly and indicated the patch on her arm. "It's automatic. Isn't science incredible?"

"Gets more incredible every day," he agreed. He got up. "I'm going for more coffee. I won't be long."

"Thanks. For all you're doing," she said seriously.

He stared down at her with quiet, guilty eyes. "It will never be enough to make up for what happened."

"That's not true," she began.

"I'll be back in a bit." He left her brooding.

"You have to try to make Cort stop blaming himself," Maddie told Odalie the next day after she'd had breakfast and Cort had gone to the ranch for a shower and change of clothes. Odalie would go when he returned, they'd decided.

"That's going to be a tall order," the other woman said with a gentle smile.

"If there was a fault, it was Pumpkin's and mine," Maddie said doggedly. "He ran out into the road and I chased after him without paying any attention to traffic."

Odalie sat down in the seat beside the bed, her face covered in guilt. "I have a confession," she said heavily. "You're going to hate me when you hear it."

"I couldn't hate you after all you've done," came the soft reply. "It isn't possible."

Odalie flushed. "Thanks," she said in a subdued tone.

She drew in a deep breath. "I drove by your place deliberately. Cort had been talking about you when I got home. I was jealous. I wanted you to see me with him." She averted her eyes. "I swear to God, if I'd had any idea what misery and grief I was going to cause, I'd never have gotten in the car at all!"

"Oh, goodness," Maddie said unsteadily. But she was much more unsettled by Odalie's jealousy than she was of her actions. It meant that Odalie cared for Cort. And everybody knew how he felt about her; he'd never made any secret of it.

But Maddie had been hurt, and Cort felt responsible. So he was paying attention to Maddie instead of Odalie out of guilt.

Everything became clear. Maddie felt her heart break. But it wasn't Odalie's fault. She couldn't force Cort not to care about her.

Odalie's clear blue eyes lifted and looked into Maddie's gray ones. "You care for him, don't you?" she asked heavily. "I'm so sorry!"

Maddie reached out a hand and touched hers. "One thing I've learned in my life is that you can't make people love you," she said softly. She drew in a long breath and stared at the ceiling. "Life just doesn't work that way."

"So it seems…" Odalie said, and her voice trailed away. "But you see the accident really was my fault."

Maddie shook her head. She wasn't vindictive. She smiled. "It was Pumpkin's."

Odalie felt tears streaming down her cheeks. "All this time, all I could think about is the things I did to you when we were in school. I'm so ashamed, Maddie."

Maddie was stunned.

"I put on a great act for the adults. I was shy and sweet

and everybody's idea of the perfect child. But when they weren't looking, I was horrible. My parents didn't know how horrible until your father came to the house with an attorney, and laid it out for them." She grimaced. "I didn't know what happened to you. There was gossip, but it was hushed up. And gossip is usually exaggerated, you know." She picked at her fingernail, her head lowered. "I pretended that I didn't care. But I did." She looked up. "It wasn't until the accident that I really faced up to the person I'd become." She shook her own head. "I didn't like what I saw."

Maddie didn't speak. She just listened.

Odalie smiled sadly. "You know, I've spent my life listening to people rave about how pretty I was, how talented I was. But until now, nobody ever liked me because I was kind to someone." She flushed red. "You needed me. That's new, having somebody need me." She grinned. "I really like it."

Maddie burst out laughing.

Odalie laughed, too, wiping at tears. "Anyway, I apologize wholeheartedly for all the misery I've caused you, and I'm going to work really hard at being the person I hope I can be."

"I don't know what I would have done without you," Maddie said with genuine feeling. "Nobody could have been kinder."

"Some of that was guilt. But I really like you," she said, and laughed again sheepishly. "I never knew what beautiful little creatures you could create from clay and paint."

"My hobby." She laughed.

"It's going to be a life-changing hobby. You wait."

Maddie only smiled. She didn't really believe that. But she wanted to.

* * *

Cort came back later and Odalie went home to freshen up.

Cort dropped into the chair beside Maddie's bed with a sigh. "I saw your doctor outside, doing rounds. He thinks you're progressing nicely."

She smiled. "Yes, he told me so. He said I might be able to go home in a few days. I'll still have to have physical therapy, though."

"Odalie and I will take turns bringing you here for it," he said, answering one of her fears that her car wouldn't stand up to the demands of daily trips, much less her gas budget.

"But, Cort," she protested automatically.

He held up a hand. "It won't do any good," he assured her.

She sighed. "Okay. Thanks, then." She studied his worn face. "Odalie's been amazing, hasn't she?"

He laughed. "Oh, I could think of better words. She really shocked me. I wouldn't have believed her capable of it."

"I know."

"I'm very proud of her," he said, smiling wistfully. He was thinking what a blessing it was that Odalie hadn't shown that side of herself to him when he thought he was in love with her. Because with hindsight, he realized that it was only an infatuation. He'd had a crush on Odalie that he'd mistaken for true love.

Maddie couldn't hear his thoughts. She saw that wistful smile and thought he was seeing Odalie as he'd always hoped she could be, and that he was more in love with her than ever before.

"So am I," she replied.

He noted the odd look in her eyes and started to

question it when his mother came in with Heather Everett. Both women had been visiting every day. This time they had something with them. It was a beautiful arrangement of orchids.

"We worked on it together," Heather said, smiling. She was Odalie, aged, still beautiful with blue eyes and platinum blond hair. A knockout, like dark-eyed, dark-haired Shelby Brannt, even with a sprinkle of gray hairs.

"Yes, and we're not florists, but we wanted to do something personal," Shelby added.

Heather put it on the far table, by the window, where it caught the light and looked exotic and lush.

"It's so beautiful! Thank you both," Maddie enthused.

"How are you feeling, sweetheart?" Shelby asked, hovering.

"The pain is easing, and I have feeling in my legs," she said, the excitement in her gray eyes. "The doctor thinks I'll walk again."

"That's wonderful news," Shelby said heavily. "We've been so worried."

"All of us," Heather agreed. She smiled. "It's worse for us, because Odalie was driving."

"Odalie has been my rock in a storm," Maddie said gently. "She hasn't left me, except to freshen up, since they brought me in here. I honestly don't know how I would have made it without her. Or without Cort," she added, smiling at him. "They've stopped me from brooding, cheered me up, cheered me on...they've been wonderful."

Shelby hugged her tall son. "Well, of course, I think so." She laughed. "Still, it's been hard on all three families," she added quietly. "It could have been even more of a tragedy if—"

"I'm going to be fine," Maddie interrupted her.

"Yes, she is," Cort agreed. He smiled at Maddie. His dark eyes were like velvet. There was an expression in them that she'd never noticed before. Affection. Real affection.

She smiled back, shyly, and averted her eyes.

"Odalie wants you to talk to one of our friends, who has an art gallery in Dallas," Heather said. "She thinks your talent is quite incredible."

"It's not, but she's nice to say so…" Maddie began.

"They're her kids," Cort explained to the women, and Maddie's eyes widened. "Don't deny it, you told me so," he added, making a face at her. "She puts so much of herself into them that she can't bear to think of selling one."

"Well, I know it sounds odd, but it's like that with me and the songs I compose," Heather confessed, and flushed a little when they stared at her. "I really do put my whole heart into them. And I hesitate to share that with other people."

"Desperado owes you a lot for those wonderful songs." Shelby chuckled. "And not just money. They've made an international reputation with them."

"Thanks," Heather said. "I don't know where they come from. It's a gift. Truly a gift."

"Like Odalie's voice," Maddie replied. "She really does sing like an angel."

Heather smiled. "Thank you. I've always thought so. I wanted her to realize her dream, to sing at the Met, at the Italian opera houses." She looked introspective. "But it doesn't look like she's going to do that at all."

"Why not?" Shelby asked, curious.

Heather smiled. "I think she's hungry for a home of

her own and a family. She's been talking about children lately."

"Has she?" Cort asked, amused.

He didn't seem to realize that Maddie immediately connected Heather's statement with Odalie's changed nature and Cort's pride in her. She added those facts together and came up with Cort and Odalie getting married.

It was so depressing that she had to force herself to smile and pretend that she didn't care.

"Can you imagine what beautiful children she'll have?" Maddie asked with a wistful smile.

"Well, yours aren't going to be ugly," Cort retorted. Then he remembered that he'd called Maddie that, during one of their arguments, and his face paled with shame.

Maddie averted her eyes and tried not to show what she was feeling. "Not like Odalie's," she said. "Is she thinking about getting married?" she asked Heather.

"She says she is," she replied. "I don't know if she's really given it enough thought, though," she added with sadness in her tone. "Very often, we mistake infatuation for the real thing."

"You didn't," Shelby teased before anyone could react to Heather's statement. "You knew you wanted to marry Cole before you were even an adult."

Heather saw Maddie's curious glance. "Cole's mother married my father," she explained. "There was some terrible gossip spread, to the effect that we were related by blood. It broke my heart. I gave up on life. And then the truth came out, and I realized that Cole didn't hate me at all. He'd only been shoving me out of his life because he thought I was totally off-limits, and his pride wouldn't let him admit how thoroughly he'd accepted the gossip for truth."

"You made a good match." Shelby smiled.

"So did you, my friend." Heather laughed. "Your road to the altar was even more precarious than mine."

Shelby beamed. "Yes, but it was worth every tear." She hugged her son. "Look at my consolation prize!"

But when the women left, and Cort walked them out to the parking lot, Maddie was left with her fears and insecurities.

Odalie wanted to marry and raise a family. She'd seen how mature and caring Cort was, and she wanted to drive him by Maddie's house because she was jealous of her. She'd wanted Maddie to see her with Cort.

She could have cried. Once, Odalie's feelings wouldn't have mattered. But since she'd been in the hospital, Maddie had learned things about the other woman. She genuinely liked her. She was like the sister Maddie had never had.

What was she going to do? Cort seemed to like Maddie now, but she'd been hurt and it was his car that had hit her. Certainly he felt guilty. And nobody could deny how much he'd loved Odalie. He'd grieved for weeks after she left for Italy.

Surely his love for her hadn't died just because Maddie had been in an accident. He'd told Maddie that she was ugly and that she didn't appeal to him as a man, long before the wreck. That had been honest; she'd seen it in his dark eyes.

Now he was trying to make up for what had happened. He was trying to sacrifice himself to Maddie in a vain attempt to atone for her injuries. He was denying himself Odalie out of guilt.

Maddie closed her eyes. She couldn't have that. She

wanted him to be happy. In fact, she wanted Odalie to be happy. Cort would be miserable if he forced himself into a relationship with Maddie that he didn't feel.

So that wasn't going to be allowed to happen. Maddie was going to make sure of it.

Chapter 9

By the end of the second week after the accident, Maddie was back home, with a high-tech wheelchair to get around the house in.

Odalie and Cort had insisted on buying her one to use while she was recuperating, because she still couldn't walk, even though the feeling had come back into her legs. She was exhilarated with the doctor's cautious prognosis that she would probably heal completely after several months.

But she'd made her friends promise to get her an inexpensive manual wheelchair. Of course, they'd said, smiling.

Then they walked in with a salesman who asked questions, measured her and asked about her choice of colors. Oh, bright yellow, she'd teased, because she was sure they didn't make a bright yellow wheelchair. The only ones she'd seen were black and ugly and plain, and they all looked alike. She'd dreaded the thought of having to sit in one.

A few days later, the wheelchair was delivered. It came from Europe. It was the most advanced wheelchair of its type, fully motorized, able to turn in its own circumference, able to lift the user up to eye level with other people, and all-terrain. Oh, and also, bright yellow in color.

"This must have cost a fortune!" Maddie almost screamed when she saw it. "I said something inexpensive!"

Cort gave her a patient smile. "You said inexpensive. This is inexpensive," he added, glancing at Odalie.

"Cheap," the blonde girl nodded. She grinned unrepentantly. "When you get out of it, you can donate it to someone in need."

"Oh. Well." The thought that she would get out of it eventually sustained her. "I can donate it?"

Odalie nodded. She smiled.

Cort smiled, too.

"Barracudas," she concluded, looking from one to the other. "I can't get around either one of you!"

They both grinned.

She laughed. "Okay. Thanks. Really. Thanks."

"You might try it out," Odalie coaxed.

"Yes, in the direction of the hen yard," Cort added.

She looked from one of them to the other. They had very suspicious expressions. "Okay."

She was still learning to drive it, but the controls were straightforward, and it didn't take long to learn them. The salesman had come out with it, to further explain its operation.

It had big tires, and it went down steps. That was a revelation. It didn't even bump very much. She followed

Cort and Odalie over the sandy yard to the huge enclosure where her hens lived. It was grassy, despite the tendency of chickens to scratch and eat the grass, with trees on one side. The other contained multiple feeders and hanging waterers. The enormous henhouse had individual nests and cowboys cleaned it out daily. There was almost no odor, and the hens were clean and beautiful.

"My girls look very happy," Maddie said, laughing.

"They have a good reason to be happy." Cort went into the enclosure, and a minute later, he came back out, carrying a large red rooster with a big comb and immaculate feathers.

He brought him to Maddie. The rooster looked sort of like Pumpkin, but he was much bigger. He didn't seem at all bothered to be carried under someone's arm. He handed the rooster to Maddie.

She perched him on her jean-clad lap and stared at him. He cocked his head and looked at her and made a sort of purring sound.

She was aghast. She looked up at Cort wide-eyed.

"His name's Percival," Cort told her with a chuckle. "He has impeccable bloodlines."

She looked at the feathery pet again. "I've never seen a rooster this tame," she remarked.

"That's from those impeccable bloodlines." Odalie giggled. "All their roosters are like this. They're even guaranteed to be tame, or your money back. So he's sort of returnable. But you won't need to return him. He's been here for a week and he hasn't attacked anybody yet. Considering his age, he's not likely to do it."

"His age?" Maddie prompted.

"He's two," Cort said. "Never attacked anybody on the farm for all that time. The owners' kids carry the roosters around with them all the time. They're gentled. But they're also bred for temperament. They have exceptions from time to time. But Percy's no exception. He's just sweet."

"Yes, he is." She hugged the big rooster, careful not to hug him too closely, because chickens have no diaphragm and they can be smothered if their chests are compressed for too long. "Percy, you're gorgeous!"

He made that purring sound again. Almost as if he were laughing. She handed him back to Cort. "You've got him separate from the girls?"

He nodded. "If you want biddies, we can put him with them in time for spring chicks. But they know he's nearby, and so will predators. He likes people. He hates predators. The owner says there's a fox who'll never trouble a henhouse again after the drubbing Percy gave him."

Maddie laughed with pure joy. "It will be such a relief not to have to carry a limb with me to gather eggs," she said. The smile faded. "I'll always miss Pumpkin," she said softly, "but even I knew that something had to give eventually. He was dangerous. I just didn't have the heart to do anything about him."

"Providence did that for you," Cort replied. He smiled warmly. Maddie smiled back but she avoided his eyes.

That bothered him. He put Percy back in the enclosure in his own fenced area, very thoughtful. Maddie was polite, but she'd been backing away from him for days now. He felt insecure. He wanted to ask her what was wrong. Probably, he was going to have to do that pretty soon.

Maddie went to work on her sculptures with a vengeance, now that she had enough materials to produce anything she liked.

Her first work, though, was a tribute to her new friend. She made a fairy who looked just like Odalie, perched on a lily pad, holding a firefly. She kept it hidden when Cort and Odalie came to see her, which was pretty much every single day. It was her secret project.

She was so thrilled with it that at first she didn't even want to share it with them. Of all the pieces she'd done, this was her best effort. It had been costly, too. Sitting in one position for a long time, even in her cushy imported wheelchair, was uncomfortable and took a toll on her back.

"You mustn't stress your back muscles like this," the therapist fussed when she went in for therapy, which she did every other day. "It's too much strain so early in your recovery."

She smiled while the woman used a heat lamp and massage on her taut back. "I know. I like to sculpt things. I got overenthusiastic."

"Take frequent breaks," the therapist advised.

"I'll do that. I promise."

She was walking now, just a little at a time, but steadily. Cort had bought a unit for her bathtub that created a Jacuzzi-like effect in the water. It felt wonderful on her sore and bruised back. He'd had a bar installed, too, so that she could ease herself up out of the water and not have to worry about slipping.

Odalie brought her exotic cheeses and crackers to eat them with, having found out that cheese was pretty much Maddie's favorite food. She brought more art books, and classical music that Maddie loved.

Cort brought his guitar and sang to her. That was the hardest thing to bear. Because Maddie knew he was only doing it because he thought Maddie had feelings for him. It was humiliating that she couldn't hide them, especially since she knew that he loved Odalie and always would.

But she couldn't help but be entranced by it. She loved his deep, rich voice, loved the sound of the guitar, with its mix of nylon and steel strings. It was a classical guitar. He'd ordered it from Spain. He played as wonderfully as he sang.

When he'd played *"Recuerdos de la Alhambra"* for her, one of the most beautiful classical guitar compositions ever conceived, she wept like a baby.

"It is beautiful, isn't it?" he asked, drying her tears with a handkerchief. "It was composed by a Spaniard, Francisco Tárrega, in 1896." He smiled. "It's my favorite piece."

"Mine, too," she said. "I had a recording of guitar solos on my iPod with it. But you play it just as beautifully as that performer did. Even better than he did."

"Thanks." He put the guitar back into its case, very carefully. "From the time I was ten, there was never any other instrument I wanted to play. I worried my folks to death until they bought me one. And Morie used to go sit outside while I practiced, with earplugs in." He chuckled, referring to his sister.

"Poor Morie," she teased.

"She loves to hear me play, now. She said it was worth the pain while I learned."

She grinned. "You know, you could sing professionally."

He waved that thought away. "I'm a cattleman," he replied. "Never wanted to be anything else. The guitar is a nice hobby. But I don't think I'd enjoy playing and singing as much if I had to do it all the time."

"Good point."

"How's that sculpture coming along?"

Her eyes twinkled. "Come see."

She turned on the wheelchair and motored herself into the makeshift studio they'd furnished for her in her father's old bedroom. It had just the right airy, lighted accommodation that made it a great place to work. Besides that, she could almost feel her father's presence when she was in it.

"Don't tell her," she cautioned as she uncovered a mound on her worktable. "It's going to be a surprise."

"I promise."

She pulled off the handkerchief she'd used to conceal the little fairy sculpture. The paint was dry and the glossy finish she'd used over it gave the beautiful creature an ethereal glow.

"It looks just like her!" Cort exclaimed as he gently picked it up.

She grinned. "Do you think so? I did, but I'm too close to my work to be objective about it."

"It's the most beautiful thing you've done yet, and that's saying something." He looked down at her with an odd expression. "You really have the talent."

She flushed. "Thanks, Cort."

He put the sculpture down and bent, brushing his mouth tenderly over hers. "I have to be so careful with you," he whispered at her lips. "It's frustrating, in more ways than one."

She caught her breath. She couldn't resist him. But it was tearing her apart, to think that he might be caught in a web of deception laced by guilt. She looked up into his eyes with real pain.

He traced her lips with his forefinger. "When you're back on your feet," he whispered, "we have to talk."

She managed a smile. "Okay." Because she knew that, by then, she'd find a way to ease his guilt, and Odalie's, and step out of the picture. She wasn't going to let them sacrifice their happiness for her. That was far too much.

He kissed her again and stood up, smiling. "So when are you going to give it to her?"

"Tomorrow," she decided.

"I'll make sure she comes over."

"Thanks."

He shrugged and then smiled. "She's going to be over the moon when she sees it."

That was an understatement. Odalie cried. She turned the little fairy around and around in her elegant hands, gasping at the level of detail in the features that were so exactly like her own.

"It's the most beautiful gift I've ever been given."

She put it down, very gently, and hugged Maddie as carefully as she could. "You sweetie!" she exclaimed. "I'll never be able to thank you. It looks just like me!"

Maddie chuckled. "I'm glad you like it."

"You have to let me talk to my friend at the art gallery," Odalie said.

Maddie hesitated. "Maybe someday," she faltered. "Maybe."

"But you have so much talent, Maddie. It's such a gift."

Maddie flushed. "Thanks."

Odalie kept trying, but she couldn't move the other girl. Not at all.

"Okay," she relented. "You know your own mind. Oh, goodness, what is that?" she exclaimed, indicating a cameo lying beside another fairy, a black-haired one sitting on a riverbank holding a book.

Maddie told her the story of the antiques dealer and the cameo that had no family to inherit.

"What an incredible story," Odalie said, impressed. "She's quite beautiful. You can do that, from a picture?"

Maddie laughed. "I did yours from the one in our school yearbook," she said, and this time she didn't flinch remembering the past.

Odalie looked uncomfortable, but she didn't refer to it. Perhaps in time she and Maddie could both let go of that terrible memory. "Maddie, could you do one of my great-grandmother if I brought you a picture of her? It's a commission, now…"

Maddie held up a hand. "No. I'd love to do it. It's just a hobby, you know, not a job. Just bring me a picture."

Odalie's eyes were unusually bright. "Okay. I'll bring it tomorrow!"

Maddie laughed at her enthusiasm. "I'll get started as soon as I have it."

The picture was surprising. "This is your grand-mother?" Maddie asked, because it didn't look anything like Odalie. The subject of the painting had red hair and pale green eyes.

"My great-grandmother," Odalie assured her, but she averted her eyes to another sculpture while she said it.

"Oh. That explains it. Yes, I can do it."

"That's so sweet of you, Maddie."

"It's nothing at all."

It took two weeks. Maddie still had periods of discom-fort that kept her in bed, but she made sure she walked and moved around, as the therapist and her doctor had told her to do. It was amazing that, considering the impact of the car, she hadn't suffered a permanent disability. The swelling and inflammation had been pretty bad, as was the bruising, but she wasn't going to lose the use of her legs. The doctor was still being cautious about that prognosis. But Maddie could tell from the way she was healing that she was going to be all right. She'd never been more certain of anything.

She finished the little fairy sculpture on a Friday. She was very pleased with the result. It looked just like the photograph, but with exquisite detail. This fairy was sitting on a tree stump, with a small green frog perched on her palm. She was laughing. Maddie loved the way it had turned out. But now it was going to be hard to part with it. She did put part of herself into her sculptures. It was like giving herself away with the art.

She'd promised Odalie, though, so she had to come to terms with it.

Odalie was overwhelmed with the result. She stared at it and just shook her head. "I can't believe how skilled you are," she said, smiling at Maddie. "This is so beautiful. She'll—I mean, my mother, will love it!"

"Oh, it's her grandmother," Maddie recalled.

"Yes." Odalie still wouldn't meet her eyes, but she laughed. "What a treat this is going to be! Can I take it with me?" she asked.

Maddie only hesitated for a second. She smiled. "Of course you can."

"Wonderful!"

She bent and hugged Maddie gently. "Still doing okay?" she asked worriedly.

Maddie nodded. "Getting better all the time, thanks

to a small pharmacy of meds on my bedside table," she quipped.

"I'm so glad. I mean that," she said solemnly. "The day you can walk to your car and drive it, I'll dance in the yard."

Maddie laughed. "Okay. I'll hold you to that!"

Odalie just grinned.

Cort came over every day. Saturday morning he went to the barn to study the charts he and John Everett had made. John had just come over to bring Maddie flowers. She was sitting on the porch with Great-Aunt Sadie. As soon as John arrived, Cort came back from the barn and joined the group on the porch. The way Cort glared at him was surprising.

"They'll give her allergies," Cort muttered.

John gave him a stunned look, and waved around the yard at the blooming crepe myrtle and jasmine and sunflowers and sultanas and zinnias. "Are you nuts?" he asked, wide-eyed. "Look around you! Who do you think planted all these?"

Cort's dark eyes narrowed. He jammed his hands into his jean pockets. "Well, they're not in the house, are they?" he persisted.

John just laughed. He handed the pot of flowers to Great-Aunt Sadie, who was trying not to laugh. "Can you put those inside?" he asked her with a smile. "I want to check the board in the barn and see how the breeding program needs to go."

"I sure can," Sadie replied, and she went into the house.

Maddie was still staring at John with mixed feelings.

"Uh, thanks for the flowers," she said haltingly. Cort was looking irritated.

"You're very welcome," John said. He studied her for a long moment. "You look better."

"I feel a lot better," she said. "In fact, I think I might try to walk to the barn."

"In your dreams, honey," Cort said softly. He picked her up, tenderly, and cradled her against his chest. "But I'll walk you there."

John stared at him intently. "Should you be picking her up like that?" he asked.

Cort wasn't listening. His dark eyes were probing Maddie's gray ones with deep tenderness. Neither of them was looking at John, who suddenly seemed to understand what was going on around him.

"Darn, I left my notes in the car," he said, hiding a smile. "I'll be right back."

He strode off. Cort bent his head. "I thought he'd never leave," he whispered, and brought his mouth down, hard, on Maddie's.

"Cort…"

"Shh," he whispered against her lips. "Don't fuss. Open your mouth…!"

The kiss grew hotter by the second. Maddie was clinging to his neck for dear life while he crushed her breasts into the softness of his blue-checked shirt and devoured her soft lips.

He groaned harshly, but suddenly he remembered where they were. He lifted his head, grateful that his back was to the house, and John's car. He drew in a long breath.

"I wish you weren't so fragile," he whispered. He kissed her shocked eyes shut. "I'm starving."

Her fingers teased the hair at the back of his head. "I could feed you a biscuit," she whispered.

He smiled. "I don't want biscuits." He looked at her mouth. "I want you."

Her face flamed with a combination of embarrassment and sheer delight.

"But we can talk about that later, after I've disposed of John's body," he added, turning to watch the other man approach, his eyes buried in a black notebook.

"Wh-wh-what?" she stammered, and burst out laughing at his expression.

He sighed. "I suppose no war is ever won without a few uncomfortable battles," he said under his breath.

"I found them," John said with a grin, waving the notebook. "Let's have a look at the breeding strategy you've mapped out, then."

"I put it all on the board," Cort replied. He carried Maddie into the barn and set her on her feet very carefully, so as not to jar her spine. "It's right there," he told John, nodding toward the large board where he'd indicated which bulls were to be bred to which heifers and cows.

John studied it for a long moment. He turned and looked at Cort curiously. "This is remarkable," he said. "I would have gone a different way, but yours is better."

Cort seemed surprised. "You've got a four-year degree in animal husbandry," he said. "Mine is only an associate's degree."

"Yes, but you've got a lifetime of watching your father do this." He indicated the board. "I've been busy studying and traveling. I haven't really spent that much time observing. It's rather like an internship, and I don't have the experience, even if I have the education."

"Thanks," Cort said. He was touchy about his two-year degree. He smiled. "Took courses in diplomacy, too, did you?" he teased.

John bumped shoulders with him. "You're my best friend," he murmured. "I'd never be the one to try to put you down."

Cort punched his shoulder gently. "Same here."

Maddie had both hands on her slender hips as she stared at the breeding chart. "Would either of you like to try to translate this for me?" She waved one hand at the blackboard. "Because it looks like Martian to me!"

Both men burst out laughing.

Cort had to go out of town. He was worried when he called Maddie to tell her, apologizing for his absence.

"Mom and Dad will look out for you while I'm gone," he promised. "If you need anything, you call them. I'll phone you when I get to Denver."

Her heart raced. "Okay."

"Will you miss me?" he teased.

She drew in a breath. "Of course," she said.

There was a pause. "I'll miss you more," he said quietly. His deep voice was like velvet. "What do you want me to bring you from Denver?"

"Yourself."

There was a soft chuckle. "That's a deal. Talk to you later."

"Have a safe trip."

He sighed. "At least Dad isn't flying me. He flies like he drives. But we'll get there."

The plural went right over her head. She laughed. She'd heard stories about King Brannt's driving. "It's safer than driving, everybody says so."

"In my dad's case, it's actually true. He flies a lot better than he drives."

"I heard that!" came a deep voice from beside him.

"Sorry, Dad," Cort replied. "See you, Maddie."

He hung up. She held the cell phone to her ear for an extra minute, just drinking in the sound of his voice promising to miss her.

While Cort was away, Odalie didn't come, either. But even though she called, Maddie missed her daily visits. She apologized over the phone. She was actually out of town, but her mother had volunteered to do any running-around that Maddie needed if Sadie couldn't go.

Maddie thanked her warmly. But when she hung up she couldn't help but wonder at the fact that Cort and Odalie were out of town at the same time. Had Odalie gone to Denver with Cort and they didn't want to tell her? It was worrying.

She rode her wheelchair out to the hen enclosure. Ben was just coming out of it with the first of many egg baskets. There were a lot of hens, and her customer list for her fresh eggs was growing by the week.

"That's a lot of eggs," she ventured.

He chuckled. "Ya, and I still have to wash 'em and check 'em for cracks."

"I like Percy," she remarked.

"I love Percy," Ben replied. "Never saw such a gentle rooster."

"Thanks. For what you did for Pumpkin's grave," she said, averting her eyes. She still cried easily when she talked about him.

"It was no problem at all, Miss Maddie," he said gently.

She looked over her hens with proud eyes. "My girls look good."

"They do, don't they?" he agreed, then added, "Well, I should get to work."

"Ben, do you know where Odalie went?" she asked suddenly.

He bit his lip.

"Come on," she prodded. "Tell me."

He looked sad. "She went to Denver, Miss Maddie. Heard it from her dad when I went to pick up feed in town."

Maddie's heart fell to her feet. But she smiled. "She and Cort make a beautiful couple," she remarked, and tried to hide the fact that she was dying inside.

"Guess they do," he said. He tried to say something else, but he couldn't get the words to come out right. "I'll just go get these eggs cleaned."

She nodded. The eyes he couldn't see were wet with tears.

It seemed that disaster followed disaster. While Cort and Odalie were away, bills flooded the mailbox. Maddie almost passed out when she saw the hospital bill. Even the minimum payment was more than she had in the bank.

"What are we going to do?" she wailed.

Sadie winced at her expression. "Well, we'll just manage," she said firmly. "There's got to be something we can sell that will help pay those bills." She didn't add that Cort and Odalie had promised they were taking care of all that. But they were out of town, and Sadie knew that Maddie's pride would stand in the way of asking them for money. She'd never do it.

"There is something," Maddie said heavily. She looked up at Sadie.

"No," Sadie said shortly. "No, you can't!"

"Look at these bills, Sadie," she replied, and spread them out on the table. "There's nothing I can hock, nothing I can do that will make enough money fast enough to cover all this. There just isn't anything else to do."

"You aren't going to talk to that developer fellow?"

"Heavens, no!" Maddie assured her. "I'll call a real estate agent in town."

"I think that's…"

Just as she spoke, a car pulled up in the yard.

"Well, speak of the devil," Maddie muttered.

The developer climbed out of his car, looked around and started for the front porch.

"Do you suppose we could lock the door and pretend to be gone?" Sadie wondered aloud.

"No. We're not hiding. Let him in," Maddie said firmly.

"Don't you give in to his fancy talk," Sadie advised.

"Never in a million years. Let him in."

The developer, Arthur Lawson, came in the door with a smug look on his face. "Miss Lane," he greeted. He smiled like a crocodile. "Bad news does travel fast. I heard you were in an accident and that your bills are piling up. I believe I can help you."

Maddie looked at Sadie. Her expression was eloquent.

Archie Lawson grinned like the barracuda he was.

"I heard that your neighbors have gone away together," he said with mock sympathy. "Just left you with all those medical bills to pay, did they?"

Maddie felt terrible. She didn't want to say anything unkind about Odalie and Cort. They'd done more than most people could have expected of them. But Maddie was left with the bills, and she had no money to pay them with. She'd read about people who didn't pay their hospital bill on time and had to deal with collectors' agencies. She was terrified.

"They don't say I have to pay them at once," Maddie began.

"Yes, but the longer you wait, the higher the interest they charge," he pointed out.

"Interest?"

"It's such and such a percent," he continued. He sat down without being asked in her father's old easy chair. "Let me spell it out for you. I can write you a check that will cover all those medical bills, the hospital bill, everything. All you have to do is sign over the property to me. I'll even take care of the livestock. I'll make sure they're sold to people who will take good care of them."

"I don't know," Maddie faltered. She was torn. It was so quick...

"Maddie, can I talk to you for a minute?" Sadie asked tersely. "It's about supper," she lied.

"Okay."

She excused herself and followed Sadie into the kitchen.

Sadie closed the door. "Listen to me, don't you do that until you talk to Mr. Brannt," Sadie said firmly. "Don't you dare!"

"But, Sadie," she said in anguish, "we can't pay the bills, and we can't expect the Brannts and the Everetts to keep paying them forever!"

"Cort said he'd take care of the hospital bill, at least," Sadie reminded her.

"Miss Lane?" Lawson called. "I have to leave soon!"

"Don't let him push you into this," Sadie cautioned. "Make him wait. Tell him you have to make sure the estate's not entailed before you can sell, you'll have to talk to your lawyer!"

Maddie bit her lower lip.

"Tell him!" Sadie said, gesturing her toward the porch.

Maddie took a deep breath and Sadie opened the door for her to motor through.

"Sadie was reminding me that we had a couple of outstanding liens on the property after Dad died," Maddie lied. "I'll have to talk to our attorney and make sure they've been lifted before I can legally sell it to you."

"Oh." He stood up. "Well." He glared. "You didn't mention that earlier."

"I didn't think you thought I was going to sell the ranch today," Maddie said, and with a bland smile. "That's all. You wouldn't want to find out later that you didn't actually own it…?"

"No. Of course not." He made a face. "All right, I'll be back in, say, two days? Will that give you enough time?"

"Yes," Maddie said.

He picked up his briefcase and looked around the living room. "This house will have to be torn down. But if you want some pictures and stuff, I can let you have it after we wrap up the sale. The furniture's no loss." He laughed coldly. "I'll be in touch. And if your answer is no—well, don't be surprised if your cattle suddenly come down with unusual diseases. Anthrax always comes to mind… And if federal agencies have to be called in, your operation will be closed down immediately."

He left and Maddie had to bite back curses. "The furniture's no loss," she muttered. "These are antiques! And anthrax! What kind of horrible person would infect defenseless animals! Maddie went inside, a chill settling in her heart.

* * *

"Nasty man. You can't let him have our house!" Sadie glared out the window as the developer drove off.

Maddie leaned back in her chair. "I wish I didn't," she said heavily. "But I don't know what else to do." She felt sick to her soul at the man's threats. "Cort is going to marry Odalie, you know."

Sadie wanted to argue, but she didn't know how to. It seemed pretty obvious that if he hadn't told Maddie he was leaving with Odalie, he had a guilty conscience and was trying to shield her from the truth.

"Should have just told you, instead of sneaking off together," Sadie muttered.

"They didn't want to hurt me," Maddie said heavily. "It's pretty obvious how I feel about Cort, you know."

"Still…"

Maddie looked at the bills lying open on the table. She leaned forward with her face in her hands. Her heart was breaking. At least she might be able to walk eventually. But that still left the problem of how she was going to walk herself out of this financial mess. The ranch was all she had left for collateral.

Collateral! She turned to Sadie. "We can take out a mortgage, can't we?" she asked Sadie.

Sadie frowned. "I don't know. Best you should call the lawyer and find out."

"I'll do that right now!"

She did at least have hope that there were options. A few options, at least.

But the lie she'd told Lawson turned out to be the truth.

"I'm really sorry, Maddie," Burt Davies told her. "But your dad did take out a lien on the property when he bought that last seed bull. I've been keeping up the payments out of the ranch revenues when I did the bills for you the past few months."

"You mean, I can't sell or even borrow on the ranch."

"You could sell," he admitted. "If you got enough for it that would pay off the lien… But, Maddie, that land's been in your family for generations. You can't mean to sell it."

She swallowed. "Burt, I've got medical bills I can't begin to pay."

"Odalie and Cort are taking care of those," he reminded her. "Legally, even if not morally, they're obligated to."

"Yes, but, they're getting married, don't you see?" she burst out. "I can't tie them up with my bills."

"You can and you will, if I have to go to court for you," Burt said firmly. "The accident wasn't your fault."

"Yes, it was," she said in a wan tone. "I ran out in the road to save my stupid rooster, who died anyway. As for guilt, Odalie and Cort have done everything humanly possible for me since the wreck. Nobody could fault them for that."

"I know, but…"

"If I sell the ranch," she argued gently, "I can pay off all my debts and I won't owe anyone anything."

"That's bad legal advice. You should never try to act as your own attorney."

She laughed. "Yes, I know. Okay, I'll think about it for a couple of days," she said.

"You think about it hard," he replied. "No sense in letting yourself be forced into a decision you don't want to make."

"All right. Thanks, Burt."

She hung up. "Life," she told the room at large, "is just not fair."

* * *

The next day, Ben came walking in with a sad expression. "Got bad news," he said.

"What now?" Maddie asked with a faint smile.

"Lost two more purebred cows. They wandered off."

"All right, that's more than coincidence," she muttered. She moved to the phone, picked it up and called King Brannt.

"How many cows does that make?" King asked, aghast.

"Four, in the past few weeks," she said. "Something's not right."

"I agree. I'll get our computer expert to check those recordings and see if he can find anything."

"Thanks, Mr. Brannt."

He hesitated. "How are things over there?"

She hesitated, too. "Just fine," she lied. "Fine."

"Cort's coming home day after tomorrow," he added.

"I hope he and Odalie have had a good time," she said, and tried not to sound as hurt as she felt. "They've both been very kind to me. I owe them a lot."

"Maddie," he began slowly, "about that trip they took—"

"They're my friends," she interrupted. "I want them to be happy. Look I have to go, okay? But if you find out anything about my cows, can you call me?"

"Sure."

"Thanks, Mr. Brannt."

She hung up. She didn't think she'd ever felt so miserable in her whole young life. She loved Cort. But he was never going to be hers. She realized now that he'd been pretending, to keep her spirits up so that she wouldn't despair. But he'd always loved Odalie, and she'd always known it. She couldn't expect him to give up everything he loved just to placate an injured woman, out of guilt. She wasn't going to let him do it.

And Odalie might have been her enemy once, but that was certainly no longer the case. Odalie had become a friend. She couldn't have hard feelings toward her...

Oh, what a bunch of bull, she told herself angrily. Of course she had hard feelings. She loved Cort. She wanted him! But he loved Odalie and that was never going to change. How would it feel, to let a man hang around just because he felt guilty that you'd been hurt? Knowing every day that he was smiling and pretending to care, when he really wanted that beautiful golden girl, Odalie Everett, and always would?

No. That would cheat all three of them. She had to let him go. He belonged to Odalie, and Maddie had always known it. She was going to sell the ranch to that terrible developer and make herself homeless out of pride, because she didn't want her friends to sacrifice any more than they already had for her.

That developer, could he have been responsible for her lost cows? But why would he hurt the livestock when he was hoping to buy the ranch? No. It made no sense. None at all.

Later, with her door closed, she cried herself to sleep. She couldn't stop thinking about Cort, about how tender he'd been to her, how kind. Surely he hadn't been able to pretend the passion she felt in his long, hard, insistent kisses? Could men pretend to want a woman?

She wished she knew. She wanted to believe that his hints at a shared future had been honest and real. But she didn't dare trust her instincts. Not when Cort had taken Odalie with him to Denver and hidden it from Maddie.

He hadn't wanted her to know. That meant he knew it would hurt her feelings and he couldn't bear to do it, not after all she'd been through.

She wiped her eyes. Crying wasn't going to solve anything. After all, what did she have to be sad about? There was a good chance that she would be able to walk normally again, when she was through recuperating. She'd still have Great-Aunt Sadie, and the developer said that he'd let her have her odds and ends out of the house.

The developer. She hated him. He was willing to set her up, to let her whole herd of cattle be destroyed, her breeding stock, just to get his hands on the ranch. She could tell someone, Mr. Brannt, maybe. But it would be her word against Lawson's. She had so much to lose. What if he could actually infect her cattle? Better to let her cattle be sold at auction to someone than risk having them destroyed. She couldn't bear to step on a spider, much less watch her prize cattle, her father's prize cattle, be exterminated.

No, she really didn't have a choice. She was going to lose the ranch one way or another, to the developer or to bill collectors.

She got up and went to the kitchen to make coffee. It was two in the morning, but it didn't matter. She was never going to sleep anyway.

She heard a sound out in the yard. She wished she kept a dog. She'd had one, but it had died not long after her father did. There was nothing to alert her to an intruder's presence anymore. She turned out the lights and motored to the window, hoping the sound of the wheelchair wouldn't be heard outside.

She saw something shadowy near the barn. That was where the surveillance equipment was set up.

She turned on all the outside lights, opened the door and yelled, "Who's out there?" The best defense was offense, she told herself.

There was startled movement, a dark blur going out behind the barn. Without a second thought, she got her cell phone and called the sheriff.

The sheriff's department came, and so did King Brannt. He climbed out of his ranch pickup with another man about two steps behind the tall deputy.

Maddie rolled onto the porch. She'd been afraid to go outside until help arrived. She was no match, even with two good legs, for someone bent upon mischief.

"Miss Lane?" the deputy asked.

"Yes, sir," she said. "Someone was out here. I turned on the outside lights and yelled. Whoever it was ran."

The deputy's lips made a thin line.

"Yes, I know," she said heavily. "Stupid thing to do, opening the door. But I didn't go outside, and the screen was latched."

He didn't mention that any intruder could have gone through that latched screen like it was tissue paper.

"Miss Lane's had some threats," King commented. "This is Blair, my computer expert. We set up surveillance cameras on the ranch at cross fences to see if we could head off trouble." He smiled. "Looks like we might have succeeded."

"Have you noticed anything suspicious?" the deputy asked.

She grimaced. "Well, I've had a couple of cows found dead. Predators," she said, averting her eyes.

"Anyone prowling around the house, any break-ins?" he persisted.

"No, sir."

The deputy turned to King. "Mr. Brannt, I'd like to see what those cameras of yours picked up, if anything."

"Sure. Come on, Blair." He turned to Maddie. "You should go back inside, honey," he said gently. "Just in case."

"Okay." She went very quickly. She didn't want any of the men to ask her more questions. She was afraid of what Lawson might do if he was backed into a corner. She didn't want the government to come over and shut her cattle operation down, even if it meant giving away the ranch.

Later, the deputy came inside, asked more questions and had her write out a report for him in her own words. He took that, and statements from King and Blair and told Maddie to call if she heard anything else.

"Did you find anything?" she asked worriedly.

"No," the deputy said. "But my guess is that someone meant to disable that surveillance equipment."

"Mine, too," King replied. "Which is why I've just sent several of my cowboys out to ride fence lines and watch for anything suspicious."

"That's very nice of you," she commented.

He shrugged. "We're neighbors and I like your breeding bulls," he told her.

"Well, thanks, just the same."

"If you think of anything else that would help us, please get in touch with me," the deputy said, handing her a card.

"I'll do that," she promised. "And thanks again."

King didn't leave when the deputy did. Sadie was making coffee in the kitchen, her face lined with worry.

"It will be all right," she assured the older woman.

"No, it won't," Sadie muttered. She glanced at Maddie. "You should tell him the truth. He's the one person who could help you!"

"Sadie!" Maddie groaned.

King pulled Blair aside, spoke to him in whispers, and sent him off. He moved into the kitchen, straddled a chair at the table and perched his Stetson on a free chair.

"Okay," he said. "No witnesses. Let's have it."

Maddie went pale.

King laughed softly. "I'm not an ogre. If you want my word that I won't tell anyone what you say, you have it."

Maddie bit her lower lip. "That developer," she said after a minute. "He said that he could bring in a federal agency and prove that my cattle had anthrax."

"Only if he put it there to begin with," King said, his dark eyes flashing with anger.

"That's what I think he means to do," she said. "I don't know what to do. The bills are just burying me..."

He held up a hand. "Cort and Odalie are taking care of those," he said.

"Yes, but they've done too much already, I'm not a charity case!" she burst out.

"It was an accident that they caused, Maddie," he said gently.

"I caused it, by running into the road," she said miserably.

"Accidents are things that don't happen on purpose," he said with a faint grin. "Now, listen, whatever trouble you're in, that developer has no right to make threats to do harm to your cattle."

"It would be my word against his." She sighed.

"I'd take your word against anyone else's, in a heartbeat,"

he replied. "You let me handle this. I know how to deal with people like Lawson."

"He's really vindictive."

"He won't get a chance to be vindictive. I promise." He got up. "I won't stay for coffee, Sadie, I've got a lot of phone calls to make."

"Thanks, Mr. Brannt," Maddie said gently. "Thanks a lot."

He put a hand on her shoulder. "We take care of our own," he said. "Cort will be back day after tomorrow."

"So will that developer," she said worriedly. So many complications, she was thinking. Poor Cort; he'd feel even more guilty.

"He won't stay long," King drawled, and he grinned. "Cort will make sure of that, believe me."

Chapter 10

Maddie was on pins and needles Saturday morning. It was worrying enough to know that Cort and Odalie were coming back. She'd have to smile and pretend to be happy for them, even though her heart was breaking.

But also she was going to have to face the developer. She didn't know what King Brannt had in mind to save her from him. She might have to go through with signing the contracts to ensure that her poor cattle weren't infected. She hadn't slept a wink.

She and Sadie had coffee and then Maddie wandered around the house in her wheelchair, making ruts.

"Will you relax?" Sadie said. "I know it's going to be all right. You have to trust that Mr. Brannt knows what to do."

"I hope so. My poor cattle!"

"Is that a car?"

Even as she spoke a car drove up in front of the house and stopped. "Mr. Lawson, no doubt. I hope he's wearing body armor," she muttered, and she wheeled her chair to the front porch.

But it wasn't the developer. It was Odalie and Cort. They were grinning from ear to ear as they climbed out of his Jaguar and came to the porch.

Just what I need right now, Maddie thought miserably. But she put on a happy face. "You're both home again. And I guess you have news?" she added. "I'm so happy for you."

"For us?" Cort looked at Odalie and back at Maddie blankly. "Why?"

They followed her into the house. She turned the chair around and swallowed. "Well," she began uneasily.

Odalie knew at once what she thought. She came forward. "No, it's not like that," she said quickly. "There was a doll collectors' convention at the hotel where the cattlemen were meeting. I want you to see this." She pulled a check out of her purse and handed it to Maddie.

It was a good thing she was sitting down. The check was for five figures. Five high figures. She looked at Odalie blankly.

"The fairy," she said, smiling. "I'm sorry I wasn't honest with you. It wasn't my great-grandmother's picture. It was a collector's. He wanted a fairy who looked like her to add to his collection, and I said I knew someone who would do the perfect one. So I flew to Denver to take him the one you made from the photograph." Odalie's blue eyes were soft. "He cried. He said the old lady was the light of his life… She was the only person in his family who didn't laugh and disown him when he said he wanted to go into the business of doll collecting. She encouraged him to follow his dream. He's worth millions now and all because he followed his dream." She nodded at the check. "He owns a doll boutique in Los Angeles. He ships all over the world. He said he'd pay that—" she indicated the check again "—for every fairy you made for him. And he wants to discuss licensing and branding. He thinks you can make a fortune with these. He said so."

Maddie couldn't even find words. The check would pay her medical bills, buy feed and pay taxes. It would save the ranch. She was sobbing and she didn't even realize it until Odalie took the check back and motioned to Cort.

Cort lifted her out of the wheelchair and cradled her against him. "You'll blot the ink off the check with those tears, sweetheart." He chuckled, and kissed them away. "And just for the record, Odalie and I aren't getting married."

"You aren't?" she asked with wet eyes.

"We aren't." Odalie giggled. "He's my friend. I love him. But not like that," she added softly.

"And she's my friend," Cort added. He smiled down at Maddie. "I went a little goofy over her, but, then, I got over it."

"Gee, thanks," Odalie said with amused sarcasm.

"You know what I mean." He laughed. "You're beautiful and talented."

"Not as talented as *our* friend over there." She indicated Maddie, with a warm smile. "She has magic in her hands."

"And other places," Cort mused, looking pointedly at her mouth.

She hid her face against him. He cuddled her close.

"Oh, dear," Sadie said from the doorway. "Maddie, he's back! What are you going to tell him?"

"Tell who?" Cort asked. He turned. His face grew hard. "Oh. Him. My dad gave me an earful about him when I got home."

He put Maddie gently back down into the wheelchair.

"You didn't encourage him?" he asked her.

She grimaced. "The medical bills and doctor bills and feed bills all came in at once," she began miserably. "I couldn't even pay taxes. He offered me a fortune…"

"We're paying the medical bills," Odalie told her firmly. "We even said so."

"It's not right to ask you," Maddie said stubbornly.

"That's okay. You're not asking. We're telling." Odalie said.

"Exactly." Cort was looking more dangerous by the second as the developer got out of his car with a brief-case. "My dad said you've had more cows killed over here, too."

"Yes." She was so miserable she could hardly talk.

"Dad found out a lot more than that about him. He was arrested up in Billings, Montana, on charges of intimi-dation and poisoning in another land deal," Cort added. "He's out on bond, but apparently it didn't teach him a thing."

"Well, he threatened to plant anthrax in my herd and have the feds come out and destroy them," she said sadly. "He says if I don't sell to him, he'll do it. I think he will."

"He might have," Cort said mysteriously. "Good thing my dad has a real suspicious nature and watches a lot of spy films."

"Excuse me?" Maddie inquired.

He grinned. "Wait and see, honey." He bent and kissed the tip of her nose.

Odalie laughed softly. "One fried developer, coming right up," she teased, and it was obvious that she wasn't jealous of Maddie at all.

There was a tap at the door and the developer walked right in. He was so intent on his contracts that he must not have noticed the other car in the driveway. "Miss Lane, I've brought the paper...work—" He stopped dead when he saw her companions.

"You can take your paperwork and shove it," Cort said pleasantly. He tilted his Stetson over one eye and put both hands on his narrow hips. "Or you can argue. Personally, I'd love it if you argued."

"She said she wanted to sell," the developer shot back. But he didn't move a step closer.

"She changed her mind," Cort replied.

"You changed it for her," the developer snarled. "Well, she can just change it right back. Things happen sometimes when people don't make the right decisions."

"You mean diseases can be planted in cattle?" Odalie asked sweetly.

The older man gave her a wary look. "What do you mean?"

"Maddie told us how you threatened her," Cort said evenly.

Lawson hesitated. "You can't prove that."

Cort smiled. "I don't have to." He pulled out a DVD in a plastic sleeve and held it up. "You're very trusting, Lawson. I mean, you knew there was surveillance equipment all over the ranch, but you didn't guess the house and porch were wired as well?"

Lawson looked a lot less confident. "You're bluffing."

Cort didn't look like he was bluffing. "My dad has a call in to the district attorney up in Billings, Montana. I believe you're facing indictment there for the destruction of a purebred herd of Herefords because of suspected anthrax?"

"They can't prove that!"

"I'm afraid they can," Cort replied. "There are two witnesses, one of whom used to work with you," he added easily. "He's willing to testify to save his butt." He held up the DVD. "This may not be admissible in court, but it will certainly help to encourage charges against you here for the loss of Miss Lane's purebred stock."

"You wouldn't dare!" the developer said harshly.

"I would dare," Cort replied.

The developer gripped his briefcase tighter. "On second thought," he said, looking around with disdain, "I've decided I don't want this property. It's not good enough for the sort of development I have in mind, and the location is terrible for business. Sorry," he spat at Maddie. "I guess you'll have to manage some other way to pay your medical bills."

"Speaking of medical bills," Cort said angrily, and stepped forward.

"Now, Cort," Maddie exclaimed.

The developer turned and almost ran out of the house to his car. He fumbled to start it and managed to get it in gear just before Cort got to him. He sped out the driveway, fishtailing all the way.

Cort was almost bent over double laughing when he went back into the house. He stopped when three wide-eyed females gaped at him worriedly.

"Oh, I wasn't going to kill him," he said, still laughing. "But I didn't mind letting him think I might. What do you want to bet that he's out of town by tonight and can't be reached by telephone?"

"I wouldn't bet against that," Odalie agreed.

"Me, neither," Sadie said.

"Dad said that Lawson's in more trouble than he can manage up in Billings already. I don't expect he'll wait around for more charges to be filed here."

"Are you going to turn that DVD over to the district attorney?" she asked, nodding toward the jacketed disc.

He glanced at her. "And give up my best performance of *'Recuerdos de la Alhambra'*?" he exclaimed. "I'll never get this good a recording again!"

Maddie's eyes brightened. "You were bluffing!"

"For all I was worth." He chuckled.

"Cort, you're wonderful!"

He pursed his lips. "Am I, now?"

"We could take a vote," Odalie suggested. "You've got mine."

"And mine!" Sadie agreed. "Oh, Maddie, you'll have a way to make a living now," she exclaimed, indicating the little fairy. "You won't have to sell our ranch!"

"No, but we still have the problem of running it," Maddie said heavily. "If I'm going to be spending my life sculpting, and thanks to you two, I probably will—" she grinned "—who's going to manage the ranch?"

"I think we can work something out about that," Cort told her, and his dark eyes were flashing with amusement. "We'll talk about it later."

"Okay," she said. "Maybe Ben could manage it?"

Cort nodded. "He's a good man, with a good business head. We'll see."

We'll see? She stared at him as if she'd never seen him

before. It was an odd statement. But before she could question it, Sadie went into the kitchen.

"Who wants chocolate pound cake?" she asked.

Three hands went up, and all discussion about the ranch went away.

Maddie wanted to know all about the doll collector. He was a man in his fifties, very distinguished and he had a collection that was famous all over the world.

"There are magazines devoted to collectors," Odalie said excitedly. "They showcased his collection last year. I met him when we were at the Met last year during opera season. We spoke and he said that he loved small, very intricate work. When I saw your sculptures, I remembered him. I looked him up on his website and phoned him. He said he was always looking for new talent, but he wanted to see what you could do. So I asked him for a photo of someone he'd like made into a sculpture and he faxed me the one I gave you."

"I will never be able to repay you for this," Maddie said fervently.

"Maddie, you already have, over and over," Odalie said softly. "Most especially with that little fairy statue that looks just like me." She shook her head. "I've never owned anything so beautiful."

"Thanks."

"Besides, you're my best friend," Odalie said with a gamine grin. "I have to take care of you."

Maddie felt all warm inside. "I'll take care of you, if you ever need me to," she promised.

Odalie flushed. "Thanks."

"This is great cake," Cort murmured. "Can you cook?" he asked Maddie.

"Yes, but not so much right now." She indicated the wheelchair with a grimace.

"Give it time," he said gently. He smiled, and his whole face grew radiant as he looked at her. "You'll be out of that thing before you know it."

"You think so?" she asked.

He nodded. "Yes, I do."

She smiled. He smiled back. Odalie smiled into her cake and pretended not to notice that they couldn't take their eyes off each other.

Odalie said her goodbyes and gave Maddie the collector's telephone number so that she could thank him personally for giving her fairy a good home. But Cort lingered.

He bent over the wheelchair, his hands on the arms, and looked into Maddie's eyes. "Later we'll talk about going behind my back to do business with a crook."

"I was scared. And not just that he might poison my cattle. There were so many bills!"

He brushed his mouth over her lips. "I told you I'd take care of all those bills."

"But they all came due, and you've done so much… I couldn't ask…"

He was kissing her. It made talking hard.

She reached up with cold, nervous hands and framed his face in them. She looked into his eyes and saw secrets revealed there. Her breath caught. "It isn't Odalie," she stammered. "It's me."

He nodded. And he didn't smile. "It was always you. I just didn't know it until there was a good chance that I was going to lose you." He smiled tightly then. "Couldn't do that. Couldn't live, if you didn't."

She bit her lip, fighting tears.

He kissed them away. "I don't have a life without you," he whispered at her nose. "So we have to make plans."

"When?" she asked, bursting with happiness.

"When you're out of that wheelchair," he said. He gave her a wicked smile. "Because when we start talking, things are apt to get, well, physical." He wiggled his eyebrows.

She laughed.

He laughed.

He kissed her affectionately and stood back up. "I'll drive Odalie home. I'll call you later. And I'll see you tomorrow. And the day after. And the day after. And the day after that…"

"And the day after that?" she prompted.

"Don't get pushy," he teased.

He threw up a hand and went out to the car. This time, when he drove off with Odalie, Maddie didn't go through pangs of jealousy. The look in his eyes had been as sweet as a promise.

Epilogue

Physical therapy seemed to go on forever. The days turned to weeks, the leaves began to fall. The cows grew big with calves. Rain had come in time for some of the grain crops to come to harvest, and there would be enough hay, hopefully, to get them through the winter. Maddie's legs were growing stronger. Little by little, she made progress.

Odalie and Cort were still around, prodding her, keeping her spirits up during the long mending process. She didn't let herself get discouraged. She created new fairies and Odalie shipped them off, carefully packed, to a man named Angus Moore, who acted as Maddie's agent and sold her dainty little creations for what amounted to a small fortune for the artist.

The developer, sure enough, left town and left no forwarding address. Gossip was that the authorities wanted to talk to him about several cases of dead cattle on properties he'd tried to buy in several states. Maddie hoped they caught up with him one day.

Meanwhile, Cort came over every night for supper. He brought his guitar most nights, and serenaded Maddie on the porch until the nights got too cold for that. Then he serenaded her in the living room, by the fireplace with its leaping flames while she curled up under a blanket on the sofa.

From time to time, when Sadie was occupied in the kitchen, he curled up under the blanket with her.

She loved his big hands smoothing her bare skin under her shirt, the warmth and strength of them arousing sensations that grew sweeter by the day. He was familiar to her now. She had no fear of his temper. He didn't lose it with her, although he'd been volatile about a man who left a gate open and cattle poured through it onto the highway. At least none of the cattle was injured, and no cars were wrecked.

"He was just a kid," Cort murmured against her collarbone. "He works for us after school. Usually does a pretty good job, too, cleaning out the stables."

She arched her back and winced.

"Damn." He lifted his head and his hands stilled on her body. "Too soon."

She looked miserable.

He laughed. He peered toward the doorway before he slid the hem of her T-shirt up under her chin and looked at the pert little breasts he'd uncovered. "Buried treasure," he whispered, "and I'm a pirate..."

She moaned.

"Stop that. She'll hear you."

She bit her lip and gave him an anguished look. He grinned before he bent his head again, producing even more eloquent sounds that were, thankfully, soon muffled by his mouth.

But things between them were heating up more every day. She had his shirt unbuttoned just before he eased over her. Her hard-tipped breasts nestled into the thick hair on his muscular chest and one long, powerful leg eased between both of hers. He levered himself down very gently while he was kissing her, but she felt the quick, hard swell of him as he began to move helplessly on her, grinding his hips into hers.

"Oh, God," he bit off. He jerked himself back and up, to sit beside her on the sofa with his head bent, shuddering.

"I'm sorry," she whispered shakily.

He drew in short, harsh breaths while his hands worked at buttoning up the shirt. "Well, I'm not," he murmured, glancing down at her. He groaned. "Honey, you have to cover those up or we're going to be back at first base all over again!"

She looked down and flushed a little as she pulled her shirt down and fumbled behind her to do up the bra again. "First base."

He laughed softly. "First base."

She beamed at him. "I'm getting better every day. It won't be long."

"It had better not be." He sighed. "I think I'll die of it pretty soon."

"No!"

"Just kidding." He turned on the sofa and looked down at her with warm, dark, possessive eyes. "I talked to a minister."

"You did? What did he have to say?"

He traced her nose. "We have to have a marriage license first."

Her heart jumped. They'd been kissing and petting for quite a long time, and he'd insinuated, but he'd never actually asked.

"I thought we might get one with flowers and stuff. You know. So it would look nice framed on the wall."

"Framed."

He nodded. His eyes were steady on her face. "Madeline Edith Lane, will you do me the honor of becoming my wife?" he asked softly.

She fought tears. "Yes," she whispered. "Yes!"

He brushed the tears away, his eyes so dark they seemed black. "I'll love you all my life," he whispered. "I'll love you until the sun burns out."

"I'll love you longer," she whispered back, and it was all there, in her eyes and his.

He smiled slowly. "And we'll have beautiful kids," he said softly. He pushed back her hair. "Absolutely beautiful. Like you."

Now she was really bawling.

He pulled her gently into his arms and across his lap, and rocked her and kissed away the tears.

Sadie came walking in with coffee and stopped dead. "Oh, goodness, what's wrong?"

"I told her we were going to have beautiful kids," he said with a chuckle. "She's very emotional."

"Beautiful kids? You're going to get married?" Sadie exclaimed.

"Yes." Maddie smiled.

"Whoopee!"

"Oh, dear!" Maddie exclaimed.

Sadie looked down at the remains of the glass coffee-pot and two ceramic mugs. "Oh, dear," she echoed.

Cort just laughed. But then, like the gentleman he was, he went to help Sadie clean up the mess.

They were married at Christmas. Maddie was able to wear an exquisite designer gown that Odalie had insisted on buying for her, as her "something new." It was an A-line gown of white satin with cap sleeves and a lacy bodice that went up to encase her throat like a high-necked Victorian dress.

There was a train, also of delicate white lace, and a fingertip veil with lace and appliquéd roses. She wore lace gloves and carried a bouquet of white roses. There was a single red rose in the center of the bouquet. One red rose for true love, Cort had insisted, and white ones for purity because in a modern age of easy virtue, Maddie was a throwback to Victorian times. She went to her marriage a virgin, and never apologized once for not following the crowd.

She walked down the aisle on the arm of Cole Everett, who had volunteered to give her away. Odalie was her maid of honor. Heather Everett and Shelby Brannt were her matrons of honor. Four local girls she'd known all her life were bridesmaids, and John Everett was Cort's best man.

At an altar with pots of white and red roses they were married in the local Methodist church, where all three families were members. The minister had preached the funeral of most of their deceased kin. He was elderly and kind, and beloved of the community.

When he pronounced Cort and Maddie man and wife,

Cort lifted the veil, ignoring the flash from the professional photographer's camera, and closed in to kiss his new bride.

Nobody heard him when he bent, very low, and whispered, "First base."

Nobody heard the soft, mischievous laughter the comment provoked from the bride. There was a huge reception. John Everett stopped by the table where Cort and Maddie were cutting the wedding cake.

"So, tell me, Cort," John said when the photographer finished shooting the cake-eating segment, "if I'm really the best man, why are you married to my girl?"

"Now, a remark like that could get you punched," Cort teased, catching the other man around the neck, "even at a wedding."

John chuckled, embracing him in a bear hug. "I was just kidding. No doubt in my mind from the beginning where her heart was." He indicated a beaming Maddie.

Cort glanced at her and smiled. "What an idiot I was," he said, shaking his head. "I almost lost her."

"Crazy, the way things turn out," John mused, his eyes on Odalie as she paused to speak to Maddie. "My sister, Attila the Hun, is ending up as Maddie's best friend. Go figure."

"I wouldn't have believed it myself. Odalie's quite a girl."

John smiled. "I thought it would be you and Odalie, eventually."

Cort shook his head. "We're too different. Neither of us would fit in the other's world. It took me a long time to realize that. But I saw my future in Maddie's eyes. I always will. I hope Odalie finds someone who can make her half as happy as I am today. She deserves it."

John nodded. "I'm very proud of her. She's matured

a lot in the past few months." He turned back to Cort. "Christmas is next week. You guys coming home for it or not?"

"Oh, we have to…my folks would kill us, to say nothing of Sadie." He indicated the older woman in her pretty blue dress talking to some other people. "Maddie's like the daughter she never had. They can't have Christmas without us," he stated. "We're just going down to Panama City for a couple of days. Maybe later I can take Maddie to Europe and show her the sights. Right now, even a short plane trip is going to make her uncomfortable, much less a long one to somewhere exotic."

"I don't think Maddie will mind where you go, as long as she's with you," John said. "I wish you all the best. You know that."

"Thanks, bro."

"And when you come home, maybe we can crack open some new video games, now that my sister won't complain about my having you over," he added with a sigh.

Cort just grinned.

The hotel was right on the beach. It was cold in Panama City, but not so cold that they couldn't sit on the patio beyond the glass sliding doors and look at the cold moonlight on the ocean.

Predictably, they'd barely made it into the hotel room when all the months of pent-up anguished desire were taken off the bridle for the first time.

He tried to be gentle, he really did, but his body was shivering with need long before he could do what he wanted to do: to show his love for Maddie.

Not that she noticed. She was with him every step of

the way, even when the first encounter stung and made her cry out.

"This is part of it," he gritted, trying to slow down. "I'm so sorry!"

"Don't...sweat it," she panted, moving up to meet the furious downward motion of his hips. "You can hang out... the bedsheet in the morning...to prove I was a virgin...!"

"Wh-wh-what?" he yelped, and burst out laughing even as his body shuddered with the beginning of ecstasy.

"First...base," she choked out, and bit him.

It was the most glorious high he'd ever experienced. He groaned and groaned as his body shuddered over hers. The pleasure was exquisite. He felt it in every cell of his body, with every beat of his heart. He could hear his own heartbeat, the passion was so violent.

Under him, her soft body was rising and falling like a pistol as she kept pace with his need, encouraged it, fanned the flames and, finally, glued itself to his in an absolute epiphany of satisfaction that convulsed both of them as they almost passed out from the climax.

She clung to him, shivering with pleasure in the aftermath. Neither of them could stop moving, savoring the dregs of passion until they drained the cup dry.

"Wow," she whispered as she looked into his eyes.

"Wow," he whispered back. He looked down their bodies to where they were joined. They hadn't even thought of turning out the lights. He was glad. Looking at her, like this, was a joy he hadn't expected.

"Beautiful," he breathed.

She smiled slowly. "And to think I was nervous about the first time," she said.

"Obviously unnecessary, since I have skills far beyond those of most mortal men...*oof!*"

She'd hit him. She grinned, though. And then she wiggled her eyebrows and moved her hips ever so slowly. Despite the sting, and the discomfort, pleasure welled up like water above a dam in a flood.

"Oh, yes," she whispered as he began to move, looking straight into her eyes. "Yes. Do that."

He smiled. "This," he murmured, "is going to be indescribable."

And it was.

When they got back, in time for the Christmas celebrations at Skylance, nobody could understand why, when Cort whispered, "first base," Maddie almost fell down laughing. But that was one secret neither one of them ever shared with another living soul.

* * * * *

Despite a no-nonsense background as a West Point graduate, army officer and Fortune 100 sales executive, **Caro Carson** has always treasured the happily-ever-after of a good romance novel. As a RITA® Award-winning Harlequin author, Caro is delighted to be living her own happily-ever-after with her husband and two children in Florida, a location that has saved the coaster-loving theme park fanatic a fortune on plane tickets.

Books by Caro Carson

Harlequin Special Edition

Texas Rescue

A Cowboy's Wish Upon a Star
Her Texas Rescue Doctor
Following Doctor's Orders
A Texas Rescue Christmas
Not Just a Cowboy

Montana Mavericks: What Happened at the Wedding?

The Maverick's Holiday Masquerade

The Doctors MacDowell

The Bachelor Doctor's Bride
The Doctor's Former Fiancée
Doctor, Soldier, Daddy

Visit the Author Profile page at Harlequin.com for more titles.

FOLLOWING DOCTOR'S ORDERS

CARO CARSON

For Katie, who was precious when she was four years old, and is even more precious now.

Chapter 1

She heard his voice before she saw him.

Through the constant hum of voices that formed the background noise of the emergency department at West Central Texas Hospital, his deep bass carried. Although he was a fireman by profession, his voice always made her think of cowboys. With its mild Texas drawl and the hint of a wink in the tone, his voice brought to mind a cowboy who'd come to town looking for beer and girls and a good time. He wasn't a serious man.

She was a serious woman. Dr. Brooke Brown, emergency physician, could hardly be anything else. The buck stopped here—right here, at the pen in her hand. When she wrote a medical order, it was followed, and the results sat squarely on her shoulders. Whether the patient lived or died was her responsibility—medically, legally, morally.

It stood to reason, then, that she was the one female

employee in the emergency department who didn't get giggly-excited when the radio announced that the fire-fighters from Engine Thirty-Seven were bringing in an-other patient. Brooke had weightier things to think on than which team of Austin's firefighters and paramedics had the most bachelors—or which had the bachelor with the sexiest voice.

But Engine Thirty-Seven did.

Brooke would never acknowledge such a thing out loud, but the two women standing at the nurses' station weren't so reserved.

"It's gonna be a great shift," one woman said. "The studs of Thirty-Seven are here to kick it off right."

"It's Eye Candy Wednesday."

"Yesterday, you said it was Eye Candy Tuesday."

"Every day that Thirty-Seven comes here is an eye candy day."

Ignoring their light banter, Brooke continued to listen to the distinctive rumbling bass of one member of the *Eye Candy Engine*. Firefighter Zach Bishop was rattling off the patient's basic information to the triage nurse, his voice coming from just behind Brooke and to her right—room three, she was sure—*compound fracture of the tibia* spoken in the same tone of voice as *Mary Ellen, don't break my heart and tell me that diamond means you're engaged, darlin'.*

Zach Bishop always conveyed the impression there was nothing to worry about. Nothing was unfixable or alarming. The patient could have confidence his injury was treatable. The nurse could flirt safely as she showed off her new engagement ring, knowing the firefighter with the movie-star looks didn't truly expect her to be-tray her fiancé.

Dr. Brown, however, knew there was always something to worry about. Specifically, Brooke worried about the people of Austin who came to the emergency room of West Central with their complaints, big and small. She had confidence that she could handle the medical complaints—a professional confidence. Zach's kind of confidence was personal—and masculine—and a distraction to the smooth operation of her department.

Was it any wonder that they'd spent nearly a year as something close to adversaries?

Adversaries wasn't the right word. They worked together smoothly. He was a good paramedic, and his shameless appreciation of the female attention that was showered upon him always came second after the patient's care. But as the handsome Mr. Bishop returned all the smiles that came his way, Brooke frowned in annoyance.

She couldn't accuse him of trying to get attention. He'd just walk in, casually pushing a gurney, and the contrast between his sun-streaked short hair and his black uniform caught the eye. Whether he wore the black T-shirt of the fire department or the black button-down shirt of the ambulance corps he moonlighted with, the short sleeves of both uniforms revealed the defined muscles of his arms— biceps, triceps, carpi ulnaris.

After his first few visits, it had become obvious to Brooke that while the man didn't seek feminine attention, he certainly didn't discourage it. He wasn't required to stop and chat with every woman who wanted to stop and chat with him, but he did.

Early in September, Brooke had leveled a look of disapproval his way as he was leaving the ER. He usually only raised a brow in an amused response to her glare, but that time, he'd leaned in just a bit too close to deliver the most ridiculous line she'd ever heard: *If I had a nickel every time a woman as beautiful as you frowned at me, I'd have...five cents.* Then he'd simply walked away, out through the sliding glass doors that led to the ambulances parked outside.

The next time he'd brought in a patient while Brooke was on duty, every woman in his vicinity had slowed her pace just enough to smile and be smiled at once more. Brooke must have frowned again, because he'd leaned in and quietly said, "Ten cents."

She'd been ready that time. "I find it hard to believe you've only been frowned at twice in your life."

"It's not the frowns that are scarce. It's that I never see women as beautiful as you are." He'd had the audacity to wink as he'd left her standing alone at the nurses' station.

And so it went. On the days she was working and Engine Thirty-Seven happened to bring a patient in, Zach would deliver a ridiculously corny line for her ears only. *I finally placed your accent.*

I don't have an accent.

You must be from Tennessee, because you're the only ten I see.

She'd either scowl or roll her eyes, because she was brunette and brainy and not the type that boys flirted with. Then they'd part company for hours or days or a week, however long it was before Engine Thirty-Seven again transported a patient to West Central during a shift that she and Bishop both happened to be working.

It was amazing, really, that they'd been carrying on this routine for the better part of a year, exchanging frowns for one-liners out of earshot of their coworkers. It was harder and harder not to smile each time; Brooke had a grudging respect for his unending supply of silly lines. Still, she didn't like the way Engine Thirty-Seven's arrival disrupted the concentration of her otherwise disciplined staff.

Case in point: the nurses in front of Brooke began debating whose turn it was to take this afternoon's patient with the broken tibia. "It's my turn to work with the hot fireman. You got the medevac guys last night."

"Yeah, but their patient was critical. It wasn't like they had time to stop and flirt."

Brooke let their silliness slide past her as she finished dashing off her discharge orders for the patient she'd just seen. Like all doctors, she wrote quickly out of necessity, but she prided herself on slowing just enough when it came to numbers so that no pharmacist or nurse would misread the dose. Mistakes were unacceptable. Scribbling was irresponsible.

"But that man is delectable." Both nurses sighed.

Yes, Zach was, in a strictly eye-candy kind of way, but Brooke had more important things to think about, and so did these nurses.

She handed the orders to one nurse. "Please discharge room two." The nurse, blonde and single, wrinkled her nose in defeat as she left the nurses' station.

Brooke nodded curtly at the other nurse. "Come to room three with me."

Brooke had assigned the older, married nurse to work room three with her for reasons that had nothing to do with the firefighter. On a straightforward case like this fracture would probably be, an experienced nurse like Loretta could handle most of the care. Brooke would only have to see the patient twice—once to do the initial assessment and once to ensure whatever treatment she ordered had been completed. This freed Brooke for the cases where only an MD could perform the work. It was efficient.

"Radiology will be about twenty minutes," Loretta said.

Brooke almost smiled. The nurse must have overheard Zach say the injury was a fracture, just as Brooke had, and she'd contacted radiology without being asked. Experience and efficiency were invaluable.

The nurse had known Brooke wouldn't touch the injury without seeing an X-ray first. No doctor would. The X-ray was necessary to verify that no debris existed that might be driven deeper into the soft tissues of the injured leg while it was being set. A compound fracture, one with the bone protruding from the skin, could only be set temporarily, at any rate. The injury would undoubtedly require surgery within a few hours. That was a job for a different type of doctor, in a different part of West Central.

"Tetanus?" Nurse Loretta asked. "Whichever antibiotic is handy today?"

"Yes on both. Whatever cephalosporin is in the machine, if there are no allergies."

Loretta had suggested exactly what Brooke would have ordered.

See? My decision was rational. It has nothing to do with keeping away from Zach Bishop a woman who is younger and single and more likely to appeal to him.

Brooke was not the type to be possessive when it came to a handsome face, a hard body or a deep cowboy voice. She tended to date men who were more bookish. Intellectually stimulating. Men she could engage in conversation without first needing to brace herself against the distraction of purely physical perfection.

Brooke paused outside room three and braced herself.

It did no good. As she walked in, her attention was caught by the most commanding presence in the room: his. It was human nature, she supposed, to notice who was dominant in every situation, and the tall man in the black firefighter's T-shirt was definitely the most physically dominant man in the room.

Distraction over. Get to work.

Brooke was in charge once she entered a treatment room, so she focused on the elderly man on the gurney.

"Good afternoon. I'm Dr. Brown. You're Harold Allman, is that correct?"

The man looked frail despite being heavyset. His white face and the stiff way he was holding himself meant he was in pain, but he still chuckled and looked up at Zach.

"Boy, times have changed," he said conversationally, ignoring Brooke's question. "Not only do we have lady doctors, but good-looking ones, too. This one's a real looker."

"That she is," Zach said.

Brooke neither frowned nor smiled. She was accustomed to hearing this kind of tedious "lady doctor" comment from men of a certain generation. Beyond the patient's bed, Loretta rolled her eyes and shook her head. Obviously, she was tired of the same old comments herself.

"Harold, how did you break your leg?" Brooke stepped forward to start the hands-on part of her exam, but Zach didn't move out of her way as he normally would. At this point, with responsibility for the patient turned over from the paramedic to the hospital staff, he'd usually tell the patient goodbye and leave. But Harold, she realized, was clinging to Zach's gloved hand with a white-knuckled grip at odds with his chuckle.

As Brooke pulled on her own latex gloves, she walked to the far side of the bed. Far be it from her to deny the old man comfort. If hanging on to a strong man like Zach gave Harold a little courage, that was fine with her.

Harold spoke with a noticeable hitch in his breath. "I'd like to tell you I did something that would impress you, young lady. I could've broken my leg sky diving. That would've been something, wouldn't it? But the truth is, I just fell down my own porch stairs."

"Were you dizzy before you fell?" Brooke asked.

"No, I'm just—I'm just turning into a clumsy old man." He sounded sad.

"Nah, anyone can trip," Zach said, and Brooke saw him give the old man's hand a quick squeeze. "Happens to the best of us."

"I'm going to look for other injuries. If anything is tender, let me know." She checked Harold's scalp, turned his head from side to side, pressed on his ribs and palpated his arm from shoulder to wrist. Judging by how tightly he gripped Zach's hand, Harold's other arm wasn't injured, so Brooke decided to forgo that part of the exam.

She lifted one edge of the paper tent that was hiding the patient's broken leg from his own view. The bone was protruding from the skin. Just seeing this type of injury could send patients into shock, so she kept the paper in place.

Pain also contributed to shock. Harold was being brave in his benignly chauvinistic way, but he was clearly suffering.

Brooke addressed Zach. "What have you given for pain, Mr. Bishop?"

"Morphine, two milligrams."

She raised a brow at him. That dose was low. "Only once?"

Zach shrugged a bit. "Didn't want to mask any chest pain." His tone said it was no big deal, nothing to worry about.

"I see," Brooke said, and she did. Zach suspected severe heart disease in this patient. A more potent dose of morphine could have meant the man would have a heart attack without feeling it. The attack would have to reach great severity before symptoms would be noticeable in a morphine-drugged, pain-free man.

The patient was already anxious and his body was under significant stress. Brooke knew Zach's shrug and easy tone of voice were meant to keep the patient's anxiety levels from skyrocketing. She envied Zach's bedside manner.

"Nitroglycerin at the scene, Mr. Bishop?" Brooke could never match Zach's *life is good* approach, but she did her part to keep the patient calm by continuing her methodical exam, palpating his undamaged leg as if she weren't discussing a potentially life-threatening event with Zach.

Anticipating Brooke's next order, Loretta opened a drawer and pulled out a pack of ECG leads, ready to place the little sticky circles on Harold's chest so they could monitor his heart, although that wasn't a typical part of treating a fracture. As if they'd choreographed it, Brooke moved to the foot of the bed as Loretta took her place.

While Loretta unbuttoned Harold's shirt and attached the leads, Brooke pressed her fingertips to the ankle of

Harold's broken leg. She took his pulse without jostling the injury, needing to confirm that blood was still circulating past the fracture to reach his extremities.

The patient looked up at Zach and scolded him. "Now, don't go embarrassing me in front of these pretty ladies. That chest pain comes and goes, I told you. I just take one of those tiny white pills, and I'm fine. Fit as a fiddle, except for my leg." But his chuckle was forced and he rubbed at the center of his chest with his free hand.

No sooner had the nurse turned on the television-like monitor over the bed than Harold's worried rubbing motion changed. He clutched at the open edge of his shirt. "Maybe…one of my pills?" he gasped.

Brooke read the jagged line of his ECG in a glance. A myocardial infarction—a heart attack—was underway. "I'm going to take good care of your heart, Harold. Let's do something about that pain, too."

From that moment, time slowed down and sped by simultaneously. It was always that way for Brooke while she led her team through an emergency. When she had to function at a high level of complex decision-making, everything seemed paradoxically simple.

At her word, the crash cart was called. Extra personnel filled the room. Decisions had to be made, one after the other, in a logical order. As a nurse tied a yellow disposable gown over Brooke's white coat, Brooke called for the right drugs at the right doses. Once morphine had eased the panicked and pained patient into unconsciousness, she quickly dressed the broken leg as a stopgap measure before the cardiac cath team arrived to rush the patient to their artery-opening, lifesaving theater.

After the patient and his bed had been rolled away to the cardiology floor, there was a moment of silence, of inactivity. As if the bed were still there, no one walked through the empty center of the room as they snapped off their gloves and discarded protective gear.

Brooke was the first to use the sink as she scrubbed her hands for the millionth time that day, the smell of the soap and the sound of the water bringing her back from that intense state of mind. She thanked her team for their work, making eye contact and nodding at each person, the equivalent of a handshake in an environment where hygiene procedures made real handshakes problematic.

Zach was not in the room. Brooke had been so very alert through it all. How had she missed his exit?

The image of Harold clinging to Zach's hand was vivid in Brooke's mind. When Harold had lost consciousness, his hand had slipped from Zach's. Brooke could remember thinking, *Now Zach can administer the oxygen.* Brooke had ordered him to do just that, and he had, of course.

When had he left the room? It was curious, how moments that were crystal clear became hazy. As more and more of her regular team had entered the room, Zach must have stepped out, no longer needed and making room for those who were. He was a good paramedic that way.

He was a good paramedic in every way. Sharp and smart in matters of medicine. Comforting in his cocky way. Patients loved him. Her staff loved him. And Brooke—well, she needed to at least thank him as she had the others.

He was probably out by the nurses' station, filling out his own paperwork. Brooke would go out there to dictate this patient's chart. She'd ignore Zach, he'd ignore her and just before he left, he'd lean in, ready to murmur some outrageous line in her ear. But this time, she would speak first.

She would thank him for a job well done. Even if he did leave a disturbing wake of feminine fluttering everywhere he went, it was a pleasure to work with someone as good at his job as he was. After eight months of frowning at the man, it was time she thanked him for being part of the team.

It was professional courtesy. Nothing more—but he'd probably be so surprised, he'd forget to deliver whatever corny line he had ready.

The thought nearly made her smile.

Chapter 2

Zach scowled at the coffeepot, too damned frustrated with himself to wait for *her* in the hallway.

He'd transferred his patient, Harold Allman, to the care of the hospital. No cause for frustration there. The handoff had gone smoothly. It had been done in the nick of time, too. The poor guy had coded right there in the treatment room. Since a heart attack probably had been lingering on the horizon for months, Harold's heart had chosen the best possible place to succumb to the inevitable. He was in good hands here, with Dr. Brooke Brown and the rest of the West Central team.

Zach should go now. There was nothing to wait for. No *one* to wait for.

Yet he couldn't seem to make himself leave this emergency room, not without a chance to tease Dr. Brown first, and *that* was the problem. That was no laughing matter.

As a fireman and paramedic, Zach belonged out in the city of Austin, first on the scene, providing initial care. Or he belonged back at the firehouse, waiting for the next call. He belonged with his crew, Murphy and Chief, who were outside, under the portico that marked the ambulance entrance. Undoubtedly, they were sitting on the chrome running boards of Engine Thirty-Seven right now, shooting the breeze with other first responders as they waited for him.

Zach should be walking out those glass doors right this second. Instead, he was in the ER staff's kitchenette, leaning against the counter, lingering against his better judgment.

Go. Just leave. You don't need to see her one more time.

Her. Dr. Brown. He was waiting around for the chance to say what? One lousy sentence. That was all he ever said, one dumb line to see if she'd smile, but damn if he didn't look forward to those stolen moments.

Dr. Brown had become something of a favorite with him, which was idiotic. She had a sharp mind and a beautiful face, true, but so did a lot of women in the world. Heck, so did a lot of women right here at West Central. Zach always enjoyed working with this hospital staff. Lighthearted conversation and playful smiles were a welcome break during an intense job.

He got neither from Dr. Brown. They weren't her style, which meant *she* wasn't his style. Zach pushed himself away from the kitchen counter that held the industrial coffee machine. His crew was waiting on him. He needed to get back to the engine. He'd catch Dr. Brown next time, see if he couldn't make her smile.

The coffeepot was nearly empty, sitting on the burner,

dangerously close to being boiled away entirely. Before he left, Zach could show some appreciation for the friendly folks at West Central. If there was one thing a fireman knew how to do, it was make a gallon of coffee. He opened the cabinets until he found the white paper filters, and made himself useful.

Go. You're stalling. It could be another hour before she's done with Harold. She's hated you from day one, anyway.

Maybe she had, but he hadn't felt the same. *Hate* was not how he'd describe that first impression. He and his crew had brought in a patient during shift change. She'd been leaving, he realized now, which was why she hadn't been wearing her white doctor's coat.

The patient hadn't been critical. They'd been wheeling him in at a sedate walk, but even if they'd been coming in at a run, Zach would have noticed Dr. Brown. Her dark hair had been pulled back tightly, and she'd been wearing a crisp white button-down shirt and a pinstriped pencil skirt. She'd only lacked the black-framed eyeglasses to complete the look of a guy's fantasy librarian or schoolteacher. Smart. Controlled. Sexy.

She hadn't noticed him at all. As he and the crew had wheeled the patient in, she'd merely stepped aside, unimpressed and perhaps slightly bored, as if firemen surrounding a gurney were an everyday sight for her. He'd wondered who the sexy librarian was. Zach was used to crowds gathering to watch him work, not to being ignored.

Go. Quit hanging around for another glimpse. She didn't notice you then; she ignores you now.

But he'd never really convinced himself that she hadn't noticed him that first day. As he'd passed her, their eyes had met for the briefest second. Met and held just a moment longer than strangers do. When Zach had turned back for a second look, she'd been turning away to head out the door. There was something about that quick turn that made him suspect she'd been staring at him after all.

True, she ignored him now. It was a very *aware* kind of ignoring, however. She had to know exactly where he was in order to stand with her back to him. She had to intentionally remain silent when the nurses chatted with him as she wrote in her charts. And he would have sworn on more than one occasion that she'd deliberately stood in his path, making it easier for him to deliver one of his teasing pickup lines before he left the ER.

Those lines had become a private game between them. Harmless. Fun. And challenging, especially now that he'd made her lips quirk in an unwilling smile more than once.

It's fun to try to make Brooke Brown smile, but it's fun to make every beautiful woman smile. No difference.

The grapevine had said she was seeing someone at this hospital when he'd first laid eyes on her last September. He'd been dating a nurse at a different hospital. Their game had started off innocently enough, just verbal sparring. It had never gone further. Heck, they never dropped the professional courtesy of addressing each other as *Dr. Brown* and *Mr. Bishop*.

Through the fall and winter and spring, nothing had changed, although the grapevine now said Dr. Brown was no longer seeing anyone in particular. Of course, Zach and the nurse at the other hospital had parted ways long ago. He always ended a relationship while things were still friendly, before any drama could develop.

This long-standing flirtation with the sexy librarian-teacher-doctor at West Central wasn't any kind of relationship, so it was completely drama-free. In other words, it was safe. Zach didn't want an emotional relationship, and Brooke Brown, MD, was no threat in that sense. They didn't care for one another beyond their running joke.

Go, then. This isn't the way you play the game. You crack a joke if she happens to be on duty, and then you leave. Why are you sticking around now?

He wasn't. He was leaving. As soon as the coffee was ready, he'd pour himself a cup and get the hell out of Dodge, before he did something stupid and tried to take this non-relationship to the next level.

He thought about her too much. With their first call of the day, Engine Thirty-Seven had been directed to another hospital, and Zach had been disappointed to lose the chance to see Dr. Brown. To tease her. To try to make her smile.

That was a red flag in his book. Zach loved women, and women loved him. But to start thinking exclusively about one woman, to be obsessed with one woman?

Been there, done that, never doing it again.

The steady drip of the brewing coffee built momentum, filling the carafe. He just needed a few more minutes.

When dispatch had directed Engine Thirty-Seven to take Harold Allman to West Central, Zach had felt a little extra adrenaline rush: Dr. Brown could be on duty.

Red flag.

Yeah, yeah. The coffee's still brewing. I'll be out of here in a few minutes.

When it came to Dr. Brown, he always seemed to linger a few more minutes. As she'd handled Harold's code, Zach should have left the room. He should have gotten out of the way immediately. Instead, he'd stood at that door and watched her for a minute longer. Then for five minutes longer.

Watching Dr. Brown's cool concentration had stirred something in him, something more than physical attraction. He was impressed with her. He'd almost felt proud of her.

And yes, her abilities as an emergency physician made her even sexier, damn it. He'd thought she was sexy the first time they'd locked gazes last September. Now it was April, and the problem wasn't just that he found her sexy. The problem was, every other woman no longer seemed as sexy to him.

Hell, if enough red flags aren't waving for you, then you might as well stick around and make a fool of yourself over a woman for a second time in your life. Fall in love, get down on bended knee. I'm sure rejection won't hurt as badly the second time. Stay and enjoy that pain again.

To hell with the coffee. He was leaving.

Zach grabbed the doorknob and pulled.

Dr. Brown was on the other side, holding that side's knob. The force with which Zach pulled the door toward himself pulled her into the room as well.

"Oh," she said, looking up at him in surprise. She only looked up a few inches. Although he was tall, she was, too, and she always wore heels with those pinstriped skirts under her white coat.

They stood there, each holding their side's doorknob for a long, mute second. Zach let go and stepped back.

She came in and shut the door. "I was looking for you."

His surprise was genuine. For eight months, he'd been bringing patients into West Central. For eight months, she'd been ignoring him.

"I wanted to tell you that your decision to under-dose the morphine increased the odds in Harold Allman's favor. Thank you. And thank you for sticking around after the handoff. I think the way you kept him calm also kept him out of severe shock."

Dr. Brown had never spoken two complete sentences to him. Zach wasn't sure what to make of it. She wasn't flirting, not like other women did. She was just talking to him. He crossed his arms over his chest.

Her gaze held his as she spoke. She didn't come close to batting her eyelashes, not one flutter, but he noticed how thick they were, anyway.

"Not a lot of people would have held a patient's hand like that," she said. "Especially a… Well, I was going to say especially a man wouldn't hold hands, but that would be gender stereotyping, wouldn't it?"

Gender stereotyping. Did she have to speak like a sexy librarian as well as look like one?

"Forget I said that," she said. "It was a job well done, whether you're male or female."

Apparently done for the day, she began unbuttoning her white lab coat, starting with the button at her chest. *Damn, damn, damn.* He was definitely male.

Through the kitchen was an even tinier room, one that held a cot and a few metal lockers. It was the physicians' lounge, in theory. In reality, it was just where the doctors stashed their belongings. Dr. Brown stepped toward the lounge door, unbuttoning as she walked.

There was no way Zach was going to leave while an attractive woman was removing clothing. He leaned back against the counter.

Since he couldn't just stare at her, he kept the conversation going. "I denied the patient adequate pain relief, so it seemed like the least I could do was let him squeeze the hell out of my hand. I'd be lying if I said it didn't hurt. The old guy could grip as hard as a female patient I had last year. She was in labor, and she nearly broke my hand with every contraction." He paused and grinned at her. "But if that sounds like gender stereotyping, forget I said that."

And then it happened. What the corniest pickup lines or the cleverest zingers couldn't accomplish, a simple conversation could: Brooke Brown smiled. She laughed, actually. Laughed as she shrugged off her white coat and let it drop down her arms.

Go. Leave now, before you fall too hard.

He couldn't just turn tail and run. That wasn't how they played their game. It would look odd. He needed to spar with her. Keep things normal.

But he stayed silent, mesmerized by a Brooke Brown who was neither focusing on medical care nor glaring at him while the rest of her staff flirted with him. She reached behind the door for a hanger, a woman doing a common task that shouldn't have been so fascinating. He didn't look away as she hung up her white coat.

"I'm glad I'm done for the day," she said, as she stepped into the tiny room and opened one of the metal gym lockers. "Are you done, too?"

She was making small talk, completely unaffected by this change in their routine. Still, he didn't take his eyes off her, not even to glance at the wall clock. By the time they drove the engine back to the firehouse, it would be seven o'clock and the end of his twenty-four hour shift.

"Yeah, I'm done, too."

He needed to stick to his plan. Coffee to go. Head for the engine after delivering the line she expected, if he could remember the over-the-top line he'd planned.

He could not. As he picked up the full coffeepot, he thought of the oldest line in the book, instead. He raised the pot in one hand and the cup in the other. "Can I buy you a drink?"

She froze in place. Her back was to him, and since he was watching her every move, he saw her hesitation. He watched her fingertips as she raised her hand to the back of her neck and fumbled for her stethoscope. She pulled a square purse out of her metal locker, keeping her back to him, her head a little bowed. "I don't think that would be a good idea. We're not coworkers *per se*, but we do work together at least a couple of times a week, and..."

Her voice trailed off as she turned around and saw him holding up the coffeepot and the cup in the gesture that had accompanied *Can I buy you a drink?*

"Oh, it was a joke," she said, and he felt every bit of her mortification. Her gaze dropped to the floor, and the cool and commanding physician looked for all the world like an embarrassed young girl, standing in front of gym lockers like an awkward teenager.

"My mistake," she murmured.

He could leave it like that, with her feeling embarrassed, and their relationship unchanged.

But she deserved better, this smart and sexy woman who hadn't seemed to like him much until today. The truth was, he'd said the line in a different manner than he usually did. Not so tongue-in-cheek. Not laughing as he spoke.

"It wasn't a joke, Brooke. Can I buy you a drink?"

Chapter 3

She was such a fool.

Can I buy you a drink?

He'd said it in that delicious deep voice, but without that good-time cowboy tone. For once, he'd sounded serious.

Still, he'd meant it as a joke. It was always a joke, it had been a joke from the very first, and Brooke was an idiot for having forgotten that for even the briefest of moments.

The stethoscope dangled from her hand. Buying herself a moment, she tucked it into her purse.

Why had she imagined a guy like Zach would have been serious for even a moment? He'd called her by her first name for the first time she could remember, and it made her want to blush like he'd whispered some intimacy in her ear. Maybe that had made her hear some-thing more than he'd meant.

He was only eye candy. A ladies' man. A fun-loving cowboy, for goodness' sake.

And she was an emergency medicine professional. She could operate under duress. She'd been trained to keep moving forward, even after a blunder.

She moved forward now, literally, to toss her purse on the counter and take the empty coffee cup from his hand. "Sure, I'll take a drink. Thanks for pouring."

His smile seemed to come as easily as ever, but the look in his eyes pinned her in place. "Am I supposed to politely assume that's a no and drop the subject?"

"It's a yes. I'd like a drink." She wiggled the white cardboard cup impatiently.

He covered her hand with his before he began to pour the steaming hot liquid, holding her cup steady with the same hand that had kept poor Harold steady. His palm was warm. His hand was large enough to wrap around both her hand and the cup easily.

Unlike Harold, she didn't find the touch of his hand calming. She'd been this close to Zach before, but only in passing, for a whisper of silliness—*I'm having a hard time finding my way out of this building because I keep getting lost in your eyes*—and then he'd be gone and she'd be left alone with a pleasant little shiver of awareness.

He didn't leave this time. He was still here, still touch-ing her, and she had nowhere to look except at him. His eyes were blue-green and as focused on her as she was on him.

"I expected more from you." He let go of her hand and put the coffeepot back on the burner.

"More what?" she asked.

"I expected a straightforward yes or no from a woman like you. Can I take you out for a drink after work?"

His casual stance and the trace of his ever-present grin sent all the usual messages: nothing to worry about, no reason to be alarmed. But the look in those blue-green eyes was different.

This wasn't a game. She was so terribly aware of the height and breadth of him, so much masculinity in a fire-fighter's shirt. Oh, it had been a long, long time since pheromones and hormones had threatened her ability to think clearly.

"Why the hesitation? You make a thousand decisions every shift, Brooklyn."

"It's just Brooke." No one here called her Brooklyn. "How did you know my real name?"

"It's on your license."

Paper copies of all the physicians' licenses were displayed on the wall. She was willing to bet no one else had read them in ages. "It's a frivolous name. I prefer Brooke."

"It's a sexy name. *Brooklyn Brown.* It fits you."

That deep voice of his was always appealing, but the way he used it now, saying her name as if it were something he could taste…

Oh, no.

She set the coffee cup on the counter.

No, no, no. She was not going to turn into a mush-for-brains puddle of female hormones at the feet of a fireman who said she was sexy.

"I could pick you up in an hour. Are we on?"

Brooke needed to say no. She knew it. Instead, she kept looking at the single most handsome man to ever ask her on a date, and…kept looking. Silent, not moving forward, not functioning at all. *Mush for brains.*

The door opened again. "There you are. Done for the day?"

That particular voice belonged to Dr. Tom Bamber, a radiologist at the hospital. He was a welcome distraction at the moment, forcing Brooke to stop staring at Zach as she turned to greet Tom. She only had a second to wonder why the radiologist had come to the emergency department before he said, "I was looking for you."

"You were?" Her surprise was genuine. He must have an unusual report for her. Radiologists typically gave their reports over the phone from their dark cave in the hospital basement, not in person. Harold Allman and his fractured tibia had been taken to the cardiac cath lab instead of X-ray, anyway. Dr. Bamber hadn't been on duty earlier, and—

"I've got tickets to the ballet tonight. Orchestra, row E." He flourished them before her like a two-feathered fan. "Score."

Score, indeed. Brooke loved the ballet, beauty created from precision. It was sweet of Tom to remember, but—

Tom kept talking. "I have my doubts that a young troupe can truly do justice to Balanchine, but we might as well go and judge their attempt. Shall we say seven? We can dine with the Philistines at the food trucks outside the theater." Tom stepped just a little too close to her. "Then I'll buy you a drink after the show."

Good grief, the man was asking her out on a date. Brooke rarely went out with friends and even more rarely on dates, but now she had two men wanting to buy her drinks. On the same night. At the same moment. Asking in front of one another.

She stole a glance at Zach, to whose presence Tom seemed to be oblivious. Zach raised her coffee cup to his lips, watching her conversation like a man watching a sporting event. He blew across the top of the hot liquid, which made his mouth look like he was about to give someone a soft, sweet kiss.

No, no, no. Don't go there.

Brooke smiled politely at Tom. His lips looked unremarkable. His mouth wasn't about to do anything except question her.

Normal lips were a good thing. Tom was exactly the sort of man she should date. They spoke the same language as doctors. They'd discussed their mutual appreciation of the ballet once, over lunch in the hospital cafeteria. They were evenly matched, even in their height. She could look him squarely in the eye.

Brooke had to glance *up* at the fireman who'd also just asked her out for a drink. She wondered what kind of place a man like Zach would take a woman like her. What was a playboy paramedic's idea of a night out in Austin? Where would it begin—and where would they end up?

No, no, no.

Zach was all wrong for her, yet she couldn't accept Tom's ballet invitation in front of Zach. She felt a little relieved, actually, that she had an excuse not to go out on a perfectly nice date with a perfectly nice man like Tom.

Likewise, even if she'd wanted to, she couldn't tell Zach yes in front of Tom.

Even *if* she'd wanted to?

She *had* wanted to. She'd almost said yes to a fireman just because he dripped sex appeal. Tom had unknowingly stopped her from making a big mistake.

"I'm sorry, but—"

The kitchen door burst open once again.

"There you are."

Brooke felt relieved; this man was almost as handsome as Zach, but also quite happily married. The head of the emergency department, Dr. Jamie MacDowell, wasn't going to offer to buy her a drink.

"Can you work late?" Jamie asked her instead. "We just got a call that there's been a multi-car accident on I-35."

"Sure, I can stay." Brooke recognized the cowardly relief she felt. Now she didn't have to turn down two men.

Jamie nodded at Zach as if they were old friends. "Surprised your engine hasn't been called yet."

An obnoxiously loud series of three tones sounded from the radio at Zach's hip.

"Now it has." Zach silenced his radio as he started for the door.

"Jinxed you," Jamie said. As Zach passed him, the two men didn't shake hands as much as do some kind of forearm-to-forearm punch. Brooke had seen that move before. It seemed that all three of the Dr. MacDowell brothers and half the emergency responders in the Texas Rescue and Relief organization had played on the same high school football team.

She should have guessed that Zach's cocky grin and his confidence with women had started in his teen years. Of course, Zach Bishop had been a high school football star.

As he turned back to her, he added a wink to the grin that had probably slayed a dozen cheerleaders. "Looks like neither one of our shifts is over. Tonight is not our night, but the offer still stands."

Then he left. Tom Bamber frowned at her. Jamie Mac-Dowell lifted one brow in speculation.

Brooke turned her back on both men and grabbed her white coat off its hanger. It was time to go to work. Zach was gone, and she was once more left alone with a little thrill of awareness, same as always.

The offer still stands.

Or maybe, things weren't the same as always.

An hour later, Brooke was making decisions in that quick yet methodical state of mind, going down the logical checklists ingrained in her brain regarding the injuries and complications of accident victims. She had no time to wonder where Zach was.

She wondered, anyway, during those moments when she transitioned from one patient to another. She'd worked a hundred shifts not caring who pushed the gurney as patients arrived. She'd worked a hundred more without replaying the last words a man had said to her. Yet tonight, she kept remembering the way Zach had said *Brooklyn Brown*. The way he'd told her the offer still stood.

Each time she walked into a treatment room, she noticed that Zach wasn't there. Each time the sliding glass doors opened and paramedics wheeled in a patient, she noticed that Zach wasn't there. When Loretta stopped to let her know that Harold Allman was doing well after his heart procedure, Brooke made a mental note to be sure to pass on the good news to Zach—later, because he wasn't there.

Still, Harold's recovery was a useful thing to have ready to discuss, because she wasn't sure what else she would say the next time she saw Zach. Whenever that would be.

It wasn't that day. When she took her purse out of the gym locker for the second time, it was after midnight, and she was so tired, the cot in the physicians' lounge was starting to look inviting. She wondered if Zach felt the same, wherever he was.

No fire engines had arrived from the crash scene. Fire engines didn't transport patients; ambulances did. But if a fire engine was first on the scene and its paramedic was the first to begin a victim's medical treatment, then that paramedic would stay with the patient, continuing medical care in the back of the ambulance on the way to the hospital. The fire engine followed the ambulance, staying with its paramedic, ready for him to rejoin the engine's crew once the handoff to the hospital had taken place.

Any time an ambulance pulled up to the hospital doors and Zach Bishop emerged with a patient, that big red Engine Thirty-Seven pulled in right behind him, like Zach was some kind of superhero with a red fire truck instead of a red cape sailing behind him.

Not tonight. Brooke assumed that meant Zach was working as less of a paramedic and more of a firefighter. Was he still on the scene, putting out a fire or cutting open a crumpled car? Or was he, like she, dragging himself home, staying awake through sheer willpower long enough to take a shower and then falling into bed with hair still wet, sleeping like the dead until it was time to wake for the next shift?

As Brooke's own wet head hit her pillow, her last thought of the day was a vision of Zach, his hair dark and damp from a shower, smiling at her from the empty white pillow next to hers.

Shall I call you for breakfast, or just nudge you?

Brooke didn't swoon for superheroes. She didn't date eye candy.

But if she wanted to, she could, because the offer still stood.

In the last unguarded moment of a long day, Brooke fell asleep with a smile on her lips.

Chapter 4

She heard him before she saw him. Tom Bamber's voice was as distinctive as Zach Bishop's, but not in a sexy way. He sounded more like—well, he sounded like a radiologist giving a report, which he was.

He wasn't giving the report to Brooke. He was speaking to Jamie. It was odd that Tom had emerged from his basement office and walked to the emergency room instead of just picking up the phone.

She had a hunch that he'd done so in order to see her. Brooke considered sneaking past the nurses' station to the kitchen in order to avoid Tom. If he was planning on asking her out again, discretion would be the better part of valor.

Okay, she was feeling cowardly. She didn't want to face the awkwardness of an offer she didn't want but shouldn't refuse. She started down the hall with careful steps, trying to minimize the sound of her heels on the tile.

Tom was exactly the kind of guy she ought to date. Her mother would approve. Nothing could be safer and more secure than a radiologist. Mom was big into security. Predictability.

Imagine taking firefighter Zach home to meet Mother.

First, the man would have to be crazy about her to want to set foot in the mausoleum that was her mother's house. Second, although women loved Zach, her mother would be the exception. Even Zach couldn't charm her from her permanent frown.

But what if he could? That would really be something.

"Overactive imagination in room two."

Brooke stopped in midstep and turned to face the nurse. Loretta might as well have been diagnosing her as the next patient.

"Sorry, Dr. Brown. Did I startle you?"

"No, not at all."

Was she blushing? She couldn't be. Dr. Brooke Brown did not blush. She also did not daydream about firemen who were so madly in love with her that they wanted to even *meet* her mother. Where was her logic, her order, her checklists? First, long before the man was crazy in love with her, she'd have to actually see the man again, maybe even call him by his first name.

First, the man would have to make an effort to see me.

It had been three days since he'd said the offer still stood and then left for the accident scene. Zach didn't have her phone number. He didn't know where she lived. He was leaving it up to chance for their paths to cross, as always. They would both have to just happen to be ending shifts at the same time for that after-work drink to become reality.

In other words, he was an easy-go-lucky, flirtatious guy, and she was an idiot for mistaking his casual invitation for anything more. Had she really thought their relationship was going to move to another level? She was a fool for daydreaming that a handsome playboy was anything but a handsome playboy.

Loretta handed her the clipboard for room two. "Four-year-old female, two hovering parents who brought their own thermometer."

Well, there was nothing like work to wake Brooke up from her daydreams. "Fever?"

"Barely one hundred degrees, the third time they asked me to verify their thermometer's readings with our thermometer. Runny nose. They printed out a list from their internet search. Could be the first signs of a cancerous tumor, you know."

"First things first. We'll have to consider the common cold."

"Good luck. Those parents are already in a temper because the urgent cases were seen first. They got here at six thirty this morning, because their regular pediatrician's office didn't open until eight. It's nine now, so… you get the picture."

Twenty minutes later, Brooke was in a temper herself. She understood anxious parents—she'd been raised by one—so Brooke had been very thorough in her exam of the child. There was no indication whatsoever of anything more serious than the common cold in the little girl. Nothing in her medical history, nothing in her family history, nothing to warrant even a basic antibiotic prescription.

Brooke had explained her reasoning. She'd answered every question the parents had. But when the parents had questioned her qualifications as a physician, when the accusations had started flying that Brooke must be unduly influenced by insurance companies, drug companies or hospital profits, her own patience had run out.

They'd asked to see another doctor.

Jamie MacDowell was in there now. Brooke stood at the nurses' station, empty-handed, denied even the patient chart that she could have slapped onto the counter in a satisfying smack.

She knew Jamie's conclusion was going to be identical to hers. Jamie would back her up in every way. It was all such a waste of effort. The parents would leave, and the next time they feared that their daughter was seriously ill, they'd go to a different hospital's emergency room. All of Brooke's careful explanations, all of Jamie's professional courtesy, would result in nothing. West Central Texas Hospital was wasting resources that could have been better spent on a dozen other people.

Worse, those parents would never relax and appreciate that they had a healthy child. Brooke couldn't help but think of her mother and how grateful she would have been to have a four-year-old girl with a common cold. Instead, when Brooke's sister had been four, her mother had spent a week sitting at the bedside of a child in a coma, until Brooke's sister had passed away.

It had been so long ago, close to twenty years now. Brooke rested her elbows on the high counter of the nurses' station and let her head drop into her hands. For just a moment, she pressed her fingertips against her temples to relieve the stress. It was impossible to treat a four-year-old little girl and not think of her sister.

If those angry parents in room two only knew how much worse their lives could be, how much more serious their troubles could get. People should thank their lucky stars when their lives were normal. Boring. Routine. Brooke's mother was right: security and predictability were the keys to a good life.

"Dr. Bamber asked that you give him a call when you have a moment," the nurse at the desk said.

Brooke frowned. She wasn't waiting on any radiology reports. "About which patient?"

The nurse, the blonde and single one from a few nights ago, beamed at her. "No patient. I think it's personal."

So, Tom was going to ask her out again, and he wasn't waiting until chance brought them together to do it. He was predictable. He was exactly what she needed in her life, if she needed any male companionship at all.

The glass doors slid open. A patient arrived on a gurney, paramedics walking on either side. No eye candy. No one from Engine Thirty-Seven.

Brooke was annoyed at the way her heart had skipped a beat when the doors whooshed open. She was disappointed at her own disappointment. This little game of Zach roulette did not amuse her. She had a chance at normalcy and predictability and a perfectly nice date with a perfectly nice guy. She should be satisfied. She'd call Tom. Soon.

"I'm going to grab a quick cup of coffee," she told the nurse.

The emergency two-way radio that resided permanently at the nurses' station sounded. Another ambulance was on its way. She lingered and listened as the nurse communicated with the crew, until Brooke heard it was not Engine Thirty-Seven.

Impatiently, she pushed through the door into the kitchenette.

There Zach was, standing there as calm as could be, reading the work schedule pinned on the bulletin board. She hadn't braced herself to see him, so the sight of him took her breath away. His hair, which had darkened to a medium brown over the winter, was once more becoming streaked by the sun now that warm weather had returned to Texas. His jaw was square, clean-shaven, and his uniform—

Zach wasn't in uniform. Brooke had never seen him in anything but black. Now he wore a pale blue shirt, cuffed halfway up his forearms and tucked into his jeans. His boots were brown, not black, and they were cowboy boots, not steel-toed work boots. He looked about as delicious as a rugged man could look.

Brooke wished, with a sudden ferocity that knocked her off guard, that she could say to hell with logic and predictability and Tom and instead take a chance with Zach. What would it be like to let him make her laugh after hours instead of settling for a quick grin at work? To flirt, to tease, to touch a man without knowing where it would lead or how long it would last?

That would be dangerous living.

He glanced her way to see who had opened the door. When their eyes met, he smiled.

She nodded coolly. "What are you doing here? You're not…" She gestured toward his jeans. "…working."

"Looking for you, of course. I hoped you'd be done with your shift, and we could catch that drink."

"It's nine in the morning."

"We could drink coffee." He stepped closer to her, close enough that she could see how the blue of his shirt made the blue in his eyes more pronounced. Close enough that the quiet bass of his voice filled the air between them. "I know a vintage record store that has a coffee bar. They play heavy metal on vinyl, but they top your lattes with just a whisper of foam. If you were just coming off a hard night shift, it would be a great combination."

"Oh."

"I came in and checked the schedule yesterday. I thought you were working overnight and might need to wind down this morning, before going to bed."

There was practically a purr in his voice. She narrowed her eyes in suspicion. Was he trying to *seduce* her at nine in the morning? Seduce her with heavy metal music played on vinyl records in one of Austin's funky coffee shops? The man must not have any sense of what she was like as a person. She wasn't the kind of woman who drank coffee in places like that.

Maybe I am. I've never tried it.

She leaned back against the wall, tucking her hands behind herself, in the small of her back. Away from him. "I switched shifts. I've got ten more hours today. I won't be done until seven, if that."

His easy grin said it was no big deal, nothing to worry about. He nodded toward the schedule on the wall. Her schedule. He hadn't left anything to chance, after all.

"I see that. I'm covering a short shift today for a friend in an ambulance company, eleven to six. I can be showered and shaved and ready to take you out tonight when you get off at seven. Say yes."

She hesitated. As flattering as it was that he'd apparently meant it when he'd said it wasn't a joke and he really wanted to buy her a drink, he was still that playboy paramedic who flirted shamelessly with everything and everyone female.

She lifted her chin, wishing she weren't so tempted to add herself to his fan club. "What if I said no?"

His smile didn't slip, but he looked a little surprised at her question. "I'd be disappointed, but I understand long shifts. If you're tired, you're tired. I was matching up our schedules when you came in. I'm starting twenty-four hours tomorrow, but we could make it the day after tomorrow."

"I meant what's your plan B for tonight, if I can't make it?"

He placed one hand on the wall near her head and leaned closer to her. That mostly-blue gaze never left her face. "I'd head over to the firehouse after work. Shower. Crash on the couch in front of some mindless sports."

"Alone?"

He tilted his head a little to the side, studying her. "Yes, alone. I want to go out with you. If you're unavailable, I don't want to go out."

She snorted a little, not the most ladylike sound, but her disbelief needed an outlet. "Be serious. If I said no, you'd get over that disappointment fast. You could take any other woman out for drinks. You'd have another date lined up before I could snap my fingers."

He wasn't smiling now. "Women aren't interchangeable. If I want to spend time with you, then no one else will do."

"I've watched you flirt with every woman you set eyes on for eight months."

"That doesn't mean I date every woman I see. When I'm interested in one woman, then she's it."

She did frown at that. "Really? Judging by your behavior around here, it's been a long time since you decided one woman was enough."

"I'd say it's been four years. Almost five."

That startled Brooke into silence. Such a specific answer—the man had his secrets, then. A past. It was hard to imagine Zach devoted to one woman four years ago.

"Are you divorced?" She felt as if she was venturing way too far into personal territory by asking him that, but wasn't that information she should know about a man before she dated him?

She glanced at his free hand. No ring, no mark left by a ring. No sign that a woman had ever placed a gold band on that finger, claiming him.

"Never married," he said curtly. He pushed away from the wall and leaned back against the counter, a casual pose that seemed much more like the Zach she knew. "Do you really think if you aren't available, then I'm going to step into the hall and ask Mary Ellen instead?"

"Mary Ellen's engaged."

Zach's easygoing smile returned. "Just one more reason I'd rather be with you."

"What are the other reasons?"

"Spend the evening with me, and I'll tell you each one."

Chapter 5

She'd said yes.

Brooke's shift had started with two hours of misery, thanks to those miserable parents, but after seeing Zach in the break room, she'd been buoyed along by a sense of sweet anticipation, eight pleasant hours so far, all because she'd thrown caution to the wind and said yes.

Maybe she didn't know herself as well as she'd always thought she did. Or maybe she'd been intrigued by a glimpse of a man who had layers that ran deeper than a handsome face and a quick, laughing wit. Or maybe…

Or maybe, it was just good, old-fashioned physical attraction. Zach had leaned over her, placed his hand on the wall near her head, and her body had responded. She could catalog all the classic signs of arousal. Blood vessels had dilated, breathing had deepened, heart rate had increased.

Incredibly, being around her had produced the same effects in Zach. She'd been staring into his blue-green eyes when she'd realized that his breathing had changed slightly, too. Since Brooke shined a penlight into patients' eyes all day long, she'd noticed that the pupils of Zach's eyes widened as she challenged him. That one telltale sign, a pupil dilation indicating an arousal of the autonomic nervous system that no one could fake, had given her more confidence than all the smiles he sent her way. She didn't trust her own instincts, the ones that said this attractive man found her attractive, too, but she could trust science.

He was into her.

She was smiling at the thought even now. Just two more hours and her shift would end and her date would begin. The anticipation was intoxicating. Brooke bent her head over the patient's chart and tried not to look as giddy as she felt inside. It was quite the emotional high to have a schoolgirl crush that was actually being returned. Endorphins, dopamine, serotonin.

She liked Zach Bishop, and he liked her back. Why had she fought that so hard? There was nothing bad about a little uptick in endorphins. How could she have so coldly considered choosing to spend her time with Tom Bamber for the sake of predictability?

The desk radio interrupted her thoughts. An ambulance was on its way in, transporting a patient who was already coding. She wiped the grin off her own face, feeling almost ashamed to be happy when others were not. She stuck her hands in the pockets of her white coat and listened while a nurse wrote the information being relayed.

The radio reported a white male, ninety-six years old,

was en route. They were bagging him, using a balloon-like device to push air into his lungs. Defibrillation had failed to produce a heartbeat. Manual chest compressions were ongoing, and had been ongoing for the entire thirty-minute ambulance ride in from a distant ranch. Brooke knew they would still be ongoing when they arrived in an estimated ten minutes; the patient was not going to spontaneously recover. Whoever was forcing that heart to squeeze by pushing on the chest would have to keep pushing.

The last of Brooke's buoyant emotions sank. It was time to do the hard work of her profession.

Ninety-six years old. A total of forty minutes of chest compressions before arrival. No one was immediately declared dead on arrival without every effort first being made, but the checklist of medical options was short in this situation.

Brooke was waiting in the crash room when they arrived. The paramedics told her the patient had been found in his bed when a family member brought his dinner tray to him. The first item on Brooke's mental checklist was also the last: assess body temperature. The thermometer's reading was repeated to be completely certain, but she knew any chance of resuscitation was gone. His body had cooled after he'd died in his sleep, peacefully, well before his family had noticed and called the ambulance. Brooke stepped back from the patient and formally announced the time of death.

That wasn't the hard part of her job. Declaring a patient dead was something she was qualified to do.

But the next logical step was never easy. She had to inform the next of kin that their loved one was gone. Grief was an unpredictable monster, and no matter how she approached a deceased patient's family, no matter how young or old the patient was, no matter how expected or unexpected the death was, the monster always landed a blow.

Brooke had learned to protect herself from it as much as possible. She always entered a room of waiting family members while wearing her white coat, a symbol of care and competence and authority that Brooke believed was reassuring to the family in a subconscious way. She shook hands, her polite yet serious demeanor generally the first step in preparing the family to hear the news she had to deliver. She did so as simply and concisely as she could, telling them when, and why.

Then the monster had its turn.

Each time, Brooke could only stand by and witness the assault. Whether the monster caused shocked silence or unrestrained wailing, Brooke stayed in the room. Inevitably, there would be additional questions about what had happened, and she was in the best position to explain why the body had failed, why a treatment had or hadn't been attempted, or anything else the family wanted to know.

As the monster finished its first round of punches, someone would make the emotional request to view the body, or else someone would ask a practical question about funeral arrangements, and then Brooke knew it was time to leave the family in the competent hands of the hospital's morgue attendants.

With her duty complete, she would return to the nurses' station, pick up the next chart in sequence, and move on to her next patient. Laceration of the forearm. Evaluation of abdominal pain. More patients needed to be cared for, regardless of Brooke's personal feelings, so there was no sense in giving in to her emotions. It was a routine she usually handled as well as anyone could.

Today should not have been different.

Brooke informed the family of the ninety-six-year-old patient that their loved one could not be revived. She waited for the first wave of grief to pass, then left the family when the hospital administrator arrived to handle the final arrangements.

It was time to move forward. Yet Brooke stood at the nurses' station, and wondered why she felt shaky.

"Dr. Brown, can you take room four?" A nurse held out a clipboard, expecting Brooke to take it the way she always, always did.

Today, she hesitated.

Just give me a minute. I need a minute.

"I'll complete this death certificate first," Brooke said evenly.

"Oh. Sure." After a second of hesitation, the nurse set down the clipboard and walked away.

Brooke's hand felt stiff and ungainly—*what on earth is wrong with me?*—as she began filling out the form, taking care to keep her writing legible so the admin clerks wouldn't transcribe any errors into the final legal document.

This death should not have been a difficult one, as these things went. The patient had lived a longer life than most people. His death had been painless, at home, and he'd clearly lived his last days surrounded by people who cared about him.

But today, Brooke was off balance. She'd made plans for tonight that were out of character. Her emotions weren't entirely under control, so the monster had grazed her as it hit the patient's family.

I wish Zach would walk in the door.

For one second, just one second, Brooke let herself imagine a man dressed in black, bigger and stronger than she was, ready to shoulder her worries and cares.

What a foolish thought. If anything, Zach was to blame for her sudden inability to handle the hardest part of her job. Because she'd felt this morning's endorphin-fueled rush of attraction, this afternoon's death seemed all the darker in contrast.

She'd failed to protect her emotional stability. She wasn't usually incapacitated by grief, because she wasn't usually extraordinarily happy, either. She should never have agreed to start seeing a man who affected her like Zach did.

She could fix that now. She could cancel her date with Zach. She could return Tom Bamber's call.

She should use her head, not her heart. Or rather, she should use her head, and not her *hormones*. Her attraction to Zach was purely physical, surely.

Then surely it's okay to go ahead and see him tonight. There's no emotional attachment. It's just physical chemistry. A little flirting with the biggest flirt of them all.

That was perfectly sensible, but her attraction to Zach didn't feel purely physical. Her emotions were all stirred up every time she was near him, and that was unacceptable.

She looked at the clock. Six thirty. His shift had ended thirty minutes ago; hers had thirty minutes left. There was plenty of time to change plans. They'd exchanged phone numbers this morning. She should call him and cancel, for her own peace of mind. She could pack all her emotions, the good and the bad, into the neat little compartments in her head where they belonged, if she stopped anticipating time with Zach.

The door to the waiting room opened. Not the door to the large waiting room, which had check-in desks and televisions and children's play areas. This was the door to the smaller waiting area, the one with four walls and soothing artwork and privacy, the one where the staff put the families of patients who were critical and might not survive.

The family of the deceased ninety-six-year-old began filing out. They'd followed the ambulance here in what must have been a small convoy of cars. Brooke had been surprised at the large cluster of adult children she'd had to shake hands with when she'd gone in to break the news. Now they were milling about, discussing who should leave, who would stay until the funeral parlor arrived, who needed coffee and where was the cafeteria, and had Bob had a chance to view the body yet? A broken little family, pulling itself back together, getting reorganized as families do.

Brooke kept her head down. She wrote faster, but she still heard the young girl's voice. "Do I get to see Grandpa now?"

None of the adults seemed to have heard her. When Brooke had broken the news, that girl had been in the waiting room, too, a lovely young person on the threshold of adolescence, with braces on her teeth and shiny long hair.

"Aunt Lucy?" the girl asked, trying again. "Can I go and see Grandpa with you?"

Brooke wished now she'd shaken the girl's hand as if she were one of the adults. *She feels the loss, too. She's grieving, too. Pay attention to her!*

The girl looked perhaps eleven or twelve years old, but that was old enough to understand and feel everything that was going on. Brooke knew, because that was how old she'd been when her four-year-old sister had died.

The monster hit her hard.

With her pen frozen over the paper, Brooke sucked in her breath at the sudden blow. It had been lurking, she realized, since this morning's four-year-old patient with the parents who didn't know how fortunate they were to have a little girl with a common cold.

The aunt patted the preteen on the shoulder almost absentmindedly, but she did answer her. "We'll say goodbye to Grandpa at the funeral parlor, honey."

The girl's family cared for her. Of course they did, just as Brooke's family had cared for her. Still, she'd been lost after her sister's death. Watching this little drama in the hall, she could see how easily an older child could be overlooked. When her sister had died, Brooke hadn't been young enough to require the attention of being fed and dressed and provided for, but neither had she been old enough to be included while the adults in her family had made funeral arrangements and tried to console her nearly incoherent parents.

Brooke's almost twenty-year-old memories suddenly weren't old enough. She felt the pain of her sister's death, a horrible contrast to the pleasure of thinking about Zach.

Zach.

Had she really been blaming him for letting the genie out of the bottle? Her emotions weren't out of control because she'd said yes to him. They were out of control because a four-year-old little girl had stirred up painful memories this morning, and this afternoon's death had made them boil over.

She looked at the clock again. It was six forty-five. Unless she texted him that she needed more time, Zach would pick her up at her apartment at seven thirty. She'd given him the address.

Loretta walked up to her. "Can you start one last patient? It's a straightforward laceration. Shouldn't take too long."

A straightforward case would still keep her here another hour. Loretta was asking because Brooke always said yes. All of the doctors, not just Brooke, routinely worked past the end of their shifts. It was the nature of a medical career. Zach would understand. He might not have ended his shift on time, either. She'd text him and push back their date by another hour.

She glanced at the family down the hall. The girl turned away from the cluster of adults. She poked listlessly at a poster on the wall.

Suddenly, an hour seemed like an eternity to Brooke. She wanted, very badly, to see the man who made her smile against her will with his corny lines. She wanted to be with a man who had confidence, who lived life with a bit of swagger. He'd buy her a drink, she'd soak up his casual charisma and life would be no big deal, nothing to worry about.

"No, I can't start a new patient now." Brooke dashed her signature hastily on the bottom of the death certificate and slapped it, facedown, in the nurse's in-box.

"Are you okay, Dr. Brown?" Loretta was watching her with concern.

"I'm fine. It's been a long shift, so I'm determined to leave on time for once."

The grieving family was breaking up, a few going

back into the waiting room, most of them, including the girl, leaving through the door to the parking lot.

Loretta looked in the same direction Brooke was looking. "That was a nice family, wasn't it? Listen, I saw Dr. Gregory come in, and MacDowell's here. You can go on and leave a little early. I'll let them know." Loretta patted her shoulder, a maternal move that surprised Brooke into taking a step back.

"Yes, I'll see you next time." She walked quickly toward the kitchen, unbuttoning her white coat as she went. She stuffed it into the next laundry bin she passed, grabbed her purse from the locker and headed for the physicians' parking lot at the same pace she usually reserved for heading to the crash room.

She wanted to see Zach. Zach had held Harold Allman's hand and kept the pain from overwhelming him. She wanted, more than anything, for Zach to hold her hand, too.

Chapter 6

Zach sat on the tailgate of his pickup truck, killing time in the parking lot of an upscale apartment complex. In the last hour before sunset on a warm Texas day, it was good to have nothing to do but watch residents pull into their slots, lock up their cars and head for their apartment doors. It was all so ordinary.

Zach needed ordinary. Ambulance work was never his favorite, but a friend had asked a favor. An ambulance shift meant every person he saw was sick and in pain. Patients were scared and worried, and so were the friends or family members who'd called for the ambulance. Family members who rode along with the patient were as anxious and alarmed as the patients themselves.

It made for a long day. He'd take twenty-four hours with Engine Thirty-Seven over seven hours in an ambulance any day, but Zach, like most paramedics, picked up extra shifts to earn a little more money. Some days, the money wasn't worth it.

The adult daughter of his last patient had ridden in the back with him, and her anxious face stuck in Zach's mind more tenaciously than the rest. The transport had been very long. Despite running with lights and sirens, it had taken over half an hour to reach downtown Austin from the country ranch, and the woman's gaze had darted between Zach and her father's gurney the entire time.

The sorrow on her face haunted him. She'd known, as he'd known, that nothing he did would save her father. He'd done it all, anyway, fifty miles of work with her sorrowful eyes upon him.

An apartment door opened. An old lady stepped out, her white hair neat and tidy, and she poured a glass of water on a potted plant by her door. Then she went inside. She'd been in no distress at all. She'd looked bored. Zach could have kissed her.

He checked his watch. He still had thirty minutes, at least, to detox before his date with Brooke. He needed it. She was cool, calm and collected, no matter how chaotic the ER became. He needed to play it cool, too. He hopped off his tailgate and slammed it shut. His arm and chest muscles, tired from performing hopeless CPR, immediately protested the forceful motion.

Slow down. Keep it light.

He wasn't here for any kind of emotional entanglement. He didn't need Brooke's cool levelheadedness to help him get over a bad shift. He was just here for a drink with a woman who reminded him of a sexy librarian. Nothing more.

A sedate sedan pulled into the spot next to his, and two couples got out. As the ladies passed him, they smiled.

The men looked at him with suspicion. All four of them, like every single person he'd seen in the past half hour, were senior citizens.

This couldn't be the right address. Brooklyn Brown, young and vital with legs that could slay a man, couldn't possibly live in a retirement community.

A gray-haired man wearing a veteran's ball cap passed Zach's truck on his way to toss a trash bag in the complex's Dumpster. On his return trip, he stared Zach down as he stalked closer and closer. If Zach were in his firefighter uniform, the man would probably salute. Zach had long noticed that old men liked seeing young men in uniform; maybe he reminded them of themselves in younger years. But since Zach was not in uniform, he could practically see the man wondering if he was a troublemaker of some kind. A hooligan.

Zach crossed his arms over his chest to stretch his sore triceps and looked up to the second floor and the door that was supposedly Brooke's. Maybe he should find the mailboxes and see if the name Brown was on the one that matched this number.

"You lost, son?" the ball-cap man asked aggressively. Once a warrior, always a warrior, at least in attitude.

Zach tried to disarm the man with friendliness. "Nope. Just waitin' on a woman." He uncrossed his arms so his stance looked less aggressive, but the move cost him.

By morning, he'd be feeling every last chest compression he'd performed today. Instead of going out tonight, he ought to be soaking in a tub of ice water like he had back when he ran two-a-day football practices.

The old man grunted something that sounded like agreement. "Women. Never on time."

"This one's not late. I'm early." Zach pointed in the

direction of her second-story door. "I'd hate to be waiting at the wrong address. Do you know if Dr. Brooke Brown lives here?"

He dropped his aching arm before he finished his question. Maybe instead of going out, he could soak in Brooke's tub. With Brooke.

And...that idea was wrong to entertain. It would only lead to frustrated pain in other parts of his body. This was their first date, and he half expected her to cancel on him. For the past four years, he'd had a never-on-the-first-date policy. Jumping into bed—and into love—with a certain blonde angel named Charisse had cured him of that impulse. Never again.

You've known Brooke for the better part of a year. She's not keeping any secrets from you.

And...that was the wrong way to let his thoughts travel, too. This was just a drink. Nothing more.

"A doctor, huh? That pretty young thing in 89E?"

Zach wouldn't have described Brooke as a pretty young thing—an elegant, professional woman was more appropriate—but her neighbor was looking at her through a lens several decades older than his. This was the right address.

"Yes, sir," Zach said. "She's a doctor. If she's late, she'll have a good reason."

"I don't know about that." The old man wasn't going to concede that any woman might have a good reason for being late. "Don't let me catch you here mooning about under her window once it gets dark, you hear?"

"I hear." Zach was close to thirty, so being given orders like he was still a teenager was kind of amusing. He crossed his arms over his chest again, welcoming the stretch in his muscles, and leaned against the back of his truck.

As the old man headed up the concrete sidewalk, a red sports car pulled into a parking space, looking as out of place among the town cars and four-door sedans as Brooklyn Brown herself must look among her neighbors. The red car was an old model, and Zach had the fleeting thought that it must be true that young doctors were drowning in med school student loans if Brooke had to drive a car that many years old.

Older model or not, it was a sports car. That was the important part. His sexy librarian couldn't help but be sexy, even with her hair always pulled back and her clothes always buttoned up.

Sexy was good. Sexy raised no red flags.

He enjoyed the view as the red door opened and a pair of very feminine legs swung out of the car. Zach savored the sight of those legs before checking out the rest of Brooke, for Brooke it had to be. He took in the tight gray skirt, its businesslike material snug over the curve of her hips, then the pastel buttoned-down shirt that stretched tightly across her chest as she slung her purse strap onto her shoulder, and then the best part of the view, red lips and dark eyes in a beautiful face.

Her face—

All his leisurely thoughts stopped cold, swamped by concern. Something was wrong. That was the expression of a woman in distress. He'd never seen it on Dr. Brown.

Zach had already taken a step toward her when she looked up and spotted him. Her expression altered instantly, from misery to…relief? Surprise? She couldn't be that surprised to see him here. They had a date.

"Oh, you're here," she said. "I'm so glad you're here."

She headed toward him in a way that made him think, for a moment, she was going to throw herself into his arms, but she stopped just inches away. They stood there, a bit too close, awkward.

Not touching. For eight months, they'd never touched. Until he'd steadied her hand as he poured her coffee three days ago, he'd never felt her skin.

For the past three days, he'd thought of little else.

"I'm early. Brooke, are you okay?"

She nodded, but she seemed to be very intent on placing her car keys in a particular pocket of her purse.

It wasn't her concentration on her purse as much as it was that ever-present, invisible barrier that stopped him from reaching for her, although God knew she looked like a woman who could use a hug. He told himself that was okay. They were Dr. Brown and Mr. Bishop, not exactly hugging buddies.

Still, he ducked down a few inches to take another look at her face. "Bad shift, huh?"

"I'll be fine. It was… It just made me think about…" She looked in the direction of her door, avoiding eye contact with him. "It reminded me of things I'd rather not think about. I'll get changed and we'll go. I could use that drink."

She half smiled at nothing in particular, and Zach told himself to follow her cue. He should smile, too. Walk her to her door. Change the subject, give her space and time to recover, let her soak in her virtual tub of ice, if that was what she needed before they went out for that drink.

But she didn't take a step. Something had happened since he'd left her this morning, something serious enough to discompose the unflappable Dr. Brown.

"The ninety-six-year-old," he said quietly. "You were

the receiving physician, weren't you? Aw, Brooke, I'm sorry."

She stared straight at him then, stunned. "How did you know? You didn't bring him in. Were you—?" She shook her head before she finished her thought. "The radio. You must've heard it over the radio."

"I was there. That was the shift I covered. I stayed in the ambulance."

"You were outside? Oh, I wish you'd come in."

The pleading note in her voice matched the look in her eyes. He felt a tug in his chest that was far deeper than a layer of aching muscle.

He shouldn't do this. He shouldn't ask this. He shouldn't get involved with this woman.

"Why?" he asked, reckless.

Her expressive eyes became more shuttered. "You're a very good medic. I like working with you."

"Right." She'd said as much three days ago, when he'd asked her out. His skills as a paramedic weren't why they were here. He played along, wanting her to talk. "So, did the other two paramedics screw up or something?"

"No, they were fine."

She went back to fidgeting with her purse, brows knit in concentration.

"It was just that the case made me sad," she said, "and you make me smile."

He hadn't seen that coming. At all.

She dashed her cheek against her sleeve although Zach hadn't seen a tear. She pretended to laugh it off; he knew her well enough to know she was pretending.

Red flag.

"Sorry," she said, wiping her dry cheek. "See? I could

have used some of your humor, such as it is. A corny line to take my mind off…things."

He was so tempted to put his arms around her that he forgot to laugh politely along with her. At his silence, Brooke hitched the strap of her purse higher on her shoulder and took the first step toward her building.

She pivoted back suddenly. "Ninety-six years old! Why did that family put themselves through it? Why did they put my staff through it? He'd died peacefully in his sleep. Did they really need me to verify that?"

Zach remembered the daughter's face as he'd pushed and pushed and pushed, compressing a heart that was finished beating, forever. "Maybe they were hoping for a miracle."

Brooke made that little sound of disbelief, the same one she'd made this morning when she'd scoffed at the idea that he'd spend the night with no one if he couldn't spend it with her.

"A miracle. After forty minutes of CPR? I can't even think where to start with that one." She reached up and yanked her ponytail holder out of her hair. The cascade of dark brown hair in the light of the setting sun had a beauty that hit Zach square in the chest.

Her hair was a little longer than he'd imagined, a little straighter. The light picked out metallic glints in the rich darkness. She shoved her hand through her hair and shook it loose.

His mouth felt dry. His body went hard. Muscles that had ached a moment before were suddenly charged. There was nothing light about it, nothing pleasant and civilized.

Hadn't he always known that Brooklyn Brown would be dangerous?

"I don't mean to dismiss miracles," she said in a more subdued tone.

Maybe she thought his silence was disapproval. He forced himself to speak. "You're just saying what everyone was thinking. Go ahead, blow off some steam."

Too late. She was already back in control, standing calmly, but the evening breeze still toyed with her hair.

"Spontaneous, unexpected recoveries do occur, but they're so rare." She still sounded like that schoolteacher-librarian despite the unrestrained hair. "That's why everyone talks about them, because they are once-in-a-lifetime occurrences. They become legend in a hospital, you know?"

"I know." His voice sounded gruff to his own ears.

"That doesn't mean I wouldn't like to see one." Once more, she ducked her chin a bit, but this time she looked up at him through her lashes and smiled almost shyly. "Although honestly, if his heart had suddenly started beating, it probably would've scared me to death."

Zach came closer. Denim brushed pinstripes as he picked up a handful of her hair and let it slide over his palm. "I don't think you scare easily."

For a long moment, she held his gaze as the last rays of the sun glowed warmly. "I was trying to make a joke."

Of course she'd been trying to make a joke. They had a routine, and this intense need wasn't part of it. He was screwing it all up.

He didn't care. He buried both hands in her hair and smoothed his thumbs over her cheekbones to the outer corners of her eyes, where he'd never seen a teardrop although she'd apologized for crying.

"I'm not much of a comedian," she whispered. "I'll let you be the funny one in this relationship."

Relationship. Was that what this was, built slowly over the course of year, one sentence at a time?

"I'm sorry I wasn't there to make you smile today," he said, "but now, I'm all yours."

She closed her eyes against the brilliance of the last ray of the setting sun, and Zach closed his mouth over hers in the kiss that ended what they'd known, and started something new.

Chapter 7

It was the most perfect kiss a man had ever given her, soft and gentle, a long, still moment of connection. Brooke felt the tender emotion behind it as surely as she felt the sunlight on her skin. As kisses went, it was pure and heartfelt.

Chaste.

And all she could think about was sex.

Zach. All she could think about was *Zach.*

She'd never wanted to take a man to bed the way she wanted Zach right now.

She wanted oblivion. She was so tired of death, tired of fighting it, tired of accepting it, sick to death of the way death shaped her life. Zach was alive and exciting. He was every peak she so carefully avoided in her quest to never hit rock bottom. She wanted him.

He was holding her face in his hands, so she placed

her hands on top of his wrists, tentatively at first. After so diligently keeping a professional distance, it was hard to give herself permission to touch him. Gaining confidence, she wrapped her fingers around his wrists, feeling the coarse, masculine hair that dusted his forearms. Her right hand grazed the watch he wore, a sport model typical of emergency personnel who needed the second hand for taking a pulse—when the patient had a pulse.

God, no. She didn't want to think about that. She didn't want to think at all.

He ended the slow kiss with a shorter one and rested his forehead against hers. "Let's skip the drink."

"Okay."

Hallelujah—but that was followed almost immediately by a little shiver of nerves. Cold feet. Impatient with herself, she pushed the feeling aside. She could do this. Why not? *Why not?*

Zach gently let go of her face. As he lowered his arms, she realized she was still clinging to his wrists, holding on as hard as Harold or the woman in labor or anyone else who needed him. She was being desperate, when she wanted to be sexy. She let go of Zach and held on to the leather strap of her purse with both hands instead.

"Dinner would be better than drinks," he said.

Oh. He hadn't been thinking what she'd been thinking. She kept moving forward despite her blunder. "Sure. That sounds good."

Zach was interested in her, without a doubt, but that didn't mean he wanted to skip every single getting-to-know-you phase to take her to bed. She ought to appreciate that a whole lot more than she did at the moment.

"Let me take you somewhere low-key," he said. "We're both wiped out."

No, I'm not wiped out. Do I look wiped out?

After twelve hours, she probably did. She didn't feel tired, though. The clean scent of his skin stimulated all her senses. She wanted to wash off her twelve-hour day and be fresh and new, too.

"Do you mind if I jump in the shower first?" she asked. "I won't be long. I'm not going to soak in the tub or anything."

He'd been looking at her very intently since she'd first spotted him, but now something she'd said had that cocky grin returning, slowly but surely, starting at one corner of his mouth. Showers? Soaking in tubs?

She cleared her throat. "I guess this is where I say, 'Why don't you come up to my place?'"

He winced in an exaggerated way. "That's one of the oldest lines in the book. It's listed right after 'Can I buy you a drink?'"

"I think it's the line that 'Can I buy you a drink' is supposed to lead to. We're doing this all out of order."

As she turned to lead the way to her apartment, Zach kept pace with her easily. "We'll figure it out."

He slid his fingers between hers, and held her hand.

Brooke was glad that Zach thought they'd figure out what they were doing, because as she stood in her bedroom, freshly showered and completely nude, she had no idea.

Were they going out to dinner as a prelude to sex? Because all the way up the stairs, he'd held her hand as if they were a couple, familiar with one another and already intimate. But then he'd stood in the middle of her living room instead of making himself at home, and she'd scurried around to find the television remote and offer him a drink—sparkling water, which was all she had. He'd declined. After a moment of silence, she'd said, "Well, um, the bedroom's through there so that's where I'll be, but only for a minute, I'll be out again."

So stupid. Of course she'd be out again. She'd sounded as if she was warning him not to come in looking for her—or else she'd sounded as if she was letting him know where she was in case he *did* want to come looking for her. She didn't know which way she'd meant it, which meant she didn't know which way he'd taken it, which meant she didn't know which underwear to put on, damn it, because she didn't know who would be taking it back off.

If she wore anything lacy, it would seem as if she'd planned it. But she didn't want to wear the plain stuff she wore to work, because she wanted to look her best for her first time with Zach. She could just imagine the two of them reminiscing in the distant future. *Remember our first time together, and you were wearing that ugly beige underwear...?*

Unbelievable. She was not only thinking about having sex with Zach, but she was thinking of it as the start of a long-term relationship.

The man had only invited her out for a drink. She snatched a bra and a pair of underpants out of her drawer and put them on. They weren't lacy, but they were black, and they matched. After all, those drinks had been upgraded to dinner.

Only because he's wiped out.

He didn't look it, although she'd noticed him shaking out his arm a little, while she'd unlocked her front door. Maybe he'd hit the gym between his shift and coming to pick her up. Her mind rejected that quickly as impossible.

He'd had no time for both a workout and a shower after his shift, and he'd definitely taken a shower after his co-workers had brought in the ninety-six-year-old.

Why had he waited outside the hospital when he'd been part of that ambulance team? Pieces of a puzzle she hadn't known she was trying to solve fell into place, and she realized, finally, why he was tired.

Why didn't he tell me?

She grabbed the dress she'd laid out, the only one she owned that just reached to mid-thigh, making it too short to be appropriate for work. It was sleeveless and snug, and she tugged it into place as she stepped into a rarely-worn pair of metallic sandals.

Zach was on the couch, but he stood immediately when she walked up to him.

"You look great, Brooklyn."

"You weren't driving the ambulance, were you?"

"What?"

"If anyone stays outside with the ambulance, it's the driver. When you said you didn't come in, that's what I assumed, but the paramedic who was doing the compressions was barely winded. She hadn't been working at it long. The other guy's shirt was so crisp and new, he must've just come on shift."

Zach smiled at her. "That's some attention to detail. This is like dating Sherlock Holmes. Is this what you were thinking about while you were in the shower?"

"I was wondering why you didn't come into the ER. You knew I was there. Why not come in like you usually do? You didn't come in because you'd just finished forty minutes of chest compressions. You were probably too tired to walk."

He shut off the television and tossed the remote control onto the couch. "Someone had to do it."

"You did all forty minutes yourself, didn't you? Why didn't you trade off?" She knew she sounded like a stern instructor, chastising a student for failing to follow a recommended procedure.

"There's not a lot of room in the back of an ambulance, you know." His tone of voice was mild, as if he spoke about a simple inconvenience. "It was just me, the patient and a family member. I had no choice."

She felt almost angry with him for taking on such a monumental task. "You must have known he was gone before you even started. You're acting like it's no big deal when it must have been exhausting. Why would you put yourself through such an ordeal?"

"I can't call it, Brooke. I can't legally decide to quit working on a patient. Only you can."

She fell silent. Whatever words of frustration she'd been about to say died on her tongue as she looked in his eyes.

"I'm a paramedic. You're a doctor. There's a big legal difference." The last of his smile faded away, and she was unable to look away from his serious gaze. "There are things you want to do, and there are things you have to do. Today, I had to do what I didn't want to do. It happens."

Her hot feeling of anger left, and in its place, something close to sorrow threatened to move in. Her throat felt thick with unexpressed emotions.

That, she could handle. She could swallow down sorrow and suppress any emotion in order to keep functioning, but she was caught off guard by the tears that welled up in her eyes. She hadn't shed tears for anyone in a very long time. They only interfered with her vision, and her vision was necessary to her job. Even today, she hadn't felt close to tears as she'd watched the girl who'd reminded her of herself at the tender age of twelve.

Instead of crying, I ran to see Zach.

"Hey, it's okay." Zach brushed her hair off her shoulder. "You had to do things you didn't want to do, too."

She dismissed his concern with a halfhearted wave of her hand. "Not much. I just had to notify the next of kin, but you—"

"Just notify the next of kin," he murmured.

"But you…forty minutes. Did it hurt?"

"It was a workout." He shrugged, but she saw that the motion wasn't totally easy.

"I can't imagine."

She could imagine it, actually. She'd done CPR on mannequins many times, and once on a human being. She'd had to throw most of her body weight into each compression for them to be effective. She eyed Zach's arms and chest. He was much stronger than she, but it couldn't have been easy, not even for a firefighter.

"Have you taken any ibuprofen yet? You should take something now to prevent delayed-onset muscle soreness."

He laughed a little and rubbed one arm. "It's not that delayed."

"You're in pain? Where exactly does it hurt?" She stood more squarely in front of him, her mind kicking into physician mode, assessing the symmetry of his body, looking to see if he was favoring an injured part.

As a doctor, she touched people all day, and touching Zach suddenly became clinical, and therefore easy. With a hand on each of his arms, she pressed his triceps and then pushed down on his shoulders, testing for muscle tone and resistance in the deltoids, watching for signs of sensitivity.

Other muscles would have been involved in the motion of performing chest compressions—trapezius across his back, pectorals in the front. But as her hands slid from his shoulders to the solid wall of his chest, she realized Zach was laughing at her.

"Brooke, stop. I'm fine." He very effectively stopped her by putting his arms around her and pulling her close. Her hands were trapped with her palms pressed against his chest. When he spoke, she could feel the bass of that cowboy voice vibrate through her hands as his breath stirred her hair. "I'm a big, tough guy who has survived worse workouts than that. I'll be a little sore tomorrow. I'll survive. It's just exercise."

"I'm sorry you had to do it. I'm ashamed of myself for expecting you to make me laugh tonight."

"Then I have to say I'm sorry, too. I wanted you to be all cool and calculating tonight. If you acted like the whole thing had been just another day at the office, then I could convince myself that was true."

The heat of his body came through his shirt to warm her palms. She felt that tender, achy need to cry again.

She needed to toughen up. She started by taking a step backward. He let her go.

"Just exercise," she said, with a bit of a scoff in her voice.

"Just notifying the next of kin," he said, imitating her tone as he stepped forward, a slow pursuit as she retreated.

Her smile felt shaky. "This is probably a really bad idea, the two of us dating. We won't have any balance when we've both had to deal with failure at work."

"Or maybe this is why we should be dating."

She took another step backward. The wall behind her gave her the backbone she seemed to be lacking. She tucked her hands behind herself.

Zach stepped closer. Had it only been this morning that he'd stood too close like this and told her to say yes?

In a moment of illumination, Brooke realized she'd been wanting to say yes for far longer than a day.

Zach's voice was huskier when he spoke quietly. "Maybe it takes someone in emergency medicine to understand exactly what we mean when we say it's been a hard day. Seeing how easily things can go bad makes you want to seize the chance for something good. Something like this."

He kissed her, a little harder than before, a little hungrier. It only lasted a moment, one sublime meeting of mouths before he lifted his head, restraint in every line of his face.

He had more restraint than she felt. She pressed her fingertips into the wall at her back when she wanted to be pressing them into the solid muscle of his body. "I understand that. It makes you want to...live life."

His blue-green gaze dropped to her mouth. She cataloged the signs of arousal. Shallow breathing, muscle tension—all his. He wanted her.

"Is that what you were thinking about while I was in the shower? That we should go out to dinner, because we both want to live life?"

"Brooklyn." He sounded stern, almost forceful. The sound of her name spoken that way was thrilling. "I knew you were naked, right on the other side of this wall. I could hear the water pouring down your body. What do you think I was thinking about?"

"Life?" she whispered, her gaze on his mouth. "Me?"

All his restraint broke, and she was swept against him by strong arms, lifted to her toes by the strongest man she'd ever been with. His physical greed for her drove further thoughts from her head. She'd never been kissed so deeply, so decisively, as if she was a prize to be claimed. The sound she made was primal, a gasp of capitulation, an exclamation that meant yes.

Zach clutched her even more tightly and then abruptly let her go. She let herself fall back against the wall for support as he leaned over her, eyes closed, breathing hard. He cursed on an exhale. "It's okay. I'm no threat to you. We're going out. We're going to get to know one another better. Over dinner."

But his words barely registered over the cacophony of her body clamoring for his. Pheromones, hormones, whatever it was that made bodies communicate, they had it. Their bodies had found their perfect mates without word or conscious thought. She wanted to feel him move inside her. She wanted to feel his power as he worked for his pleasure.

He was trying to cool things off. Slow things down. "Zach."

He opened his eyes and she waited for the second it took him to focus on her.

"Do you want to know what I was thinking while I was in the shower? I was taking bets with myself whether or not we'd really make it to dinner before we did this." She hooked her fingers into his belt loops and gave them a quick yank, rocking his hips into her.

His body gave in. As if her words had cut some wire that was holding his frame taut, he fell against her, pressing her into the wall. She thought he'd dive into her mouth immediately, but first he cupped the side of her neck in his warm palm. She felt the fine tremor in his hand.

He spoke against her lips. "Be sure. It's only our first date. We can wait."

"I've been waiting half a year for this." Burying both hands in his hair, she pushed away from the wall, pressing her soft chest against his hard one. He bent to scoop an arm behind her knees, and she was lifted off her feet, being carried into her own bedroom as she toed off the ankle strap of first one sandal, then the other. She landed on the bed with a bounce that was probably a little less gentle than he'd intended. He was clearly on edge and fighting to keep his control.

She'd wanted oblivion, but the lights were on, and she was on top of the bedding. There were no sheets to hide under, just Zach above her, pulling off his shirt, shucking off his jeans. Zach pressing her into the mattress with his bare body while she was still dressed. This was no mindless escape. She was acutely aware of him, of who he was and what they were about to do.

Her eyes fluttered shut because she could only feel, feel, feel his body against hers. Her whole world narrowed to the sensation of his bare skin and his heavy weight. She wrapped her arms around his shoulders and drove her fingers into his hair, needing to hold on to him.

He shoved one side of her short dress above her hips and grabbed the edge of her black underwear, jerking it midway down to her thighs and then to her knees. She bent her leg, wriggled one foot free of the elastic and then kicked them off.

There was a rip of foil, a shifting of position, and then Zach was saying her name again. "Brooklyn, Brooklyn, look at me."

She opened her eyes, and he pushed inside her without wasting the time to further undress her. She watched his face as the exquisite first slide of their bodies overcame him, forcing him to close his eyes against the pleasure so great it was nearly pain.

He set the pace, stroking into her with purpose, keeping their rhythm as he lifted himself onto one arm. He studied her face with each stroke, and she was helpless to hide her reactions as he changed the nuances of angle and depth until that primal groan escaped from her again.

He grabbed her dress and bra strap, both, and pulled them off one shoulder to expose her breast. With another groan and another stroke, he bent his head and kissed her there, openmouthed, wet and warm.

It was too much. It wasn't enough. She moved under him, needing more Zach. Everything was Zach, everything she could taste and see and touch. She wanted him so badly, so mindlessly, that she didn't know who reached their peak first, only that there was an unbearable moment of blinding white pleasure, and then she was slowly returning to herself. Her bedroom. She was on her bed, and her arms were around Zach Bishop.

He was catching his breath, his face buried in that space between her neck and shoulder, his body heavy on hers after their release.

She found some small reserve of energy, just enough to lift her hand and lay it on the nape of his neck. She stroked his hair with her fingertips, a bit dazed.

She'd been reckless, giving herself wholly to the man who'd needed her. She'd stayed in the moment, alive and aware. Knowing he was taking pleasure in her had driven her as much as the sensations of her own body.

"I've never had sex like that before," she whispered.

Zach lifted his head and smiled down at her with sleepy-lidded eyes. "No one's ever had sex like that. That was ours. It could only happen between us."

He settled onto the pillow next to her, tucking her into his side, giving her a feeling of security and rightness that was at once familiar and new.

She kissed his cheek as they lay entwined, and felt happy.

"If I had a nickel every time I felt this good," she whispered into his ear, "I'd have five cents."

Chapter 8

It took Zach two weeks to realize he was in trouble.

The two weeks since he'd asked Brooke out for a drink that actually had yet to happen had been, simply put, bliss. That first night, after they'd finally ditched her dress, they'd ordered pizza in and gotten to know one another. Thoroughly.

He still got a grin on his face when he thought about it.

The next morning, he'd started a twenty-four-hour shift, but when it ended, he'd grabbed the go bag most emergency responders kept packed with clothes and a spare shaving kit, and he'd headed back to her place. They both had two consecutive days off. For forty-eight hours, it had been as if they'd just invented sex, and they had to try it in every possible position to see which ones they liked the most. Over, under, standing. In a chair, in the shower, in the car—because he'd insisted they go out to dinner like decent folk the second night—until he was simply drunk on the pleasure of her body. For two weeks, the sex had been fulfilling.

That hadn't worried him. That was no trouble at all.

It was the in-between times he should have been afraid of. The text messages when one or both were working should have raised a red flag. The way she warmed the arch of her bare foot on his leg while they shared the couch was too cozy, too easy, as he watched baseball and she read medical journals. The way she'd lost it and dissolved into giggles at the nurses' station when he'd stopped to whisper a line in her ear had made him too damned happy.

He knew now that she was ticklish behind her ear, and since they were lovers, he'd gotten much, much closer to deliver his line that day. He'd practically nibbled on her ear—*Hello, angel. What time are they expecting you back in Heaven?*—and she'd ducked to get away from the tickle. She'd stifled her giggle almost instantly, but her blush had charmed him for long minutes. Later, she'd made him solemnly promise never to do that again.

He hadn't done it again. He had too much respect for her position at the hospital. The gossip mill had already done its job, and he didn't need to demonstrate that they were an item. The nurses flirted with him less outrageously, and no other men asked Brooke out—except that idiot doctor with the ballet tickets, who'd needed a confrontation to get the point.

Toward the end of their first week together, Brooke had laughingly complained during a phone call that she'd spent the better part of her morning dodging the persistent Dr. Bamber. Something in her voice made Zach suspect it wasn't actually funny to her, so he'd stopped by a deli and brought lunch to the ER's kitchen. Bamber had walked in to find Zach, not Brooke.

Without preamble, Zach had laid the cards on the table. "If Dr. Brown wants to go to the ballet, I'll take her."

"You?" Dr. Bamber had sneered. "What do you know about the ballet?"

"Not much, except Brooke likes it, and I like Brooke."

The doctor had put up more of a front than Zach had expected. "And you think that makes you the right man for her? Can you even name a ballet, or is *The Nutcracker* your idea of high art?"

"*The Nutcracker?* It opens with a Christmas party, right?"

Bamber managed to nod, one distinct downward motion of the nose he'd stuck in the air.

Zach laid on the Texas drawl. "The first half of *The Nutcracker* is boring as hell, but the second act is like some kind of a classical music greatest hits album. I'll give her something better to do for the first half, and we'll show up at intermission to enjoy the rest of the show. Got it?"

"If you're still around in December."

"I'll be around."

Bamber had left the room and Brooke had entered a minute later. She'd enjoyed the sandwich he'd brought her—her favorite was pastrami on rye, as if she'd been raised in Brooklyn and not just named after it—and he'd enjoyed the silent satisfaction of knowing Bamber would stay in his radiology office in the basement from now on.

That instinct to claim her should have scared him. That assertion that he'd still be seeing her in December should have warned him.

But after two weeks of moments like those, it was a

simple ride in Engine Thirty-Seven that had opened his eyes to just how much trouble he was in.

He was working a half shift, just twelve hours overnight, providing extra fire coverage for the city of Austin on a Saturday night, when the good citizens seemed the most prone to light fireworks or wreck their cars. It was a good shift, rarely boring, and he and Chief and Murphy were joined by a Texas Rescue volunteer, Luke Waterson, who'd been on Zach's football team in high school. Zach knew that when the shift was over, he'd find Brooke at his house, in his bed on Sunday morning, so that made the shift as perfect as work could be.

He'd been thinking of Brooke when Engine Thirty-Seven had rolled past a church on its way back to the station after fueling up. He wished he could blame it on that. In the late sun of on early Saturday evening, a bride and groom had stood on the church steps, smiling for a photographer and dozens of their friends and families.

Brooke will look beautiful in a wedding gown.

Red flag. Finally, he'd seen the red flag. But it was a fact: Brooke would look beautiful in a wedding gown. Any man would think so if he saw her.

Any man.

The idea of Brooke wearing a white gown for any man other than him had caused a red-hot pain in his heart, and Zach had finally realized, after two weeks, he was in trouble.

He was falling in love with Brooke Brown, imagining forever in a white wedding gown. He'd done that once before, on a tropical island with a blonde angel. Charisse Johnson, with a beautiful soul as well as a beautiful face, had held his heart in her two perfect hands for one perfect week. Love at first sight had been followed by seven days and nights of bliss, until he'd learned the "beautiful soul" part was utter bull.

Zachary Taylor Bishop, I would marry you on a beach. My gown would be simple, almost like a nightgown, blowing in the ocean breeze. I'd be barefoot and wear flowers in my hair, if I married you.

There's no if, Charisse. We're getting married, I promise you. You're going to be the most beautiful bride I ever saw.

She had been a beautiful bride, too. One week later, Charisse Johnson had gotten married in a church, with shoes on her delicate feet and a goddamned diamond tiara in her golden hair.

She hadn't been marrying him.

Zach had spent that same week frantically tracking her down, desperate to know what had made his angel slip out of his bed and sneak off the island without any explanation. He'd found her in her hometown in Alabama, just in time to stand outside a church and watch her enter on her father's arm.

Never again.

Then, if not you, some other man will marry Brooklyn Brown.

Despite the pain that fact caused in the vicinity of Zach's heart, he couldn't be in love with Brooke. It had only been two weeks, and he couldn't possibly be stupid enough to fall so hard, so fast. Not twice in his life. Not after learning his lesson the worst way possible.

Therefore, it wasn't love. He could control what he felt for Brooke. Contain it. That's what firemen did. Like any other nuisance fire, he'd just keep a watchful eye on it, and let it burn itself out.

Brooke was not sleeping in his bed when Zach pulled into his drive. She was sitting on the wooden steps of his porch, clutching a cup of coffee. Although she'd changed into jeans, her hair was still pulled back tightly from her shift. If his heart sped up a tick at the sight of her, he told himself it was simply because she was a beautiful woman.

Zach got out of his truck, tossed the keys on the front seat and shut the door. He lived just a short distance from Austin's city limits, but one didn't have to go far to be in the country. At this rural address, he didn't worry about his truck getting stolen from his own drive. His house was really more of a bachelor's hunting and fishing cabin on a few acres of undeveloped land, but Brooke seemed to like it. They spent as much time here as they did at her place.

He stopped at the bottom step. Judging by the look on her face, Brooke didn't like anything right about now.

"Bad shift, huh?"

She didn't answer him. Her gaze didn't waver from some distant point. He noticed her feet were bare, although there was still a definite chill in the air in the April morning.

"How bad, Brooke? Talk to me."

"It wasn't your engine, then, that cut them out of the car?"

He shook his head. Any shift that he didn't have to operate the Jaws of Life tool was a good shift. She obviously hadn't been so lucky.

He'd spent the past twelve hours telling himself he wasn't in love with her, but now, seeing her so shell-shocked, he sure felt something. He wanted to comfort her.

I'll keep a watch on it. It won't burn out of control.

"Why don't we go in?" he suggested. "It's almost chilly enough to start a fire. Would you like me to?"

"It was a child."

He winced at her words. "That's hard. I'm sorry." He climbed a few steps to sit beside her and put his arm around her shoulders. The coffee mug she held was empty. Her hands had to be cold. Her hands, her feet, the expression on her face.

She must have been the one to tell the next of kin. Something about notifying the family of the ninety-six-year-old man had gotten to her two weeks ago; to have to do the same for a child's family must be a hundred times worse.

There wasn't a thing he could do about it.

"I'm sorry you lost a patient, sweetheart."

"I didn't lose. I won."

"You did?"

"You bet I did." She gripped the handle of the mug with one hand and began slamming it into the palm of her other hand rhythmically. "I stopped that bleeding. I restored that airway. I stabilized her, and I got her up to the OR in record time. She made it. I won."

The rock that had settled in his chest crumbled away. "That's fantastic. You should be—"

"I just—I just—I *hate* kids! You know that pediatric specialty hospital? I wish they'd take every last child there. If there were some kind of adults-only ER, I'd work there in a heartbeat." She stopped pummeling her palm with the coffee cup, but she didn't seem to know what to do with it, as if she'd suddenly become aware it was in her hand and had no place to set it down.

"Throw the mug. I don't care."

"I hate kids." She plunked the cup on the step to punctuate her sentence.

Zach moved up one more step to sit above her. He pulled out the elastic band in her hair, dropped it into the coffee cup and started combing his fingers through her hair, the way she'd done herself, standing in front of her apartment building when she'd been stressed out by the ninety-six-year-old patient. It didn't seem to have any effect on her rigid bearing, but he kept at it.

"The patient was five," she said. "Car accident. My sister Chelsea was four when she got hit by a car."

He let all the hair in his hands slip through his fingers. "I didn't know you had a sister."

"I don't. She didn't win."

He wrapped his arms around her stiff figure and pulled her back to his chest. She didn't soften or lean against him. He kissed the top of her head and her temple, but not her ticklish ear.

"I didn't know." He said it like an apology. It was one. He'd been feasting on her body and relishing her company for two solid weeks, and he should have known she had this terrible scar.

"It's not the kind of thing that you tell people." She reached for the coffee cup instead of him. "Hi, I'm Brooke, I'm a doctor, I live in Austin and I have a dead little sister. It just doesn't come up."

He closed his eyes. "That patient must have been hell for you today."

"Not at all. I'm fine in the heat of the moment. I have no problem thinking clearly. I get right to work."

"I'm sure you do. And afterward? Like now?"

"I'm just angry. Not sad." She didn't shake him off, but she didn't relax into him, either. He would have thought she was frozen in place, except her hand was on the coffee cup, rocking it back and forth on the wooden step, turning it in her white-knuckled grip. He let go of her and went back to stroking her hair, gathering it up, using his hand instead of the elastic band to keep it all together.

"Afterward," she said, "I can't stand the thought of what could have gone wrong. So many things could go wrong. Kids are so damned vulnerable. Twice as vulnerable as an adult."

He stopped what he was doing and let her hair fall loose. "Throw the coffee cup, Brooke."

"I don't want to." She sounded as angry as a petulant child.

"Then I will." He picked up the mug, stood, and hurled it at a tree about fifteen yards away. It hit the trunk and broke into a few big shards that rained down to the ground. "There. That's better."

"That was so unnecessary."

He looked down at her, hoping she was no longer staring straight ahead. She wasn't. Instead, her eyes were closed, dry lashes resting on flawless skin. Without the coffee cup, her hands were clasped neatly around her knee, the serene pose of a woman who insisted she was not sad.

Her knuckles were white, betraying the force it required to keep herself together.

"Brooke, darlin'." He bent and grasped her upper arms and pulled her to her feet. He cupped her head in one hand and kissed her brow.

"Why are you being so nice to me when I'm telling you these awful things about myself?" she whispered.

"Because I—"

Because I love you. And damn it, one week or two

weeks or not, it sure as hell felt like love, even though he knew from experience that it couldn't be real.

"Because I'm your friend as well as your lover."

Then he lifted her into his arms and carried her into the house. As the morning sun woke the rest of the world, the two of them needed to sleep after long nights at work. He kept her warm in his bed, wrapped in his arms while he felt her breathing slow as she drifted off, and the powerful feeling in his chest where her cheek rested felt very, very real.

When the nightmare woke her, he put her back to sleep by stroking her hair, *I love you* and *I love you* in each silent caress.

Chapter 9

Brooke had the next day off. The annual Firefighter's Community Day was always held the first Saturday in May. One of the parking lots of West Central Texas Hospital was transformed for the main event. Tents and food vendors lined the edges. In the center, a three-story tower had been constructed from two sets of metal staircases topped by a platform.

Zach was about to run up those stairs. For fun.

Brooke looked around at the array of firefighters in full gear, their baggy pants and bulky overcoats and hard helmets all various shades of beige or black, orange or yellow, depending on their city's chosen color scheme. Zach was in beige, she knew, but she honestly couldn't tell which man in beige was him.

Like athletes before a sporting event, the firefighters were stretching, running in place, or testing out the first flight of stairs. Referees in black-and-white shirts gestured toward the digital timer at the finish line.

Then one man in beige threw back his head and laughed, and she knew that was Zach. He was representing Texas Rescue for this race. She was here to cheer him on.

It was an odd role for her. She was usually required to do something. When did she ever just stand still and clap for someone else? She was inexperienced, frankly, when it came to being this kind of girlfriend. Heaven knew her last boyfriend, dependable David, had never done anything that attracted spectators. It wasn't a criticism; she never did anything that required spectators, either. It had been easy to be a good partner to David. He was a hospital administrator. Her mother had approved of David.

Her mother. Brooke had another support role to play today. She planned to keep pretending to Zach that this wasn't the most dreaded day on the calendar, and then, once Zach had left for his overnight shift at the firehouse, she would visit her mother. Already, her mother was furious with her for spending only dinner with her instead of the entire day.

You know how difficult this day is. How can you expect me to visit her grave by myself?

I don't expect you to, Mom. I'll go with you after dinner. There will be plenty of daylight left.

Her mother had been appalled, disappointed, and in every way furious with Brooke. That was nothing new.

In previous years, Brooke had tried to limit the amount of her involvement in her mother's misery, which meant she'd felt her mother's wrath. In the end, Brooke always caved in. She loved her mother, and she'd loved her sister, too.

But this year, she had something specific to do on the anniversary of her sister's death. It couldn't be postponed. She couldn't reschedule it. Zach's firefighter competition gave her that concrete reason she needed to finally limit the amount of time she spent in maudlin reflection, offering comfort to her mother that would never be accepted.

This one year, just this one year, Brooke wanted to try spending the anniversary of her sister's death in the sunshine with an excited crowd. She wanted to live life. She wanted that life to be normal.

A siren sounded, and Zach and his opponent took off at a run, each throwing a man-size dummy over their shoulders as they raced up the staircases to the top of the tower. Zach took the stairs two at a time despite his heavy uniform and heavier dummy. His strength and speed amazed her, although Brooke had always known he was in great shape. She'd intimately traced the muscles of his legs. She'd admired the bulk and definition of the quadriceps. She'd cupped the powerful gluteus maximi in her hands, feeling the muscle flex as each stroke brought them to that shattering moment of abandon...

No one knows what I'm thinking. I refuse to blush.

She tilted her head back with the rest of the crowd. Zach and his competitor were now perched on the platform, each raising a bundle of fire hose to the top of the tower by hauling in three stories of rope, hand over hand. She remembered the flex of muscles of Zach's bare chest and shoulders as he held himself over her in bed.

She felt the flush on her cheeks. Okay, so all her knowledge of Zach's body was sexual. She hoped Zach's crew would assume she was just warm from the temperature. Although it was early in the day and early in May, the temperature would reach the mid-80s by afternoon.

Zach ran down the tower stairs, a half flight ahead of the other guy because he'd hauled in the fire hose more quickly, but it was close. Brooke glanced from the digital timer at the finish line to Zach and back again. The other man gained a few steps and the crowd cheered louder as the race got closer, but his competitor's late effort wasn't enough. Zach crossed the finish line first.

Brooke let out a single whoop of relief. She clapped while the crowd hooted and hollered. She looked around at all the fist pumps and wolf whistles, and clapped harder. Although Zach was bent over at the waist to catch his breath, he raised his arm to acknowledge the cheers.

He straightened to accept a bottle of water. When he took off his helmet and smiled at the crowd, women whistled. He looked almost unbearably handsome with his hair wet and crazy, his skin shining with a healthy sweat. Brooke's heart did a little flip in her chest, and she was very proud in that moment to be this firefighter's girlfriend.

She wouldn't be his for long, of course. Zach's reputation as a playboy had been earned, and they never talked about their emotions, but for now, Brooke intended to enjoy this bit of normalcy.

When her time with Zach was through, she'd go back to being her mother's only surviving child. For the rest of her life, there would be plenty of time to mourn for the lost possibilities.

Zach won two more rounds.

Brooke watched the races while surrounded by various members of Texas Rescue. Zach's partners from Engine Thirty-Seven, Chief and Murphy, grew more boisterous with every round, but Brooke found herself clasping her hands together in silent anxiety. Her facade of normalcy was slipping.

She couldn't relax, because she couldn't stop thinking like an emergency physician. The more rounds Zach had to complete, the more fatigued his muscles became. Muscle fatigue led to accidents. She didn't like the height of the tower, and she worried that a slip on the metal stairs would make a man fall—would make *Zach* fall—to the asphalt below. Her medically trained brain maintained a catalog of the kinds of injuries that would result.

Murphy and Chief had no such concerns.

"Quarterfinals next," Chief said.

"Hell, yeah." Murphy let go of his girlfriend long enough to high-five Chief. Then Murphy slid his arms around his girlfriend again, hugging her back to his front.

The same way Zach wrapped his arms around me on the porch yesterday morning.

But it wasn't the same.

Murphy was holding his girlfriend simply to get a better look at her cleavage, Brooke was certain. Brooke could hardly avoid getting an eyeful herself. Murphy couldn't have been more than twenty. He wore his firefighter's T-shirt, but his girlfriend was dressed like some kind of Japanese anime character. Her thick bangs and pigtails looked childish, but her black lipstick made her look as if it was Halloween, and her low-cut top showed cleavage worthy of any comic book heroine. It was almost endearing to listen to them whisper their sci-fi sweet nothings to one another as they copped inappropriate touches, which they thought no one else noticed. They were acting their age. They were normal.

When Zach had held her like that, he hadn't been checking out her body. He'd been offering her comfort, which she'd needed after freaking out over a pediatric patient who could have died like her sister had.

Not normal.

Zach won his quarterfinal matchup. Murphy and Chief went crazy, like men watching a touchdown at a football game. In contrast, Brooke immediately checked her watch to calculate how much rest time Zach would get before the semifinals. Of the two reactions, she knew Murphy and Chief's was the normal one.

She excused herself to wait for the semifinals in the friends and family tent that Texas Rescue had set up. Nearly everyone seeking shade was female, so Brooke gave herself a point toward being normal on that score. The other girlfriends had some amazing cleavage on display, just like Murphy's girlfriend. Brooke felt a little prudish in her modest blue tank top and red shorts. As she entered the tent, the cleavage crowd were gathered around a girlfriend who was showing off a diamond ring, looking delighted to be moving on to the other group in the tent: the wives.

The wives were a fairly frazzled lot. The men in the competition were all young, so their wives were young, too, each one juggling one or two small children. Toddlers fussed and tried to escape their strollers. Sippy cups and snack boxes abounded. A diaper was being changed in a corner of the tent, something that made the microbiology major in Brooke shudder, but hand sanitizer was being passed around liberally as well. The wives, she noticed, didn't have time to admire each other's rings.

She didn't envy them, but she could respect them. Brooke had chosen a career that made it nearly impossible to be a good mother. She worked nights, weekends, holidays. No child would be able to depend upon her to bake cupcakes for school or show up for a dance recital. That was perfectly okay. Brooke didn't want to be a mother.

If she never had a child, she would never end up like her own mother.

All of these women, each one who fussed over a child, who retrieved a sock from the dirt or who wiped a messy face, were vulnerable. One slipup, and their child could be harmed. Could even—like her own sister—be killed. And the women would never be the same again, just as Brooke's mother had never been the same.

At this moment, precisely eighteen years later, Mother was waiting for her, waiting to weep over the child who'd never made it to kindergarten.

Brooke shivered, goose bumps running down her spine. She took a bottle of water from one of the Texas Rescue coolers and sat on a metal folding chair in the middle of the bubbly girlfriends and the tired mothers and the fussy children. She lingered a while, because as isolated as she felt, this was still better than sitting alone with her mother on the anniversary of her sister's death.

Mother had wanted her to stay with dependable David. Mother would have loved Tom the radiologist. But why? So that Brooke would get married and have children and be as vulnerable as her mother had been?

No, thank you.

She knew who she was. She had her life mapped out. She was a dedicated physician, a woman who'd chosen career over family. She was lucky to be dating Zach, who understood the demands of her job. Their casual relationship worked for them.

Not so casual, yesterday.

She'd felt so brittle, afraid she'd crack if she talked about her sister after treating the accident patient. Zach hadn't asked for details, but at the touch of his hands in her hair, she'd started talking, anyway. Zach had broken the coffee cup for her. It had fallen apart, but she hadn't. Not really, if she didn't count the tears she'd shed in her dreams.

Sleeping with a woman who had nightmares about a long-deceased sister wasn't the kind of relationship Zach had signed up for, and Brooke wouldn't subject him to it much longer. She'd just get through the rest of this day, survive the ordeal with her mother tonight, and then, starting tomorrow, she'd be herself again.

Brooke finished off her bottle of water and stood, ready to leave. She didn't belong with either group in this tent, but a moment of indecision held her still. She couldn't go back to the spectators and high-five with Murphy and Chief. There was no point in leaving early to see her mother, because she wasn't the daughter whose presence her mother missed.

She didn't belong anywhere.

But Zach understood her. She wished she could see him; he'd hold her hand.

Instead, she was holding an empty water bottle. She could at least find a recycle bin for it. Then she heard him, that deep cowboy bass carrying over the children's babble and the girlfriends' chatter. She turned, and the sight of him knocked her off balance. He wore his fireman's beige turnout pants, their baggy fit making his red suspenders a necessity, but his T-shirt fit tightly, his chest muscles defined under the black material. Zach was laughing not with a group of women, which wouldn't have surprised her at all, but with a child.

One child, thrilled with the adult attention, was a magnet for more. Child after child came over to see Zach.

He crouched down, tickled one child in the stomach, and pretended to double over from another child's tiny fist punching his chest. Then he saw Brooke.

He stood and patted various kids on the head, wading through his sea of admirers until he reached her. He'd changed into a clean, dry T-shirt, she could tell up close, but his hair was still a tousled mess. He was, as always, the most handsome man she'd ever seen. He pulled her close and kissed her, mouth closed in deference to his young audience, but hard enough to let her know this was no absentminded peck.

"Knock, knock."

Brooke looked down to see a small child rapping his fist on the beige canvas of Zach's turnout pants.

"Who's there?" Zach asked.

"Thammy."

"Sammy who?" Zach picked up the black-haired boy and held him high to finish the joke face-to-face.

"Thammy MacDowell."

Zach laughed. "Is that right? I just met a boy named Sammy MacDowell a minute ago, right outside this tent, and he told me the same joke."

"That was me!" The little boy splayed his hands over his shirt eagerly.

"It was? Are you sure?"

Zach, big and grown, kept up the silly conversation with the child, who couldn't have been more than three. Slowly, Brooke sank back onto her folding chair, the cold metal seat chilling the backs of her thighs.

Zach belonged here. Brooke had always known that women liked him, of course. Men liked him, too, whether it was old Harold Allman clinging to him for courage or

Jamie MacDowell commiserating with him over some sports team's loss.

But kids…

Kids adored him. It was easy to see why. He talked to them directly. Zach laughed at whatever little Sammy MacDowell said to him.

Brooke's empty water bottle made sharp popping sounds as it crumpled in her hand. *I hate kids.* Had she really said that out loud to him?

Zach did not hate kids. Still, that didn't mean he wanted a family of his own, did it? Not Zach, the heartthrob of Engine Thirty-Seven. Not Zach, who could have any woman he wanted. He was just being patient with this particular child because Sammy was Jamie Mac-Dowell's son, and Jamie and Zach were old high school teammates. It was a football thing, right?

Sammy's mother came over to retrieve her son. Zach talked with her easily, in no rush to hand the child back. She was young and pretty, the perfect all-American wife. Brooke sat there, taking in the picture they made: Zach and the woman and the toddler.

Brooke's image of Zach as a ladies' man crumbled. He was a good man, hardworking and handsome, a natural with kids. Someday, he'd marry a woman he loved, father children he loved, and live happily ever after in a house with a white picket fence. He'd have a good life. A normal life.

It would never include her.

Holding nothing but crumpled plastic in her hand, Brooke stood and silently stepped away.

Chapter 10

Brooke paused outside, blinking, letting her eyes adjust to the sun after the shade of the tent.

The bright Texas sun couldn't blind her to the truth: she lived under a black rain cloud. Had been living there so long, she forgot it sometimes, until days like today. Some people just had less good fortune than others, and her good fortune had run out eighteen years ago today.

Zach's had not. The longer she stayed with Zach, the longer she prevented him from meeting the right girl, the one he could marry and have a family with. She needed to take her black cloud and go.

I don't want to leave him.

Her mother had accused her of being selfish today. For once, her mother might be right.

A bright green recycle bin sat a few yards away. Brooke walked close enough to toss in her water bottle. With nothing else to do, she stood by the bin of discarded plastic, lost in gloomy thoughts, when strong arms slipped around her from behind.

"Are you feeling religious?" Zach asked quietly.

She must look as serious as her thoughts. Not really religious thoughts, but certainly reflective—

Zach squeezed her. "Because you look like the answer to my prayers."

She really ought to be used to these jokes by now.

He let go of her only to grab her hand and pull her along behind him. "Come on, we're making a break for it." He smiled at her over his shoulder and tugged her behind him at an easy jog, heading toward the edge of the parking lot and the red fire engine with the number thirty-seven painted on its side. He didn't stop until they'd run around the cab to the side of the engine away from the crowd.

"Finally," he said, crowding her against the warm metal of the truck. His kiss was greedy yet skillful, a blend that threatened to wipe out all her resolve to let him go and find someone better.

She slid her palms along his black T-shirt, skimming over the red suspenders that crossed his shoulder blades, relishing the feel of the defined muscles of his back, his shoulders, his neck. This side of the truck was private enough. Brooke wanted him, badly, and he obviously wanted her, too.

She let her thumbs drift along his jaw, telling herself she should end this now. Well, soon.

Oh, to heck with it.

Just for today, then. Just for the rest of the afternoon, she would cling to her fantasy and pretend she was a normal woman in love with a normal guy.

In love?

No, she couldn't go there. Zach had said he was her friend as well as her lover. That was all she needed.

But, oh, she could love him. She wanted the best for him, even when that meant she couldn't have him.

If she wasn't in love with him, she was close, so dangerously close that her legs felt weak at the realization. She clung to his neck a little harder.

"Baby," he murmured against her mouth approvingly, as if her weakness meant something good instead of something dreadful. "I'm addicted to this. Two hours apart is too many. I've been watching you in the crowd, wanting to jump that barrier and grab you up every time you did that proper little clap."

His thoughts were so much less gloomy than hers, she had to wait a beat to shift gears and let her thoughts match his. To let her thoughts be normal.

"I'm trying to get the hang of cheering," she said, forcing herself to smile. "I can't get that 'whoop, whoop' thing down that Murphy and Chief do."

"Don't change. Your clapping is cute."

"Cute? Me?"

"It's like having a princess applaud me." And then he kissed her with a carnality that would make any princess mindlessly toss away her crown.

Abstract concepts like future wives and children went up in smoke. In the here and now, his mouth was delicious, his body was hard and warm, and his hair felt soft under her fingers. Its color was lightening from brown to blond with each day of approaching summer sun. The man himself was everything bright and light, chasing away her black cloud with a sensual, physical joy that was every bit as addicting as he said it was.

A wolf whistle pierced the air. It didn't occur to Brooke that it was directed at them, because she'd never done anything in her life to cause that kind of reaction from a stranger, until Zach cooled their kiss and then finished it with a chuckle.

"I guess the hospital parking lot isn't the best place for this." He kissed her one more time, lightly, a G-rated kiss in case any families wandered by.

Brooke kept her arms around his neck and pressed her forehead into the solid muscle of his shoulder, hiding her face. "I hope that was no one I know. I'm a doctor. I'm not supposed to act this way."

She peeked at him when he said nothing. He was smiling at her in a way that looked distinctly smug and terribly masculine. He was a great kisser, and he knew it. This was no family man. Zach Bishop, playboy paramedic, darling of the ER nurses, was back.

Thank goodness. She could handle this version of Zach.

"You don't have to look so proud of yourself," she said, arching one brow in mock disapproval.

His smile only deepened. "If you say so, Dr. Brown."

She kept her arms loosely around his neck, enjoying their physical compatibility. She shouldn't wish for anything more.

I wish this wasn't so temporary. Life will change; it always does.

At any moment, he could get hurt. The race itself looked risky to her. In the blink of an eye, Zach could be taken away from her, gone like her sister.

It was easy to keep her supposedly stern expression. She really did wish she could order him to stay safe at all times. "As a doctor, I have to advise you that we should be icing down your muscles before the semifinals."

He only shrugged, neck muscles bunching and relaxing in the circle of her arms. "That's okay. I'm fine." He turned to sit on the chrome running board of the fire engine, giving her plenty of room to sit beside him.

He stretched his legs out in front of him and leaned his broad shoulders against the side of the truck. He was so healthy, such a contrast to the ill and injured patients with whom she spent the majority of her time. Yet with one false step on that staircase, one stumble over a heavy dummy's dangling limb, he would be hurt. The possibility made her heartsick.

She couldn't tell Zach that. Zach wouldn't want to be with a woman who obsessed over statistically unlikely accidents. All of the other girlfriends were smiling and enjoying themselves, but Brooke felt compelled to do something to minimize the risk of harm.

"I'll get some ice, anyway," she said. Their kiss had left her hair a little messy. As she reached up to tighten her ponytail, she offered an explanation she thought would sound good to an athlete. "You'll thank me for it tomorrow when you aren't as sore as you'll be without the ice."

He tugged her ponytail loose again with a smile. "I'm not sore."

"It's not tomorrow yet."

He laughed. "I run stairs all the time, Brooke, almost every day of the week. It's part of the workout we do when we're on shift. I feel fine, really."

He'd be feeling differently in the blink of an eye if he placed one heavy boot on a stair at the wrong angle and his muscles were too fatigued to catch himself. Brooke stood, ready to get the ice, and tried another approach. "Think of it this way. You'll be faster if we reduce the inflammation in your quads now."

His nonchalant smile stayed in place, but she could see that he was watching her more closely. Maybe she was being too insistent.

"I forget that I've got a physician in my corner," he said. "You'd be very good to have if this were a serious competition. There is a competition circuit, but this is more of an exhibition day. If I'm in a race where fractions of seconds count, I'll let you ice me down all you want. Right now, it doesn't really matter. We've already won the best prize."

"Semifinals are the best prize?" She tried not to let her frustration show. The man didn't want ice, and that was that.

"My engine gets a shift covered because I made semifinals." He reached up to grab her hand and tug her down to sit beside him once more. He didn't let go of her hand.

She kept her gaze on their intertwined fingers. "No wonder Murphy and Chief went so crazy after that last race."

"The rest is just a matter of bragging rights."

"If you don't care whether or not you win the next round," she began, and she heard the hesitation in her own voice, the insecurity. She kept moving forward, anyway. "Then why bother doing it again? Sit it out the rest of the day. Good enough is good enough."

It could be dangerous. Please don't risk it.

"What's wrong, Brooke?"

That surprised her. "Nothing."

He had her in his sights now, studying her intently. "I'm not going to be a no-show. I'm going to try to win."

She studied her watch. He still had thirty minutes left before the siren would sound and send him up the tower again. The second hand swept its way around the numbers. Thirty minutes left for an athlete's body to clear lactic acid from the interstitial spaces in the muscle tissue—

"Brooke." His other hand covered her watch.

She had nowhere else to look except into his blue-green eyes.

"You keep checking your watch. Do you have to be somewhere?"

"No." It wasn't a lie. She had nowhere to be for hours and hours yet.

He didn't look as if he quite believed her, but he let her wrist go.

"Getting into the semifinals means Engine Thirty-Seven doesn't have to work tonight. Everyone will be headed out for a beer, but we could go somewhere else, just the two of us."

Brooke looked away. Her black cloud loomed above them both. "I can't. I made plans."

"You're working? Did you pick up a shift for someone?"

She was caught. She'd been so sure she'd arranged everything so he wouldn't be dragged into her misery. He never should have found out. "No. It's…it's personal. I just have to…go somewhere."

"On a Saturday night." His voice was flat, no cowboy, no good times in the tone. "You have something personal to do on a Saturday night, something without me. Something I wasn't supposed to know about."

"I thought you'd be working overnight." She'd never hated this day of the year more than she did at the moment.

Abruptly, Zach stood. She watched him turn his back

on her and shove his fingers through his short brown-blond hair. Just as abruptly, he was down on one knee beside her. "I thought it went without saying, but let me say it now. I want to be the only one, Brooklyn Brown. Since that first night, we've been together every single day, and I like it that way. That's the only way I want it to be. You and me, exclusive."

"Oh, Zach. You shouldn't be worrying about this right now. You've got a race to run in—"

"Screw the race."

Because he was on one knee, they were face-to-face as she sat on the running board. His eyes were narrowed with intensity, his mouth a grim line, no longer sensual or smiling. Brooke guessed this was how he looked when he was cutting someone out of a car or sledgehammering his way into a burning building. Her defenses were too flimsy for this. She'd wanted to pretend she was happy, but he was seeing right through to the real Brooke, the one who'd tried to hide a secret.

"Damn it." The words were quiet, spoken softly under his breath. "I thought it was so obvious that we were together. If I can't stop you from going out tonight, I can sure as hell start trying to change your mind."

"It's not like that."

But wasn't it? Hadn't she realized today that she shouldn't keep dating him when she wasn't the one who could give him a family?

It was flattering, thrilling, to hear him ask her for a clear commitment, but she'd forced this issue accidentally. She'd hoped to skate by for the rest of the weekend before doing the right thing. She knew she wasn't the right woman for him. Heck, she wasn't the right woman for anyone. He was offering her a commitment that would only hurt him in the long run. She had to let him go.

This was the worst day on the calendar in every way.

"Zach, you deserve so much better than me."

If that wasn't the opening salvo in a breakup speech, then Zach didn't know what was. God knew he'd said it enough times to enough different women. Hearing Brooke say it to him made the ground drop out from underneath him, right where he knelt.

"Don't say that." His words sounded so familiar. A half dozen likable women had responded the same way to him. *Don't say that, Zach, you're perfect for me.*

Brooke couldn't seem to look him in the eye. "I'm not the right woman for you."

"We're good together." He nearly cringed at the cliché.

"I know," Brooke said. "Just because we're good together doesn't mean we should be together for the long term."

Were there no original phrases when it came to this breakup dance? The words were old, but the pain was new to him. In the past, he'd felt some remorse if he'd let a relationship go on too long and the soon-to-be-ex-girlfriend had fallen for him harder than he'd realized. Regret? Yes, he'd felt that, but letting a girl go gently had never really caused him significant pain. But this…

Zach would have driven his fist into the red metal of Engine Thirty-Seven if he thought it would make the sharp pain in his chest go away. This was too much like watching Charisse in her bridal finery as she walked into a church to marry someone Zach hadn't known existed.

There'd been no words then. He'd stood on the sidewalk

in silence. Charisse had never seen him. Zach would never know who or what or why.

"Who is it?" he demanded this time. "Who did you make plans with tonight?"

When Brooke was silent, Zach realized his hands were in fists. He forced his fingers to relax. "It's okay. I'm not going to beat the guy up. Who are you going out with tonight?"

"It's my mother."

"Your mother?"

Brooke crossed her arms over her chest and studied something in the distance with her chin high, but the gesture looked more miserable than defiant. "I really can't cancel on her. Really. It has to be today."

"There's no other man?"

Brooke finally looked him in the eye. Glared at him, actually. "We spent last night together, Zach. We ate breakfast together this morning. Of course I'm not seeing another man tonight. What kind of degenerate person do you think I am?"

Relief and confusion were a strange mix. He gestured in the general direction of the competition tower, as if he wasn't certain what the structure was. "What are we fighting about?"

"We're not. I didn't mean to distract you. Your focus should be on this competition. We can talk about it later."

"Talk about *what*?"

When she didn't answer him, he stood up. He needed to think on his feet. His mind was racing, jumping to conclusions, each one worse than the last. He forced himself to slow down, to go in reverse over these past few minutes.

First and foremost, Brooke wasn't seeing another man.

Zach was relieved. Or rather, in his mind, he knew he was relieved, but his heart hadn't quite caught up to the knowledge yet. All the muscles surrounding his rib cage were still tight, as if the end of this relationship would be a physical punch he had to defend himself against.

Because that was what loving a woman felt like. He was braced against another Charisse, anticipating the pain of loving someone who didn't feel the same.

Screw that. He had no time for the ghost of Charisse and her fake promises of love and children and a future together. Brooke wasn't cheating on him. She was justifiably mad he'd jumped to that conclusion. *Of course I'm not seeing another man.*

Before that, what had she said? *You deserve so much better than me.* That was still a breakup line, even if she didn't have another man waiting on the bench. And before that, she'd talked about ice a lot. She was fixated on the ice, and she acted like having dinner with her mother tonight was a terrible secret he'd uncovered.

He threw his hands up in surrender. "I'm lost, Brooke. What do we need to talk about?"

She checked her watch again.

"I've got all the time in the world," he said.

"No, you don't. You have to be at the starting line in twenty-five minutes. I'm sorry all this about my mother came up. I don't want you to lose focus."

"Lose focus?" He hadn't exactly been focused on the part about seeing her mother, but apparently she was.

She looked like a child, sitting so close to the ground. He held his hands out for her to take and waited until his silence caused her to look up. As soon as she noticed his hands, she placed hers in his, almost a reflex.

He pulled her to her feet. "I'm focusing on exactly what I should be focused on right now."

Keeping this burn under control. Keeping the fire contained.

"You've been distracted all morning. Talk to me."

She gave his hands a little squeeze, but when she would have let go, he held on. If she wouldn't look him in the eye, he wanted to keep some kind of contact with her.

"I'm sorry," she said. "I'm not usually like this."

"I know you aren't. I've known you for how long now? Nine months." More of the tightness around his chest eased at the reminder. He wasn't rushing in like the fool he'd been with Charisse. He hadn't fallen for Brooke in a matter of days. True, they'd only been together as a couple for two weeks, but he'd known her for much longer.

In nine months, he'd never seen Brooke so discomposed, not until yesterday morning, when he'd come off his night shift to find her sitting on his porch steps. "You're thinking about that little girl."

Her hands jerked in his.

He let them go. "Have you called and checked on her today?"

"Oh, that little girl. The car accident. Yes, she came through her first round of surgery with no complications. She's awake with normal orientation."

"That's good. Really good."

"Yes. Sometimes they never wake." There was a little catch in her breath. She pressed one palm against her temple as if she could squeeze something into place. "This is so embarrassing."

He shrugged. "Some patients are like that. You can't forget them easily, especially children."

She remained silent. His gut told him she didn't know

how to blow off steam. She wouldn't throw the coffee mug yesterday; he had. The one time she'd vented her frustration about the ninety-six-year-old, she'd cut herself short almost immediately. She'd apologized then, too.

She ought to be able to talk to him. They were in the same line of work. He understood.

Come on, Brooke. Open up. You'll feel better.

Since she was silent, he decided to say a few words to get the ball rolling. "I hate when kids are the victims, too. They're innocent. They're never the one who caused the car accident. Even if they've gotten themselves in trouble, stuck on a roof or something, it's not really their fault. They can't foresee how things can go wrong."

"I think you're exactly right. You're a natural with children. Do you see that? This whole day, watching you with your friends' kids, has forced me to face the truth. You need the chance to settle down. You need children of your own."

She was looking at him now, facing him fully. Zach recognized her expression, the one she wore on duty when she had to make a tough decision or deliver bad news. Today's decision had to do with settling down and having children.

Well, damn. That had come out of left field.

"Are you offering?" he asked, after a moment of baffled silence.

"Me? Absolutely not."

That shouldn't have hurt. Children weren't even on his radar, yet he clenched his teeth a little against the sucker punch that she'd *absolutely not* consider having any with him.

The bottom line, apparently, was that she thought he needed children, and she wasn't willing to provide them.

"Is this why you said I deserved someone better than you? For the sake of my future children?"

"I've decided against having children myself," Brooke said, a teacher explaining a scientific concept. For once, he didn't find that bossy librarian tone appealing.

"Is that right?" His cowboy drawl was deliberate. "But you assume I'm planning on having a passel of kids. Or do you think I'll just leave a string of accidents behind me, given the way you assumed I slept with every woman I spoke to?"

She kept her chin up and her gaze direct. "I know you better than that now. I think you'd be a good father. You should marry a nice girl and have babies, be happy and have a good life."

"But not with you."

"I'm never going to have children, so there's no reason for you or any man to commit himself to me. We may have had some fun, but the reality is, I'm a waste of your time."

And then she did that quick dash of her hand to the corner of her eye again, the same movement she'd done outside her apartment building when she'd apologized for crying, although he'd never caught a glimpse of a tear.

She was sad?

The pieces started to fall into place.

The band around his chest eased, but the pain shifted from being hurt by her to hurting *for* her. Zach took a deep breath. "Let me get this straight. You are telling me you never want to get married and never want to have children, and that's supposed to motivate me to break up with you?"

"Perhaps that's oversimplifying," said his librarian,

"but yes, there's no sense in you spending time with me when I'm all wrong for you."

These words weren't the usual breakup lines. They bothered him. She was referring to herself as a waste of time, as all wrong.

"When you say I deserve better than you," he said, "you really mean it."

"Yes, of course."

Jeez. The pain in his heart really was for her, no question.

"Brooklyn, no one really thinks they aren't good enough, don't you know that? It's just a line people use when they want to look around for someone better to date. Someone different to date, at least."

She frowned at him as if he'd just told her the sky wasn't really blue or that gravity didn't really make things fall.

He persisted. "Deep down, don't you believe you're a good person, good enough to date anyone you want?"

He stood her silence for one second. Two.

Enough.

He'd always preferred to take action, to handle the most immediate problems first.

So first, he kissed her.

He was the man who stopped the bleeding at the scene, not the office-based practitioner who waited for test results before making a decision. Brooke was like him, whether she realized it or not, a physician who handled the most urgent issues in the ER and deferred the rest to other specialists.

The space between them needed to go, so he pulled her into him, one arm securing her body to his, his other hand cupping her jaw and turning her face to the angle he needed to kiss her deeply. Thoroughly. And yes, damn it, lovingly.

With that connection restored, he spoke against her mouth, brushing brief kisses on her lips between sentences. "You are an amazing woman, Brooklyn Brown, so amazing that I was a little afraid to start dating you, because I knew I'd never want to stop. I don't want to stop seeing you."

Her little gasp was silent, but he felt the quick inhalation beneath his lips.

"It's crazy to think I could find someone better than you. You understand me. You know what it's like to lose a patient and what it's like to save one. And I understand you, too. I've got so much respect for you. It takes guts to jump in and try to make a difference, and you've got that kind of courage."

"That's just being a doctor."

"No, it isn't." He smoothed his thumb over her cheek, feeling the soft, feminine skin. "Even more amazing, that courage is wrapped up in an incredibly beautiful package. Everything about you is soft and strong at once. You're more than pretty, Brooke. You're sensational. When I've got you in my bed, it's beyond pleasure. You respond to my touch like I'm doing everything right."

"Because you are, and you know it. Our sexual compatibility shouldn't be—"

He smiled against her lips. "Sexual compatibility. How many syllables is that? Do you know what I thought the first time I laid eyes on you? You were leaving the ER, all neat and professional in your pinstriped skirt, and you looked like my fantasy of a sexy librarian."

She went very still at that. "Really?"

"It's a shame you don't need glasses. Just so you know,

if you start wearing reading glasses when you're older, I'm going to be all over you."

"You're literally over me now."

"Damn right."

She almost, nearly, not quite chuckled. It was definitely a little sound of amusement, and he kissed her quickly.

Now that he'd gotten her to lighten up, he turned serious. "And I'm never, ever going to be willing to share you. When I thought you had a date with another man tonight, I might as well have been stabbed in the chest." And that was as close as he was willing to admit that she had his heart. He would keep this fire contained.

She pushed against him, and he let her go, but only far enough that he could rest his hands on her waist and his forehead against hers. This was an intimate conversation, and he wanted to keep the space between them intimate.

Her hands clutched his shoulders. "I don't know what kind of women you've dated in the past, but I wouldn't sleep with two different men in twenty-four hours."

Charisse would have. Charisse *had*. And he'd thought she loved him.

"I know that, baby, I know. It's not just about sleeping with someone else. I want you in every way, not just in bed. It hurts to imagine you going out to dinner and a movie with some other guy. You might like him better than me, and that would—"

He stopped himself. *Ease up. Contain it.* "I don't want to know how that would feel."

"Oh, Zach."

"I wouldn't feel that way if you were just a nice girl I was wasting time with until I could find someone better.

Don't tell me to spend my time looking for other women. I've already found the right one."

Her hands clutched his shoulders harder. He knew her physical responses from weeks in bed. He knew he'd done something right, *said* something exactly, perfectly right.

"No," she whispered, pressing her forehead harder against his as if she could transfer her thoughts that way. "You're focusing on everything we have in common. I'm thinking about everything we don't. You'd make a great father—"

"You'd make a great mother."

"Don't say that. You don't have to say that."

Why was she fighting this so hard? It was as if she wanted him to think less of her. He couldn't.

"I mean it, Brooke. I've watched you with kids in the ER for nine months. Days, nights, the ones who were hurt bad and the ones who were barely sick. You're consistently kind. You have—I don't know how to say it—you have a different touch with them than adults. You'd make a great mother, but neither of us are planning on having children. That's more we have in common."

"Why don't you want a family? You could have it all."

Hell, no.

But that was a knee-jerk response, and he knew it. For Brooke, he tried to say something more specific. "I tried the marriage fantasy on for size. It didn't fit."

"Four years ago?"

Her quick and accurate guess didn't surprise him.

"What happened?" she asked.

He never talked about it. No one in his family knew what had happened while he'd been on that trip, but he'd never convince Brooke that marriage wasn't in his future unless he explained some part of it.

With a sigh, he let go of her. A little space here wouldn't be a bad thing. He didn't want her touched by anything that had to do with Charisse.

"There was this woman." He didn't bother with the happy beginning. That had all been a lie, anyway. "It was a whirlwind thing during some time off. We decided to surprise everyone by coming home married. The day we were going to buy her white dress and meet the preacher on the beach, she ran away."

"Did you find her?"

"Within days. Turned out she'd already picked out a dress and booked a preacher for another man long before I came on the scene. I showed up in time to watch her marry him."

He'd shocked Brooke, that much was easy to see.

"How about you?" he asked. "Why don't you want the two kids and minivan?"

"Nothing like that. I've never had my heart broken like that."

"Good." He meant it. He didn't like the idea of Brooke being betrayed. He leaned against the familiar red metal of his engine and crossed his arms over his chest, settling in to watch Brooke. She'd been somber since the race, but now she was growing more animated.

"I never would have guessed you'd been through something like that," she said.

He wondered if she realized she was pacing.

"Don't you see, Zach? This is where we're opposites. This is what we don't have in common. Even after an episode like that, you still enjoy life. You still like women. Heck, you love women."

"Generally speaking, yes. That particular one, not so much."

"You laugh more than I do."

He was grinning a little, now that she mentioned it. "And you're more serious than I am."

"Yes, exactly."

He waited, but she seemed to think that she'd laid out her concern completely. She'd stopped pacing.

"That's it?" he asked, just to be sure.

"I'll drag you down. Do you remember the first night that we—the first night you came to my apartment? I said I was hoping you'd make me laugh after that shift. It's unfair for me to expect you to make me laugh all the time. We're so unequal."

"I was hoping you'd be cool and calm. I was counting on you to help me gain some professional perspective on that god-awful ambulance shift." He pushed away from the engine and eliminated the space between them again. She didn't object when he pulled her into a plain bear hug. "We're good together. We balance each other out."

"Not that day." Her voice was muffled against the side of his neck. "I didn't help you cool down and you didn't make me laugh."

"True. We just fell into bed and had amazing sex." He smiled at the memory and then down at Brooke, who started to smile, too. "It's an excellent third option."

"See? You're making me laugh again."

"Good." He meant that, too. She seemed to have more than her share of self-doubts and past hurts, and he intended to learn more in due time. For now, he'd solved the immediate problem. She wasn't going to break up with him. "We'll laugh when we can and stay cool when we can't. We'll understand crazy shifts and when all else fails, we'll have crazy good sex. You and me, only you and me, exclusive. Right?"

She hesitated.

He hugged her harder. "C'mon, Brooke. You can't say no to that."

"People do change their minds on the marriage and family part."

"If you decide you want the two-point-five kids and the minivan, you let me know. We firefighters are good at performing dynamic risk assessments as the situation changes. What do you say? Will you be mine?"

"I think this is an offer I can't refuse."

"Good."

"But that dynamic risk assessment better include roses and chocolate."

"Very funny." Since he had her in a bear hug anyway, he picked her up and spun her around once. "But remember, I'm supposed to be the funny one."

"Duly noted." Her stern words were at complete odds with the smile she gave him.

Her smiles were too rare, but that would change from here on out. This was love, yes, but it would be good for them. Not too consuming. No one had to get hurt.

A warning siren sounded from the top of the tower.

He set her down. "I think you agreed in the nick of time."

She checked her watch. "Oh, my gosh. You've only got four minutes."

"That's plenty. Chief will have my coat and helmet ready." He took off at a jog, knowing Brooke would jog, too, and stay beside him.

"Is this going to be enough of a warm-up for you?" she asked, and he didn't need to look at her face as they skirted the edge of the crowd to know her smile was gone.

"It's perfect. Don't worry about me."

"I shouldn't have distracted you. I'm so sorry."

There it was again, another glimpse of insecurity. He'd never suspected it, he doubted anyone would, but the decisive Dr. Brooke Brown had real insecurities. She thought she was a waste not just of his time, but of any man's. Who the hell had put that idea in her head?

He came to an abrupt halt. "Just so you know, you are a thousand times more important to me than winning the semifinals. If it had taken me another hour to get you to say yes, then I would have taken another hour, and dropped out of the race."

"Oh, Zach."

As answers went, he liked it. It sounded as if he'd said something right.

"Come on. The starting line is waiting for us."

Chapter 11

After the races, Zach had to babysit.

The baby was a red-and-blue helicopter named Texas Rescue One, and its pilots apparently trusted only Zach to stay with their precious machine while they grabbed lunch.

Zach had won the semifinal race after jogging straight up to the starting line, much to Brooke's relief. If he'd lost that race, she would have felt guilty for accidentally igniting a big relationship talk when she should have been making sure he was preparing properly for the race: resting, reducing inflammation, rehydrating.

Nowhere in the list of sports medicine principles did intense emotional conversations come into play. Neither did kissing. She'd tried to stop him, hadn't she? She'd tried to redirect his focus to his race, but then he'd told her she was amazing. Sensational. What a thing for a man like Zach Bishop to say. *To her.*

While Zach babysat the helicopter, letting the crowd pose for selfies but keeping them out of the cockpit, Brooke stood in line at one of the food trucks to buy Texas-sized hot dogs. Standing in the sun, smelling great food on all these grills, feeling secure that dating Zach wouldn't cause him any regrets in a childless future, it was easy to pretend this Saturday wasn't a tragic anniversary.

The community fair was helping her keep the grief at bay. When she remembered where she had to go tonight, when she remembered that today was the day the cutest kid sister had ceased to be, the monster took a swipe, but it couldn't quite get a good swing at her.

"I'll take two foot-longs, please. Extra relish."

She made her way back to the helicopter, carefully keeping her hot dogs from falling out of their oblong paper trays. Already, she had her doubts that just one would be enough for Zach after the thousands of calories he'd burned in the morning's competition.

After winning his semifinal, Zach had lost the final race to a firefighter from Killeen, but his congratulatory handshake to the victor had been sincere, and he'd waved at the crowd to acknowledge their cheers. It was as if there was no room in him for anger or pouting or kicking a dummy in disappointment, as one of the other firemen had done. He wasn't devastated although he'd come so close and then lost the final round.

How did he manage to shrug off disappointment like that? To switch from the high of winning the semis to the low of losing the finals?

Any moment of happiness could change into a moment of tragedy. Her sister's death had taught Brooke that life was short. Her career in the ER reinforced that truth too frequently. Zach had to know it as well as she did, but he wasn't afraid to enjoy the happy moments. Maybe, just maybe, some of that optimism would rub off on her.

If they stayed together long enough, that was.

Ha. She was already anticipating the fall. *Enjoy it while it lasts.*

Speaking of enjoying things while they lasted, she checked her watch. She had a couple of hours, at least, before she needed to shower and don something black and drive to her childhood home. Hours to go, still.

Zach spotted her and gestured toward the nearest picnic table. She sat and took her first bite of something she'd never advise a patient to eat. Zach picked up a small child and set his helmet on the little boy's head for a photo in front of the chopper. He kept his hand on the heavy helmet brim to keep its full weight off the child's fragile frame.

Determinedly, Brooke kept chewing. If she'd thought for one second that she was vulnerable to a biological clock or maternal instincts, she'd be feeling it now. Every sense in her would be looking at him and screaming, "That's some major fatherhood potential there. Life partner stuff."

She wasn't thinking that, because she wasn't going to have children. But Zach should. *Just look at him, so protective, so caring. So undeniably adorable.*

He'd said he didn't want to have children. She wasn't depriving him of anything.

The pilots returned, two women in flight suits. If their gender surprised her for a second, it amused her for the next. Naturally, Zach would be around a helicopter with a female crew. She should have guessed.

As one woman stayed with Texas Rescue One, Zach

began walking Brooke's way with the other pilot. She was petite and blonde and confident. She carried herself as if she was in charge.

Probably the same way I carry myself on duty. Was that the kind of woman Zach preferred?

Come to think of it, the gossip mill always had Zach paired up with a trauma nurse or some other type of career woman, someone who had a high-adrenaline job or was some other kind of go-getter. He was never known for dating bimbos. No one too young. No one too empty-headed.

Brooke had thought she was an anomaly for a ladies' man like Zach, someone unique and out of the ordinary for him. Maybe she'd hoped being a novelty would keep him interested in her, but in reality, an ER doctor was just Zach's style.

Or a pilot.

She glared at her hot dog. Had she not just promised herself she would try to emulate Zach? Yes, every peak was followed by a valley, but she would enjoy the happy moments. She would worry about the crash later. For now, Zach preferred an ER doctor, and he was determined that they see each other exclusively.

Brooke set her hot dog in its paper tray and dusted off her hands. She stood and held out her hand to shake with the blonde pilot.

"Captain Elliott," Zach introduced her.

"You can call me Sam, of course," the pilot said with a smile. "It's Samantha, but people unfortunately love that Sam Elliott name—like the actor, you know. You can't tell me a mustache joke I haven't heard."

"I'm Brooke. I'll try to forget every mustache joke I've ever heard."

Sam turned to Zach. "I like her already. She looks awfully sane to put up with your crazy."

Brooke smiled politely. Zach was so much more sane than she was, it wasn't even a contest.

Sam was jerking her thumb toward Zach. "Shark Bait gets sad if we don't dangle him on a wire from the bottom of the chopper at least once a month. That's certifiably crazy."

"That's a certified rescue swimmer," Zach returned mildly. "You want Texas Rescue to have a rescue swimmer on the roster, then you gotta let me hang out on the end of a wire at least once a month."

"Shark Bait?" Brooke asked, while inside she was hoping she was hearing all this rescue swimmer stuff wrong.

Sam grinned. "We hook him on the end of a line and lower him into the water. He's just glorified bait."

Brooke frowned at Zach. "I thought the Coast Guard took care of water rescues."

"Off the coast, sure. They run the school that certified me." Zach's words were casual, but he was watching her closely, as he had when she'd been too persistent about the ice.

Smile. Be normal. The man isn't in any danger at the moment.

Sam was enthusiastic. "We do search and rescue, mostly, for folks who get lost in the wilderness. Half the time we find them in a spot where the only way out is up. Zach drops down and hooks 'em up, and we haul them into the chopper."

"I didn't know you did that." She was talking to Zach more than the pilot. Shouldn't she have known he was a rescue swimmer? "You've never brought someone here."

"We haven't?" Sam looked at Zach and poked him in

the arm. Brooke told herself it was a sisterly move. Poke, poke. "Yeah, yeah, remember that frostbite couple right before Christmas? We brought them here."

"Dispatch sends us to Breckenridge most of the time," Zach said, naming another Austin hospital. "I never get a chance to impress Dr. Brown in my flight suit."

"You won't get it next weekend, either. We have to do all the paperwork training. No ride in a basket."

"Killjoy."

"Cheer up," Sam said. "Maybe we'll get a real call or a nice natural disaster before that, and then we won't have to do training this month at all."

All the worry Brooke had felt during the races returned in force. Zach was a rescue swimmer. Paramedic and firefighter, she'd known about, but the rescue swimmer thing seemed far more dangerous. Her mental catalog of checklists for drowning victims was grim. People just couldn't cheat water. Not that anyone could cheat fire, either. Or smoke inhalation.

Or twisted metal in car wrecks.

Her gaze settled on a little girl wearing a pink dress. Her pigtails bounced as she played among the river rock landscaping that filled the median strips in the hospital parking lot.

The monster hit Brooke hard.

Oh, Chelsea, you precious baby.

Chelsea had brought her treasures all the time, treasures like river rocks. Although she'd been in middle school, Brooke had appreciated her sister's pure joy when she found a rock that was more precious than all the rest by virtue of having an interesting chip or crack. Chelsea had given all the special rocks to her.

"It was nice meeting you. Catch you later." Sam headed back to her copilot.

Brooke was amazed anew at how it was possible to conjure a passable smile and a polite nod of the head and fool the whole world into thinking she wasn't losing to a monster.

She kept it up, sitting down at the picnic table and picking up her hot dog. She smiled and nodded as Zach thanked her for his own foot-long. He couldn't be bothered to sit, but he perched on the edge of the table above her. His watch caught the sun for a flash as he took a bite, and Brooke read the time upside down. Of course, his watch had a second hand like hers, sweeping its way steadily around the face, ready to clock the pulse of a mortally injured patient.

"Confession time," Zach said.

She looked up at him with genuine curiosity. What kind of confession did he have to make? Maybe he'd signed up for another race. Maybe he was going to tell her nothing more earth-shattering than cotton candy was his secret weakness. Or maybe he was going to confess that in addition to firefighter, paramedic, and rescue swimmer, he also rode bulls in a rodeo. Danger seemed to be more addictive to him than her kisses.

Her smile was in place. "I'm listening."

"Not me. It's time for you to confess. What's up? You can't be worried that I'll miss the start of another race, but you keep checking your watch anyway, and then a little worry wrinkle appears right here." He pressed his finger to the space between her brows with a grin, but then he dropped his hand and his smile faded away. "This dinner with your mother isn't just a dinner, is it?"

He'd hit the nail on the head, but she didn't want to talk about it. "Men aren't supposed to be so intuitive."

"Are we going back a few decades? Okay, girls are supposed to be nurses, not doctors."

"Very funny."

"You're worried about the time, aren't you?"

She scowled at her hot dog. It was loaded with bright yellow mustard and chopped green relish, the ultimate picnic food. She couldn't choke down a bite right now, no matter how badly she wished she could.

Zach could. The dozens of people who'd been in line at the food stand could. But Brooke?

She was worried that a man might drown, and sad because a little girl had been playing among some rocks.

She'd always wanted to fit in, but having a sister die had made her a pariah at a young age. As an adult, it was simple to look back and understand that her school friends hadn't known what to say. They'd avoided the girl who'd had such bad luck.

Then her father had passed away, too. Maybe they'd been scared that something so terrible was contagious. She'd learned all the common fears during the standard psych training in medical school. She understood.

But today, she didn't want to be so logical about her lonely years as the unlucky teen. She'd tried to make friends. She'd failed.

Maybe it wasn't all my fault.

"Maybe I'm the one who is fine," she snapped at Zach, "and you're the one who's obsessing over how many times I look at my watch."

She plunked her hot dog back in its paper tray. She hated that Zach could see right through her. She hated that she'd given him such a sharp answer just now, and she hated that she'd have to apologize when all she wanted in the world was to enjoy a hot dog today.

"What time are you supposed to see your mom?" he asked, and the kindness in his tone was just about her undoing.

"I told her I'd be there by six."

"Same time my shift should've started. Why were you trying to hide dinner with your mom from me?"

She was so thankful that he wasn't meeting her bad mood with one of his own, she put her hand on his thigh and squeezed gratefully, buying herself a moment to swallow down the emotion that clogged her throat.

"It's not really dinner. I'm driving her to the cemetery. Today is the anniversary of my sister's death. The eighteenth anniversary."

He tossed the rest of his hot dog back onto its tray, next to hers.

"Baby, you should have told me."

She probably should have, but she'd spent eighteen years not telling people the worst thing that had happened to her.

"Do you want to leave now? You must want to be with her."

She laughed at that, but it was a pathetic sound. "I wish I could skip the whole thing. It's a maudlin ritual. After we go to the cemetery, she wanders around the house and looks at old photos. I'll offer her tea and she'll say no. She even waves away the box of tissues until the tears get really bad. At some point, I won't be able to stand it, and I'll turn on some lights. She'll protest, but she won't turn them off.

"Then I'll go into the kitchen and cook something from whatever is in the pantry. She won't eat it until it grows cold and needs to be reheated. One year, I tried bringing over groceries and a new recipe we could make together, but that was really offensive to her. She prefers this martyrdom routine, I think. You should see her huddled in her corner of the couch, sipping little spoonfuls of canned soup after she's turned it away for a couple of hours."

Zach didn't say anything. Brooke kept her focus on his thigh, on the tight little square she was drawing there with one fingertip. She traced it again, so she wouldn't have to look up and see how appalled he was at her complaints.

"I sound like an awful person, don't I?" she said quietly, ninety-degree angles forming sharp edges over and over.

She'd done it again. She'd confessed the sad truth, just as she'd done during the intimacy of a preteen slumber party, and now she'd lose the friend. There would be a little distance between Zach and her, that distance that death puts between those with a black cloud over their lives and those without.

The situation was sorrowful, and pity was the natural response for anyone who found out about it. Pity led to distance, and because people had pitied her and then distanced themselves from her over and over, she knew what to expect.

She didn't want Zach's pity. She wished she could erase everything she'd just said.

"I do love my mother." The squares stopped abruptly. "I do. Every year, I've tried to comfort her. I thought we could leave the house and go to a museum once, just the two of us, when they were having an exhibit of historical gowns. I thought it would be interesting and kind of academic, nothing frivolous like going to see a comedy and eating movie popcorn."

"But she disagreed."

"She thought that plan was disrespectful."

"And this year?" he prompted her.

When she didn't say anything, he said it for her. "This year, you decided to spend the day here. With me."

"I wanted to see what it was you'd been doing all those push-ups and pull-ups for. I wanted to see what it would be like to be a normal girlfriend. The weather's perfect, and I wanted to be outside, but not at a cemetery."

She stopped herself before blurting out every horrible thought in her head. She'd already said *I hate kids* and accused her mother of being a martyr. That was too much already. She couldn't say she hated her sister's grave with its inscription about an angel too perfect for this world and its statuette of a little cherub that looked nothing like her sister.

Zach sat heavily beside her on the bench. He smoothed his hand over her ponytail, then wrapped the length of it around his hand, just one turn, and tugged her head to rest on his shoulder. "I'm assuming your mother didn't approve of a community picnic. Ah, my poor Brooke."

"Don't make me cry," she said, but she leaned on him as he let her ponytail unravel into a smooth spiral. "I'm trying to be normal."

As she rested on Zach's shoulder, Murphy and his Gothic girlfriend walked in their direction, beers in hand. Zach sketched Murphy a bit of a salute, a casual move that Brooke thought nothing of until she saw Murphy's eyes widen. He quickly pushed his girlfriend to walk in a different direction.

Brooke knew what that salute had meant. *Don't come*

over. Got my crazy girlfriend in the middle of a melt-down here.

It was sad that she was grateful to be spared making any small talk with Murphy at the moment.

A little spurt of rebellion followed the thought. She didn't want to be grateful. She didn't want to be the black cloud on this picnic.

I can do this. I'm not crazy.

To prove it, she sat up and slid their paper trays back in front of them, ready to eat. "I've got a couple of hours left, at least. Are there any more races to watch? It sounds like live music is starting up."

"Hey, Brooke?"

"What?"

"You want me to go with you tonight?"

Time stood still. So did her heart, and when it started beating again, she knew that one of her heart's desires had always been to have a friend like Zach.

"It's so nice of you to offer." She had to stop and swallow down that emotion again. "But you can't come."

"Why not?"

"It's going to be kind of like a funeral. I'm going to change into a black dress first and everything."

"I own more than jeans. I'll wear black, too. It'll be fine."

"It's not…it's not going to be fun. You'll see us at our worst."

He started toying with her ponytail, using the end like a paintbrush across her shoulder. "I expect it to be emotional. I'd rather not have you behind the wheel of a car when you're going through an emotional wringer. I'll be able to drive you and your mom to the cemetery with a clear head."

"Oh." She'd never thought of anything so practical. "But you'll starve. Soup cans, remember?"

"We can take your mom out to dinner. We'll pick a really quiet, formal place. Something not too disrespectful."

He understood.

He understood, and her heart wanted to burst with it.

"We'll never get her out of the house."

But what if they could? Her heart beat faster. Hope was a persistent thing, even after all these years of defeat.

"Let's go to the cemetery first," Zach suggested. "She'll be out of the house and in the car, so we'll tell her we have reservations somewhere nearby. If she really hates the idea of a restaurant, we'll drive through a takeout place and bring that back to the house instead. Either way, it will be better than reheated soup, right?"

"Oh, Zach."

I love you, she wanted to say. It was the most inappropriate time to tell a man she loved him, the date of her sister's death, while they were planning to visit a cemetery and trick her mother into a new routine. Inappropriate, the day he'd shared that a woman named Charisse had said she loved him but married someone else.

But Brooke loved him now, too. They would have no words, no wedding, no kids. But she loved him just the same.

Chapter 12

Zach tried not to enjoy the rest of the day.

Clearly, Brooke's mother preferred it that way, and this was her show.

But as Mrs. Brown handed him a photograph of her deceased child— "Here's dear Chelsea playing in the backyard when she was just two" —he couldn't help but smile at the big sister in the photo, a ten-year-old Brooke with a blanket tied over her shoulders as if she was a superhero. He'd done that, too, at the same age.

Zach cleared his throat and killed his grin, making sure his expression was neutral when he handed the photo back to Mrs. Brown.

God knew the cemetery visit had been rough. He'd done the driving, but to better accommodate three people, they'd taken Brooke's car instead of his truck. When they'd parked at the cemetery, he'd opened the back door for Brooke's mother, of course, in time to hear her fiercely whisper to Brooke that "that man" needed to let them have their time alone.

She'd undoubtedly wanted him to hear. Zach had done his part, politely pretending he hadn't heard. He'd suggested that they go on without him to pay their respects; he'd wait in the car. It spared Brooke from being embarrassed and forced to ask him to stay behind, at any rate.

Through the windshield, he'd watched as Brooke, all in black, had stood before a headstone, keeping her arm around her mother, who was tall and trim and stiff with dignity. Long minutes had passed, and Brooke had started patting her mother on her back. Her mother had walked toward the headstone, leaving Brooke standing with her hand patting empty air.

As Brooke dropped her arm, her mother slumped, then knelt and wept on the headstone. Brooke stood alone, as still as a slab of stone herself, and waited.

And waited.

Zach looked at his watch.

And waited. An appalling amount of time passed while Brooke stood there, ignored, staring at her sister's tombstone and her mother's back.

Enough.

Zach got out of the car and went to fix the immediate problem, which was that Brooke was alone in an awful situation. In silence, he stood next to her and held the hand that had been left empty. Her mother didn't notice for fully fifteen minutes longer. When she got to her feet and turned around, Zach ignored her outraged gasp.

"Do you want to visit your father's grave now?" he asked Brooke. She'd lost both her father and her sister in the same year, he knew that much.

Mrs. Brown pressed a hand to her chest with a whimper.

Zach had too much experience as a paramedic to be truly concerned. Real whimpers of pain sounded different. This one was theatrical, to let him know he'd made some kind of terrible mistake.

"He's not buried here. He was cremated, so..." Brooke trailed off uncomfortably. Uncharacteristically.

Zach glanced around the parklike grounds. Usually there were buildings of some sort that housed ashes. "So where do we go to pay our respects?"

"This is Chelsea's day, not my husband's. His remains are interred elsewhere." Mrs. Brown stalked toward the car, her energy and backbone completely restored by Zach's offense.

"I'm sorry, baby. I assumed they'd be buried in the same cemetery. Do you want me to drive you to his place now?"

That sounded strange, *his place*, like her father had his own house or something.

"That really would push my mother too far. He died a little less than two weeks later. He's not part of this day."

They started walking toward the car, still hand in hand. It sounded odd to him to only mourn one family member at a time, but he was here for Brooke. Questioning her about her mother's choices wouldn't make this easier on her. "We'll do this again in two weeks, then."

She took a deep breath, an obvious attempt to prepare herself for something, and stopped him by tugging on his hand. She stepped in front of him, facing him with her doctor's difficult news expression.

"He committed suicide."

"Brooke." He couldn't think of anything else to say.

Say it isn't so. Say you haven't had to deal with this in your life. He hated that she'd been through so much pain.

"I didn't want to shock you, but I thought you should know. My mother does not pay her respects today or any day."

Her expression took on the bitterness in her voice, adding to the ache he felt for her.

"Do you visit him?"

She nodded.

"If you want to visit now, I'll take you there. Your mom can wait in the car."

"No, I don't want to. It's been a long enough day already, and we haven't even attempted dinner yet."

Her mother, apparently tired of waiting for them by the car, chose that moment to open the door herself, get in, and slam it shut.

Brooke's worry wrinkle appeared. "Maybe we better take her home now."

"And start the reheating of the soup? You've been running for hours on two bites of a hot dog."

"I've upset her enough by having you here." She surprised him by suddenly raising their joined hands to her lips and kissing him hard on the knuckles. "But I'm not sorry that I said yes. Thank you for coming."

They'd only taken a few steps when she stopped once more. "Wait a second." She dug in her pocket and pulled out one of those river rocks that were used in landscaping. She dashed back to her sister's grave and placed it on the headstone.

He didn't ask for an explanation. He just escorted her back to the car in silence and drove straight to the restaurant to get her some decent food. He gave her mother no choice in the matter.

The rest of the evening was going as Brooke had predicted, and Zach resumed playing his part. He'd rocked the boat enough. Besides, it was almost entertaining to look at photos of a very young Brooke. He was sitting in the center of an oversize sofa from the nineties, sunk into the deep cushions and large throw pillows, with Brooke on one side and Mrs. Brown on the other.

"Here's my sweet Chelsea's last Christmas on earth." Mrs. Brown passed him the framed five-by-seven.

"She really was cute, Mrs. Brown." Zach studied the photo of two sisters, a preschooler and a preteen, wearing pajamas in front of a tinseled tree. "Look at that Elmo doll. I remember seeing those on the news. There were riots at the stores over the shortage of Elmos. How did you manage to get one? I'll bet there's a story behind that."

Mrs. Brown only stared at him as if he'd started speaking in gibberish, alien being that he was.

He passed the photo to Brooke. "What are you holding up for the camera?"

"That was a Tama-something. Those little digital pets in a key chain."

"I remember those." He turned back to Mrs. Brown. "You must have been a great Christmas shopper. Those were the hottest toys around."

She sniffed. "Thank goodness I got that Elmo toy. It was her last gift from Santa. Nothing was too good for sweet Chelsea."

And Brooke. Sweet Brooke deserved her cool toy, too. Say it.

When Mrs. Brown kept staring at the photo in silence, Zach handed it back to her. "Looks like both of your daughters had a great Christmas that year."

"That digital pet thing was a waste of money. They

actually died when they weren't fed often enough. I can't imagine who thought it would be clever to entrust children with toys that had to be kept alive. Brooke's died within weeks, and I had to deal with her disappointment."

Okay, then. Clearly, no one was supposed to share a fond memory or talk about a happy time. He would have loved to hear about Mrs. Brown's *battle royale* in a toy store over key chain pets and furry red dolls, but that wasn't going to happen.

He'd been to funerals and wakes before, of course, which was really what this was: the eighteenth wake for Chelsea Brown. Always, at gatherings for relatives or even fallen firefighters, funny stories had managed to pop up through the grief. Smiles and tears mixed together as treasured memories were shared.

Not here.

Zach hauled himself out of the quicksand of the couch cushions and started strolling about the living room, trying to imagine the house with a lively family of four in it while Brooke was growing up. It was a clean, spacious, upper-middle-class house, even if the decor was a couple of decades old. He had a feeling that couch was the last couch *on earth* on which sweet Chelsea had sat.

Check yourself, Zach. You haven't walked a mile in her mother's shoes.

He was trying.

The bookshelves and mantel were covered in framed photos. Baby photos, kindergarten photos, and a really charming one taken at Halloween with Brooke dressed like a baby—a lanky, braces-wearing baby who was really in middle school, beaming at the camera.

He smiled back at the Brooke in the photo. She held a pacifier and a stuffed bunny in her hands. Chelsea was in a bunny costume at her feet, smiling up at her, too. Poor Brooke. She'd obviously lost her biggest fan the day her sister had died.

Behind him, he heard the real Brooke offer to heat up the leftovers. At the restaurant, her mother had sat on the edge of her chair and refused to even pick up the menu, but once Brooke had ordered things she liked, she'd relented and at least tasted her entrée. Brooke had insisted on bringing the rest home.

"It will taste better now than if you wait until tomorrow to reheat it. I can bring it to you right here on the couch."

"Taste! I couldn't care less about how food tastes."

Zach kept staring at the Halloween photo. He wanted to like Brooke's mother. He wanted to sympathize with her for her loss, but he was having a hard time being a good audience for what was obviously a well-rehearsed routine.

"I'm not like you," Mrs. Brown said to her only living child. "I couldn't enjoy my food at that restaurant, chomping away like nothing upset you."

Zach turned around. "Where are the photos from high school?"

Mrs. Brown, interrupted mid lecture, glared at him. "She was only four when she died."

"From Brooke's high school."

Zach caught Brooke's eye. Quite intentionally, he smiled at her. "I want to see what kind of nineties prom gown you wore. Did you want to be a sexy Britney Spears, or were you already doing your classy librarian look?"

The corners of her eyes crinkled with the smallest of smiles. "I had the same straight slip dress that everyone else had that year. Floor-length and shiny. Very, very shiny satin."

"Let's see it."

She glanced at her mother, her ghost of a smile fading away. "I don't think any of those pictures made it into frames."

"How about a graduation photo?"

Brooke frowned at him and shook her head quickly.

Her mother dabbed at her eyes with the tissue Brooke had pressed into her listless hand a while ago. "Yes, there should have been photos of my babies grown up in caps and gowns. Oh, the milestones that never happened. The year that Brooke finished medical school, Chelsea would have graduated from high school, you know. That was such a difficult year. I could hardly think of anything else."

Zach rubbed his jaw.

Mrs. Brown looked at the photo in her lap mournfully. "Two graduations in the same year. Those photos would have made a beautiful double-framed display, don't you think?" She dissolved into tears so that Zach barely made out the word *think*.

He could hardly keep cool and think himself. Brooke was alive. She had graduated high school, college, med school. Nothing in this house indicated that Mrs. Brown had a daughter who'd achieved so much. A daughter who was still here, waiting to be noticed, waiting to be valued.

Zach hated the stricken expression on Brooke's usually fearless face. She was beautiful and smart, a lifesaver in the hospital, respected by everyone who knew her. There was more to her, though, a side he'd bet very few people glimpsed. He'd only come to see it himself these past few weeks. She had an almost childish curiosity to see more, to do more. She took a great interest in every Austin hot spot they visited, always wanting to know everything about the band or the building or the bartender's best drink. Today, instead of sitting in this house for hours, she'd wanted to see a firefighter competition. She'd wanted to cheer him on.

She wanted to live life.

Now, he got it. Looking around this house, it was easy to see that once her sister had ceased to exist, Brooke had ceased to exist as well, at least for her parents. Perhaps if Chelsea couldn't live, then Brooke didn't deserve to live, either.

The injustice of it infuriated him, but if Brooke could keep her emotions calm and cool, so could he. "I'm sorry Chelsea didn't have the chance to graduate."

"Thank you," Mrs. Brown said, still dabbing with the tissue.

He kept his voice even. Friendly and curious. "But why don't you have Brooke's photo on display?"

Both women gaped at him.

"If I'd graduated from medical school, my mother would have a poster-sized blowup of my graduation photo in your face when you walked into the house, I bet." He shrugged. "That's just the way moms are."

He saw it then, the narrowing of Mrs. Brown's eyes, the shrewd look, the way she sized him up, the interloper in her kingdom.

That's right, ma'am. I don't take kindly to the way you've treated your daughter. To the way you treat her still.

He waited where he was, standing in front of the mantel with its row of photos, young braces-Brooke beaming at him through a long-ago camera lens. The next move was Mrs. Brown's.

Or so he thought; it was Brooke who made the next move. "Zach and I have to be going."

"You can't." Mrs. Brown looked as surprised as Zach felt. "It's too early. I'm not ready to retire for the evening."

"I am. We were up early for a community event over at the hospital. I've had enough." Brooke extricated herself from the couch and looked down at her mother. "The leftovers are in the fridge, when you get hungry. I'm glad the weather held for us today. It was beautiful, wasn't it? Good night. I love you."

She bent to kiss her mother's cheek, straightened the Christmas photo where it sat on the end table, and turned to Zach. "Ready to go?"

He knew he was witnessing a turning point in her relationship with her mother. She was drawing a new boundary line, setting a limit to how much time she would spend with someone who didn't appreciate her.

He appreciated her. He loved her, and all the incredible courage she possessed to keep trying, to keep striving, no matter how unfair life had been to her.

She led the way to the front door, but her mother called out before they reached it. "It's in the bedroom."

They stopped.

"What is?" Brooke asked.

"Your graduation photo. It's in my bedroom, on the bureau, if your...if your young man wanted to see it before you go." She waved her white tissue toward the hall, a little flag of surrender. "Go ahead and show it to him, if he wants to see it."

Zach felt Brooke slip her hand into his.

He nodded gravely at her mother. "Thank you, ma'am. I'd like that very much."

* * *

Zach didn't take his eyes off the road as he drove, but he felt Brooke shift in the passenger seat of her own car, restless. Restless good, because she'd gotten past something she'd been dreading? Or restless bad, because she'd relived so many hard moments?

They were driving back to their side of Austin, so he'd have to turn toward either his house or her apartment shortly. He broke the silence. "Your place or mine?"

She shifted in her seat again. "That line may be even older than 'Can I buy you a drink?'"

Restless good, then. She was making a joke.

"Lady's choice. Your place or mine. We're getting close to the Mopac, so choose soon."

"Your truck is at my apartment. I have to work tomorrow, anyway."

"Your apartment, then." After a few more minutes of silent driving, they pulled into her complex, which he'd taken to privately calling Senior Citizen Land. Such a strange place for her to live—

No, it wasn't. It made perfect sense now. No children. No triggering of painful memories.

She stopped him on the sidewalk and gestured toward his truck. "I'm just going to sleep and get up for work in the morning. You might want to head back to your place."

Everything in him rebelled at the idea. She'd opened up to him today, lost her cool veneer and let him see the real woman underneath, with all her past sorrows and current worries. If she retreated into her retirement home, she'd close out the world once more, and him with it.

"I'm not much fun tonight," she said. "You should have a night off from all this drama."

"This isn't drama. You didn't cause this. It's just life."

"Whatever it is, you don't need it. You already helped me after that car accident patient got to me yesterday. You were really wonderful with my mother today."

"I pissed her off."

"That was kind of wonderful, to be honest. I think she liked you by the time we left."

"Good."

Brooke's smile was fleeting. She rubbed her arms against the light chill in the night air.

"Do you really want to be alone tonight?"

She closed her eyes in pain or resignation or some other emotion. "I'm trying to give you a chance to take a break, a graceful exit after a solid forty-eight hours of probably the most difficult girlfriend you've ever dated. Take it."

"Unless you're planning on leaving me at the altar, you don't get to wear the most difficult girlfriend crown. It's been taken."

Her eyes flew open at that.

He cupped her face in his hands. Had he really been foolish enough to think he'd contain these feelings for her? This fire wasn't going to burn itself out, not anytime soon. Not ever. She was too special—but she didn't know that. She'd lost her fan club at age twelve.

"These past two days have been intense. You've been the girl with the tragic past for a long time, haven't you? That's not how I've ever seen you. When I met you, you were a kick-ass ER doctor who didn't fall at my feet. That's who is telling me to leave now, too. But I know something else about you. You want what I want."

"I do?"

"You don't want to be the girl with the tragic past. You want to be the woman who has fun outdoors on a Saturday in May, and you want to have that fun with me. You know why? Because we're two of a kind. We're ready for some happiness in our lives, and part of that happiness is finding someone who understands us. Someone who isn't afraid to try again and again. Someone who'll never run away. Someone who's brave enough to stay."

And suddenly, he didn't know if he was talking about her wants or his own, but it didn't matter because she reached to hold his face in her hands, too, and they were kissing, warm and full and fulfilling.

The distinctive sound of a trash bag being thrown with some force into a Dumpster was followed by a disgruntled man's voice. "Take it inside!"

They did.

Sex was out of place on a day like today, but there was comfort in the little routines of living. Formal black clothes were shed and well-worn flannel pants, undemanding in their shapelessness, signaled sleep. So did a cold glass of water, the reaching for a lamp switch, the sharing of a pillow.

Brooke's breath was warm on the skin of his neck. Her fingers smoothed their way over his hair, a soothing good-night gesture. He kissed her gently, and then she kissed him twice more, once as he cupped her cheek, once as he rested his hand on the side of her neck. Her loose sleep shirt slid off her shoulder, and then she was turning to him in the dark, her unhurried hands pushing aside bedding and shirts and flannel in sleepy silence. Everything was softness, skin, and warmth between them.

It wasn't a night for sex, but for making love.

Afterward, he felt her breathing slow as she drifted to sleep with her cheek resting over his heart. He lay with his arm tucked behind his head, contemplating the ceiling of the apartment he wanted her to give up.

They should live together. They were always grabbing clothes and leaving vehicles at one place or the other. She liked his house. It was small, two bedrooms and one bath, but the land was pretty enough, and Brooke spent a lot of time on the porch enjoying the modest view of a simple creek. Money wasn't plentiful for a firefighter, but he could swing some renovations, doing the work himself. An updated bathroom, a bigger tub. Yeah, it would be nice.

There were no kids around his cabin to send Brooke into a dark place. The house was so remote, there was no worry about it being quiet enough when they had to sleep during the day. If it was their only address, they'd always know where to find each other. They'd always know where they'd be sleeping. Together.

As he tried to imagine the conversation, the invitation, it left a bad taste in his mouth. "Hey, Brooke. We should live together. You like my place, right?"

It was all wrong. Living together sounded like a matter of convenience, not a commitment. Knocking out a closet wall to make a bigger bathroom wasn't as symbolic as sliding a gold band on a ring finger.

He rubbed his ring-free hand over the smooth skin of her bare shoulder as she slept.

"Brooklyn Brown, you're a beautiful woman. I love everything about you. I love your grace under pressure, I love the way you fight for your patients, and I love the way you fight for your chance at happiness. I love the way I feel when I'm with you. I love you. Will you marry me and live with me forever?"

Yes, that sounded right.

He'd told her today that marriage would never again be in his future. Was tomorrow too soon to tell her how wrong he'd been?

Chapter 13

Emergency rooms operated under their own set of Murphy's Laws. Chief among them was this: if the day was so slow and dull that personnel were sent home, patients would flood the waiting room as soon as the staff left.

As they juggled the sudden deluge of patients, Brooke happened to pass the only other physician on duty. "Mac-Dowell, this is your fault. You had to send Dr. Gregory home, didn't you?"

Jamie held his hands up in surrender. "You'd think I'd know better by now. My bad."

As Brooke picked up the next patient chart, she realized she was smiling.

Good.

That's what Zach would say. Not, *how can you be happy when work is swamped?* Not, *how can you be happy when yesterday was your sister's memorial day?*

Nope. If he knew she felt really content today, like a woman who was grounded, who had real friends—or just like a woman who'd slept well—he'd say "good" and then take her for a bite to eat at some unique taco joint that featured an amazing musician.

One day after her mother had tried to play a game of "Who Grieves the Most," life was good. Being Zach's girlfriend was even better.

Brooke was nearly through with a patient who'd arrived in the middle of her first migraine, with intense pain and visual disturbances that would terrify anyone if they didn't know the cause. Jamie rapped on the door and asked her for a moment of her time.

"Got a patient coming in by air," he began without preamble, all business. "Another by ambulance. Two minutes."

"Which one do you want?"

"You get the roof."

Brooke rapidly signed discharge orders for her migraine patient and headed for the elevator. The helicopter landing pad was on the roof of the hospital. The hospital security guard was standing by to override the elevator and take Brooke and her team straight up.

The nurse who'd manned the radio stepped in. "That got nerve-racking in the middle, didn't it?" she said to the orderly with her as the doors closed.

"Fill me in." Brooke pulled her stethoscope out of her pocket and slung it around her neck. She checked her watch. The second hand was sweeping around, steady. Ready.

"Seventeen-year-old male, lost while hiking, stuck on the side of a cliff overnight. Your basic exposure call, some abrasions. The harrowing part was the rescue swimmer. I guess a gust of wind came up the cliff face and slammed him into the rocks. He caught the patient by one hand and the pilot had to do some maneuvering—I don't know. It was hard to follow on the radio, but everyone got back on board the chopper. Here they come now."

Brooke didn't need to look to know which chopper it would be. The Travis County Sheriff's helicopter wasn't coming in. The medical transport from a rural hospital wouldn't land. The rescue swimmer wasn't with the Coast Guard this far from the ocean. She shielded her eyes against the blasting wind made by the rotor blades as the helicopter with the red-and-blue logo of Texas Rescue and Relief touched down.

Her nurse and orderly speed-walked onto the landing pad after it touched down. Brooke waited by the elevator, obeying protocol despite the sick pitch of her stomach. *Slammed into rocks…got back on board…*but what if he hadn't? Oh, God, what if he hadn't?

She'd left Zach in her bed, sleeping peacefully. Yet here he was, dressed in an orange flight suit and a black harness, his face hidden by a white aviator helmet, pushing a gurney toward her from under the helicopter's slowing blades, jogging along with her orderly and her nurse.

Jogging with a limp. Hamstring, quadriceps, knee?

But it wasn't until he stood next to her in the elevator, shifting his weight off his left leg, that she saw the tear in his left sleeve and the gash in his triceps. Blood was still flowing freely, only coagulating around the edges of the wound.

Brooke had already put her hands on the teenaged hiker, which meant her latex gloves couldn't touch anyone else. She jerked her chin toward the nurse. "Are your gloves clean? Get that towel on his arm before he bleeds on something."

The nurse folded one of the clean towels that were tucked into the gurney and placed it over the gash in the back of Zach's upper arm. Zach automatically reached around to hold it in place, as cool and calm as if it didn't hurt at all. When the elevator stopped at the ER and the orderly pushed the gurney into a treatment room, Zach quietly murmured in her ear. "What's a nice girl like you doing in a place like this?"

"Stitching up your arm. Don't leave this ER until you're seen, Bishop."

"It's that bad?" he asked, craning his neck to try to see the back of his arm.

"Let's go." She stepped up to the teenager on the gurney and started taking his pulse, two fingers on his wrist, eyes on the second hand of her watch.

"Seventeen-year-old male, exposure times eighteen hours, dehydration."

As Zach rattled off his report, Brooke kept her eyes on the teenager. She wanted to take a closer look at Zach's arm, but she had to do this job first.

Zach had already started all the right medical treatments, primarily IV fluids and blankets for warmth. Fortunately for the teenager, the night temperatures had stayed in the sixties, far from freezing but still significantly lower than human body temperature. His body, skinny in its adolescence, had worked hard to stay warm as the hours passed, but it was already recovering. The moment the nurse verified that the patient's body temperature was as normal as his pulse and blood pressure, Brooke ditched her latex gloves and started donning a fresh pair.

She pulled the towel away from Zach's arm. "Come with me. You're worse off than he is."

"Nah, just some bruises—"

"Don't argue with my medical assessment." All the private treatment rooms were full, so she led him to the curtained-off area that was used for overflow. "Sit."

Zach leaned his hip on the exam table as casually as he'd done on the picnic table just yesterday. She started opening drawers, looking for the heavy-duty bandage scissors. Behind her, Zach made a sound of pain, a quiet curse deep in this throat.

She turned to see him using two hands to lift the heavy helmet from his head.

"Don't use that arm," she said sharply.

"Yeah." He'd already dropped his left arm and was tilting his head to finish hauling the helmet off with only his right hand. He dropped it less than gracefully on the exam table. "You're right about that."

"Now sit. All the way. You're going to be here for a while." She slid her finger under the elasticized cuff of his sleeve and positioned her scissors.

Zach jerked his arm. "Don't cut it."

When she glared at him, he tried to do his charming smile, as if she was any old female in the hospital. "These flight suits aren't cheap. Texas Rescue runs on donations, you know."

Fine. If he was going to treat her as if she was any old female, she'd treat him like any old patient. "Mr. Bishop, your suit is already ruined. I'm not going to aggravate the wound further by dragging this sleeve over it."

She began cutting. The orange tear-resistant fabric resisted her scissors, but she kept at it, revealing his strong forearm inch by inch.

"Sorry," Zach said.

She didn't stop cutting, didn't look up to those blue-green eyes. He was a paramedic; she was a doctor, doing her job. "You know the standard procedure."

A nurse came from the main hall to the overflow area.

"I need a suture tray."

"Coming right up, Dr. Brown." The nurse left, snapping the curtains closed with a jangling of metal rings.

"I'm going to get you a pair of black-framed glasses," Zach said, sounding like that good-time cowboy. "You do the angry schoolteacher really well. It's got a definite appeal."

She kept her eyes on her work. "You're not supposed to be enjoying this."

They both spoke quietly, aware the curtains offered no privacy beyond the visual.

"Can't help it. Dr. Brown in action is pretty damned sexy. I always thought so." He winced when she lifted the shoulder strap of the harness to finish cutting the flight suit. "I'd be enjoying this a lot more if it didn't hurt quite so much. I barely felt it until you made me sit."

"Your body isn't pumping out adrenaline anymore." She carefully pulled the bloody sleeve away from his arm and dropped it in a trash can lined with a red biohazard bag. "It doesn't need to. You're safe now."

He was safe in her hands, but if something had happened to him out there, dangling from a wire—

Later. She couldn't go there now. She was working.

"I want to get this harness off you before I wash out the wound. Otherwise, it will just contaminate it again when you take it off."

Zach started to reach for the fasteners with both hands before she could stop him. He sucked in a hiss of pain at the same time she grabbed for his wrist to hold his injured arm still. "Don't move that arm."

"Right."

She'd been avoiding making eye contact with him, but as they worked together to unfasten the harness with its metal D-rings, she had to glance at his face to assess his reaction to any pain she was causing. He was looking at her, too.

She refolded the towel and held it over the gash protectively as she lifted the harness and pulled it down his arm. She felt his gaze on her.

"I'm okay, Brooke, really."

"Says the man who was bashed into the side of a cliff." With the harness free, she placed it and his helmet onto the only chair in the curtained area. She snapped her gloves off and donned a fresh pair. "I need you to lie facedown so I can rinse this before I suture it."

Zach fit his large frame on the exam table as best he could, positioning himself so she could slide a plastic pan under his arm.

"Were you on the radio?" he asked.

"No, but word travels fast when it's as exciting as a near-death episode." She began pouring sterile saline over the gash, letting the water run freely into the pan.

"That kid wasn't near death. I had him under the arm. I could've held that grip for twenty minutes, if I had to."

"Not the teenager. You. They said you got thrown into a cliff and the pilot couldn't pull you back in right away."

"That's not near death. That's more like a hard hit in a football game. The rigging held me fine."

"While you held the teenager? How much weight did you put on that harness?" The metal rings on the webbed straps were only a few inches in diameter, hardly impressive in their thickness.

"It's made to hold more weight than that, baby. So am I."

The nurse returned with the suture tray. She gathered up the plastic pan and scissors while Brooke mixed the numbing agent and filled the syringe. The nurse didn't leave, but stood there with her hands full.

"You might want to look away for this part," the nurse said. Brooke glanced up to see her smiling at Zach, inviting him to look at her instead.

Women falling for his handsome face. Situation normal.

That sense of normalcy helped Brooke focus as she began injecting the painkiller in strategic sites around the injury. She did not think about this being her lover's arm. This was merely tissue—epidermis, dermis, triceps—that needed numbed before sutures could be placed.

When she finished, she put the needle in the sharps disposal unit and addressed Zach formally. "The medicine needs a few minutes to be effective. I want you to rest in place. I'll be back."

She pushed the curtain aside, walked the few steps it took to get into the main hallway, and leaned against the cold, solid wall. Numbing that gash shouldn't have required so much concentration. She'd pushed four-inch-long needles into countless body parts. It was necessary to cause a temporary pain that protected the patient from a more unbearable pain.

It had taken a surprising amount of effort. This, then, was why doctors weren't supposed to work on loved ones.

The nurse stopped to deliver a message. "The patient asked me to find you. He wants to talk to you."

Brooke nodded. "Would you please see if Dr. Mac-Dowell is available for a consult right now?"

The nurse's surprise was understandable. Stitching a gash was hardly something that doctors consulted one another about, but if Jamie was free, Brooke would rather he did the suturing. Jamie and Zach were friends, so there was no completely disinterested provider available, but she was the patient's girlfriend. Surely, that made her too close to Zach.

On the other hand, Zach and Jamie had known each other for years. More than a decade. She'd only been dating him for weeks.

She remembered last night. Her bed. Their warmth.

Yes, she should be the last option when it came to operating on him.

The nurse returned quickly. "Dr. MacDowell's not going to be free for a long time. Car accident. The patient lost a lot of blood and his body's shutting down." She proceeded to describe some of the dramatic measures that had already been taken.

"Thank you." Brooke held up a hand to cut her off in the middle of her enthusiastically gory report. It looked like either Brooke was going to stitch Zach up, or she was going to leave him sitting with an open wound, waiting for Jamie for another hour, possibly more.

This was strictly business.

She whisked the curtain open once more.

"Here's the deal. You need stitches, no question, but since we have a personal relationship, I'm technically only supposed to do it if there are no alternatives. The only other provider on duty right now is Jamie. He's in the middle of a critical case. Since it's Sunday afternoon,

I doubt there are any surgeons hanging out in the hospital, but I could page one."

Zach raised one brow. "Or you could do it yourself."

She met his look squarely, wanting to evaluate her own emotional control as she looked into those blue-green eyes. After a moment's gut-check, she said, "Yes, I could."

"Well, then, make it pretty. You're the one who's going to have to look at it."

She did it.

Brooke had done worse. Only two days ago, she'd blocked out every memory of her sister and worked on the little girl from the car accident. And now, she'd blocked out the fact that the raw flesh under her needle was the body of the man she loved.

Zach meant more to her than any other man ever had. He was as important to her as family. Family was vulnerable. She'd lost her sister. Her father. How close had she just come to losing Zach on the side of a cliff?

It didn't matter. These were just sutures. A simple fix for a simple injury.

Still, she was glad it was over.

"Don't bandage it yet. I want to see it. Got a mirror?" Zach was off the table before she could stop him, although putting weight on that left leg caused him obvious pain. He hopped over to the mirror by the sink, anyway, and twisted to admire her handiwork.

She opened the drawer for another pair of scissors. "You're favoring your left leg. Is it your hip, knee or ankle? All three?"

"Mostly hip."

She nodded. That was good. The hip was a bigger

joint, far less likely to have gotten dislocated or torn than a knee or ankle. Bruises could heal on their own, no surgery required.

"Let me see it," she said, gesturing for him to return to the exam table.

"Brooke, put the scissors away. I'm not getting back in the helicopter with no pants on."

At the idea of him climbing back into Texas Rescue One, something inside her snapped. How dare he endanger himself again? How dare he put her through this again?

"You're not getting back in that helicopter at all."

"My truck is parked at Texas Rescue. Chopper One is my ride back to the office. Besides, I have to make sure y'all don't steal our gurney. I've got to take that back up."

"You are not pushing a gurney. I just stitched you up, damn it." She kept her voice to a hiss, mindful of the useless curtains around them. The heat inside her could have sent them up in flames. How dare he?

How *dare* he put her through this?

"Brooke—"

"You are grounded, Bishop. Doctor's orders. I won't let you undo all my work. Texas Rescue has to abide by my medical orders if you won't."

"Brooke, baby—"

"I don't want you to be in danger. Do you see that? I can't keep you safe if you keep this up. That arm is going to be at half strength, if you're lucky, for weeks. You would be a danger to yourself and your crew."

"Hey, Brooke?"

"What?"

"I love you, too."

The heat inside her froze. Ice-cold. Slowly, she sank

to the edge of the chair, his helmet at her back, his harness digging into the back of her thigh.

Oh, no. She loved him, and he loved her, too. And that meant only one thing would happen next: death.

No, no, no.

She pressed her hand to her temple, trying to keep herself focused. The hand that had held forceps and needle steady now shook with the terror of losing another person she loved. It was irrational, and she knew it. She'd get her act together in a moment. One moment.

"I didn't mean to make you sad." Zach sounded sad himself, as sad as she'd ever heard him. He went to one knee beside the chair, but he sucked in a little breath and grimaced as he put his hand to his side.

Ribs. Only ribs caused a patient to do that move. "You need an X-ray." The words were automatic. The first step on the checklist was obvious.

"Nah, I'm fine. I've had broken ribs before. It's nothing like that."

She stared him down.

"You're going to make me get an X-ray before I go, aren't you?"

She nodded in silence.

Her moment of irrational fear was up. She was ready to talk now, ready to be sane.

"Do you know why I don't want to have a child?" she asked quietly.

"Memories of your sister make it too painful for you. I never asked, but were you in the car with her when it happened?"

"No, it wasn't that kind of car accident. She'd wandered away from us in a parking lot. A car hit her. I saw it happen. I couldn't keep her safe."

"I'm so sorry."

"I know, and thank you for that. But all that is in the past now. I'm talking about now. I'm talking about the future."

"Good."

"Have you ever heard that having a child is like having your heart walk around outside your body? I see the parents in here. They might as well be the ones who are hurt or sick, because they hurt that badly for their children. Love makes you vulnerable, terribly vulnerable, and if there is anything my past has taught me, it's that I can't risk being that vulnerable again."

The nurse interrupted them, her cheerful voice calling from the other side of the curtain. "Is it okay if I come in?"

"Nope," Zach replied, sounding shockingly carefree. "I'm dressing. Give me a few minutes."

"Okay."

The curtain length was hemmed to be more than a foot off the tile floor. Brooke watched the nurse's white-clogged feet walk away.

"Go on." Zach took her hand as he stayed kneeling.

"That's really all there is to it. It's not that I wouldn't love a child. It's that I couldn't guarantee his or her safety, so I won't risk it. And Zach—I don't want to risk loving you, either."

"I understand." So much sadness in that cowboy voice.

"But I don't have much choice in the matter. I love you already."

He jerked a little at her words. "You realize that?"

"Yes, I've known it for a while now. But—wait, do you mean you'd already decided I loved you?"

"I was right."

"You're really too confident, you know that?"

He silenced her with a kiss.

She broke it off. "But 'I love you' isn't what I'm trying to explain. You brought up some good points last night on the sidewalk. You said you wanted someone who wasn't afraid to be happy. I have to tell you, I'm scared to death. I'm in love with a man who could be taken from me in the blink of an eye—if not hit by a car, then bashed into a cliff. No matter how hard I try, I can't keep you safe. You have my heart, and you're walking around with it in all kinds of dangerous situations."

He used his good hand on the arm of her chair to leverage himself to his feet. She stood, too.

He was more than just alive. He was larger than life as he stood over her, half bare-chested in the remains of a flight suit. He looked at her, almost right through her, and started shaking his head. Being Zach, he started to grin. "You're forgetting something important."

"What's that?"

"I'm no child. You aren't responsible for my safety. I'm all grown up, and I grew up to be a pretty good size. If your heart's in here, it's got a lot of protection." He punched his bare pectoral muscle lightly with his fist.

That confidence, that cocky attitude, was too appealing. She didn't want to throw reason to the wind and give in to the seduction of a powerful man.

"Your career isn't exactly safe. Didn't I just stitch up your arm? When you aren't hanging from a helicopter, you're a firefighter. You run into burning buildings."

"In a fire suit. With tanks of air and a GPS locator and a team of trained firefighters backing me up. I train hard for a reason, and it's not just to look good for women, darlin'. I'm glad you enjoy this body, but it isn't just for fun. All those push-ups and pull-ups weren't to win a tower race. I'm in shape because that keeps me safe when I'm hanging on to a cable to grab a guy off a cliff. I'm strong so that I only cut my arm instead of plunging to my death."

Oh, the way her heart plunged when he said *my death*.

"Don't say that." She took a step away, ready to yank those curtains aside and leave, but Zach stopped her with a firm grip on her arm. She jerked her arm free before she realized he'd used his injured arm to stop her. His grip had felt strong.

"How deep was that gash?" he asked.

"Deep enough for stitches." She tucked her hands in the pockets of her white coat.

"Be straight with me."

"It wasn't as deep as it looked at first, but it truly needed stitches."

He flexed the biceps of his bare arm briefly. "See? It'll take more than a piece of rock to penetrate these iron pythons."

"Don't joke about it." She was mad at him for laughing. So very mad. But medically, he had a point. It was harder for an object to penetrate dense musculature.

He could read her too easily. He got serious again to press his advantage. "When I'm on the job, it's no different than when you get in your car. You drive a well-built vehicle. You wear a seat belt. You obey the traffic laws. You do everything you can to protect yourself during a potentially dangerous activity. It's not like you stand on the car's hood and try to surf the wrong way down a street."

"Even if I do everything right, I could still be in a car accident."

"You could, but not without a seat belt and airbags and everything that would help your odds. You can't promise me that nothing bad will ever happen to you. But I love you, anyway. There's no other option for me, so despite the worry, I'm going to enjoy every minute with you."

"It would kill me if something bad happened to you."

"But it's unlikely that it will. I promise you, I will never do anything deliberately to cause you pain, and that includes taking unnecessary risks at work. Take a chance on me, Brooke. See what it's like to love someone who isn't so fragile."

She was going to cry. Hope was pounding so hard inside her chest, she could feel tears fighting to well up, strong emotions that needed an outlet. She'd spent so many long years suppressing them, though, that she wasn't sure how tears would feel. She dashed the back of her hand against the corner of her eye. It was dry.

Zach bent and kissed the corner of her eye, anyway, as if she had a tear there that needed to be taken away.

"I already love you," she whispered. "That's what's so scary."

"Yeah, but Brooklyn Brown doesn't scare easy. We're going to grab that happiness, and no one's going to take it away from us. Stay with me, and be happy."

"Oh, Zach."

He smiled as if she'd said much more than that, and kissed her until real tears of hope ran down cheeks that had been dry for far too long.

Chapter 14

The bathroom at his cabin really was too small. A man couldn't step out of the shower without being confronted by his own naked image in the mirror. Zach stood there, nude, and had to admit he looked pretty damned bad. No wonder Brooke had grounded him. He was black and blue down his entire left side. It looked worse today than it had in the three days since the wind had decided to remind them all who was boss.

He started to towel off in his usual brisk way, but his ribs objected within seconds. And his thigh. His upper arm. He ended up dabbing himself dry as gingerly as a pinup girl with a powder puff. Then he pitched his towel with all the force of his throwing arm into the laundry basket with perfect accuracy.

Of course, when the basket was only two feet away, it wasn't much of a win.

The bathroom renovation idea that he'd started mulling over was rapidly becoming a real project in his mind. He'd rather wait until he and Brooke were married, so they could plan it together, turning his bachelor space into a home for man and wife.

That could be a while, though. She needed time to get used to the idea that his career included all kinds of safeguards, and he was considerably heartier than a child. Confidence would come with time, reinforced with every shift where he returned home healthy.

He had the time off now. Even without being married, he could get the project going and ask Brooke's opinion on everything. They could spend their days off looking at faucets and tile and all that other stuff. Maybe it would even help her see that he wasn't as much of an adrenaline junkie as she seemed to think he was. He'd enjoy the challenge of laying tile as much as he would bungee-jumping.

Then, when they married—because he was going to ask her someday, and she was going to say yes—the new bathroom would be a wedding gift.

Besides, she'd grounded him for four more days, and he was bored as hell.

He dressed one-handed, gritting his teeth as he pulled on jeans over his bruised hip. A T-shirt was easier to manage than a button-down. Then he struggled into the sling he had to admit was helpful in preventing him from mindlessly grabbing things with his injured arm. It was a lot easier to dress with Brooke's help, but she was already at the hospital this morning and wouldn't get home from work until eight at night, if she made it out of there on time.

Even with a bum arm, he'd be able to get a lot done by then. He'd have no interruptions for the planning phase.

With pencil, notepad, and measuring tape in hand, he started to sketch the existing floor plan, but ten minutes into it, someone knocked on his front door.

So much for no interruptions.

With his arm in a sling, he had to set his notepad down and stick the pencil in his teeth in order to open the door with his one good hand.

The woman on his porch was a knockout, petite and platinum blonde, an angel dressed in a white halter dress.

"Don't you remember me?" Charisse Johnson clasped her perfect hands together under her perfect breasts. As she gazed up at him as if he were some kind of demigod, a tear dropped from her lashes and rolled down her cheek. "Oh, Zach!"

The pencil clattered to the floor.

"And so I just had to come and see you. My yoga instructor said the most beautiful thing during savasana. Love cannot be destroyed."

Zach leaned against his kitchen counter, watching Charisse as she helped herself to his home, refilling the water glass she'd asked for, part of the long time no see, what did you do to your arm, aren't you going to ask me in routine. It was bizarrely fascinating, like watching a creature from another world, a unicorn in his kitchen.

"He explained it like this. Love is like water. It can be deep and stay in one place, all for one person, or it can flow, trickling out to touch lots and lots of people." Charisse made little rippling motions with her delicate fingers, the ones that had caressed him before sliding a gold band on another man's hand. "But no matter what shape it takes, it cannot be destroyed."

"I take it you're more into the trickling."

She nodded earnestly. "I try to fill my world with love, and leave love everywhere I've been."

There was no way she'd missed his sarcasm. During their whirlwind romance, he'd always thought she was intelligent, just not academically inclined. This delightfully dim-witted chatter was just an act. He had no patience for it.

"It's time to get to the point, Charisse."

"The point? It's all about love. That's the only thing that matters." She walked toward him, right up to him, getting in his personal space. She traced the strap of his sling with one finger. "Look at you, getting hurt in the line of duty, all to save someone you didn't even know. That's a form of love, too. *Agape*. Oh, Zach, you have so much love in you. Surely there's still some for me?"

"No." He stopped her finger and pushed her hand away.

She tossed her platinum hair back and bit her lower lip with her perfect, white teeth. "Not even a little bit?"

"No." It was true. So bone-deep true. He'd once loved her, or the idea of her, absolutely. She'd thrown that love away so hard, it had been obliterated. If he put it in the terms of her stupid water analogy, that love had exploded into a spray of water droplets so tiny, they'd evaporated into the atmosphere.

He'd known this for a long time. It wasn't a revelation that he had no lingering feelings left for Charisse. If this visit was teaching him anything, it was that maybe he could forgive his younger self for being so taken by her. She was every bit as pretty and vivacious as he remembered. He could cut himself a break for having been so blinded back then, instead of hating himself for having been a sucker.

Blonde bombshell or not, if he'd met her for the first time today, the man he was now wouldn't waste more than a smile on Charisse Johnson. She was all surface, no depth.

He looked for more in women since his brush with Charisse, and he'd found it all in Brooke. Pretty had been upgraded to sensational. A woman who was vivacious when ordering drinks at a bar had been replaced by a woman whose vitality energized an emergency department. Giddiness couldn't compete with substance, not that Brooke was always serious. He could recall her applauding in the middle of a bunch of whooping firefighters at the races. That had been truly charming. Even when it came to cheerleading, Charisse wasn't as cute as Brooke.

But she was trying. "No? I don't believe you. Mary Beth saw you on my wedding day. You remember Mary Beth? She was on the island that week, too. All my bridesmaids were. It was the bachelorette party."

"I figured that out."

"They were true friends that week. I almost married you, but they sat me down and gave me a reality check that morning. But the morning of my wedding, my real wedding, Mary Beth said she'd never seen a man look the way you looked. She said you were standing under an old southern oak tree, and you didn't take your eyes off me. Oh, I wish I'd seen you."

They'd now entered the sickening portion of the visit. He found that although the love was long gone, the bitterness remained strong.

"I'm not reliving this with you, Charisse. It no longer matters." He brushed past her to head for the front door, which she would be leaving through shortly.

"Zach, I'm divorced."

I'm not surprised.

"The divorce was final two weeks ago."

He opened the door with more calm and cool than he was really feeling. "I'm sorry, Charisse. I'm not interested in picking up where we left off."

Finally, she dropped her act. Her eyes narrowed and her mouth tightened, but only for a second. She tossed her hair and became charming once more.

"I wasn't asking if you were interested. I've found a man who loves me. He really loves me. I know he's the right one. In fact, we're leaving for our destination wedding today. Tony is taking me all the way to Fiji to say our vows on a tropical beach. I've always wanted to be barefoot in the sand while a man pledged himself to me— oh, sorry. No offense."

"None taken."

"But I need a little favor. Destination weddings are so glamorous. They are not a place for children—and Zach, I'm a mother now." She pressed her fingertips to her chest and smiled like a virtuous, platinum Madonna.

That one was a stretch. Charisse with maternal instincts? Whatever. Some other man's problem.

"I need your help. I need someone to care for my child while I'm gone."

It was such an outrageous request, Zach had no reply. This was why she had come? If she still lived in Alabama, she'd come a long way.

"Who could I turn to? I thought of you right away."

"No."

"For one thing, you're a fireman, and they always show photos of firemen caring for children on Facebook."

"This is insane, Charisse. The answer is no, I will not babysit your kid while you go get married in Fiji."

"For another thing," she said, and despite her smile, he could see that she was irritated with him for interrupting her pretty speech, "you loved me, and for a man to do what Mary Beth said you'd done, to track me down and come after me… Well, a love like that can't be destroyed completely."

"You can take that up with your yoga instructor."

What a frigging nightmare this was. Thank God, thank God, *thank God* Charisse had stood him up four years ago.

He wanted Brooke. Just the thought of Brooke was like a balm to his soul right now. He was going to get Charisse out of his house, get into his truck, and drive to the hospital. He'd bring Brooke anything in the world she wanted to eat for lunch, and he'd feed her every bite while telling her how priceless she was.

"And I've got the child to prove that our love still exists, something special between you and me, forever. Our child." She closed the distance between them and shut the front door with a flourish, the exclamation point on the end of her speech.

Memories started crowding in. Zach didn't focus on memories of having sex with Charisse, but memories of using birth control with her. Condoms—yes, they'd used condoms. She'd been on the pill, too.

At least his younger self hadn't been dumb enough to take her word for the pills. He'd moved into her hotel room on the third day of that vacation, and he'd seen the round prescription compact by the sink, next to her toothbrush. But they'd used condoms as well before that, because pills didn't protect against…but then, she was an angel, and they were going to elope, and it was silly to worry about catching a disease from his almost-wife. His faithful, innocent one-and-only.

His younger self had been an idiot. He was lucky he hadn't caught any diseases after they'd ditched the condoms. But when it came to pregnancy, she'd still been on the pill. He was covered there.

"The baby was born exactly nine months after the wedding. My husband and I hadn't been planning on children so soon, but it was fun. Lots of baby showers.

"Then, about a year after she was born, well, our marriage hit a little rough patch. We smoothed things over, but Gary started saying she didn't look like him. Everyone, and I do mean everyone, told him that children's looks change a lot at that age, but he was as obstinate as a mule. By the time she was three he demanded a paternity test, can you believe it?"

How many yoga instructors had he caught you with in those three years?

Zach said nothing. He was in a state of suspended animation, watching a scene in someone else's life, waiting to see what would happen next. It was kind of a blessedly numb state to be in.

"He took her to the lab himself and got the paternity test. As they say on TV, he wasn't the baby-daddy, after all." She heaved a great sigh.

"So then he made a big fuss about it, and I just had to get away for a little while. While I was gone, he took her over to my parents' house and freaked them out by saying he wasn't going to care for another man's child. You can just imagine the scene when I got back from the cruise. Long story short, the divorce became final two weeks ago, right on the baby's fourth birthday, and

I couldn't be happier. Tony treats me so much better than Gary ever did. Fiji will be a dream come true.

"But my parents are being so old-fashioned, saying they've done their part and the parent should raise the child, not the grandparents. Not even just for one more month. So I thought to myself, I'm not the only parent, am I? Tony helped me track you down. Oh, Zach. It is good to see you."

Zach sat down heavily on his couch and shoved his hand through his hair. Fifteen minutes ago, all he'd wanted in life was to design a new bathroom to surprise Brooke. Now he was dealing with more drama than he'd dealt with in the past four years. Four years and nine months, to be precise.

This is drama, Brooke. Over the weekend, she'd apologized for putting him through drama, when it had only been life. Charisse created drama. She'd been born with every advantage a person could have to succeed in life, but she tossed the good things in her life away, time after time, thoughtlessly.

And maybe there was something to Charisse's water theory, because a very tiny part of him pitied her.

He still wasn't babysitting her child while she ran off to Fiji. "I'm not buying it, Charisse. Just because your ex-husband wasn't the father, that doesn't mean I am, either."

"Who else would it be? What kind of woman do you think I am?"

"The kind who sleeps with one man days before she marries another." He let that comment sink in. Whether he pitied her or not, he was fed up with her cockeyed view of the world. "It's entirely possible there is another baby-daddy candidate out there besides me and your ex."

"Oh, that's a terrible thing to say."

"There has to be, in fact. You either got pregnant on your honeymoon or within a week or two afterward, but it wasn't before. You were on the pill when you were with me. It's very effective, so I doubt I'm the father. You had your fling with me the week before the wedding. What's to stop you from having a fling the week after?"

"It's you, Zach."

"I saw you take a pill in the hotel room."

"One." She stared down at him, looking triumphant as she gave him the details with gusto. "I had a lot going on that month. Between the wedding nerves and the beach vacation and the alcohol, I skipped a bunch of pills that month, actually. The OB-GYN said that's how I got pregnant. You're it, Zach."

It was possible. The room seemed to lose its air. For one stunning moment, he had trouble drawing in a breath, and it had nothing to do with his bruised ribs.

Charisse was also an accomplished liar. Zach needed proof. "The first thing we're going to do is a paternity—"

He cut himself off at the sound of a small thump from the porch, followed by the wail of a child. It was the instantly recognizable true wail, the cry that indicated real pain.

The kind that made paramedics jump into action.

Chapter 15

The child's cry pierced its way right through the front door.

Zach was already on his feet, moving Charisse out of his way and yanking open the door. He cleared the porch stairs by jumping down them in one leap.

The little girl was lying in the grass to the side of the stairs. The natural land tended toward scrub brush and hard dirt, but in the shade of the stairs, the wild grass had grown to a decent height for May. Zach hoped it had cushioned her fall.

She was unmistakably Charisse's daughter, from her platinum curls to her white sundress. When she saw Zach, her blue-green eyes opened wide. He knew he looked like a giant stranger to her, which he was. A little gasp of fear choked off her cry of pain.

Kids were always intimidated when a firefighter suddenly appeared. It took another beat for him to remember he wasn't in uniform. This wasn't a regular call.

He gave her the Friendly Fireman smile, anyway. "Hey, sweetheart. I came to help you. Can you tell me what happened?"

She nodded despite her now rhythmic sobs. "I—felled—down."

"You sure did."

"I got hurt."

He should have latex gloves and a medical kit. Without a stethoscope, without anything at all, it was just him and the child, and he had one arm in a sling just to make it really difficult.

Come on, Bishop, you can assess a pediatric patient with one arm tied behind your back.

He put his hand on her ankle, just above the little white-strapped sandal, a steady touch to establish his friendly presence. Plus, kids had such delicate skin, he could usually feel their pulse anywhere. Her cries were tapering off. Her breathing was less shallow and rapid already. That was good.

"Where does it hurt the most?"

Charisse stomped down the stairs as heavily as a dainty woman in white sandals could stomp. "For heaven's sake, Zoe. What did you do now?" She crouched down, stuck her hands under Zoe's shoulders, and started hauling her out from under the stairs.

"Wait." Zach grabbed Charisse's arm, but she'd already pulled the little girl out. "You don't move a patient like that."

"Patient? Kids fall down and get hurt all the time. Trust me. It's no big deal." She started brushing grass and dirt off the skirts of the girl's dress with little smacking swipes of her hand. "And they are always getting dirty. Look at you. I wanted you to look so pretty with Mommy."

Zach looked around his property, seeing the creek in a whole new light. "She was out here alone this whole time? You left her on the porch?"

Charisse picked up her daughter and perched her on her hip. With her palm, she wiped the tears off the girl's cheeks briskly, but in an unmistakably motherly way. Zoe didn't seem to like the face-wiping, but Zach supposed no kid would. Maybe Charisse was a capable parent, after all.

"I left her in the car. Somebody was very, very naughty and disobedient and didn't stay in the car like Mommy told her to."

Or not.

Zach saw red. "You never, ever leave a kid in a car. It's May. It's Texas. My fire engine has been called out too many times to break a window in a hot parking lot to free a kid." He wouldn't say it in front of Zoe, but twice they'd arrived to find a victim unconscious. They'd called in air transport for those.

Charisse kept up her fake Mommy voice. "Well, Mr. Zach, if you look at the sky, you'll see that it's not too hot today at all. It looks like rain."

"It's against the law. Don't do it again. Ever."

Anger mixed with physical pain. He hurt everywhere. Jumping from the height of his porch when half his body was black and blue hadn't been his smartest move. It hadn't hurt in the moment, but it did now. That burst of adrenaline must be wearing off. That's what Brooke would say.

Brooke. His chest hurt all over again. He wished she were here, assessing the situation in her cool way, keeping them all on point when Charisse went off on her poor-me stories.

Brooke, who would have run down the stairs and found a little girl lying on the ground, as she'd once seen her sister.

He remembered the photo of Chelsea Brown in the white bunny costume, gazing up at Brooke so adoringly. He looked at Zoe, her dress as white as the costume, and his vision blurred with sudden emotion. Would Brooke see the resemblance?

Of course she would have, if she'd been here. She'd said she was fine in the moment when she had to treat a child, but he knew the nightmares were the price she paid. Zach was glad she was at work. It was going to be hard enough tonight to tell her about this day. He'd get Charisse and her daughter on their way, but he'd be following up to get that paternity test.

And if the test came back the way he was becoming certain it would...

He reached up to grab the band of his sling, needing to readjust the weight on his neck.

Charisse had been fussing with her child's hair. She sighed. "That's as good as you're gonna get, Zoe. Ready? Let's do our special smile." Then Charisse pressed her cheek against her daughter's and smiled like a dazzling toothpaste model.

Little Zoe obediently bared her teeth in a painful grimace.

"Look, she's my mini-me. We both have dimples, Mr. Zach." She reached up and held her daughter's face in her thumb and finger, giving it a squeeze. "We're just alike, except she has blue-green eyes, doesn't she, Mr. Zach? Have you noticed what else you have in common? Have you, have you?"

Charisse's baby voice was grating on nerves that had so recently been grated against a cliff.

"Your names both start with the letter *z*! Zoe and Zachary. Zzzoe. Zzzachary."

"Enough. I get it."

"I did that on purpose. When I was pregnant, I had a feeling the baby was yours. You were just so much better in bed than Gary. That honeymoon was such a dud."

"Enough." Children weren't deaf. Even he knew that.

Charisse rolled her eyes. "She doesn't know what I mean."

Kids still repeated things. It was damned funny at the firehouse when someone else's kid did it. He didn't think Zoe would hear laughter if she said something to her new stepfather about how Zach or Gary performed in bed. Or a yoga instructor.

He couldn't keep his eyes off Zoe. Whether it was from a personal or professional compulsion was a toss-up, but as a paramedic, he couldn't miss how she was holding her arm against her chest. "Zoe, does your arm hurt?"

She turned her silent gaze on him and nodded, upper lip quivering.

"Her knee is skinned, too. Come back in the house. I'll take a look at it. Then, we need to talk privately."

Charisse had no first aid skills. Zach lifted Zoe with one arm onto the sink counter in the bathroom that was absolutely, positively going to get remodeled as soon as possible. He was dabbing hydrogen peroxide on Zoe's knee when Charisse noticed the clock in his bathroom and commented that it was nearly lunchtime.

If she thought he was going to invite her to stay for a little homemade meal, she was crazy. Or even more crazy than she already was. "You and your daughter will be able to find lots of restaurants on the way back into Austin, but you're going to need to stop at an urgent care center and get an X-ray first."

Zach was sizing a sling from a first aid kit to keep Zoe's arm immobile when Charisse abruptly decided to get her phone out of her car.

"I'll be right back." She smoothed her daughter's hair where it had gotten mussed up by the sling. "I want to use the map thingamajig to find out where the nearest urgent care center is, if you really think she needs an X-ray."

"I can tell you where," Zach said in exasperation, but the front door had already slammed shut. He shook his head until he realized Zoe was looking at him. "Can I get you anything, sweetheart?"

She only stared at him with those blue-green eyes. Zach looked over her head into the mirror. Was his eye color that unique? He looked back down to find her studying him with unwavering intensity.

"Maybe you'd like a drink? I've got milk."

"Thank you very much, Mr. Zach."

The sentence was so clear and proper, it startled him. "Just Zach. No mister."

"Our arms match."

He picked her up, careful to keep both their injured arms immobile. "This is gonna be a challenge, but we can do it."

He was carrying her into the kitchen when he heard the sound of a car's trunk slamming shut. That was an odd place to keep a phone, but perhaps Charisse had wanted to keep it out of reach of Zoe while she'd been left in the car.

He gave Zoe a bit of a squeeze. Poor thing. Although

it wasn't hot today, she must have felt very lonely in that car, parked at a stranger's house.

Zach set her on her feet so he could do the one-armed retrieval of the milk. As he shut the fridge door, he heard the slamming of Charisse's car door, but it wasn't until he heard the car's engine that he suddenly remembered.

"Fiji."

Milk sloshed onto the countertop as he slammed the carton down and sprinted for the door.

She couldn't. She couldn't be that bad of a mother. No one left their child with a virtual stranger.

"Charisse!"

He skidded to a stop at the top of the stairs. There was no need to jump down them a second time today. Charisse was driving away, fast. The dust her tires had kicked up in his dirt drive was already settling back down, covering the items she'd left behind.

The first drops of rain began spattering the tiny princess suitcase that waited next to a child's car seat. They couldn't have looked more out of place on his property.

The rain began pelting Zach, but he didn't hurry as he walked down the stairs, retrieved the suitcase and seat, and returned to the house where, with a silent audience of one, he began cleaning up the milk he'd so carelessly spilled.

Brooke didn't want to tempt Murphy's Law, but things were so slow in the ER, she considered asking Jamie if she could cut her shift short. She didn't want to jinx everyone by leaving, but even the rainstorm hadn't picked up the pace. Usually, rain meant car accidents, but not this afternoon. It had only rained hard enough to keep all the people with minor problems like colds from coming into the ER.

The doctors were assigned patients evenly, but in typical Murphy fashion, hers had happened to all be quick cases. The three treatment rooms on Jamie's side of the hallway were still occupied, but according to the nurses' station whiteboard, none of Jamie's cases were difficult, either. They were just waiting on standard lab work. There was nothing Brooke could jump in and help with, really.

In short, Brooke was bored, and she missed Zach.

She took out her cell phone and leaned on the nurses' station counter. Often, twelve hours at work could go by without a single chance to send a text message. Today wasn't one of those days for her, but apparently Zach was tied up. He was taking forever to acknowledge her texts.

Wanna take me out tonite? Heard the Bond movie was good.

She'd started with that, thinking it would make her guy happy and give him something to do during his medical convalescence that wouldn't stress the stitches she'd given with such care.

An hour later, she'd gotten this reply: Let's stay in.

She wished she could think of something sexy to say. The best she came up with was I like the way you think, followed by a winking smiley face. Oh, so sexy.

Silence for at least half an hour.

Great but also need to talk. Want your advice.

Frowning, she'd immediately typed, Are you ok?

It seemed like an eternity before he'd responded, I'm healthy. Promise.

That had been an hour ago. She checked her phone

again. Still nothing else. She drummed her fingers on the counter. When Jamie came out of his treatment room, jinx or no jinx, she was going to suggest he let her go home—and by home, she meant Zach's place. Something was off.

Tom Bamber came sauntering up to the station with a set of X-rays in his hands. A slow day in the ER meant a slow day down in radiology, too.

"Hi, Tom."

He nodded rather formally at her, which was pretty much all he'd done since she'd turned down his invitation to the ballet weeks ago.

"What's on the films?" she asked. The day was so slow, she was willing to read an X-ray for fun.

But Tom had eyes for the single nurse on duty. "These are for MacDowell." He smiled at the nurse as he caressed the manila jacket that protected the sheets of black film.

The nurse returned his smile, barely. She was not interested in chatting with Dr. Bamber.

Brooke pretended to be absorbed by her unchanging text screen. It was a new low in slow days when watching Tom attempt to court a nurse was entertaining.

The nurse patted the countertop. "If you leave the films here, I'll be sure to give them to Dr. MacDowell as soon as he gets out of the treatment room."

"That's very, very thoughtful of you, but I can wait right here, at your desk, and give him the report in person. So tell me, what kind of food do you like to eat?"

As pickup lines went, Bamber was no Zach Bishop.

The nurse stood. "Actually, you know what? I should take those in and put them on the light box for Dr. Mac-Dowell."

She took the films out of Bamber's hands and made

her escape, briskly walking down the hall the other way, to the curtained-off overflow area. Bamber cleared his throat, nodded formally to Brooke once more, and returned to his basement, empty-handed.

Time dragged on. The nurse returned. "Zach's little girl is such a cutie."

Brooke looked up from her phone screen. "Pardon me?"

"The little girl Zach brought in. She's so cute. Aren't you dating Zach? From the Eye—uh, that is…"

"Eye Candy Engine," Brooke murmured, immediately turning to look out the sliding glass doors. Engine Thirty-Seven was not out there. Nor had any choppers come in.

Zach was moonlighting for an ambulance, then. That was why he was so unavailable by text. That was why he didn't feel a need to get out of the house and go to a movie tonight. She could just imagine him stuck at home this morning, going stir-crazy, and one of the ambulance companies calling to see if he could sub for a short shift. A little extra cash, a little excitement.

She hadn't sent her medical orders to any of the private ambulance companies, just to Texas Rescue. He wouldn't technically be violating her orders if he worked an ambulance shift.

What if he needed to perform CPR again? The demand on his sewn-up triceps would be significant. He'd be able to do it—he wasn't endangering a patient—but it could set his own recovery back.

"Do you mean the Zach with the dark blond hair?" she asked the nurse. Cryptic text messages or not, it sounded too sneaky. Her Zach would've just told her that he was taking an ambulance shift.

"Yeah, the buff guy. The funny one. I'm going to check on room three now. Excuse me, Dr. Brown."

Brooke glanced at the whiteboard. No X-rays were listed. More significantly, no one was listed as being in the overflow area.

This was absurd. If Zach was here, she'd go say hello. She slipped her phone in one of her white coat's oversize pockets and headed for the curtained area.

She heard him before she saw him. The tone of his voice said there was nothing to worry about, everything would be okay. His actual words were, "Your grandma is going to send the doctors a piece of paper saying we can start fixing your arm."

He was with an unaccompanied minor, then. How very like Zach to stay until the patient was more comfortable.

"This is Dr. Brown," she said to the curtain. "May I come in?"

The pause seemed long.

"Sure, come on in."

As always, her first glance at Zach gave her system a charge. And lately, the electric awareness was accompanied by a relief that she could see with her own eyes that he was safe. And hers.

At the moment, a little girl seemed to think he was hers. Already sitting nearly in Zach's lap, a little angel with white-blond hair scooted even closer to him, the paper cover on the exam table crinkling under her white dress. Like Zach, her arm was in a sling, the plain cotton kind found in first aid kits. She stared up at Brooke with huge blue eyes.

In the fraction of a second it took for Brooke to smile reassuringly at the scared child, her brain registered details in rapid fire. *Pretty girl. Curls like my sister. Zach's great with kids. He's not in uniform. Not working after all.*

Wait, then why—

The miniature angel burst into tears. She buried her face in Zach's side and started scooching around to hide behind him. Brooke watched Zach use the fingers of his sling hand to soothe her curls as he kept his other arm around her securely.

"Oh, dear. I better go." Brooke backed toward the curtain. Jamie wouldn't appreciate her upsetting his patient.

"No, wait." Zach looked at her with something very like pleading in his eyes, but pleading for what? For help soothing the patient? He was usually better at it than she was.

He was in a sling. How silly of her. She quickly went to the sink to grab the box of tissues that was kept to the left in every room. "Here you go."

Zach hunched closer to the crying girl and spoke so quietly, it was almost a whisper. "Hey, Zoe? Can I tell you something?"

He waited.

After a moment of indecision, Zoe looked up at him and nodded. This big grown-up could tell her something.

Brooke shook her head in awe. How did Zach know how to do these things? Asking the child if he could tell her something had made the child quiet down in order to have her curiosity satisfied.

"Dr. Brown is my friend. I really like her. But she's my friend, not your doctor. That means she isn't going to look at your arm. You already have a doctor, Dr. Mac-Dowell. He doesn't have to look at your arm again, either. That part is over. Now we're going to do the fixing part, as soon as we hear from your grandma."

Jamie, while wearing a white coat like Brooke's, had undoubtedly had the miserable task of testing the range of motion of the arm and wrist, something necessary but painful. No wonder the child wasn't thrilled to see another doctor in a white coat.

"Zoe. That's a pretty name." Brooke remembered Zach crouching down in the tent on Saturday, talking to kids on their level. She pulled up the rolling doctor's stool and had a seat. It was set so low, she was a bit below the little girl. She pulled a tissue out of the box and held it out casually. "Your face is kind of wet. Would you like to dry it? You seem pretty old. I don't think you need me to do it."

When the girl took the tissue and started dragging it all over her entire face, Brooke sat up taller and crossed her arms over her chest. "Wow. That's very impressive. You really are a big kid."

She could feel Zach's gaze on her so hard, she looked up. She raised a brow in question at his intense expression and shrugged one shoulder. *What? I'm not a total idiot with kids.*

She pushed her luck. "How old are you?"

"I'm four." Zoe held up all five fingers and then concentrated very hard on tucking her thumb in.

Brooke felt the tug at her heart. Four, like Chelsea. But it was just a tug. No horrible monster lurked in the corner today. Maybe because the monster knew that Zach was here, and he'd find a way to kick its butt, even with his arm in a sling.

She gave Zoe the whole tissue box. The child pulled a tissue out very carefully, set it down, and pulled out another one. Her interest in figuring out how the next tissue popped up was written all over her transparent expression.

Brooke hoped Zach could read her own expression. She wanted him to see that she didn't need to shut down her emotions in order to deal with this patient. It was almost enjoyable, actually, to meet a child this adorable.

Brooke smiled at Zach. "Let me guess. You brought me something fabulous to eat, and Jamie pulled you out of the kitchen and put you to work, knowing what a hit you are with ladies of all ages."

He shook his head no, but when she thought he was going to say something, he only clenched his jaw.

Zoe piped up. "I had milk in the kitchen, but Mr. Zach spilled it. I didn't spill it."

Brooke patted the child's knee, the one without the gauze patch. "That's okay. The hospital has people who clean up everything really well."

Zach cleared his throat. "She means my kitchen. At the house. She hurt her arm falling off the porch steps."

"Oh."

Zach paused, obviously considering his words carefully. "Her mother came to pay me a visit this morning."

Brooke couldn't remember him ever failing to look her in the eye before, but he looked away, frowning at the hand wash sign over the sink.

The obvious question would be who was the mother and where was she now, but Brooke suddenly didn't want to ask. There seemed to be a monster of a different kind lurking at the edges of her mind. She didn't want to know anything.

The child had lots to say as she pulled tissues out of the box. "I was very naughty and I opened the car door all by myself." Tissue. "And I fell and it hurted and I got my dress dirty." Tissue. "It's my new dress I got 'cause Gary isn't a daddy. Mommy said so." Tissue. "Who cares because we don't want dummy old Gary, anyway. Tony is rich. He's already raised his kids."

"Jeez." Zach looked up to the ceiling. "Someone's parent lacks a filter."

Brooke was riveted, dazed, shocked—whatever it was, she tried to keep up with Zoe, who was on a roll now, speaking faster than she could pull the tissues.

"Gary is a dud. Zach is more better, and he let me eat ice when he putted it on my arm. Zach is big. He sure will be surprised to see me. I'm nice." She paused, mulled that over and then looked up at Zach. "Are you surprising about me?"

Zach's fingers brushed against the girl's curls again. "You are very nice, and I am surprised to meet you."

"Good."

That one simple word sounded so strongly like Zach. Brooke looked more sharply at the little girl whose blue eyes were a common color in anyone with such blonde hair. A common color. Not blue-green, just blue. With a touch of green.

All her chatter about daddies was messing with Brooke's mind. Four years sounded so significant, suddenly, and not just because her sister had been four when she died.

Brooke didn't want to put the pieces together, but they kept falling into place, fitting together with too much ease. Zach had been left at the altar four years ago. This little girl was four years old.

It couldn't be. Babies required time to arrive, nine months of time: conception, gestation, contractions.

Her white coat had fallen open to reveal her pinstriped skirt as she sat. She smoothed her hands over her lap, buying herself a moment, but she was too well trained to do anything but move forward. She looked at Zach, although he didn't look at her. "That wedding you told me about, the one that didn't happen four years ago, was it maybe a little more than four years?"

She sounded so calm. So absurdly calm, as if her whole world weren't about to change.

Zach turned that blue-green gaze directly on her, and she saw no laughter, no wink. And she knew.

"I did the math this morning. It's been four years and nine months."

Brooke pushed with her foot and the chair rolled back a little way. She stood.

Zach stood up, too, but kept one hand on the child to keep her from falling from the tall exam table. Yes, safety was so important.

Brooke took a step backward, tripping on one stool wheel and making a little clatter. Zach tried to reach for her with the hand that wasn't holding the child, but it was in the sling.

That was okay. He shouldn't let go of the child for her. Children were so vulnerable.

Brooke hadn't wanted children, so that she'd never end up like her mother.

This situation was worse, so much worse. If Zach had a child, then he could end up like her father.

Chapter 16

Brooke stayed in the room while the monster had its turn. She remained standing, stoic in the trappings of her authority, the white coat, the stethoscope, ready to answer any questions the family might have as they dealt with the situation.

The family, in this case, was a new one that consisted of Zach and Zoe.

The grief wasn't for the death of a loved one, but for the end of life as it had been. Zoe was devastated that her grandma's paperwork had arrived, but that her grandma was still somewhere far away. With a child's logic, she had assumed her grandma would give the doctors permission to fix her arm by coming to see the doctor here.

Zach's grief was harder to pinpoint. There was a physical tension in his body that matched his evident mental tension as he considered everything he said, every paper he signed, and every decision he made. Each decision seemed to cause him pain.

Brooke wished she could do more, but she wasn't the one who could make people relax and laugh; that was his specialty. Hers, Zach had said, was to maintain a cool professionalism in stressful situations. So she stayed present, stayed calm, and refused to give in to the monster that wanted so badly to make her crack.

Because she was grieving, too. The life she and Zach had begun making, the happiness that she'd just started capturing, was not going to be. Zach had said her heart was safe with him, because he wasn't fragile. That was before he'd known Zoe existed. Now, if anything happened to Zoe, Zach would suffer. Zoe made Zach as vulnerable as the child.

Brooke had seen, firsthand, what happened to fathers who lost the love of their life, when the love of their life was an innocent four-year-old with golden curls.

Ashes.

The monster had his way. She'd loved her father, but it hadn't been enough reason for him to keep living after Chelsea died.

She loved Zach, but that didn't mean she'd be able to save him, either. She simply couldn't let anything bad happen to Zoe.

Ever.

"Kids need naps."

That was Jamie's parting advice in the curtained cubby as Zach and Zoe, with his sling and her pink fiberglass cast, got ready to leave.

"And snacks," Jamie added, in a critical discussion with his former football teammate.

If Brooke hadn't been able to hear what they were saying, she would have assumed they were two athletic men huddled to talk sports. Instead, they were having a serious discussion about child care.

"If we don't feed Sammy every couple of hours, there's hell to pay. And once they get this tired fussy thing going, just give up and go home and put them down for a nap. Leave the store, leave the restaurant, whatever. Naptime is sacred."

"Got it."

"I'm not saying I'm an expert on anybody else's kid, but someone looks like she's heading for a meltdown. I suggest you go straight home."

Zoe was rubbing her eyes and getting her own fingers tangled in her hair and twisting herself around in Zach's arm in general irritability.

"You better go," Brooke said, and she pulled the curtains back.

"Thanks again, Jamie. For everything." Even with Zoe in the crook of his right arm, Zach was able to extend his hand to shake Jamie's. He turned to Brooke. "I'll see you tonight."

It had been her idea for him never to engage in public displays of affection at her job, but as he walked away, she wished he'd kissed her anyway, with Jamie standing there and Zoe in his arms.

Zoe was looking over Zach's shoulder at Brooke as he carried her down the hall. Her head dropped onto Zach's shoulder and she did the slow, sleepy blink, but she waved bye-bye at Brooke.

Oh.

It was so special to have a child notice her. It was Chelsea all over again. Even at age twelve, Brooke had understood why her father had loved Chelsea the most, because she'd thought Chelsea was extra lovable, too. It made sense that the baby was Daddy's favorite, because the baby was Brooke's favorite.

And now the baby was Zoe. If Brooke was touched by Zoe's little wave, then Zach must be head over heels in love with his daughter already.

Zoe was now the most important person in his life. It made sense to her. That was the way things should be.

Jamie took the films off the light box and returned them to their envelope. "I owe you an apology. Zach asked me to help him find a way to take you somewhere private before you saw Zoe. He really wanted to tell you himself."

"He did tell me."

"I mean alone. We had a call in to the day care center to see if they'd watch Zoe after we put the cast on her, and I was trying to keep him out of the way until then."

"You were hiding him? That only works in movies." She wasn't trying to make a joke.

Jamie looked a little sheepish. "I'm sorry you got such a surprise."

"I'm fine, Jamie."

"For what it's worth, I thought you handled it really well."

The day care center he'd just mentioned was part of the pediatric ward, for use by children who were recovering from non-contagious conditions. Hospital employees could use the center for their children a certain amount of days per year. It kept absenteeism to a minimum.

Zach's medical leave ended in four days. What would he do with a child when he had to work?

"Do I have to be married to Zach in order to put Zoe in the day care center? Is it enough to just be living together?"

"I didn't know you two were living together."

She felt as if she'd been caught in a little white lie with Zach's friend. "We haven't really discussed it, but it wouldn't be a stretch if I checked the box that said we were cohabitating."

"I think they'll allow any minor that lives in your household. The hospital just doesn't want you to miss work because you couldn't find a sitter. Listen, it's so slow here, you should end your shift now."

It was exactly what she'd planned to suggest before she'd met Zach's new daughter.

He has a daughter.

There was a jolt every time the reality hit her. It was a monumental change.

She hesitated. "The two of them probably need time alone. I don't want to get in the way. I don't think she needs another stranger around."

"If you two want to talk as adults, naptime is just about the only time you won't have an audience."

"It will jinx you if I leave. You'll be flooded."

"Zach will owe me one, then. Go."

"How many tortilla chips can I feed her before I'm officially a bad father? We finished the whole bag yesterday when we came home from the hospital."

They were in the kitchen, starting a pot of coffee and getting out cereal bowls. Zach was free of the sling today, and Brooke had been silently assessing how he used his arm. No problems, so far.

He held up a plastic chip bag that had nothing but crumbs in the bottom. "Make that two bags."

Brooke started to laugh, but Zach didn't laugh with her. "Wasn't that a joke?"

Zach glanced into the living room, where Zoe was playing with a dollhouse app on Zach's phone. She wasn't listening to them.

"I did it again. I keep referring to myself as her father. What if I'm not?"

"So you want the answer to be yes?"

He answered her with a groan of frustration as he pulled her into his arms in a giant bear hug. They stood like that for a long moment, and he rested his cheek against her. He'd given Brooke bear hugs like this before, enveloping her in security when she was vulnerable. She thought this might be a little different. Maybe in this hug, she was the bear. She squeezed him harder with both arms.

"I didn't know she existed until yesterday, but if the lab says no and I have to send her back to Alabama, to a grandmother who is tired of being stuck with her while her mother ignores her, I think it will tear me up."

He squashed Brooke a little tighter to him. If she was the bear, then she was a teddy bear. Teddy bears didn't need to talk to provide comfort, which was good, because she didn't know whether to encourage his hopes or temper his dreams or offer some platitude when she'd never been in his shoes.

"I'll still be here," she said, "either way."

It hadn't comforted her parents much when they'd lost their daughter, but it was all she had.

"And as a doctor, I can say with authority that there is no scientific evidence that a one-day diet of tortilla chips will cause permanent harm to a child."

"Hey, Brooke?"

"What?"

"I love you."

* * *

It was pouring rain during naptime. Zoe was tucked into her bed, which for now was a futon from Zach's long-ago first apartment. It had been serving as a gamer's couch in the spare bedroom, where his video games were now stacked in a corner to make room for a pink suitcase's contents.

Rain often brought hail and flash floods to Central Texas, but on this afternoon, it was soothing, so much so that, despite being on edge over test results, Zach and Brooke were sound asleep together on the living room's couch when the cell phone rang.

It was Jamie with the lab results. Zach was the father.

He hung up the call and stayed where he was, flat on his back, motionless. Brooke sat up and stayed on the edge next to him, listening to the rain.

"Are you happy?" she asked tentatively, when the silence stretched on. He looked a bit like a boxer who'd been knocked out in the ring.

"I don't know how to do this."

"But you will."

"I'm not qualified. I've been given this life, this human being, and I could screw it all up."

It was overwhelming. Brooke couldn't lie and say it wasn't, so she told him something else that was also true.

"Yesterday, do you remember how the lab tech swabbed your cheek for the test first? He wanted to show Zoe that it wouldn't hurt, and then he started giving Zoe that pep talk, the one we all do sometimes. I was thinking that the tech was making it sound like having her cheek swabbed was going to be the best thing that had ever happened in her life.

"But then I looked at you, and I realized the tech

wasn't exaggerating. If this paternity test proved that you were the father, it really would be the best thing that could happen in that little girl's life. It might be throwing you into a tailspin at the moment, but you're going to be an excellent father."

His knockout didn't last long. Restless, he got to his feet. "I've done a great job so far. Just great. I spent four years being oblivious to the fact that she even existed."

"How could you have known?"

"I should have checked. I should have followed up, even though Charisse was on the pill." He drove one hand through his hair in that way Brooke found so achingly familiar. "I don't have any other bastard children running around. I'm sure of it, and not just because I take precautions. Every other woman I've been with, I've stayed on good terms with. We've got mutual friends. I see them around. I know nobody's had a baby. But Charisse, the one I actually got pregnant, is the only one I never saw again. Damn it. Damn me."

Brooke pushed aside the jealous pain at the idea of the women who'd come before her by using cool logic. He hadn't known Brooke, so any women before her had nothing to do with her. There were no other women now that she was his girlfriend.

Maybe cool logic could help him forgive himself for not knowing Zoe had been conceived. "Let's suppose you had followed up. You saw her get married. If you'd managed to run into her again and seen her with a baby, what would you have thought?"

He considered seriously. "That she and her husband had a baby."

"That's what she would have told you, too. She wouldn't have risked a thing." From the conversation

Zach had relayed yesterday, it was obvious that Charisse did whatever was best for Charisse.

Zach dropped into the armchair facing her. "But she knew. Her doctor told her she could have gotten pregnant anytime that month. She should have had a paternity test the day the baby was born. Four years, she took away from me. I missed all of it. I missed the whole baby thing, the first steps, all of it."

Had she ever thought Zach Bishop was not a serious man? She'd been as wrong about him as he'd been about Charisse. He'd been lighthearted not because he lacked depth, but because he chose to live his life with a positive outlook. She'd wasted a lot of time, ignoring him simply because he chose happiness.

He'd be happy again. He had a daughter who was going to bring him joy and love, like Chelsea had brought joy and love into her family. Brooke just needed to help Zach get through this dark period. She'd seen what bitterness had done for her mother. She didn't want that to take hold in Zach.

"Charisse was wrong, but it would have taken a lot of courage for her to risk her new marriage by confessing there was a chance the baby wasn't her husband's."

"She's not the courageous type."

"Zach, not many people are that courageous."

"You are."

She shrugged off his compliment, but it was a wonderful, warm feeling to hear his unconditional confidence in her. "You never know what you'll really do until you are in the situation yourself. I don't think I'll ever be called upon to show that particular kind of courage."

"You're already showing courage, just by being here."

"With a handsome man and a cute kid? It's not that tough."

"It is for you. You had a nightmare last night, baby. Do you remember?"

She did. It had been the most vivid recollection she'd had in a long time.

The accident in real life hadn't been gory. In fact, everyone at the time had thought her sister had been lucky and merely knocked unconscious, until it became clear at the hospital that she was in a coma. What made last night's nightmare so vivid wasn't blood or gore.

Before bed, Brooke had helped Zoe put on her pajamas and brush her teeth. The sensation of little arms hugging her, the feel of baby-smooth skin as she kissed a cheek good-night, these were the things that had made memories of Chelsea more vivid. In her nightmare, Chelsea always disappeared without warning. Last night, the sudden, sucking loss of hugs and cuddles had felt as fresh as when Brooke was twelve.

She dashed the back of her hand across her cheek, but it was dry. Relieved, she attempted a smile to fool Zach. "It wasn't so bad. Probably just a leftover effect from last weekend."

Zach left the arm chair to sit with her. He kissed the corner of her eye. "Baby, you aren't a very good liar. Talk to me. What do you think about all this?"

"I told you the truth. I think it's the best thing that can happen for Zoe."

"That's not what I meant." He cupped her jaw in one hand and rested his forehead against hers. "You don't have to be calm. You're not on duty. Being around Zoe has to be hard for you."

"I'll adjust. I had nightmares before Zoe, too."

"I made you a promise when you sewed me up. I said I would never deliberately do anything to cause you pain."

"But you didn't do this deliberately."

"But the pain is the same for you, anyway. Brooke, I'm so sorry about all this. I've been thinking about it. Maybe you should ease yourself into the situation. Sleep at your own place for a while. God knows I'll miss you, but God knows I don't want to see you hurting, either."

She remembered her nightmare, that keening loss of a child's love. She'd do anything to prevent that from happening to Zach. Anything.

"I'll be happier if I'm here with you."

Or she would be, as long as she could keep Zoe safe.

Chapter 17

On the surface, Zach's week had gone as well as it could possibly go for a man who'd just found out he had a four-year-old child.

Physically, he was fine. His arm was healing fast, his bruises fading to green and yellow. His week's medical leave was over, and he was cleared to go back to work by Brooke.

His work schedule hadn't been a problem yet, either, also thanks to Brooke. He worked twenty-four on and forty-eight off at the fire station. Brooke had rearranged her schedule to be off work for the twenty-four hours that he was on duty.

Brooke had thought ahead. She'd set up a video chat between him and Zoe while he was at the firehouse, in case the child became upset at yet another adult suddenly disappearing. The video chat had been fun, but not emotionally necessary. Zoe was surprisingly stable, and Zach believed it was because she'd lived almost entirely with her grandparents while Charisse had been lining up her next husband. If Charisse had dragged her around as an afterthought during her husband hunt, Zach had no doubt that his daughter would have more emotional issues.

His daughter. The best part of his week was simply being with his daughter.

Each day, he learned more about what a preschooler could and couldn't do. He'd been surprised she could use a fork and knife pretty well, but she couldn't manage the bathtub faucet. She could entertain herself with leaves and rocks outdoors, but she had to be watched so she didn't stand in an ant pile or get too close to the creek. From the moment she woke to the moment she slept, Zach was on constant alert, but he was constantly enchanted by her as well. Her smiles were irresistible. Her peals of laughter had to be the happiest sound on earth.

On the surface, life was great.

Deep down, things weren't right with Brooke.

The surface of her was calm. She didn't seem to have any problem being around Zoe. She helped her dress, did her hair, played endless rounds of a board game she'd bought in the hospital gift shop. Zach should be grateful.

Instead, he was worried. He'd held Brooke during nightmares. He'd been to her sister's grave. He'd broken a coffee mug for her one morning. But now, with the snap of her fingers, she had no issue at all. It couldn't be true.

If she was still having nightmares, they didn't wake him. He was afraid he was just sleeping harder than before. Days as a father were definitely more demanding than days as a bachelor with a smokin' hot girlfriend.

They'd had precious little time to be a couple, just the

two of them, before Zoe had taken center stage in his life. At the firefighters' picnic, he and Brooke had planned to delay kids indefinitely, and they'd agreed to talk about any changes of heart on that subject. Five days later, he'd presented her with a child. There'd been no talking. Charisse had blown that out of the water.

They'd have that talk now, then. Charisse didn't get to screw up the lives of the people he loved any longer—not Zoe's, not Brooke's.

He was sitting on the porch steps when Brooke pulled into the drive in her red car. He took a sip from his cold beer as she opened the door and swung her legs out. He admired the view, letting his gaze take that leisurely trip from the tips of her professional pumps, up those trim legs, past the pinstriped skirt. He savored the heat in his body that burned at the sight of her. This was the woman for him. She always would be.

He lifted his gaze to her face. That worry wrinkle marked the space between her brows as she looked toward the creek and around the property. She glanced right past him, up to the porch. He knew the exact moment she spotted Zoe, because she nearly drooped with relief—for less than a second.

By the time she took her first step toward him, that smooth, serene smile was in place.

That was the problem. The invisible barrier hadn't been there before. She'd flirted with him, been annoyed with him, aroused by him, worried for him. She'd been real. He'd take any of those over this merely pleasant Brooke.

He wanted to say welcome home, but she was just visiting his house. The change of clothing she carried on a hanger over her arm meant she'd stopped at her apartment on the way here.

"Hi, baby." He twisted off the cap of another cold bottle and held it out to her. "Welcome to happy hour."

"Oh." She patted the clothes she carried. "Let me just hang these up and check on Zoe."

He shook his head and stood up. "You'll miss the view. Turn around." He took the clothes from her and hung them from the edge of the porch railing.

She dutifully accepted the beer and turned to face west.

"Isn't it something?" he asked. "They lifted the flash flood warnings for the night. After that morning rain, we've got something spectacular to look at."

The sunset couldn't hold Brooke's attention. She turned to look up at the porch. He stole a brief kiss, since she hadn't offered.

"Zoe's fine. The railing is solid. The only way off the porch are these stairs. Jamie's wife suggested the library today. It was a hit. Zoe's got a ton of books up there." He sat on a step, and she took the one below him. He set his beer down and began to pull her ponytail holder loose, already anticipating the slide of her dark hair between his fingers, the way she'd sigh at the sensation and lean against his knee. It was a fine way to start a talk.

"Any interesting patients today?"

"Not really." Her hand hovered over the ponytail for a moment, but then she dropped it into her lap. Zach took that as permission to proceed. She settled against his leg, but he could tell she wasn't resting her full weight on him.

"Any pediatrics?"

"Strep throat. A boy who was luckier than Zoe and only had a sprain, not a fracture."

That was it. She only trusted him with half of herself. There was none of that brutal honesty from before. *I hate kids*, she'd said, but only after giving everything she had to save one. Only after fighting to keep a stranger's child from the same fate as her sister. He'd understood.

"Brooke!" Zoe came down the stairs, pink cast swinging in the twilight.

"Watch that arm," Zach said. "It's a weapon."

Brooke smiled at his joke, and Zoe started to sit on her step, but then so subtly that he almost missed it happening, Brooke had Zoe up on Zach's step instead. A minute after that, Brooke was in the house to get them all something to munch on, something that would appeal to a child. There'd be no sharing a beer at sunset. No overdue conversation.

The same thing had happened this morning, now that he thought about it. He'd been kissing Brooke in the kitchen. Zoe had come in and Brooke had immediately backed off and let Zoe throw her arms around Zach's legs instead.

The evening snack led to Zoe's bath time, and although there was barely space for Zach to stand in the doorway of the bathroom, he felt the distance. Zoe was nearly buried in bubbles in the tub, her waterproof pink cast glowing through the white foam, and Brooke was on her knees on the hard tile, performing acrobatic stretches to wash Zoe's hair.

Already, they had a little routine. Brooke would pull the plug, wrap Zoe in the towel, and hand her to Zach, who'd carry her to her makeshift bedroom. It seemed as if they were a team, but their roles were separate.

He looked down at Brooke and felt a longing for her that made him hurt. He was losing her. She loved him, she loved his daughter, but the distance wasn't in his imagination.

He hit the wall. Literally.

Woman and girl, both, looked at him, startled. He thumped the side of his fist more gently on the wall a second time.

"It's hollow. I had made plans to knock this out."

"You did?" Brooke poured clean water from a plastic cup over his daughter's hair, shielding his child's eyes with the flat of her hand.

"It would make room to put in a double sink. New tile. I had plans."

"It sounds great. Why don't you do it?"

Separate tasks, again. Not, *I'd love to help do that*.

Jeez, he was being as melodramatic as Charisse. This wasn't Brooke's house, and he hadn't invited her to make it hers. Why should she assume he wanted her to help?

He needed to lighten up, so he inclined his head toward little Zoe and winked at grown-up Brooke. "Been putting those tools to work building a distinctly feminine bed and dresser set this week instead. You can buy a lot of pink plastic toys for the price of a bathroom light fixture."

Serious thoughts would intrude. He was a father now. "That reminds me. I've got to get her declared as a dependent on my health insurance before that hospital bill comes in."

Brooke got to her feet, wrapped Zoe in one of his dark navy towels, and handed him his daughter. "Here you go. One completely adorable tax deduction, squeaky clean."

Later, when it was just the two of them, she'd been sitting on his bed, brushing her hair before bed.

He wanted to try again, when no little girl would join them on the porch steps. He sat behind her and took the brush out of her hand, ready to take over a task that always struck him as sensual with Brooke, and tried to think how to open the conversation about children that they needed to have.

She turned toward him first. "What if I gave up my apartment?"

He was stunned at the abrupt question. "You want to live with me?"

"I kind of already am. I was at my apartment today, and I realized it's really just an expensive closet now."

She turned back around, and he began stroking her hair, choosing his words with care. "Charisse's parents are certain that she and this Tony guy don't want primary custody of Zoe. Maybe your place is a safety net. If you get rid of it, it would be harder for you to move out if you changed your mind. Are you sure living with Zoe isn't going to become too much?"

He ought to be thrilled to have Brooke here full-time, but it didn't sit right with him. It was a commitment of one sort, but it wasn't marriage.

It's rent.

"Zoe is so sweet, it's been much easier than I'd thought. You'd have to let me pay some bills here when I don't have any more there. We could work on that bathroom together."

They turned the lights out. The sheets were smooth and cool, her body warm and pliant. She molded herself to his side.

"Whose bed should we keep?" she asked. "I like your couch better than mine. I don't think my table will fit in your kitchen."

"We'll have a lot of decisions to make, I guess." He looked forward to it, or he would, when he got used to the idea. It was everything he wanted—but it wasn't. Still, he must have been making too much of a big deal over a few days of distance. If she wasn't afraid to let go of her apartment, if she was willing to live with a small child, then the sky was the limit. He wanted to marry her. He'd find a way to pay for an engagement ring, and then he'd find the right time to ask her.

When you find the woman you understand and who understands you back, you don't let anything stand in your way.

As he kissed her, he thought it was time to stop waiting for the perfect time. She was obviously not as fragile as he'd thought when it came to Zoe. He'd buy that ring right away, and then he'd tell her that he wanted more than a roommate. He wanted forever.

She broke off the kiss and touched him in the dark, running her fingers through his hair to settle on the nape of his neck, a motion he'd come to love in the weeks of their love.

"This is going to work out so well," she said softly. "When we have to work at the same time, the hospital day care center will take Zoe if we're cohabitating."

Zach pulled back as if she'd slapped him. Alarms went off—real alarms, from the two-way radio he was required to keep on standby for Texas Rescue.

He and Brooke both slept with their phones on during flash flood season, because they could be called in for emergency shifts. For Texas Rescue, a two-way radio connected Zach to the crew of the chopper.

Cursing, he silenced the alarm as Brooke reached for her phone.

"Looks like I'm on standby tomorrow." Her face was illuminated by the phone screen.

"Flash flood warnings are back on," Zach said, reading the two lines of green text on his handheld radio.

They returned their devices to their end tables and settled into their pillows once more. Those updates had been sent at exactly midnight, an automated procedure. He and Brooke were too experienced in these drills to be alarmed.

Zoe was not experienced at all. She came trembling into the bedroom, barefoot in her pink ruffles, and climbed onto the mattress that was almost too tall for her to scale. Zach cursed again, silently this time, for forgetting the alarm would wake her. That alarm was designed to wake the hardest sleeping adult around. Even he found it too jarring. Maybe he could keep it partially muffled in the future, wrapped in a towel.

Without trying to tuck Zoe back into her new bed, Brooke settled her onto her pillow and put her arm around her. Zach wasn't sure it was a good precedent to set, but knowing tomorrow had the potential to be a taxing day, sleep was more important than having a parenting discussion with Brooke now.

Brooke had her arm on Zoe, so Zach put his arm on Brooke, and he fell asleep hoping for the best.

Hours later, in the gray of a stormy dawn, he woke to the kick of a diminutive foot in his stomach. His daughter—would he ever get used to those words?—was sound asleep, blond curls on Brooke's pillow. He touched one, amazed anew at the miracle that was his child.

And then the sleep of fog was burned away in a flash. Brooke had done it again, as she had on the steps, as she had in the kitchen. She'd replaced herself with a child.

Enough. The middle of the night was as good as any time to find out for once and for all why he was losing Brooke.

Chapter 18

The nightmare left her so lonely.

Brooke woke, knowing she was only halfway done with the misery. First, the nightmare had to be endured from beginning to end. She would be smiled at. Treasured. Then all that would be taken away in a flash, and although she knew it was hopeless, she would beg for the love to stay.

Now that she was awake, she had to recover. *It was just a dream. Take a breath. Nothing bad has happened.*

Except it had. Her heart had been broken. The emotions were real and fresh and sharp.

She rolled onto her back in the new twin bed. Zoe's night-light cast five-pointed stars on the ceiling. Her pillow smelled like baby shampoo. Everything that Zoe touched was transformed into something charming, something innocent. The magic of her childish world touched everyone lucky enough to be in her circle.

This was the magic that Brooke's father had decided not to even try to live without. Eighteen years ago today, he'd decided there was no reason to stay if his little girl was gone. Brooke had not had enough magic left by the age of twelve to keep him.

The sky outside was more black than gray. The rain was steady, the kind that could last all day. That meant flash floods were possible all over the city of Austin. Roadways would become impassable in a matter of minutes as dry creek beds suddenly filled to overflowing. She wouldn't be able to visit the cemetery where her father's ashes were interred.

The relief made her cry.

She was so tired of being brave. So tired of doing the right thing. She just wanted to go back in time. Not eighteen years—no, no, no. She just wanted to go back two weeks or so. She wanted to laugh with Zach and have crazy good sex and enjoy the world. Delicious food, delicious music, delicious man. That had been magic for her.

She wanted Zach.

The bedroom door suddenly opened and Zach stepped into the light, stars splashed across his chest and arms and half his face. He didn't look loving and magical. He looked furious.

"What are you doing in here?" he demanded in a tone that was angry despite its quiet volume.

"I'm sorry," she whispered, feeling like a child who'd been caught doing something bad.

That was ridiculous. She wasn't hurting his daughter's bedroom. She sat up and pushed the blankets off. The little motion stirred the air and she realized her cheeks were wet. Real tears. She put her hands to her cheeks.

"Brooke." Her name seemed to have been ripped from

his star-covered chest. He crossed the small room and joined her on the bed, scooping her against that chest in one motion. "A nightmare. Is that why you left our bed, so you wouldn't wake me with your tears? Darlin', don't you know I never want you to cry alone?"

She couldn't do it. The dream was too recent. She couldn't play it off as if she wasn't devastated. She couldn't pretend she didn't want to completely succumb to every horrible emotion in her heart.

She cried. Oh, how she cried, and Zach kept her cheek pressed to his heart, strong arms holding her as she sobbed, warm hand soothing her hair.

When she was spent, she wiped her face on a corner of the soft sheets and looked out the window rather than at Zach. The rain was relentless.

"Did you get called in?" she asked. "Is that why you're up?"

"I came to find you. You keep leaving whenever Zoe's around. You have to be honest with me. Zoe is stirring up all your emotions about your sister, isn't she?"

"No, it's not Zoe. If anything, she's reminded me of everything good about Chelsea. It makes me feel...content, knowing that the world still has lovely, magical little girls. Innocence isn't gone, after all. It's right here."

Zach brushed his fingers over her cheek. "Then why the tears? Weren't you dreaming about your sister again?"

"No." Her words were a whisper. Her throat hurt with the truth. "I was having nightmares about you."

He was silent.

"It was your love that suddenly disappeared. I think it's because you're a father now. You have more than one person to care for."

"Brooke. Please, Brooke. If you don't believe anything

I ever say or any promise I ever make, believe this—Zoe cannot replace you in my heart. It doesn't matter how much I love Zoe, I love you, too. I need you. I want to see your face every day."

The sweetness of his words was soothing, but the nightmare was still so fresh. "You know, my father loved all of us. My mom, my sister, me. As long as we were all together, he could love us all. But once we were parted, he said he had to choose. Mom and I were here. Chelsea was in heaven. He couldn't be with all of us anymore. He chose Chelsea."

Miserable, she pulled her knees up to her chest and hugged herself. "That's how he explained it in the note he left behind."

Zach nodded, one sharp nod of understanding. He stood to pace in the small room, stars moving across his body as he took two steps away and then turned back to her.

"You think I would choose my little girl over you, because your father chose his little girl over you. That's why you've been stepping away every time Zoe is near. You assume I'd rather hug her than you. You assume I'd rather sit next to her than you. You're wrong. I haven't chosen between you two. I never will."

You never know what you'll do until you're in that situation yourself...

"I know his note was wrong. He wasn't really choosing between me and Chelsea. Thank God for medical school. The classes we took on biochemistry of the brain, the pharma classes on how and why antidepressants work, they helped me see my dad's death in a whole new light. I know why he really took his life. Losing Chelsea triggered a profound medical depression, something beyond even the huge grief that is considered normal after the death of a child. He killed himself because he was mentally ill."

"Eighteen years ago? Today was the day, wasn't it? I lost track of time."

She nodded and kept her arms firmly around her knees. It was a long time ago, and yet she could so easily remember being in this position as a preteen, hugging bony knees that didn't quite fit her body yet.

"When did you start medical school? Eight years ago?"

"Nine."

"Nine years out of eighteen. The first nine years, you believed your father's note. You really thought you lost him because Chelsea was more precious than you."

Her tears started fresh. There was no reason for them. Just because Zach understood her so well? That ought to make her happy, not sad.

"You are in my heart, Brooke. So is Zoe. That is where you both will stay, always. Even if the worst should happen, I'll never be without either one of you."

"Zach, that is beautiful."

"I want you to remember it, if you ever start to think your father's note was true."

"Once I'm fully awake, I can put it in perspective. I know he was sick. But those first few minutes in the dark, it's different."

"Then from now on, I'll carry Zoe back to her own bed when she comes into our room. You need to sleep with me. When you have a nightmare, you turn to me. Wake me up if I haven't heard you dreaming. The first thing I'll tell you is that I refuse to ever make a choice between you and Zoe. I'll tell you a hundred times that you are too precious to leave."

The two-way radio alarm sounded in the next room. Texas Rescue was asking him to leave right now.

Brooke knew she'd been saved by the bell, or in this case, the alarm.

Zach understood her almost too well. He'd so accurately guessed that a rational knowledge of mental illness didn't easily wipe out nine years of believing an irrational man's final words. It was only a matter of time before Zach figured out that her new mission in life was to make sure nothing bad ever happened to Zoe.

There was no reason to believe that he would handle grief as self-destructively as her father had, but she intended to keep Zoe so safe, she'd never find out. If she was a little irrational in achieving her goal—for example, sitting Zoe next to Zach on the porch steps so that he'd catch her before she could fall again—well, it wasn't hurting anyone.

Two hours after Zach was called in for Texas Rescue One, Brooke was called into the ER. She was bringing Zoe with her to stay in the hospital day care center. The ER was not yet swamped, but when bad weather was expected to cause injuries in the population, the hospital called in the staff before roads became impassable. Not knowing how long she'd be at work, she wore scrubs and sneakers instead of her usual skirt, and packed a set of pajamas in a tote bag for Zoe.

She was still driving toward the outskirts of Austin when she hit the first intersection that was under a few inches of flowing water. It was so tempting to drive through, but the motto Turn Around, Don't Drown was well known in Central Texas. Any amount of flowing water on a road was considered to be dangerous.

She debated a second longer. Who was she kidding? She had Zoe with her; she wasn't taking any chances with safety. Although cars around her drove through the intersection, Brooke turned around.

The relentless rain made finding an alternate route all the more challenging. Twice more, Brooke was stopped and turned around. The police were requiring it now at several points.

"My, my. It certainly is raining cats and dogs."

Zoe's perfectly enunciated line must have been one of her grandmother's sayings. It sounded adorable from such a tiny girl. The comedic relief was appreciated as Brooke continued to work her way north, trying to find a way to go around the flooding to get to the hospital.

"Oopsie. That car felled down."

Brooke crept slowly around a car that had spun out into a gulley. Rushing water was nearly as high as its hood. Police were already on the scene, so Brooke kept going.

At last, she came to a new road that had been built to run alongside a creek bed, rather than crossing it. Brooke joined the line of slow-moving cars that were taking advantage of the clear road. The new construction narrowed to a single lane after a mile. Traffic went from a crawl to a stop.

Brooke craned her neck to see how far ahead the cars were stopped. Then she checked her rearview mirror to see how many were behind her.

She double-checked the mirror.

A brown wave of churning water was coming up the road, knocking cars crookedly out of its path. It was relentless, looking just like the footage of the tsunami that had made the world news a few years ago. It was fast. And Brooke's car was a sitting duck.

She turned back around and pressed the back of her head to the headrest to prevent whiplash. "Hang on, Zoe. There's going to be a bump. Put your head back, like I'm doing."

The impact sent them forward a couple of feet, and then the water rushed past them. They'd been on a road. Now they were in a river, her car like a boulder scattered among so many other boulders.

"You're doing great, Zoe. Good girl."

"What is the water for?" Her voice sounded a little panicky and completely bewildered.

Brooke tried to set the right tone. "It's from all the rain. It will go away again. We just have to wait. It may be a while, but we're safe in the car."

Please let us be safe. Please don't let me be the one who harmed Zoe.

Waters receded as quickly as they rose in flash floods. Sometimes. On the other hand, the evening news often showed roads that had flooded under and stayed that way.

The seams of the doors were watertight. So far. She'd had no choice but to take the hit. Now she had no choice but to wait it out. She adjusted the rearview mirror so she could see Zoe.

A second push, gentler than the first, nudged them farther along. A car behind them bumped into them, the heavy vehicle moving in slow motion in the speeding water.

Brooke's car began to move.

It was a strange feeling, like being levitated. They

floated a few feet and came to a stop, but the reprieve was short-lived. The muddy water lifted them once more. They bumped other cars on their way, traveling on water that reached halfway up the trees that marked where the side of the road had been.

She had no control. She had a preschooler completely entrusted to her care, and she had no control in a raging river of muddy water.

Her front bumper hit the tree and stuck. For a moment, she was grateful for the stability, until she realized the back half of the car was sinking.

"Zoe!" She took off her seat belt and scrambled over the center console to reach Zoe's car seat. She released the straps and pulled Zoe into the front with her. The car was still dry, but the back end was sinking lower and lower into the water. She could see churning waves inching up the trunk lid toward the rear window. The back door started leaking, water trickling in steadily. It was only a matter of time now. Did she have five minutes? Ten?

They were hit with a loud thunk, and the back end was shoved downward another foot. The trickle became a stream. Five minutes seemed unlikely.

Stay or go?

Movie sequences flashed through her mind, Hollywood images of people gasping for breath, trapped in their car as the water reached the interior roof.

Go.

She hit the car window button. It worked. The front half of the car was still above water, so they could get out through the driver's side window. "You're doing everything right, Zoe. Keep hanging on to me, tight as you can. Don't let go for anything."

It was a tight squeeze, but they pushed out headfirst. Brooke paused in a sitting position, her rear on the edge of the door, and she lifted Zoe onto the angled roof. "Hold my hand instead of my neck. My hand, take my hand. That's a good girl."

The car was now at a diagonal, its front half higher in the air. The V created by the windshield and the hood of the car was her goal. With a great deal of kicking and more muscle than she'd ever used at once, Brooke leveraged herself out of the door window, onto the roof, and then over the edge onto the windshield. She ended up sitting on the windshield wipers, clutching Zoe in both arms, gasping for breath.

She couldn't rest.

When the back half was full of water, its weight would pull the entire car down, and them with it. They needed to make it to the tree.

Impossible.

She pushed the fear away. She could at least get to her feet, stand on the windshield, and push Zoe with all her might to the highest branch she could reach.

It was impossible. She'd have to throw the child too many feet just to clear the hood of the car.

There had to be another option. Choking down her fear, she started watching the water, looking for any debris that might be large enough to support their weight, something they could cling to like a raft. As she stared, the surface of the water took on a different look, getting choppier, breaking up into a mist, and Brooke realized a helicopter was overhead, the downward draft from its blades flattening the water surface.

She looked up to see the blue-and-red helicopter hovering above, lowering a metal basket toward them. A man in an orange flight suit and white helmet stood on the edge of the metal basket, his gloved hand holding on to the cable.

"Zoe, look. It's your daddy."

Chapter 19

"He's coming to rescue you."

Them. She meant he was coming to rescue them, but as long as he saved Zoe, that was all that mattered. Her innocent life couldn't end this way, not because Brooke had chosen the wrong road.

The car was nearly vertical now. The basket clanged against the front bumper and settled against the hood. Brooke wondered why Zach didn't jump from the basket onto the car to take Zoe from her arms. She couldn't see his face through the full visor, only his mouth. His lips were in a firm line.

Take her, save her, please.

She slid a foot toward him, and the car shifted. Zach gestured for her to stop. She froze in place. The tree must barely be holding the heavy car. If Zach added any of his weight to it, they'd go under. Very carefully, Zach hung on to the cable with one hand and extended his arm.

"Let go of me now, Zoe. Reach for Daddy. That's your daddy."

"It is not!" Zoe clung to Brooke's neck, her pink cast choking her air supply.

The car shifted under Brooke's feet again. There was no time to explain anything. She shouted over the noise of the chopper blades. "Let go of me. *Now.*"

Zach was even more decisive. He lunged for Zoe, grabbed a fistful of her clothing and tugged. Brooke pried Zoe's arms from around her neck, and within a second, Zach had lifted Zoe and plunked her in the basket. He crouched on the edge of the metal basket railing, buckling her in rapidly with two hands. His crouch seemed like an impossible feat of no-hands balance, until Brooke realized his harness was tethered to the cable.

With the first click of the Zoe's seat belt, Brooke's legs threatened to buckle. Zoe would live.

Then Zach turned back toward her and held out his hand again. The basket could hold two? She would live. Thrilled, she bent her knees, prepared to leap for Zach's outstretched hand. In the fraction of a second that it took to gauge the distance for her leap, the car went down. Zach, who'd been so very close, was suddenly unreachable, high above her as she sank below.

But Zoe is safe.

The water closed over her head. She fought it, kicking against the downward pull of the car until she broke the surface and took a great, gasping breath. She grabbed on to a branch and looked up in time to see Zach disconnect his safety harness and drop into the water, ankles crossed, a graceful entry.

The branch didn't hold her. Zach did.

Somehow, someway, he was holding her up, riding the

current with her until the river pushed him into the side of a bread truck. The current pinned her against him.

"Perfect," he said, as if he really meant it.

The truck wasn't floating, so they stayed in one place as Zoe and the basket disappeared into the helicopter. The pilot banked the chopper and circled around. The empty basket came down again, blowing more wildly in the rain without a man to weigh it down. It banged against the side of the truck, and the water pinned it in place as well. It was at least six feet away, which looked to Brooke like six acres.

To Zach, it must have been only six feet, because he crossed it while carrying her. With one last push of muscle, she made it up and over the side of the basket, collapsing in the metal cage that felt as welcoming as a feather bed.

Zach buckled her in before she could fumble for one end of the seat belt. He hauled himself onto the side, and she was lifted into the safety of the sky with Zach crouched protectively over her the whole way.

Now that he'd saved her life, Brooke knew Zach was going to kill her.

She'd driven Zoe into a flash flood. He'd nearly lost his daughter because of her. Speech had been impossible in the chopper, but he'd raised the visor of his helmet as if to say something, anyway. Zoe had instantly tackled him once she recognized him, and during the rest of the ride his daughter had clung to his neck and taken all his attention. Fortunately. Brooke was too tired to be murdered just now.

They touched down in an empty field that had been set up as a loading point, judging by the trucks and ambulances that edged the field in a neat row. Gurneys stood at the ready. Brooke wasn't injured, so she didn't need one. She climbed down from the helicopter herself, and an attendant in a Texas Rescue polo shirt began escorting her away from the still-moving blades. Brooke made it about ten feet when her legs gave way.

A gurney wasn't such a bad idea.

Men were pushing one toward her, but she knew Zoe was still in the helicopter, so she gestured for them to go past her as the volunteer helped her back to her feet.

The gurney abruptly stopped. Brooke turned to see Zach had stopped it with his boot on one wheel. He had Zoe in one arm, his other hand protecting her face from the downdraft of the beating helicopter blades. His own visor was down again, so Brooke could see nothing but the firm set of his mouth as he jerked his head toward her. *Put her on the gurney,* his body language said, just before he took off running to get Zoe out of the wind and into an ambulance.

Brooke sat on the gurney, feeling foolish and weak as they rattled over the ground. She dreaded facing Zach after endangering all their lives. He was just as furious as he had a right to be.

With the push of a few levers and the click of a few latches, she and her bed were lifted into the back of an empty ambulance. The volunteers stood outside the open bay doors, waiting for an all clear. The driver started the engine.

Zach came sprinting toward her from the ambulance that must be holding Zoe. "Wait! *Wait!*"

He tore off his helmet as he vaulted into the back of the ambulance with her. "Brooke, thank God—"

"I know. I'm so sorry—"

"You were amazing. Amazing."

He kissed her, hard. She was too surprised to kiss him back.

"But I almost got Zoe killed," she gasped.

"Baby, you saved her. I saw the whole thing as we were circling into position. I saw you crawling out that window and pushing her onto the roof. Have I told you that you're the most courageous person I know?"

His praise made her impatient. "I drove into the path of a flood, Zach. Don't make me out to be some kind of hero."

He backed away a little bit and studied her with a frown. "Fifteen cars are stuck on that road. Nobody had any way to know the water would come down like that. The only thing you did wrong was try to hand me Zoe when I was trying to grab both of you."

"Both of us? At once?"

He smacked his bicep with a shade of that cocky grin. "Iron pythons, remember? The two of you together don't weigh enough for me to notice."

She couldn't smile. She just couldn't, not when her heart was still pounding from the brush with rushing water. Or was each beat her heart's way of begging her to believe, for once, that Zach meant it when he said she was amazing? Zach reached for a blanket and drew it over her shoulders. "I told you this morning, I'm never going to choose between you. That would be hell for me. I could tell you thought you had to get in the basket one at a time, so I grabbed poor Zoe just to get it over with. We only had seconds."

He pushed the wet hair from her cheeks and kissed her again, as if it was a great novelty to be able to touch her. "Turns out we didn't have that long. When you went down with that car, baby, that was the worst moment of my life."

The strong hands on her wet hair held just a little bit tighter, and he looked away. Cleared his throat. Exhaled hard.

Then he looked back at her with blue-green eyes full of raw emotion. "I'm the one who may be having nightmares from now on."

She shook her head in denial, just a little tremor of a shake because his hands were holding her steady. "Better me in the water than her. She's your flesh and blood. I'm just some doc you've been dating a few weeks."

He hissed in a breath at that. He glowered at her for a long, long moment and then nodded his head as if he'd come to a decision.

"You're going to have to marry me, then, Brooke."

It was her turn to gasp.

"I've been telling myself to be patient, but more time isn't what we need. There are words I want to say and you need to hear, the words *man and wife, flesh of my flesh and bone of my bone.* I'll love you forever—until you stop being so damned surprised by it. And if forever isn't long enough, then I'll love you a little longer."

They were in the back of an ambulance, sopping wet and exhausted. She'd never heard of a proposal like this, but the most handsome man who'd ever asked her out was now asking her to marry him.

Her heart dared to beat harder. If they married, there would be no inevitable fall, no dreaded valley of grief, because their relationship would never be over. She could choose a new life as his wife, as a mother—well, a stepmother, but who knew what else the future might hold?

If it held Zach, it would hold all kinds of happiness.

She loved him so much that she'd always worry about him, and Zoe, too, but she also loved him so much that she could never say no and walk away. Never.

But *never* wasn't the word he was waiting to hear. In a moment of confusion, as the helicopter's blades sped up and sirens sounded nearby, she realized Zach's handsome face was blurry because she was crying, although she'd never felt so happy inside.

She lifted up her hands, laughing through her tears at her own loss of composure. "I don't know what to say."

His smile came slowly, the smile of a confident man. "Just say yes."

"Oh, Zach."

"That'll do."

He kissed her again, the first kiss of their forever.

* * * * *

YOU HAVE JUST READ A HARLEQUIN® SPECIAL EDITION BOOK.

Discover more heartfelt tales of **family, friendship** and **love** from the Harlequin Special Edition series. Be sure to look for all six Harlequin® Special Edition books every month.

⊞ HARLEQUIN®

SPECIAL EDITION

"Are you going to switch the babies back?"

Shelby froze.

Liam felt momentarily sick.

It was the first time anyone had actually asked that question.

"No, ma'am," Liam said. "I have a better idea."

Shelby glanced at him, questions in her eyes.

"Where is my soup!" Kate's mother called again.

"You go ahead, Kate," Shelby said, stepping out onto the porch. "Thanks for talking to us."

Kate nodded and shut the door behind them.

Liam leaned his head back and he started down the porch steps. "I need about ten cups of coffee or a bottle of scotch."

"I thought I might fall over when she asked about switching the babies back," Shelby said, her face pale, her green eyes troubled. She stared at him. "You said you had a better idea. What is it? I sure need to hear it. Because switching the babies is not an option. Right?"

"Damned straight it's not. Never will be. Shane is your son. Alexander is my son. No matter what. Alexander will also become your son and Shane will also become my son as the days pass and all this sinks in."

"I think so, too," she said. "Right now it's like we can't even process that babies we didn't know until Friday are ours biologically. But as we begin to accept it, I'll start to feel a connection to Alexander. Same with you and Shane."

He nodded. "Exactly. Which is why on the way here, I started thinking about a way to ease us into that, to give us both what we need and want."

She tilted her head, waiting.

He thought he had the perfect solution. The only solution.

"I called the lab running the DNA tests and threw a bucket of money at them to expedite the results. On Monday," he continued, "we will officially know for absolute certain that our babies were switched. Of course we're not going to switch them back. I'd sooner cut off my arm."

"Me, too," Shelby said, staring at him. "So what's your plan?"

"The plan is for us to get married."

Shelby's mouth dropped open. "What? We've been living together for a day. Now we're getting married. Legally wed? Till death do us part?"

Don't miss
THE BABY SWITCH! by Melissa Senate,
available April 2018 wherever
Harlequin® Special Edition books and ebooks are sold.

www.Harlequin.com

Need an adrenaline rush from nail-biting tales
(and irresistible males)?

Check out **Harlequin® Intrigue®**
and **Harlequin® Romantic Suspense** books!

New books available every month!

CONNECT WITH US AT:

Harlequin.com/Community

 Facebook.com/HarlequinBooks

Twitter.com/HarlequinBooks

Instagram.com/HarlequinBooks

Pinterest.com/HarlequinBooks

ReaderService.com

**ROMANCE WHEN
YOU NEED IT**